Jennie Lucas's parents … up surrounded by book… At twenty-two she met… marriage, she graduated from university with …… English. She started writing books a year later. Jennie won the Romance Writers of America's Golden Heart contest in 2005 and hasn't looked back since. Visit Jennie's website at: jennielucas.com

Maya Blake's writing dream started at thirteen. She eventually realised her dream when she received The Call in 2012. Maya lives in England with her husband, kids and an endless supply of books. Contact Maya: mayabauthor.blogspot.com
twitter.com/mayablake
facebook.com/maya.blake.94

Kim Lawrence was encouraged by her husband to write when the unsocial hours of nursing didn't look attractive! He told her she could do anything she set her mind to, so Kim tried her hand at writing. Always a keen Mills & Boon reader, it seemed natural for her to write a romance novel – now she can't imagine doing anything else. She is a keen gardener and cook and enjoys running on the beach with her Jack Russell. Kim lives in Wales.

One Night...

One Night...
to Marriage

JENNIE LUCAS

MAYA BLAKE

KIM LAWRENCE

MILLS & BOON

First Published in Great Britain 2022
By Mills & Boon, an imprint of HarperCollins*Publishers*, Ltd
1 London Bridge Street, London, SE1 9GF

www.harpercollins.co.uk

HarperCollins*Publishers*
1st Floor, Watermarque Building,
Ringsend Road, Dublin 4, Ireland

ONE NIGHT... TO MARRIAGE © 2022 Harlequin Books S.A.

To Love, Honour and Betray © 2012 Jennie Lucas
One Night with Gael © 2016 Maya Blake
One Night to Wedding Vows © 2016 Kim Lawrence

ISBN: 978-0-263-30569-2

MIX
Paper from
responsible sources

FSC
www.fsc.org

FSC™ C007454

TO LOVE, HONOUR AND BETRAY

JENNIE LUCAS

To my husband.

Thanks for Europe.

Thanks even more for home.

Thanks for making all my dreams come true.

CHAPTER ONE

CALLIE WOODVILLE had dreamed of her wedding day since she was a little girl.

When she was seven, she placed a long white towel on her head and walked down an imaginary aisle in her father's barn, surrounded by teddy bears as guests and with her baby sister toddling behind her, chewing on flower petals from a basket.

At seventeen, as a plump, bookish wallflower with big glasses and clothes hand-sewn by her loving but sadly out-of-date mother, Callie was mocked and ignored by the boys at her rural high school. She told herself she didn't care. She went to prom with her best friend instead, an equally nerdy boy from a neighboring farm. But Callie dreamed of the day she would finally meet the darkly handsome man she could love. She knew that somewhere out there in the wide world, he waited for her, this man who would wake her with the sensual power of his kiss.

Then, when she was twenty-four, that man had come for her.

Her ruthless billionaire boss had kissed her. Seduced her. He'd taken her virginity, as he'd already taken her heart, and for one perfect night she was lost in passion and magic. Waking up in his arms on Christmas morning, in the luxurious bedroom of his New York brownstone,

Callie thought she might die of pure happiness. For that one perfect night, the world was a magical place where dreams came true, as long as your heart was pure and you truly believed.

One magical, heartbreaking night.

Now, eight and a half months later, Callie sat on the stoop outside her former apartment on a leafy, quiet street in the West Village. The sky was dark, threatening rain, and though it was early September it was hot and muggy. But her cleaned-out apartment felt almost ghostly in its emptiness, so she'd come outside to wait with the suitcases.

Today was her wedding day. The day she'd always dreamed of. But she'd never dreamed of this.

Callie looked down at her secondhand wedding dress and the wilting bouquet of wildflowers she'd picked from the nearby community garden. Instead of a veil, pearl-laced barrettes strained to hold back her long, light brown hair.

In a few minutes, she'd marry her best friend. A man she'd never kissed—or even *wanted* to kiss. A man who wasn't the father of her baby.

As soon as Brandon came back with the rental car, they'd be wed at City Hall, and start the long drive from New York to his parents' farm in North Dakota.

Callie closed her eyes. *It's best for the baby,* she told herself desperately. Her baby needed a father, and her ex-boss was a selfish, coldhearted playboy, whose deepest relationship was with his bank account. After three years of devoted service as his secretary, Callie had known that. But she'd still been stupid enough to find out the hard way.

A car turned off Seventh Avenue onto her residential street in the West Village. She saw an expensive dark luxury sedan and watched it go by, then exhaled. It wasn't Eduardo's style of car, and yet, as clouds covered the noonday sun, Callie looked up at the sky and shivered. If her ex-boss ever found out their single night of passion had created a child…

"He won't," she whispered aloud. Last she'd heard, he was in Colombia, developing offshore oil fields for Cruz Oil. After Eduardo possessed a woman in bed, she was pretty much dead to him, never to be remembered again. And though Callie had witnessed this scores of times during her time as his secretary, she'd still thought that she might be different. That she would be the exception.

Get out of my bed, Callie. She'd still been naked and blissful and sleepy in the pink light of Christmas morning when he'd shaken her awake, his voice hard. *Get out of my house. I'm through with you.*

Eight and a half months later, his words were still an ice pick in her heart. Exhaling, Callie wrapped her arms around her baby bump. He would never know about the life he'd created inside her. He'd made his choice. So she'd made hers. There would be no custody battle, no chance for Eduardo to be as domineering and tyrannical a father as he'd been a boss. Her child would be born into a stable home, with a loving family. Brandon, her best friend since the first grade, would be her baby's father in all the ways that counted, and Callie would be a devoted wife to him in return. In every way but one.

She'd been doubtful at first that a marriage based on friendship could work. But Brandon had assured her that they didn't need romance or passion to have a solid partnership. "We'll be happy, Callie," he'd promised. "Really happy." Over the months of her pregnancy, he'd worn her down with kindness.

Now, as Callie leaned back against their suitcases on the stoop, her eyes fell on her Louis Vuitton handbag. Brandon kept telling her to sell it. It would look ridiculous on the farm, she knew. It had been a gift from Eduardo last Christmas. *Totally unnecessary*, she'd wept, amazed that he'd noticed her gaze lingering upon the shop window months before. *I reward those who are loyal to me, Callie*, Eduardo had replied. *A woman like you comes along only once in a lifetime.*

Squeezing her eyes shut, Callie turned her face upward, feeling the first cool raindrops against her skin. Such a ridiculous trophy, a three-thousand-dollar handbag, but it had been a hard-won symbol of her hours of devotion, of their partnership. But Brandon was right. She should just sell it. She was done with Eduardo. With New York. Done with everything she'd once loved.

Except this baby.

A low roll of thunder mingled with the honk of taxis and distant police sirens on Seventh Avenue and the hiss from the subway vent at the end of the street. She heard another car pull down the street. It stopped, and she heard a door slam. Brandon had returned with the rental car. It was time to marry him and start the two-day journey to North Dakota. Forcing her lips into a smile, she opened her eyes.

Eduardo Cruz stood beside his dark Mercedes sedan, powerful and broad-shouldered in an impeccable black suit.

The blood drained from Callie's cheeks.

"Eduardo," she breathed, starting to rise. She stopped herself. Maybe he couldn't see her pregnant belly. She prayed he couldn't. Wrapping her arms loosely over her knees, she stammered, "What are you doing here?"

Silently Eduardo stepped onto the sidewalk. His long-limbed, powerful body moved toward her with a warrior's effortless grace, but she felt every step like a seismic rumble beneath her.

"The question is—" his dark eyes glittered "—what are *you* doing, Callie?"

His voice was deep, with only a hint of an accent from his childhood in Spain. It was a shock to hear that voice again. She'd never thought she would see him again, outside of her haunted, sensual dreams.

She lifted her chin. "What does it look like I'm doing?" She jabbed her thumb toward the suitcases. "Leaving." Her voice trembled in spite of her best efforts, and she hated Eduardo for that, as she hated him for so much else. "You've won."

"Won?" he ground out. He slowly circled her at the end of the stoop. "A strange accusation."

Beneath his gaze, her body shuddered with ice, then fire. She stiffened, glaring at him. "What else would you call it? You fired me then made sure no one else in New York would hire me."

"So?" he said coldly. "Let McLinn provide for you. You are his bride. His problem."

A chill went down her spine.

"You know about Brandon?" she whispered. If he knew about her coming marriage, did he also know about her pregnancy? "Who told you?"

"He did." He gave a harsh laugh. "I met him."

"You met? When? Where?"

Eduardo gave her a hard smile. "Does it matter?"

She bit her lip. "Was it a chance meeting…or…"

"You might call it chance." His casual drawl belied the cold accusation in his eyes. He looked up at the expensive town house behind her. "I stopped by your apartment and was surprised to find you had a live-in lover."

"He's not my—"

"Not your what?"

"Never mind," she mumbled.

Eduardo moved closer. "Tell me," he said acidly, "did McLinn enjoy living here? Did he relish living in the apartment I leased as a gift of gratitude for the secretary I respected?"

She swallowed. A year ago, she'd been living in a cheap studio in Staten Island, so she could send most of her salary to her family back home. Then Eduardo had surprised her with a paid yearlong lease for a gorgeous one-bedroom apartment close to his own expensive brownstone on Bank Street. Callie had nearly wept with joy, believing it was proof that he actually cared. She'd later realized he'd only wanted to eliminate her commute so he could get more hours out of her.

"What could you possibly have to say to me now?" She frowned. She'd been home all week—packing boxes, directing the movers, being informed by the airlines that she was too pregnant to fly, calling car rental agencies. "When were you even here?"

"While you were in bed," Eduardo ground out.

Her heart lifted to her throat.

"Oh," she whispered. It suddenly made sense. She slept in the bedroom, while Brandon had the couch. "He never mentioned meeting you. But why? What do you want?"

His black eyes glittered at her. He was staring at her as if she were a stranger. No—as if she were a bug beneath his Italian leather shoe. "Why didn't you ever tell me about your lover? Why did you lie?"

"I didn't!"

"You hid his existence from me. The very day after you moved into this apartment, you had him move in with you. But you never mentioned him, because you knew it would make me question your commitment and loyalty."

She stared at him then her shoulders sagged. "I was

afraid to tell you." She swallowed. "You're so unreasonable in your demand for absolute loyalty."

His mouth was a grim line. "So you lied."

"I never invited him to move in! He…he surprised me." After Callie had called Brandon in North Dakota to tell him about the apartment her generous boss had just leased for her, he'd shown up on her doorstep the next day, telling her he was worried about her in the big city. "He missed me. He was going to get his own place, but then he couldn't find a job…."

"Right," Eduardo said sardonically. "A real man finds a job to support his woman. He doesn't live off her severance package."

She gasped at the insult. "He's not like that!" Throughout her pregnancy, Brandon had cooked, cleaned, rubbed her swollen feet, held her hand at the doctor's office. All the things that she'd have wanted her baby's real father to do, if he'd been anyone besides Eduardo. She scowled. "In case you haven't noticed, there aren't many jobs in New York for *farmers!*"

"So why stay in New York?"

Soft, lazy raindrops fell around them, pattering against the hot sidewalk. "I wanted to stay. I hoped I would find a job."

"And so you have. As a farmer's wife."

"What do you want from me? Why did you come— just to insult me?"

"Oh, didn't I mention why?" His eyes were cold and black. "Your sister called me this morning."

A chill went through her.

"Sami—called you?" Callie's conversation with her sister last night had ended badly. But Sami wouldn't betray her. She wouldn't…would she? She licked her suddenly dry lips. "Um. What did she say?"

"Two very interesting things that I could hardly believe." Eduardo took a step closer to her on the stoop and said softly, "But clearly one of them is true. You're getting married today."

Her body started to shake. "So?"

"You admit it?"

"I'm wearing a wedding gown. I can't exactly deny it. But how does that affect you?" Her lips trembled as she tried to shape them into a mocking smile. "Mad because you weren't invited?"

"You sound nervous." He slowly walked a semicircle around the end of the stoop. "Is there something you are keeping from me, Callie? Some secret?" He moved closer. "Some lie?"

She felt a contraction across her body, her belly tightening. Braxton-Hicks contractions, caused by stress, she told herself. Fake labor, the same that had sent her racing to the hospital last week, only to have the nurses sigh and send her home. But it hurt. One hand went over her belly; the other went to her lower back as she panted, "What could I possibly have to hide?"

"I already know you're a liar." A beam of golden light escaped the gray clouds and caressed his handsome face, leaving dark shadows beneath his cheekbones and jawline as he said softly, "But how deep do your lies go?"

The wilted bouquet of wildflowers nearly fell from her numb fingers. She gripped them more tightly in her shaking hands. "Please," she whispered. "Don't ruin it."

"Ruin—what—exactly?"

Her teeth chattered. "My...my..." *My life. And my baby's life.* "My wedding day."

"Ah, yes. Your wedding day. I know how you used to dream about it." He looked down at her. "So tell me. Is it everything you hoped it would be?"

She felt painfully conscious of the used wedding dress, several sizes too large, with a lace and polyester bodice that kept sliding off one shoulder. She looked down at the wilting flowers, at the two shabby suitcases behind her.

"Yes," she said in a small voice.

"Where is your family? Where are your friends?"

"We're getting married at City Hall." She lifted her chin defiantly, pushing aside the sudden desire to cry. "We're eloping. It's romantic."

"Ah. Of course." He showed his teeth in a smile. "The wedding would not matter to you and McLinn, would it, as long as you have your honeymoon."

Honeymoon? She and Brandon planned to break up their drive on a pull-out sofa at his cousin's house in Wisconsin. Passion was nonexistent between them—she thought of Brandon like a brother. But she could hardly admit to Eduardo that there was only one man on earth she'd ever wanted to kiss, only one man she'd ever dreamed about: the man glaring cold daggers at her right now. "My honeymoon is none of your business."

Eduardo snorted. "Anything for you would be romantic where Brandon McLinn is concerned. Even an ugly dress and a bouquet of weeds. He's always been the one you wanted. Even though he is a man without a job, unable to stand on his own two feet. You *love* him—" his voice was scornful "—though he is barely a man."

Callie's jaw clenched. She started to rise to her feet then she remembered she couldn't let him see her belly. Trembling with fury, she glared up at him. "Rich or poor, Brandon is twice the man you'll ever be!"

Eduardo's eyes burned through her. Then he spoke coldly.

"Stand up."

She blinked. "What?"

"Your sister told me two things. The first is true." Raindrops splattered noisily into the trees above. "Stand up."

Callie sucked in her breath. "Forget it! I'm not your secretary, I'm not your lover...I'm your *nothing*! You have no power over me, not anymore. Stop harassing me before I call the police!"

Eduardo's dark eyes glittered as he moved closer, standing over her, so close his pant legs brushed her knees. He leaned forward. "Are you pregnant with my baby?"

Staring up at him, Callie sucked in her breath. He *knew*.

Her sister had betrayed her. She'd told Eduardo everything.

She'd known Sami was angry, but she'd never thought she'd do it. Yesterday, her sister had called to wish her good luck on her trip. Callie had been jittery and afraid she was about to make the worst mistake of her life. When she'd heard her sister's loving voice, she'd blurted out her plan to elope with Brandon because she was pregnant by her boss. Sami's reaction had been furious.

I won't let you trap Brandon this way, with a baby that's not even his!

Sami, you don't understand –

Shut up! Even if your old boss is a jerk, it's his baby and he deserves to know! I won't let you ruin so many lives with your selfishness!

Callie had been shocked, but she'd never once thought Sami would go through with her threat. Her baby sister adored her. She'd trailed after Callie and Brandon every day for years with hero worship in her eyes. She might be angry, but she'd certainly never betray her. Or so she'd thought.

She'd been wrong.

"Are you?" Eduardo demanded harshly.

Callie felt another hard contraction. She tried to breathe through it, but the childbirth classes she'd attended with Brandon seemed useless. The fake contractions, which were supposed to get her body ready for eventual labor weeks in the future, were getting stronger.

"Very well. Do not answer," Eduardo said coldly. "I would not believe a word from your lying mouth, in any case. But your body…" He stroked her cheek, and an electric current coursed through her. Callie looked up with a gasp, her lips parted. "Your body won't lie to me."

He removed the bouquet of wildflowers from her unresisting hand and dropped it to the ground. Taking both her hands in his own, palm to palm, he gently lifted her to her feet.

Callie stood before him on the sidewalk, shaking and vulnerable and clearly pregnant in an ugly white wedding dress. Closing her eyes, she waited for the explosion.

But when he spoke, his voice was cool. "So it is true. You are pregnant." He paused. "Who is the father?"

Her eyes flew open. "What?" she stammered.

"Is it me? Or McLinn?"

"How can you ask…?" She faltered, blushing. "You know I was a virgin when we…when we…"

"I thought you were, though I wondered later if I'd been deceived." He set his jaw. "Perhaps you were saving yourself for your wedding night, and the day after we made love, you went home to your fiancé, and lured him into bed. Perhaps in a fit of remorse, or perhaps to hide what you'd done in case there was a child."

"How can you even say that?" she gasped. "How can you think I'd do something so disgusting—so low?"

"Is the child is mine? Or is it McLinn's?" His gaze was like ice. His sensual lips twisted. "Or do you not know?"

Her heart wrenched.

"Why are you trying to hurt me?" She shook her head. "Brandon is my friend. Just my friend."

"You've been living with him for a year. Do you expect me to believe he slept on the couch for all that time?"

"We took turns!"

"You are lying! He is *marrying* you!"

"Out of kindness, nothing more!"

He gave a harsh laugh. "*Por supuesto,*" he mocked, folding his arms. "That is why men marry. To be *kind.*"

She stepped back from him. Her throat throbbed with anguish. "My parents don't know I'm pregnant. They think I've just given up the job hunt and decided to move home." Her eyes burned as she shook her head fiercely. "I can't go back there as an unwed mother. My parents would never live it down. And Brandon is the best man on earth. He—"

"I don't give a damn about him. Or you. I care about one question. Is. This. Baby. Mine?"

Callie took a deep breath. "Please don't," she whispered. She despised the pleading note in her voice but couldn't stop herself. "Don't make me give you an answer you don't want. Let me give her a home. A family."

"Her?"

She could have kicked herself. Reluctantly she looked at him. "I'm having a baby girl."

He exhaled, setting his jaw. "A girl."

"It doesn't matter! You don't want to be tied to me. You've made that clear! She's nothing to you, any more than I am. You must forget you ever saw me—"

"Are you out of your mind?" he growled, grabbing her shoulders. "I won't let another man raise a child that could be mine!" He searched her gaze fiercely. "When is the baby due? What is the exact date?"

Thunder rolled across the dark clouds hanging low over

the city. Callie felt herself on a precipice of a choice that would change everything.

If she told Eduardo the truth, her baby would never enjoy the idyllic childhood that Callie had had, surrounded by endless prairie, playing in her father's barn, knowing everyone in their small town. Instead of parents who were best friends, her precious child would have parents who hated each other, and a tyrannical, selfish father.

If only she were the liar Eduardo thought she was, Callie thought miserably. If only she could give him a false date, and say Brandon was the father!

But she couldn't lie. Not to his face. Especially not about something like this. Grief twisted her heart as she whispered, "September 17."

Eduardo stared down at her. Then his eyes narrowed and the grip on her shoulders tightened.

"If there's even the slightest chance McLinn is the father, tell me now," he ground out. "Before the paternity test. If you're lying—or if you are simply wrong—and this baby is not mine, I will destroy you for your lie. Do you understand? Not just you, but everyone who loves you. Especially McLinn."

Her throat ached. She knew her ex-boss's ruthlessness. She'd seen him use it against others for three years, and finally—inevitably—against her. "I would expect nothing less."

"I will take your parents' farm. McLinn's. Everything. Do you understand?" His dark eyes glittered. "So choose your words carefully. Tell me the truth. Am I the—"

"Of course!" she exploded. "Of course you're the father! You're the only man I've ever slept with! Ever!"

Staggering back a step, Eduardo stared down at her. His jaw hardened. "*Still*? Do you honestly expect me to believe that?"

"Why would I lie? Do you think I actually *want* you to be her father?" she cried. "I wish with all my heart it was Brandon, not you! He's the one I want—the one I trust— the best man in the world! Instead of a selfish workaholic playboy who turns on everyone in his life, who doesn't trust anyone, who has no real friends—"

Her voice cut off as his fingers tightened into her flesh. "You were never going to tell me about the baby, were you?" His voice was dangerously soft. "You were just going to steal my child from me and put another man in my place. You were going to erase me completely from her life."

A shiver of fear went through her, but she glared at him. "Yes! She'd be better off without you!"

He sucked in his breath then bared his teeth into a smile.

"And that," he said, his black eyes gleaming, "is your greatest lie of all."

They stood glaring at each other on the sidewalk, like mortal enemies. She heard the soft patter of heavy rain-drops sliding from the green leafy trees above the brick town houses, and she knew he was right.

For eight months, Callie had told herself that Eduardo wouldn't want a baby. That his workaholic bachelor life-style would be hampered by a child. That he would be a horrible father and she was doing the right thing for everyone. But part of her had always known that wasn't true. After being orphaned himself, and brought to New York at the age of ten, Eduardo Cruz would want to be a father. He'd never surrender a son or daughter.

It was just *Callie* he would sweep aside and discard.

And that was what frightened her. With Eduardo Cruz's wealth and power, if he took her to court to battle for full custody, there was no question who would win.

His dark eyes cut her to the bone. "You should have told me the day you realized you were pregnant."

She looked up at him, her heart twisting beneath the weight of guilt and regret and the grief of broken love. "How could I," she whispered, "after you abandoned me?"

His eyes widened. Then he glowered at her, his expression merciless. "You are clever and resourceful. You could have found a way to contact me. But you did not. You tried to hide her, as you hide everything."

She felt another sharp pain as her belly tightened. "And now I've told you the truth, will you try to take her from me?"

His jaw tightened. Then a smile curled his lips. Reaching out his hand, he stroked her cheek. A sizzle of electricity spun across her skin, vibrating down her spine, and she was filled with longing and desire, irrepressible need like fire. All her traitorous body wanted to do, even now, was turn toward him like a flower toward the sun.

"You will be punished, *querida*," he said softly. "Oh, yes."

Callie stared up at him, breathless beneath his touch, trapped beneath the dark force of his gaze. Then she exhaled when she saw a cheap two-door hatchback driving up her street. The cavalry had come to save her. She nearly sobbed with relief. "Brandon!"

Eduardo whipped around. A low, guttural word came from his lips, a word in Spanish she'd only heard him use when he'd just lost a huge deal, or the time a brokenhearted starlet had tried to break into his bedroom. Turning back, he grabbed Callie's handbag, then her arm. "Come with me."

Before she even knew what was happening, he'd pulled her across the sidewalk and opened the back door to his black sedan. "Start the engine," he ordered his driver.

Realizing his intent, she desperately tried to rip her arm away. "Let me go!"

But Eduardo's grip was like steel. He shoved her into the backseat and climbed in beside her, crowding her with his massive body that seemed far too big for the space.

Eduardo leaned over her, his eyes black with fury as he gripped her wrists. "I'm not giving you another chance to hide my baby."

Callie breathed in the woodsy, exotic scent of his cologne, overwhelmed by his closeness, by the sensation of his thigh pressed against hers. It was just as she'd dreamed about in the years she'd worked for him, and unwillingly dreamed every night in all the months since he'd fired her. Their faces were inches apart. Callie's heart thumped in her chest. She felt lost in a dream.

Then Eduardo closed the door with a bang behind him.

"Drive," he told his chauffeur tersely.

"No!" With an intake of breath, she whirled around in the backseat. Her last vision through the back window was of Brandon standing by the rental car with his door ajar, staring after her with his black-framed glasses askew, his expression anguished. Beside him, their two old suitcases still sat forlornly on the curb.

Their car turned the corner, and Brandon was gone. Callie's body felt tight with pain that seemed to emanate white-hot from her heart as she turned back to Eduardo with a choked sob. "Take me back. Please."

His eyes were merciless. "No."

"You've kidnapped me!"

"Call it what you want."

"You can't keep me against my will!"

"Can't I?" he said softly.

She shivered at the look in his eyes. He turned away

as if bored, but she saw the hard set of his jaw, heard the clipped tension of his voice as he said coldly, "You will remain with me until the matter of the baby is resolved."

"So I'm your prisoner?"

"Until my paternal rights are formalized—yes."

"So you don't believe I'm a liar after all," Callie said bitterly.

"Not about the baby. But there are all kinds of lying. You lie with silence. I wonder," he said blandly, "if there's anything else you've been hiding from me? My perfect, loyal secretary."

She wrapped her arms over her belly, which felt hard and tight beneath the polyester blend of her wedding dress. "What do you know about loyalty? You've never been loyal to anyone but yourself!"

"I was loyal to you, Callie," he said in a low voice. "Once."

Staring into his fathomless dark eyes, she was suddenly lost in memories of their days together, in the office, sharing sushi at midnight, traveling the world on his private jet.

"That was when I mistakenly believed you were worth it." His tone hardened. "I learned my lesson."

"What lesson?" she cried out, bewildered. "The instant I slept with you, I went from being your trusted secretary to a disposable one-night stand. After everything we'd been through together, how could you treat me exactly like all the rest?" She lifted her tearful gaze to his and spoke from the heart. "Why did you sleep with me?" she whispered. "Did you ever care for me at all?"

He stared at her.

"You were a convenience," he said roughly, turning away. "Nothing more."

The words felt like a knife blade in her heart, serrated, rusty, tearing through her flesh. She'd loved him with such devotion, and the night she'd given him her virginity, she'd thought a miracle had happened: that he'd fallen for her, too.

"Every woman in this city thinks she can tame you. The rich, handsome playboy," she choked out. She shook her head. "The truth is you'll never trust anyone long enough to care. You desert a woman the instant you've had your minute of cheap pleasure!"

Eduardo's eyes narrowed. Then his gaze traced slowly over her lips, her neck, her breasts.

"Longer than a minute, I assure you," he drawled. "Or don't you remember?"

Their eyes met, and her cheeks flooded with warmth. Heaven help her, but she remembered every hot, sensual detail of the night he'd made love to her. She still dreamed of it every night against her will. How he'd stroked her virginal body, how he'd peeled off her clothes and kissed every inch of her skin, how he'd made her scream with pleasure, crying out his name as he suckled her, as he licked her, as he filled her until she wept with mindless joy.

Heaven help her, but she couldn't forget.

His gaze dropped. Callie sucked in her breath when she realized the neckline of her tatty, oversize wedding dress had slid down her shoulder to reveal far too much of one plump breast and a full inch of her white cotton bra. She yanked the neckline up, scowling. "I can't believe I ever let you seduce me."

"Seduce?" His lips twisted with amusement. "What a charming description. I didn't seduce you. You jumped into my arms the instant I touched you. But call it *seduction*, if it makes your conscience easy."

She gasped in outrage. "You are such a—"

"Oh, I'm sure you regretted it afterward. McLinn must have taken it hard." He shook his head. "Amazing," he mused, "to think he was willing to marry you while you were pregnant by another man. He must be insanely in love with you."

A twinge of unease went through her. "He's not in love with me. He's my best friend."

"And you must have felt so guilty." Reaching over, he twirled a tendril of her brown hair. "So full of remorse that you ruined your chaste, loyal, boring love affair of years for a single night of hot, raw lust with me."

She jerked away. "You are so full of yourself to think—"

"Why did I treat you exactly like the rest? I'll tell you." Eduardo's eyes met hers evenly. "Because you are no different."

"I hate you!"

He snorted a laugh, but his eyes were icy. "Then we agree on something at last."

Tears fell down her lashes as she looked down, suddenly deflated. "All I wanted was to give my baby a good home," she whispered. "But now, instead of two loving parents, she'll be pulled like a tug-of-war rope between a mother and father who hate each other. Two parents who aren't even married. The world can be cruel. She'll be called *illegitimate*. She'll be called a bastard…"

Eduardo's eyes widened. "What?" he exploded.

"She'll always feel she's not good enough, as if she were some kind of accident, some kind of mistake. When the truth is you and I are the ones to blame." She looked up at him with a sob. "I don't want her to suffer. Please, Eduardo. Can't you just let me marry Brandon? For her sake?"

He looked at her for a long moment, his expression half-wild.

Then his jaw set. He abruptly leaned forward in his seat to say something in rapid-fire Spanish to his chauffeur then turned away, dialing into his phone and speaking again in the same language, too fast for her to understand. Praying she'd made him see reason, that he'd changed his mind and would let her go, she watched him, tracing the harsh lines of his silhouetted face, the handsome, sensual, cruel face she'd once loved with all her heart.

When Eduardo turned back to her, his dark eyes were strangely bright. "I have happy news for you, *querida*. You are going to be married today after all."

She let out a sob of joy. "You're taking me back to Brandon?"

He gave a hard laugh. "You think I would allow that?"

Callie frowned, confused. "But you just said—"

"You are going to be married today." Eduardo gave her a smile so icy cold it reminded her of the winter wind whipping across the empty, frozen prairie. "To me."

CHAPTER TWO

CALLIE gasped. Marry Eduardo? The father of her baby? Her ex-boss? The man she despised more than anyone on earth?

Shocked, she stared at him as she waited for the punch line. Licking her lips nervously, she finally said, "I don't get the joke."

Eduardo's lips curved humorlessly. "It's not a joke."

She spread her arms wide in the backseat of the car. "Of course it is!"

Eduardo grabbed her left hand, looking down at her cheap engagement ring with its microscopic diamond. "No, Callie, *that* is a joke."

Trying to rip her hand from his grasp, she glared at him. "A ring is a symbol of fidelity, no wonder you hate it!"

"You'll have a real one."

"I'm not going to marry you!"

"Oh, right. I forgot you're a *romantic*. I should ask you properly," he said sardonically. His dark eyes gleamed as he wrapped her hand in his own and pressed it against his chest. Before her horrified eyes, he went down on one knee in the back of the car. "*Querida*, my darling, my dear, will you do me the deep, deep honor of becoming my wife?"

She felt the heat of his hard chest through his suit, and her heart fluttered—even as her cheeks burned at the mockery in his voice. Anger gave her strength, and she jerked her hand from his grasp. "Go to hell!"

He moved back to his seat. "I'll take that as a yes."

Rain pattered against the roof of the car, horns honking around them as the car moved through traffic. The rain-splattered streets passed in a gray blur.

Callie realized Eduardo meant it.

He actually wanted her to be his wife.

"But you—you don't want to get married!" she stammered. "You've said as much to every woman you've dated. You practically had it tattooed on your chest!"

"I always planned to marry the mother of my children."

"Yes—but you wanted to marry some ritzy Spanish duchess!"

The edges of his lips lifted. "The best laid plans," he said. "You are having my child. We must wed."

He made it sound like a punishment—for him. She lifted her chin. "Gee, thanks," she said sarcastically. "I'm touched. Five minutes ago, you didn't even believe you were the father. You said you wouldn't believe a word I said. Now you want to marry me?"

"I've decided that not even you, Callie, would lie to me about our baby's paternity. Not when the truth is so clearly unpleasant to you."

She folded her arms, glaring at him. "I'm having your baby, all right, but nothing on earth could make me be your wife."

"Strange. You were keen to get married a few minutes ago."

"To Brandon!" she cried. "I adore him. I'd trust him with my life!"

"Spare me his list of virtues," Eduardo said, sounding bored. "Your love makes you blind."

"He might not be rich and heartless like you, but that's

exactly why he'll make a wonderful father. Far better than—"

She cut herself off as a painful contraction arced through her body.

"Far better than me?" Eduardo said with dangerous softness. "Because I am not good enough to be her father. And that was your excuse for lying to me and marrying your lover."

"He's not my lover—"

"Perhaps not physically. But you *love* him. So you were going to steal my child. And you accuse me of being heartless," he said contemptuously. "You are breathtaking."

The words were not a compliment.

Callie held her breath as new pain assailed her. Her baby wasn't due for two and a half weeks, but this was starting to feel very different from the Braxton-Hicks contractions she'd had last week. *Very* different.

Was it possible…?

Could it be…?

No! She forced herself to take a deep, calming breath. It couldn't be real labor. It was sixteen days too soon. Stress was causing her body to react, that was all. She had to calm down, for the baby's sake!

She shifted in the backseat of the car, trying to alleviate the stabbing pain in her lower back. "You don't want to raise a baby and you certainly don't want me as your wife. It's only your masculine pride that makes you—"

"My masculine pride." Eduardo bared his teeth into a smile. "Is that what you call it?"

"You don't want to marry me, I know you don't. You're just in shock. You haven't had time to think what it would mean for you to raise a child. To have a family."

"You think I've had no time to consider what it means

for a child to feel abandoned by his parents? To feel alone? To have no real home?"

Callie closed her mouth with a snap. Of course he knew. Licking her lips, she tried helplessly. "I could give our baby a wonderful home—"

"I know you will." His eyes were fathomless and stark. "Because I will provide that home. As her father."

There was no winning this war. Now that Eduardo knew about her pregnancy, he would never give up his rights as a father.

"So what do we do?" Callie said miserably.

"I told you. Marry."

"But I can't be your wife."

"Why?"

"I—I don't love you."

"Good," he bit out. "Your sainted McLinn can keep your love. Just your body and your vow of fidelity are enough."

Her heart was pounding in her throat. "You really want to marry me?" she whispered. The thought made her tremble. In spite of everything, she couldn't forget the romantic dreams she'd once had of Eduardo taking her in his arms and saying, *I made the worst mistake of my life when I let you go, Callie. I love you. Come back to me. Be mine—forever.* "As in forever?"

Eduardo gave an ugly laugh. "Be married to you forever? No. I have no desire to live the rest of my life in hell, chained to a woman I'll never be able to trust. Our marriage will last just long enough to give our child a name."

"Oh." She shifted in her seat then frowned. That changed things a bit. "Like—like a marriage of convenience?"

"Call it what you like."

"For a week or two?"

"Let us say three months. Long enough for it to actually

look like a real marriage. And for our baby's first months to be the best possible, with us both in the same home."

"But—where would we live? My lease is gone. You sold your brownstone in the Village."

"I just bought a place on the Upper West Side."

She blinked. "You were moving back to New York, because you thought I'd be gone."

His lips twisted. "I bought it as an investment. But you are correct."

Callie stared up at him, her heart pounding. "This is never going to work."

"It will."

She took a deep breath. *Marriage.* Would it be good for their baby, as Eduardo believed? Or would it only make their frayed relationship even worse, creating yet more accusations and distrust between them?

"But how would our marriage end?" she said. "With an ugly divorce—throwing plates and screaming at each other? That wouldn't help anyone, least of all my baby."

"*Our* baby," he corrected, then bared his teeth in a smile. "Our prenuptial agreement will outline our divorce. We will agree from the beginning how it will end."

"Plan our divorce before we're even wed? That seems so sad...."

"Not sad. Civilized." He lifted a dark eyebrow, rubbing the rough, dark edge of his jawline. He gave her a tight smile. "Since we are not in love, there will be no hard feelings when we part."

Three months. Callie swallowed. She tried to imagine what it would be like to live in Eduardo's house. Even as his secretary, she'd never lived with him on such intimate terms. And though she was no longer the naive, trusting girl who'd fallen in love with him so stupidly, he still had such frightening power over her. Callie's foolish, traitorous body yearned for him like a sugary, buttery cake that was impossibly bad for her but she couldn't stop craving just the same.

"And if I refuse?" she whispered. "If I get out of this car and flag a taxi back to Brandon?"

His expression cooled.

"If you are truly so selfish that you'd put your desire for love ahead of the best interests of our child, I will have no choice but to question your fitness as a mother, and challenge you for full custody." She started to protest, but he cut her off calmly. "I have limitless funds and the best law firm in the city at my disposal. You will lose."

She felt another contraction and this time, the pain was so deep and sustained that she closed her eyes, bracing her body against it as she panted, "You're threatening me?"

"I'm telling you how it will be."

"We're here, sir," Sanchez, the driver, said from the front seat, as he pulled the sedan to the curb.

Looking out her window, Callie saw the same courthouse where she'd gotten a marriage license yesterday with Brandon. The thought of deserting her best friend to marry Eduardo was insane. But she could either become Mrs. Eduardo Cruz for three months, living in the same household and sharing custody of their newborn, or she could possibly lose her child forever.

"And…afterward…" she said haltingly, "how would we arrange custody?"

Eduardo gave her a smile that didn't meet his eyes. "Once you show that our child means more to you than some lover, and that you are a reasonable and concerned parent, I am sure we can work something out." As Sanchez got out of the front seat and walked around to open the door, Eduardo's voice turned hard. "You have thirty seconds to decide."

Shivering, she stared at him with her hands wrapped over her belly. She felt her baby moving inside her, and she was desperate to protect her. She glared at him, feeling trapped and frightened and furious all at once. "You've left me no choice."

The door opened behind Eduardo.

"I knew you'd see reason," he said sardonically. Climbing out, he turned back, holding out his hand. "Come, my bride."

For an instant, Callie was afraid to touch him—afraid of what it did to her. But as he waited, she reluctantly put her hand in his own. His hard, hot palm pressed against her skin, his larger fingers intertwined around hers. As he pulled her from the car to the sidewalk, she looked up at his face, remembering the first time she'd touched his hand.

Callie Woodville? The powerful CEO of Cruz Oil had been visiting his outpost in the Bakken fields of North Dakota. Callie was the local office liaison, sent from the nearby town of Fern. He'd held out his hand, looking sleek and urbane in a black suit, with his helicopter still noisily winding down behind him. *I've heard you run the entire office here, and do the work of four people.* His sudden, gorgeous smile lit up his darkly handsome face. *I could use an assistant like you in New York.*

She'd looked into the warmth of his dark eyes. Dazzled, she'd taken his outstretched hand. And that had been it. The thunderbolt she'd always prayed for. She'd loved him from that first moment. How she'd loved him…

Now, with Eduardo's hand still wrapped around hers, Callie was barely aware of people rushing by them on the busy New York sidewalk. The two of them were connected like the moon and the sun, as stars and comets streaked around them in the vastness of space. The two of them. Just like always.

But his handsome face had changed over the last year. It was subtle. Perhaps no one else would have even noticed. But she saw the tighter set of his jaw. The deeper crinkle around his hard eyes. His high, angled cheekbones seemed chiseled out of stone, and so did his jawline, already dark with five o'clock shadow. At thirty-six, he was even more ruthless and powerful than she remembered. His masculine beauty was breathtaking. Looking up into his deep black eyes, Callie trembled. It would be too easy to fall under his spell again, and forget the way he demanded total devotion from others, while offering none in return.

Eduardo's expression darkened. Reaching down, he tucked a tendril of her wavy brown hair behind her ear. "You will be mine, Callie. Only mine."

A shudder went through her. She was helpless, lost in his gaze. Lost in his touch. Lost in her traitorous heart's memory of how, for years, she'd lived for him, only for him.

A cough behind her broke the spell, causing her to jump away. An unsmiling bald man in a plain blue suit stood behind her. She recognized John Bleekman, Eduardo's chief attorney.

"Hello, Miss Woodville," he said expressionlessly.

"Um. Hello," she said, wondering why he was there.

He turned to Eduardo, holding out a file. "I have it, sir."

Taking the file, Eduardo opened it and glanced over the papers for several minutes. "Good." He handed it to Callie. "Sign."

"What is it?"

"Our prenuptial agreement."

"What? So fast?"

"I had Bleekman start drawing up the draft after I spoke with your sister this morning."

"But you didn't even know if it was true about the baby– much less that you wanted to marry me!"

"I always like to be prepared for every possibility."

"Yes." She scowled. "To make sure you get your way."

"To mitigate risk." He pushed a fountain pen into her hand. "Sign it. And we'll go get our marriage license."

Callie looked through the thick stack of papers of the prenuptial agreement. She started to read the first paragraph. It would probably take an hour to read it all. Frowning, she thumbed through the pages uncertainly. She saw the amount of money he intended to give her as alimony and child support and looked up with a gasp. "Are you crazy? I don't want your money!"

"My child will grow up in a safe, secure, comfortable home. That means she must never worry about money. And neither can you." He set his jaw, watching her with visible annoyance as she turned back to page two and continued reading through the document. "Do you intend to read every single word?"

"Of course I do." Lifting her head, she glared at him, even as pedestrians jostled them on the sidewalk. "I know you, Eduardo. I know how you operate—"

Her voice choked off as another sharp pain hit her body, so intense her spine straightened as she nearly gasped aloud. The contractions were getting worse. Surely this wasn't Braxton-Hicks. She was in labor. Real labor. The baby was on her way. Callie put one hand over her belly and exhaled through her teeth.

"What's wrong?"

Eduardo's voice had changed. Trying to hide the pain rolling through her in waves, she looked up.

His handsome face was looking down at her with concern. He was worried about her. His dark eyes were warm, warm as they'd been during the time when she'd been his infallible secretary, when she'd been the one woman he needed, the only woman he trusted. Before they'd slept together in the happiest night of her life, and then she'd lost everything.

The intensity of his gaze caused her heart to twist in her chest. She could cope with his cold anger or cruel words, but not his concern. Not his kindness. A lump rose in her throat, and she suddenly had to fight tears.

"Nothing's wrong," she said. "I just want to get this over with." Gripping the pen, she turned to the pages marked with yellow tags and rapidly scrawled her signature. It was all she could do to keep the pen steady, with her knees shaking. She shoved both the signed prenuptial agreement and pen against Eduardo's chest, then turned away to focus on her breathing.

Breathe in, breathe out. She tried to let the pain go through her without fighting it or tensing her muscles, but it was impossible. *Stupid useless breathing classes!*

"You didn't read it," Eduardo said behind her, sounding almost bewildered. "That's not like you."

A policeman mounted on horseback came clopping in their direction, even as yellow taxis and large buses whizzed down the street, honking noisily. But all the moving colors of the busy world seemed to slide like water around her. She didn't answer.

Eduardo touched her shoulder, turning her around. "Callie," he said huskily. "What is it?"

She couldn't speak over the ache in her throat. She'd loved him, in spite of his faults. She'd thought she was his one indispensible woman. Until he'd discarded her. She couldn't let herself care for him. And she couldn't let herself believe, even for an instant, that he cared for her.

"I just hate you, that's all," she bit out, pulling away. Pain ebbed from her body, and she exhaled, forcing her shoulders to relax. "Let's just get this sham of a wedding over with."

Without waiting for him, she started walking up the steps toward the courthouse.

"Fine." When he caught up with her, the brief concern in his voice was gone. He strode ahead to open the door, and when she saw his face, it was hard and cold again. She was glad. She couldn't bear his tenderness, not in his eyes and not in his voice. Even after all this time, it twisted her heart into a million pieces.

Three months, she told herself, her teeth chattering. *Then I'll be free.*

She followed him into the courthouse, with his lawyer trailing behind. Twenty-two minutes later, they walked back out with the license. Callie knew it was exactly twenty-two minutes, because she'd started timing her contractions with her watch.

Eduardo didn't touch her as they walked down the steps. He didn't smile. He barely looked at her. After bidding the lawyer farewell, he led her toward the black car at the curb. "I have made arrangements for us to be married privately at my home," he said coolly, as if discussing a business arrangement. Which, Callie reminded herself savagely, was exactly what it was.

She tried to follow, desperate to get their nightmare wedding over and done with, but another contraction hit her. Panting, she grabbed his arm. "I don't think I can."

He looked at her, his eyes flinty. "It's too late for second thoughts."

Sun burst through the clouds as light rain fell, sprinkling against her hot skin. She felt the contraction build inside her, and she could no longer deny what was happening. She gripped his jacket sleeve tightly. "I think…I think I'm in labor."

He sucked in his breath, searching her gaze. "Labor?"

Wheezing, she nodded. As the pain built, her knees went weak beneath her and she felt herself start to collapse toward the sidewalk.

Then she felt Eduardo's strong arms around her as he lifted her against his chest. It felt good, so good, to be cradled in his arms that she nearly wept. He looked down at her, his jaw tight.

"How long?" he demanded.

Her body was starting to shake with the pain and she saw from his expression that he could feel it, too. "All... day...I—I think..."

"Damn you, Callie!" he said hoarsely. "Why do you hide everything?"

She was in too much agony to answer. His jaw clenched and he turned away, racing to the curb. "Sanchez! Door!" he shouted, and his driver sprang into action. Seconds later, she was in the backseat of the black sedan. Eduardo took her hands in his own as he asked urgently, "Which hospital, Callie? The name of your doctor?"

She told him, as Eduardo turned to shout the information at his driver, growling at him to drive faster, *faster*.

"Just hold on, *querida*," Eduardo said softly to her, stroking her hair. "We're almost there."

But Callie was lost in pain as the car flew down the streets of New York, taking sharp turns and honking wildly until the car sharply stopped. The car door flung open, and she was dimly aware of Eduardo shouting that his wife needed help, help *now* dammit!

"But I'm not your wife," Callie breathed as she was wheeled into the hospital. She looked up at him, blinking back tears even as the pain started to recede. "We only have a license. We're not married."

Callie heard him gasp before she was whisked away by

a nurse to a private examination room. As the contraction eased, she changed into a hospital gown. When the nurse came back through the door, Callie got a single glimpse of Eduardo pacing in the hallway, barking madly into a phone at his ear. Then the door closed, and the round-faced, smiling nurse came to check her. She straightened. "Six centimeters dilated. Oh, my goodness. This baby is on the way. We'll notify the doctor and get you to your room. I'm afraid it might be too late for anesthesia…"

"Don't—care—just want my baby to—be all right…" But before Callie had even been wheeled to her private labor and delivery room, the new contraction had already begun. Each one was worse than the last, and this one hit her so badly it made her whole body shake. Rising to her feet, reaching toward her bed, Callie covered her mouth as nausea suddenly roiled through her.

Quickly Eduardo came behind her. He snatched up the trash can and gave it to her just in time for her to be sick in it. Afterward, as the pain receded, Callie sat down on her hospital bed and cried. She cried from pain, from fear, and most of all from knowing that she'd just been vulnerable in front of Eduardo Cruz…and was about to be even more vulnerable.

But there was no way out now.

Only one way through.

"Help her!" Eduardo bit out at the nurse, who gave him an understanding smile.

"I'm sorry. I don't think there's time for meds. But don't worry. The doctor is on his way.…"

Eduardo snarled a curse that involved the doctor's lacking moral qualities, intelligence and bloodline. Growling, he went to the door and peered out into the hallway for the third time before Callie heard him mutter, "Thank God. What took so long?"

"All good things take time." A smiling, white-haired man in a suit followed him back into the private delivery suite. Eduardo went to Callie, who was stretched out across the hospital bed with her feet in stirrups, taking deep breaths and trying to relax before the next contraction.

"That's not my doctor!" she cried.

Eduardo knelt beside the bed. "He's going to marry us, Callie."

She looked between them in shock. "Right now?"

He gave her a crooked half smile, pushing sweaty tendrils of hair off her face. "Why? Are you busy?"

Callie looked at the trim man with the white beard and bow tie. "Is he authorized to just randomly marry people?"

The corners of his lips quirked. "He's a justice of the New York Supreme Court. So yes."

"There's a twenty-four-hour waiting period after the license—"

"He's waived it."

"And my previous license—"

"Handled."

"Everything always goes your way, doesn't it?" she grumbled.

Leaning over the hospital bed, he kissed her sweaty forehead. "No," he said in a low voice. "But this time it will." He turned back to the judge. "We are ready."

"The doctor will be here any second," the nurse warned.

"I'll do the express version, then." The judge stood in front of the beeping, flashing displays that monitored both Callie's heart rate and the baby's, and gave the plump nurse a wink. "Will you be my witness?"

"All right," the nurse said with a girlish blush. "But make it quick."

"Quicker 'n quick. So. We're gathered here in this hospital room to marry this man and this woman." The judge peered down at Callie's huge belly. "And none too soon, I'd say…"

"Just get on with it, Leland," Eduardo snapped.

"Do you, Eduardo Jorge Cruz, take this woman—what's your name, my dear?"

"It's Calliope," Eduardo answered for her through clenched teeth. "Calliope Marlena Woodville."

"Is it really?" The judge looked at her sympathetically through wire-rimmed glasses. "How very unfortunate for you."

"From my mother's—favorite soap opera," she panted.

"Right. So do you, Eduardo, take this woman, Calliope Marlena Woodville, to be your lawfully wedded wife?"

"I do."

Callie felt the pain starting to build again, and grabbed Eduardo's shirt. Looking at her, he put his hand over hers, then said angrily to the judge, "Hurry, damn you!"

"And do you, Calliope Woodville, promise to love Eduardo Jorge Cruz, forsaking all others, till death do you part?"

Eduardo looked down at her with his dark eyes. Once, this had been all Callie ever wanted, to promise her love and fidelity to him forever. And now it was happening. She was promising to love him forever, though she knew it was a lie.

It *was* a lie, wasn't it?

"Callie?" Eduardo said in a low voice.

"I do," she choked out.

Eduardo exhaled. Had he wondered, for a brief instant, if she might refuse? No, impossible. He was too arrogant, too sure of his control over women, to ever doubt….

"I see you already have the ring," the judge said, then blinked in surprise at the tiny diamond on Callie's hand.

"I must say, Eduardo," he murmured, "that's unusually restrained for you."

She was still wearing Brandon's engagement ring! Horrified, Callie tried to pull it off her swollen finger, but it was stuck. "I'm sorry—I…forgot…"

Without a word, Eduardo eased the ring from her finger and tossed it in the trash. "I will buy you a ring," he said flatly. "One worthy of my wife."

"Don't worry." She gave him a weak smile as she felt the pain start to build again. She panted, "Our marriage will be so short it really doesn't matter…"

"That's the spirit," the judge said jovially. "Ring can come later. Or not. Well, kids, we'll just skip through and assume the part about forsaking all others and staying together for better or worse. And since with Eduardo I already know it'll be for richer, not poorer, I reckon that's about it."

Callie stared at the judge, then Eduardo. The wedding ceremony had passed by in a flash. Just a few words spoken, and two lives—soon, three—forever changed. How could something so life-changing be so fast?

The judge gave them a big grin. "You may now kiss the bride."

She nearly gasped. *Kiss?* She'd forgotten that part! He was going to kiss her?

Eduardo turned to her. Their eyes met. He slowly leaned over the bed, and for an instant, all the pain fled Callie's body in a breathless flash.

When his mouth was an inch from hers, he hesitated. She could feel the warmth of his breath against her skin, causing prickles up and down the length of her body.

Then he lowered his lips to hers.

Eduardo kissed her, and prickles turned to spiraling electricity, sizzling her nerves like a current sparking up and down her body. His lips were hot and soft, in pledge of their promise, inflaming her senses from within. It lasted only a brief moment, but when he pulled away, Callie's hands were shaking, and not from pain.

"Congratulations, you crazy kids," the justice said, beaming at them. "You're married."

Married. Callie's body flashed cold over the magnitude of what she'd just done. She'd married Eduardo. She was his wife.

Just for three months, she reminded herself desperately. The prenuptial agreement had been clear about the timetable. At least in the paragraphs she'd skimmed before the contraction had hit her... She tensed as another contraction hit, burning through her like wildfire. She gasped, biting back a cry as her doctor came in, a brown-haired man in his late fifties. Glancing at the monitors, he checked her. Then he smiled. "Seems you're good at this, especially for a first-time mother. All right, Callie. Time to push."

Her eyes went wide as fear ripped through her. Instinctively she reached for Eduardo's hand, looking up at him with pleading eyes.

Eduardo took both her hands in his. "Callie, I'm here." His voice was deep and calm as his dark eyes looked straight into hers. "I'm right here."

Panting, she focused only on his black eyes, letting herself be drawn into them. As she started to push, bringing her baby into the world, she'd never felt any pain so deep. She gripped her new husband's hands so tightly she thought she'd break his bones, but Eduardo never flinched, not once. He never left her. As she held on to him for dear life, nurses moving around them at lightning speed, monitors beeping, she focused through her tears on his single, blurry image. Eduardo was her one solid, immovable focal point.

He never looked away.

He never backed down.

He never left her.

And in the end, the pain was worth it.

A healthy seven-pound-eight-ounce baby girl was finally placed in Callie's arms. She looked down at her daughter in amazement, at the sweetest weight she'd ever known. Cuddled against her chest, the baby blinked up at her sleepily.

Leaning over them, Eduardo kissed Callie's sweaty forehead, then their baby's. For a long, perfect moment, as medical personnel bustled around them, the newly married couple sat together on the bed with their brand-new baby.

"Thank you, Callie, for the greatest gift of my life," Eduardo said softly, stroking the baby's cheek. He looked up, and his dark, luminous eyes pierced her soul. "A family."

CHAPTER THREE

EDUARDO CRUZ had always known he'd have a family different from the one he'd grown up in. Different.

Better.

His home would have the joyous chaos of many children, instead of a lonely, solitary existence. His children would have comfort and security, with plenty of food and money. And most of all: his children would have two parents, neither of whom would be selfish enough to abandon their children.

The first time Eduardo had seen a truly happy family, he'd been ten, hungrily trolling the aisles of a tiny grocer's shop in his poor village in southern Spain. A gleaming black sedan had pulled up on the dusty road, and a wealthy, distinguished-looking man had entered the shop, followed by his wife and children. As the man asked the shopkeeper for directions to Madrid, Eduardo watched the beautifully dressed woman walk around with her two young children. When they clamored for ice cream, she didn't yell or slap them. Instead she'd hugged them, ruffled their hair then laughed with her husband as he'd pulled out his wallet with a sigh. Handing out the ice creams, the man had whispered something in his wife's ear as he wrapped his arm around her waist. Eduardo had watched as they left, getting back in their luxury car and disappearing down the road to their fairy-tale lives.

"Who was that?" Eduardo had breathed.

"The Duke and Duchess of Quixota. I recognize them from the papers," the elderly shopkeeper had replied, looking equally awed. Then he turned to Eduardo with a frown. "But what are you doing here? I told your parents they'd get no more credit. What's this?" Grabbing the neck of Eduardo's threadbare, too-short jacket, he pulled out the three ice cream bars melting in his pocket. "You're stealing?" he cried, his face harsh. "But I should have expected it, from a family like yours!"

Humiliated and ashamed, Eduardo's heart felt like it would burst, but his face was blank. At ten years old, he'd learned not to show his feelings from a mother who raged at him if he laughed, and a father who beat him if he cried.

Scowling, the shopkeeper held up the ice cream bars. "Why?"

Eduardo's stomach growled. There was no food at home, but that wasn't the reason. He'd been sent home from school early today for getting into a fight, but his father hadn't cared about what had caused the fight. He'd just hit Eduardo across the face and kicked him from the house. He was too disabled—and too drunk—to do anything but lie on the couch and rage against his faithless wife. Eduardo's mother, who worked as a barmaid in the next village, had been coming home less and less, and three days ago, she'd disappeared completely. The boys at school had taunted Eduardo. *Not even your mother thinks you're worth staying for.*

When he'd seen the *Madrileños* eating ice creams, Eduardo had had the confused thought that if he took some home, his family might love each other, too. *¡Idiota!*

Crushing, miserable fury filled him. He suddenly hated them—all of them.

"Well?" the grocer demanded.

"Keep it, then!" Reaching out a grubby hand, Eduardo knocked the ice cream bars to the floor. He'd turned and run out of the shop, running as fast as his legs could carry him, gasping as he ran for home.

And it was then he'd found his father...

Eduardo blinked. He looked around the comfort and luxury of his chauffeured, three-hundred-thousand-dollar car. His eyes were strangely wet as he looked down at his two-day-old baby, sleeping peacefully in her car seat as Sanchez drove them home from the hospital.

Her childhood would be different.

Different.

Better.

He'd never let the selfishness of adults destroy her innocent happiness. He would protect her at all costs. He would kill for her. Die for her. Do anything.

Even be married to her mother.

As the car drove north on Madison Avenue, Eduardo's eyes looked past the baby to Callie on the other side. He'd once thought she was the only person he could really trust, but the joke was on him.

She'd lied to his face for years.

And not just to him. A few hours after the birth, Callie had called her family to tell them about her new marriage and new baby. White-faced and trembling, she'd refused to speak to her sister then started crying as she spoke to her mother. When Eduardo had heard her father yelling on the other line, leaving Callie in tearful, pitiful sobs, he'd finally snatched the phone away. He'd intended to calm the man down. But it hadn't exactly turned out that way.

He scowled, remembering Walter Woodville's angry

words. Setting his jaw, Eduardo pushed the memory aside. The man was clearly a tyrant. No wonder Callie had learned to keep things to herself. His eyes narrowed.

Then he looked back at his sleeping daughter, and his heartbeat calmed. For the past two days he hadn't been able to stop staring at her tiny fingers. Her plump cheeks. Her long eyelashes. The way she unconsciously pursed her tiny mouth to suckle, even while she slept.

Eduardo took a deep breath.

He had a child. A family of his own.

He had a wife.

He'd married Callie to give their baby a name, he reminded himself, then he scowled. And yet she was still nameless.

He glared at his wife and bit out, "María."

Callie looked back sharply, her vivid green eyes glinting like emeralds sparkling in the sun. "I told you no. My baby will not be named after your Spanish dream wife. No way."

He exhaled, regretting he'd ever told his trusted secretary that he wished to marry María de Leondros, the young, beautiful Duchess of Alda. They'd only met socially once or twice, but marrying her would have been a satisfying way to prove how far he'd come since the days he'd stolen ice creams. "María is a common name," he said evenly. "It was my great-aunt's name."

"Bite me."

"You're being jealous for no reason. I never even slept with María de Leondros!"

"Lucky her." She folded her arms, glaring at him. "My daughter's name is Soleil."

Irritated, Eduardo set his jaw. Was it so strange that he wished to name his child after his Tía María, who'd brought him to New York, who'd worked three jobs to support him? María Cruz had encouraged him to see his high-school job pumping gas in Brooklyn not as a dead-end, but a place to begin. After she'd died, he'd gone from driving a gas truck, to owning a small gasoline distribution business, which he'd sold at twenty-four to become a wildcatter. His first big find had been in Alaska, followed by Oklahoma. Now Cruz Oil had drilling operations all over the world.

Yet Callie stubbornly refused to be reasonable. Instead she pushed for the name *Soleil,* which meant nothing personal to anyone—she'd just found it in a baby name book and liked the sound! He set his jaw. "You are being irrational."

"No, you are," she retorted. "You're already giving her a surname, and I chose her name months ago. I'm not changing it because of your whim."

He lifted his eyebrows incredulously. "My *whim*?"

"Soleil is pretty!"

"Did it, too, come from your mother's favorite *tele-novela*?"

"Go to hell," she said, turning to stare out the window as they drove through the city. Silence fell in the backseat. Eduardo took a deep breath, clenching his hands into fists. His wife's stubbornness exceeded common sense! Because of her, they'd had to leave the hospital without yet filing a birth certificate.

His jaw set grimly, he turned back to her. "Callie—"

But her eyes were closed, her cheek pressed against the car window. He heard the rhythm of her breathing, and realized to his shock that she'd fallen asleep in the middle of their argument.

He looked at her beautiful face, against the backdrop of Central Park, the vivid green trees and lawn reminding him of her eyes. Her light brown hair fell in soft waves against her roses-and-cream complexion. As usual, she wore no makeup, but no ingénue on Broadway could hold a candle to her natural beauty. She wore the baggy knit pants and long-sleeved T-shirt his staff had brought to the hospital, but he knew the hidden curves of her generous figure would put any scrawny swimsuit model to shame.

For months he'd tried not to remember her beauty, but being this close to her, the reality overwhelmed him. His wife was the most desirable woman on earth. Even with those dark hollows beneath her eyes.

A sharp edge rose in his throat. Turning, he looked out at the brilliant dappled early evening light glowing gold through the trees. Callie had given birth to their child without anesthesia. He still couldn't comprehend that kind of bravery, that kind of strength. For the last two nights, as he'd slept in a chair beside her bed, Callie had barely slept at all. The baby had had some difficulty learning how to nurse, and Callie had been up almost every hour. He'd offered to help, and so had the nurses, but she'd insisted on doing everything herself. "She's my baby," Callie had whispered, her face pale with exhaustion. "She needs me."

Looking at Callie now, asleep with her face pressed against the window, Eduardo was forced to acknowledge feelings he'd never thought he'd feel for her again.

Admiration. Appreciation. *Respect.*

Things she'd clearly never felt for him.

"I've heard all about you, Eduardo Cruz." Walter Woodville had hissed over the phone two days ago. "Do you expect me to be grateful to you for doing the honorable thing and marrying my daughter?"

Eduardo knew Callie's family meant everything to her, so he'd contained his temper. "Mr. Woodville, I understand your feelings, but surely you can see…"

"Understand? Understand? You seduced my daughter. You used her and tossed her aside." Walter Woodville's voice was sodden with anger and grief. "And when you found out she was pregnant, you weren't even man enough to come and ask me for her hand. You just selfishly took her. *You stole my daughter.*"

Those particular words ripped through Eduardo like a blade. Then rage built through him in turn. "We never expected it to happen, but I have taken responsibility. I will provide for both Callie and the child—"

"*Responsibility,*" Walter spat out. "All you can offer is money. You might own half our town, but I know the kind of man you really are." The old man's voice caught, then hardened. "You'll never be a decent husband or father, and you know it. If you're even half a man, you'll send her and the baby home to people who are capable of loving them."

Then to Eduardo's shock, the man had hung up, leaving him standing in the hospital room, staring at his phone, wide-eyed with rage. No one spoke to him like that—well, no one except Callie.

But the old man wasn't afraid of him. He knew Eduardo's faults and flaws. And there could be only one person who'd told him.

Funny to think how he'd once trusted her. He'd wanted her in his bed almost from the start, but he'd needed Callie Woodville so much in his office, in his life, that he'd forbidden himself to ever act on his desire.

Until last Christmas Eve.

In a lavish, gilded ballroom of a Midtown hotel, Eduardo had found himself stone-cold sober at his own Christmas party, surrounded by Cruz Oil's vice presidents and board members and their trophy wives. The men in tuxedos, the women dripping diamonds and furs, had danced and drunk the spiked eggnog, alternatively boasting about the latest promising data in Colombia or gleefully discussing the expensive toys they planned to buy with their next stock bonuses.

Eduardo had watched them. He should have been in his element. Instead he'd felt lost. Disconnected.

He had everything he'd ever wanted. He controlled everything; he was vulnerable to no one. He'd thought being strong and powerful and rich would make him content, or at least, impervious to pain. Instead he just felt…alone.

Then he saw her on the other side of the ballroom.

Callie wore a simple, modest sheath dress. She stopped, her emerald eyes wide, and a flash went through him like fire.

In this cavernous ballroom, filled with tinsel and champagne and silvery lights, nothing was warm. Nothing was real. Nothing mattered.

Except her.

"Excuse me." Shoving his untasted glass of mulled wine into his CFO's hands, he'd walked straight through the crowd. Without a word, he'd taken Callie's hand. He'd pulled her out of the ballroom, and she didn't resist as he led her out into the white, icy winter night. Not waiting for his limo, he'd hailed a taxi to Bank Street, where he'd carried her to his bed. There, amid the breathless hush of midnight, he'd made love to her. He'd taken her virginity. He'd held her tight, so tight, as if she were a life raft that might save him from a devouring black sea.

He'd never felt anything like that night, before or since. Their passion had resulted in a baby.

It had resulted in a wife.

Eduardo's eyes narrowed as he looked at Callie, still sleeping as the car exited Central Park into the city streets of the exclusive Upper West Side.

You seduced my daughter, Walter Woodville had accused. The truth was that she had seduced Eduardo. With her innocence. With her warmth. With her fire.

But she was a liar. She'd hidden so much from him. He could never trust her again.

Only his baby mattered now. With her dark hair, she was his spitting image. Eduardo had known she was his child long before that morning's paternity test confirmed it. But if Sami Woodville hadn't called him two days ago out of the blue, his baby would be living in North Dakota right now. She'd be Brandon McLinn's daughter.

Eduardo's jaw clenched. Even if Callie was in love with another man, he could hardly believe she'd betrayed him so deeply. But he didn't have to trust her. He had a private investigator on staff who could tell him everything he needed to know about Callie. He'd never be fooled by her again.

He would keep his friends close, his enemies closer and his wife the closest of all.

The sedan arrived at his twenty-floor building on West End Avenue. As Sanchez opened the door, Eduardo carefully, breathlessly, lifted his sleeping baby out of the car seat. He walked slowly so he didn't wake her, cradling her head against his chest as the doorman held open the door. The baby was so tiny, he thought. So helpless and fragile. And he loved her. Love swelled his heart until it ached inside his ribs. He let himself love her as he'd never loved anyone.

His plump, gray-haired housekeeper, Mrs. McAuliffe, was waiting in the luxurious lobby. "The nursery is ready. Och, what a sweet babe!"

"Do you know how to hold a baby?" he demanded.

"Why, I'm insulted, Mr. Cruz! You know I raised four children of my own."

"Here." Gently he thrust the sleeping baby into her arms, watching anxiously. As the older woman cooed softly in admiration, Eduardo turned and raced back outside.

The September sun was still hot, pouring golden light through the white clouds. His driver was reaching for his wife's door when Eduardo stopped him. "I'll do it, Sanchez."

"Of course, sir."

Eduardo looked down at Callie through the car window. Her head had fallen back, her beautiful face now leaning against the leather seat. Dark, long eyelashes fluttered against her pale skin. She looked so young. So tired.

As he lifted her into his arms, she stirred but did not wake. Her eyelashes fluttered and she murmured something in her sleep, nestling her cheek against his chest as her wavy light brown hair fell back on his shoulder.

She weighed next to nothing, he thought. Looking down at his wife, his heart gave a strange thump. While Sanchez drove the car to the underground garage, Eduardo carried Callie inside. He took his private elevator to the top floor.

He'd closed on this two-story penthouse a week ago as an investment. The penthouse had been languishing on the market for two years with a thirty-six-million-dollar price tag before he'd bought it for a steal, at the fire sale price of twenty-seven million. He hadn't intended to live here for long. But now…his plans were rapidly changing.

"I'll take the baby to the nursery, sir," his housekeeper said softly when he came out of the elevator. He nodded then carried his wife across the large, two-story foyer with its Brazilian hardwood floor in a patterned mosaic. Going up the sweeping stairs, he started down the hall toward the guest room.

Then he stopped.

The master bedroom would be better for Callie in every way. It was larger, with a huge en suite bathroom and a wall of windows overlooking the city and the Hudson River. Most importantly, it was adjacent to the study, which had been turned into the nursery. Shifting Callie's weight in his arms, Eduardo turned back. Carrying her into his bedroom, he put her down on his king-size bed. *Sí.* It was better.

Callie shifted, murmuring in her sleep as she turned on his soft feather pillow with its thousand-thread-count Egyptian cotton pillowcase. Eduardo closed the heavy curtains around the windows, darkening the room. He covered her sleeping form with a blanket, then for a long moment, he looked down at her, listening to her steady, even breath.

He'd only meant their marriage to last three months. He hadn't thought he could endure it for longer.

But in the forty-eight hours since the birth, his perspective had changed.

His daughter was small and innocent and oh, so fragile. Eduardo knew what it meant to feel like unwanted baggage, like a stray without a home. He wanted his daughter to feel safe and protected, not split between divorced parents, between two lives. He wanted her to have not just a name, but a real home. A real family.

And no matter what Eduardo thought of Callie, he knew she loved their baby. He'd seen it in the way she'd fought through the pain of childbirth with such bravery. In the way she'd sacrificed her own body, her own sleep and peace, in order to nurture and cherish their child. Even in the way she'd fought with him over her name.

Eduardo's jaw set. If Callie could endure pain, so could he. He turned away. There would be no divorce. They both would sacrifice. He would give up his desire for a wife he could trust. She would give up her dreams of love. Love was an illusion, anyway.

Responsibility was not.

She might not like his plan. Eduardo exhaled, remembering her horrified reaction when he'd first proposed marriage. She wouldn't accept a permanent union without a fight. So he would give her time to accept their loveless marriage. To appreciate what he could offer. To forget the people she'd left behind.

His hand tightened on the doorknob. He'd give her the agreed-upon three months to see the benefits of their marriage. And if, at the end, Callie still wanted her freedom?

He glanced back through the shadowy bedroom with narrowed eyes. Then he'd ruthlessly keep her prisoner, like a songbird in a gilded cage. Walking into the hallway, Eduardo shut the double doors behind him with quiet, ominous finality.

Now that Callie was his wife, he never intended to let her go.

CHAPTER FOUR

CALLIE sat up straight in bed.

Disoriented, she put her hands to her head, feeling dizzy and half-asleep as she looked around the strange, dark room. Where was she? How did she get in this bed? Her breasts were full and aching, and she was still dressed in the same long-sleeved T-shirt and knit pants she'd worn from the hospital. She had no memory of how she'd gotten here, but she'd thought she heard her baby crying....

Her baby! She sucked in her breath. Where was her baby?

"Soleil?" she whimpered. She jumped up from bed and screamed, "Soleil!"

Light flooded the room from the hallway as double doors opened. Suddenly Eduardo's arms were around her.

"Where is she?" she cried in panic, struggling in his arms. She looked up at the hard lines of his face, half-hidden in shadows. "Where have you taken her?"

"She's here." Eduardo abruptly released her, crossing the bedroom to fling open a door. "Here!"

Her baby's cries became louder. With a gasp, Callie ran through the door. As he turned on a lamp, she saw the bassinet. Sobbing with relief, she scooped her baby up into her arms.

The baby's cries subsided the instant she was cradled

against her mother's breast, but she was clearly hungry. Callie sat down in a soft glider near the lamp and started to pull up her T-shirt. She stopped, looking up awkwardly at Eduardo. "I need to feed her."

His dark eyes shimmered in the dim lamplight. "Go ahead."

"You're watching."

"I've seen your breasts before."

She glared at him. "Turn around!"

He lifted an eyebrow then with a sigh he turned away.

Once he was safely facing the other direction, Callie lifted up her shirt, pulled down her nursing bra and got her baby latched on to her breast. She flinched at first then relaxed as her tiny daughter started gulping blissfully.

"Sounds like she was hungry."

"Don't listen!" Callie cried, annoyed.

He gave a low laugh. "Sorry."

Moments passed in silence, and Callie took a deep breath, suddenly ashamed. "I'm sorry about earlier. I just panicked. I woke up in a strange place and didn't know where I was."

His spine stiffened, but he didn't turn. "You fell asleep in the car, on the way home. I carried you upstairs. Don't you remember?"

The last thing she recalled was arguing with him as they drove through Central Park. He'd been pressuring her about their baby's name—as if Callie would ever name her sweet newborn after a spoiled Spanish heiress! But the soft hum of the engine had been hypnotic.

"I guess I was tired." She rubbed her hand over her eyes. "I slept so hard that I almost thought you'd drugged me so you could steal the baby. Funny, right?"

His voice was cold. "Hilarious."

"I'm sorry," she whispered. "I didn't mean to accuse you of…" Her throat constricted.

He turned to face her, but he definitely wasn't looking at her breasts. "Of stealing the baby?"

She swallowed. "Yes."

His eyes glimmered in the dim light. "Don't worry about it."

He was being nice, which made her feel even worse. For months, she'd hated Eduardo, calling him a coldhearted jerk to her parents and friends, telling them stories about his worst flaws, telling herself he didn't deserve to be a father.

But *she* was the coldhearted jerk. Her lips parted. If not for Sami's meddling, she would have done the dreadful thing she'd just accused him of: she'd have stolen their baby. He never would have even known he had a daughter.

How could Eduardo stand to look at her?

"I was wrong not to tell you." It took all her courage to meet his eyes. "I'm so sorry. Can you ever forgive me?"

"Forget it," he said harshly. He folded his arms. "We both made mistakes. It's in the past. Our marriage is a fresh start."

"Thank you," she whispered, feeling like she didn't deserve his generosity. Awkwardly she looked around them. The nursery was straight out of a celebrity magazine, with soft yellow walls, stuffed animals, and the sleek comfort of an expensive designer crib and bassinet. "This is nice."

"I had my staff redecorate the study while we were at the hospital."

"Your staff?"

"Mrs. McAuliffe."

"I've always known I liked her," Callie said with a

smile, trying to lighten the mood. "So next door is the guest room?"

He shook his head. "It's the master bedroom."

Her heart plummeted. "I...I was sleeping in your bed?"

"*Sí.*"

"Oh." She swallowed and tried to pretend it was no big deal that she'd slept sprawled across the same bed where Eduardo Cruz slept naked every night, when he wasn't entertaining lingerie models. Feeling self-conscious, she moved her baby to the other breast, quickly covering up any flash of skin with her cotton shirt. Cheeks flaming, she glanced up at Eduardo, but thank heaven, he was carefully looking away. "Well, thanks," she said with forced cheerfulness. "I'll move to the guest room later."

"You will stay in the master bedroom," he said evenly, "close to our baby."

"Then where would you sleep?" A sudden dreadful thought struck her. "You surely can't think you and I will—"

He cut her off. "I will take the guest room."

"I don't want to inconvenience you."

"You won't." Coming forward, he touched the infant's soft, downy head. "I want you to be here. Both of you."

Looking up at him, she breathed, "You—you do?"

"Of course I do." Eduardo looked at her, and his dark eyes cut straight through her heart. "I've dreamed of having a family like this. Of keeping them safe and warm. Protecting them." He squared his shoulders. "And I will."

The cold, ruthless edges of his expression had melted away, changing to something warm, something fiercely tender. He looked like another man, she thought in wonder. The man he might have been if his childhood had been less of a tragedy.

Compassion mixed with longing and the echoes of her love, rising in her heart. But she couldn't let it win. She wouldn't. She took a deep breath. "Thanks for taking such good care of me." With a trembling smile, she looked down at the baby falling asleep in her arms. "And Soleil."

"Marisol," he said abruptly.

She blinked. "What?"

"Marisol. It's a classic Spanish name. A blend of your favorite name—Soleil—and my aunt's name. María."

Callie licked her lips. "Marisol," she tried. She didn't hate it. She tried again, "Marisol...Cruz."

"Marisol Samantha Cruz," he said softly.

She looked up, her eyes wide with shock. "After my sister?"

"She brought our family together."

"Sami betrayed me!"

"She's family. You will forgive her." He looked down at her. "We both know you will."

Callie stared at him in consternation. No. No way! She'd never forgive her sister for going behind her back and telling Eduardo about the baby—never!

And yet...

How could she be angry at Sami for betraying her, when telling Eduardo the truth had been the right thing to do? Even if Sami's motives hadn't been totally pure. A tremble went through Callie. Even if her sister's motivation had only been because she was in love with Brandon.

Sami was in love with Brandon. Callie had to face it. For years, she'd seen the way Sami hung on Brandon's every word, but she'd told herself it couldn't possibly be serious. Her sister had a crush. Puppy love. Callie hadn't seen the truth. She doubted Brandon did, either. They'd never noticed Sami's devoted, anguished love, right in front of their very eyes.

But Brandon deserved to be loved like that, as every husband wanted to be loved by his wife. Callie had been selfish to accept his proposal, to think, even for an instant, that friendship would be enough for a marriage. How could she have even thought of allowing him to make that sacrifice? A sob escaped her throat. She'd very nearly ruined so many lives.

Looking down, Eduardo put his hand gently on her shoulder.

"I've heard you talk about your little sister for years," he said quietly. "You send her gifts, write her letters. You're putting her through college. We both know you're going to forgive her."

Callie looked up at him, blinking back tears. "You're right," she whispered. "I was so angry at her. But she didn't do anything wrong." She closed her eyes. "It was all me."

Silence fell. When she opened her eyes, Eduardo's forehead was furrowed, as if he couldn't understand her. Their eyes met, and she felt that strange tugging at her heart. With an intake of breath, she turned away. "Fine."

"Fine?"

"Her middle name can be Samantha." Callie touched her baby's plump, soft cheek. "Marisol Samantha Cruz."

"I don't believe it." A ghost of a smile lifted the corners of Eduardo's lips. "Are we in agreement? I can fill out the birth certificate?"

Looking up at him, she smiled back. "Yup."

"Wonders never cease." For a long moment, their eyes met in the soft light of the nursery, with their baby slumbering between them. Then clearing his throat, he glanced at his platinum watch. "It's nearly ten. You must be starving."

"Not really…" As if on cue, her stomach growled. "I guess I am."

"I'll make you something."

"You? You'll cook?" she said faintly.

She must have sounded dubious, because Eduardo smiled. "I am not completely helpless."

"You must have changed a lot in the last nine months. The man I knew could barely find his own kitchen." She shook her head with a snort. "I'm amazed you even survived without me."

He looked at her.

"It wasn't easy," he said gruffly. Turning, he paused at the door. "Come down when you are ready."

Callie stared at the empty doorway, bewildered at this friendlier mood between them. Looking down at her sleeping newborn, she rocked back and forth in the soft cushioned glider, cuddling her close. She gazed in wonder at her downy dark hair. Her daughter had Callie's snub little nose and round face, with her father's dark coloring and olive-colored skin. She would be a beauty. How could she not be, with such a father?

In all the years Callie worked for Eduardo, she'd never once seen him put someone else's comfort above his own. But in the last two days, he'd asked her to marry him. He'd slept in a chair for two nights at the hospital. He'd brought her to his home. Turned his study into a nursery. He'd given Callie his bed while he himself was relegated to the guest room down the hall. He'd asked her to teach him how to swaddle their baby and change her tiny, doll-size diapers. Coldhearted billionaire tycoon Eduardo Cruz, changing a baby's diaper? That was something she'd never imagined in a million years!

It won't last, Callie told herself fiercely. When the novelty wore off, Eduardo would chafe at the responsibility and intimacy of family. He would crave the freedom of sixteen-hour workdays and endless one-night stands. He would return to the selfish, cold playboy he was at heart. Very soon—likely before the three months was even up—

he would divorce Callie, and be relieved to make his parental support of Marisol the distant, financial kind.

Once that happened, Callie and her baby would go back to North Dakota. To her family. To the people who loved her.

Or did they?

She swallowed. Her phone call to her family, just hours after the birth when she was still exhausted and in pain, had officially been a disaster. Callie tried to explain that she'd just had a baby and gotten married to a man they didn't know except by reputation, and planned to live in New York for the foreseeable future. Her mother had just sobbed as if her heart was breaking. As for her father...

Her shoulders tightened. Her father never reacted well when his wife was crying. But he'd never spoken to Callie like that before—as if she were such a disappointment he didn't even want to call her his daughter. As if he yearned to disown her.

An ache filled her throat. She'd never planned to get pregnant, but keeping her baby a secret had just made it a million times worse. And that phone call had changed something between them. She felt estranged from her family, and it was like half her heart was missing.

But she also felt angry. How could her family have turned on her like this? They were supposed to love her. Why couldn't they see her side?

And her father had been so harsh to Eduardo. Callie still didn't know exactly what he'd said. She just remembered how Eduardo's expression had changed when they were talking on the phone, from conciliation to cold fury.

Walter Woodville had never liked the way Cruz Oil had swept into their town, bulldozing through the county with money and influence, luring young people from family farms with the promise of high-paying jobs. But Callie had made that initial dislike worse. Her cheeks burned as she recalled her bitter words about Eduardo after he'd fired her. Was it any wonder that stalwart, old-fashioned Walter, who'd married his high school sweetheart and still farmed land once owned by his grandfather, had been horrified by the idea of such a man knocking up his daughter, and worse—marrying her?

And as for Brandon...

Her cheeks reddened further with shame and regret. Brandon was certainly back in North Dakota by now, after driving across the country alone. She wondered what he'd told her parents. What he felt inside. Was he worried about her? Was he angry? Or worse—brokenhearted?

Amazing to think he was willing to marry you while you were pregnant by another man. He must be insanely in love with you.

Callie shook Eduardo's words away. Brandon wasn't in love with her. Friends just tried to help each other. But no—that was a cop-out. She swallowed. He'd been kind, and she'd taken advantage. She needed to call him and beg for forgiveness.

Another person she'd hurt. She slowly rose to her feet, her body sore, her legs shaking with exhaustion. As she tucked her sleeping daughter into the bassinet, she suddenly remembered the tender light in Eduardo's dark eyes when he'd held Marisol for the first time. Remembered how he'd dozed on a chair in their hospital room, cuddling their daughter against his naked chest so the baby could feel the warmth and comfort of skin on skin. Strange. In this moment, she felt closer to Eduardo than anyone else. Eduardo.

Creeping softly out of the nursery, she went to the bedroom, where she found the suitcase of new clothes his staff had brought to the hospital. Opening it on the enormous

bed, she selected a pink cashmere lounge set and sighed.
It probably cost the equivalent of a week's salary. But the
cashmere felt soft.

Taking a hot shower in the marble en suite bathroom
was pure heaven. After combing her wet hair, Callie put
on the soft cashmere set over a white cotton t-shirt and
went downstairs.

It wasn't just a penthouse, she thought in amazement.
It was a mansion in the sky. She went down the sweeping stairs to the great room, with a fireplace and floor-to-
ceiling windows that showed the sparkling lights of New
York City by night.

"What do you think?"

She jumped and turned. Eduardo walked toward her
with two martini glasses. He was wearing dark jeans and
a black T-shirt that showed off his exquisitely muscled
body. "It's incredible," she breathed. "Like nothing else
I've seen."

"Good." He gave her a slow-rising smile. "I'm glad you
like it, since it's yours." She blushed, but still couldn't look
away from his powerful body, or the masculine beauty of
his face. *Hers.* If only that were true!

He held out an orange-filled martini glass. "Here."

"I can't drink while I'm nursing."

He held up his own drink, a clear martini with an olive.
"This is mine." He pushed the orange-colored drink into
her hand. "This is juice."

"Oh. Thanks," she said, suddenly realizing she was
dying of thirst. She drank it all in one swallow, then wiped
her mouth and realized she was hungry, too. "Something
smells delicious from the kitchen," she said hopefully, setting down her glass.

Eduardo was staring at her. "I made quesadillas and
rice."

"Great!"

"You might not like them." He smiled again, but for the first time she noticed that his smile didn't reach his eyes. His hand was gripping the stem of his martini glass, his shoulders tense. "Like you said, I'm helpless in the kitchen. Not like some men, who are undoubtedly born chefs."

Callie frowned, puzzled at his sudden change in mood. "Is something wrong?"

He showed his teeth in something like a smile. "Not a thing."

"You just seem—strange."

"I'm fine. Shall we have dinner?"

"Sure," she said reluctantly. Maybe she was so tired she was starting to imagine things. Or maybe it was her guilt talking. With a sigh, she looked around. "Have you seen my purse? I just need to make a quick call."

"Your family?"

"No," she said, irritated at the suggestion. "I called them from the hospital and look where it got me. No. Brandon."

Eduardo's dark eyes flashed in the shadowy room. "No."

"He must be back in Fern by now. I'm sure he's worried about me, and I'm worried about him—"

"He's fine," Eduardo said coolly. He finished off his martini and placed the empty glass on the marble mantel. "I just spoke with him."

She stared at him. "You did?"

"He'd been calling for hours. I got sick of the phone ringing. Ten minutes ago, I answered the phone and told him to stop."

"What did he say?"

"An earful," he said grimly. He set his jaw. "What exactly did you tell him about me?"

Her cheeks grew hot. "I was angry after you fired me. I might have called you a world-class jerk."

"A jerk?"

"And a workaholic with no heart, who lures a new woman into bed each night, only to put her out with the trash each morning," she whispered. She shook her head. "I'm sorry. I shouldn't have said it."

Eduardo gave her a hard smile. "You just told him the truth." Reaching for his empty martini glass, he pulled the olive off the toothpick with his white teeth and slowly chewed. "I am all of those things. Just as you are secretive, naive and ridiculously sentimental."

Protestations rose to Callie's lips then faded. After the way she'd acted, how could she argue with that—any of it?

He came closer, his face silhouetted by the huge windows that sparkled with the lights of the city. "But we must endure it."

"Endure it?" she whispered.

"Each other," he said coldly. "For Marisol's sake."

Pain cracked through her heart. Just a moment before, she'd been filled with hope. But now she saw she really was alone. No one was on her side. No one.

Stiffening, she held out her hand. "Give me my phone."

"No."

"Fine," she bit out. "I'll find it myself."

Moving through the swinging door, she went into a large, luxurious kitchen, with top-of-the-line appliances, a wine fridge, and a pizza oven, overlooking the sparkle of the city and black void of the Hudson River. Her eyes widened as she saw her bag on a granite countertop. She snatched it up, digging all the way to the bottom.

"It's not in there," Eduardo said, watching her.

Still digging, she didn't bother to look up. "Where is it?"

"I threw it away."

Her hand stilled. "Are you kidding me?"

His voice was like ice. "I won't let you call him."

"You can't stop me!" Her eyes were wide as she gasped with outraged fury. "You had no right!"

"I'm your husband. I had every right."

"I'll get a new phone!"

His black eyes glittered. "Try it."

"This is ridiculous. I'm not your prisoner!"

"For as long as we are married, I expect your loyalty."

"He's my best friend!"

"And you are my wife."

"You can't possibly feel threatened by—"

"No, why would I?" His voice was low and full of dislike. "Just because he is the man you *adore*, the man you *trust*, the man you wanted to be Marisol's father. The man you tried to marry two days ago."

"Only because I was pregnant—"

"You were engaged *years* ago, Callie," he snapped. "Before I even met you!"

Her mouth fell open. "What?"

Eduardo leaned his hand on the kitchen countertop. "Last Christmas Eve, when we made love," he ground out, "I couldn't sleep with you in my bed—"

"So why didn't you kick me out?"

He ground his teeth. "I went for a walk. I decided to stop at your apartment to collect a few of your things. I was going to ask you to stay. I never expected to find a man living there with you."

"You—what?"

His jaw was hard as he shook his head. "After our years together, I'd actually thought I could trust you. But just hours after you gave me your virginity, I met your live-in love. Your longtime fiancé."

She gaped at him.

"What, no witty comeback?" he jibed.

"Brandon wasn't my fiancé. Not back then!"

His eyes grew wild. "Stop it, damn you! Will you never stop lying? *I met him!*"

"But we only got engaged a few weeks ago!"

Eduardo folded his arms, his expression as hard as the wooden floors. "Then how do you explain it? Either you are lying, or he was. Which is it?"

She licked her lips. "Brandon wouldn't lie," she said weakly. "Unless—" She covered her mouth with her hand.

If we're not married by thirty—Brandon had taken her hands in his own—*let's marry each other.*

Sure, she'd laughed. On the night of their senior prom, thirty had seemed a million miles away. *Why not?*

She'd thought it was a joke. But could Brandon have taken it seriously? Could that be why, the day after Eduardo had gotten her an apartment, Brandon had suddenly shown up in New York with no job and a suitcase full of jeans? Because he'd heard in Callie's voice that she was falling completely in love with her boss, and wanted to protect his territory?

No. It couldn't be. Brandon loved her as a friend. Just a friend!

She glared at Eduardo. "Either you misunderstood him, or Brandon was trying to warn you off. To protect me from a sleazy boss."

"Sleazy?" he gasped.

She folded her arms. "But there's never been anything romantic between Brandon and me. Let me call him and prove it!"

"He's in love with you." His eyes were like ice. "You're either lying, or blind. But I won't be played for a fool ever again. You will not communicate with McLinn in any way.

Not by phone, by computer or via carrier pigeon. And not through your parents. Do you understand?"

Callie couldn't believe he was being so unreasonable. Tears rose to her eyes. "But I just left him there," she whispered. "Standing in the street on our wedding day. He deserves an explanation!"

"He saw you leave with me. That is all the explanation he needs. And if not…" He allowed himself a cold smile. "I just told him everything he needs to know."

A chill went down her spine. "What did you say to him?"

Turning away, he scooped up quesadillas and rice on a plate and shoved it toward her on the countertop. "It's simple. Contact him during our marriage, just once, and you are in breach of our agreement."

"Fine, I'll be in breach! Keep your stupid alimony. I don't care about your money!"

"Do you care about custody?"

She sucked in her breath. "What?"

He lifted an eyebrow. "It seems you did not read our prenuptial agreement very carefully before you signed it."

She struggled to remember the words of the prenup, but the truth was she'd barely skimmed the first pages. "I was in labor! In pain, under duress! Whatever I may have signed, it will never stand up in court!"

He gave her grim smile. "Shall we find out?"

Callie couldn't believe he could be so heartless. No, on second thought, she could. What she couldn't believe was her own stupidity—in believing it was possible for Eduardo Cruz to be anything *but* heartless! Blinking back tears, she tried to keep her voice from trembling. "Just let me talk to him once. You can listen on the other line. I just need to tell him I'm sorry." She closed her eyes. "When I think of what I did to him…"

"Yes, I can only imagine how badly you feel," Eduardo said sardonically. "Knowing you caused him pain by flinging yourself enthusiastically into bed with me and conceiving my child instead of his. A pity raising Marisol is now a responsibility more important than the romantic longings of your heart!"

His sardonic tone tore at her soul like nails on a chalkboard. "Why do you even care?" she spat out. "Our marriage will be over in months. For that matter, why did you even marry me? Why make such a song and dance about giving our child a name and a father and a home, when we both know you'll never last for long?"

His hand tightened into a fist on the counter. "What are you talking about?"

"I know you too well," she said. "I know the life you love. Traveling around the world, beating your competitors, buying expensive toys you barely take time to enjoy, any more than the women whose names you can't remember. Keeping score with your billions in the bank." She lifted her chin. "Am I leaving anything out?"

His dark eyes were cold. "My priorities have changed."

"For how long? A few days? A week? How long will you last before you abandon us?"

"*Abandon*?" he ground out. "You mean, how long until I let you rush into another man's arms?"

She shook her head. "I'm sick of your stupid jealousy!"

"And I'm sick of constantly being told it's impossible for me to be a decent husband, oh, no, not like some unemployed farmer who hangs on your every word. Too bad for you he's not Marisol's father!"

It was the last straw.

"Yes, it is!" Callie cried, blinking back tears. Grabbing her plate of quesadillas and rice—which indeed looked very poorly cooked—she yanked violently through the cupboards until she found a fork, then stomped across the kitchen. Stopping at the swinging door, she turned and yelled, "Three months can't come soon enough!"

Then with a sob, she ran upstairs, where she could eat and cry in peace with the one person in this world who still loved her—her baby.

CHAPTER FIVE

Three months later

IT HAD been a horrible three months of watching Eduardo be a perfect, loving, devoted father to their baby, who'd gone from tiny newborn to chubby baby who slept better through the night. Three months of being treated with distant courtesy as his wife. Three months of being tortured with memories, of silent hurt and anger and repressed longing by day—and haunted dreams at night. Three months.

Over.

Looking at herself in the bedroom mirror, Callie zipped up her silver dress, a slinky, strapless gown with a sweetheart neckline that emphasized her bustline. She put on the three-carat diamond stud earrings that matched the ten-carat diamond ring on her hand. Leaning forward, she applied mascara and red lipstick. Stepping back into crystal-studded high heels, she straightened. She stared at her own unsmiling image.

It was like looking at a stranger.

Callie thought of herself as plain and plump but the mirror now plainly told her otherwise. Her light brown hair was long and lustrous, blown-dry straight twice a week at the best salon on the Upper West Side. Her arms and legs had become toned and sleek from carrying Marisol and taking her on long autumn walks. She went to the park almost every day, rain or shine, eager to escape the penthouse, where she felt useless, trapped in the same house as a husband who did not care for her.

But her transformation into his trophy wife was complete. She no longer looked the part of the farm girl, or even the secretary. She was Mrs. Eduardo Cruz. The oil tycoon's unloved wife.

But tomorrow morning, her three-month marriage sentence would be over. She and her baby would be free.

Callie's green eyes were pools of misery.

Every night, she'd slept alone in his big bed as he slept in the guest room down the hall. Every day when Eduardo came home from work—earlier than he ever had, before dinner—his face lit up with joy as he scooped Marisol up in his arms. At night, when the baby couldn't sleep, she heard him walking the halls, cuddling her against his chest, singing her to sleep in his low baritone. Callie had a million new memories that would always twist her heart, because after they divorced, she'd never see them again.

Eduardo had been unfailingly courteous. He'd never brought up Brandon, her family, or any other subject that might cause an argument. Instead, every night as she sat beside him at the dinner table, he read the paper over dinner and kept the discussion to small talk. And her gaze unwillingly traced the sensual curve of his lips and shape of his hands, her body electrified with awareness as she breathed in his masculine scent and felt his warmth.

He never touched her. All he expected of Callie was for her to take care of their child and occasionally accompany him to charitable events. As they were doing tonight.

In the intimate world of New York society, the official Christmas season was kicked off in early December by the annual Winter Ball, which raised money for children's charities across the five boroughs. Tonight was the last night Callie would wear an elegant gown and accompany Eduardo in his dashing tuxedo. The last night she'd have to look up at her husband and pretend her heart wasn't breaking.

Tonight was the end.

Fitting that their marriage would end at a Christmas party, she thought dully. Just as it had begun with one. Tomorrow, as outlined by the prenuptial agreement, she would move out and Eduardo would begin divorce proceedings.

Standing in front of her bedroom mirror, Callie exhaled. She didn't believe for a single second that he'd been faithful to her. She knew him too well. He wasn't the type of man who could go without physical release for a month, much less three. He must have had lovers since their marriage—but where? How? It tortured her.

She put a trembling hand to her forehead. What did she care? Tomorrow, she'd be packing for North Dakota. For home. She missed her family. Sami. Her mother. Brandon. Even her father. She'd missed so much. Harvest. Autumn. Apple dunking and hot mulled cider. Thanksgiving with her father carving the turkey and her mother's prize-winning pumpkin pie. But she'd been resentful and angry. She'd wanted them to call and apologize. They had the number. But they hadn't called, and neither had she.

But tomorrow, she'd go. She'd noted the date in her planner and circled it with a black pen. This sham marriage would be over.

No doubt Eduardo, too, had been watching the calendar. He'd done a wonderful job as a father but he must be exhausted, hiding his love affairs, working only nine hours a day instead of his usual sixteen, eating dinner at home every night. Honestly, she'd never expected him to last this long.

Callie shivered as if she felt the cold December wind blowing through the canyons of the city.

He'd never tried to touch her during their marriage, not once. They'd only had that single night together, the night they'd conceived Marisol. One perfect night, the fulfillment of all her innocent dreams. One night. And so much she would never forget. The sudden hot hunger of his gaze across the hotel ballroom. The warmth of his sensual lips as they kissed in the back of a taxi heading south on Fifth at a breakneck pace. The woodsy, clean scent of his black hair as he carried her up the stairs to his bedroom and how silky it had felt clutched in her fingers as he covered her naked body with his own. The low rasp of his breath as he cupped her breasts. His hard gasp as he pushed inside her. The sound of her own scream ringing in her ears as her world exploded like fireworks, like a million dreams coming true at once.

Tomorrow, she'd go home and try to find a regular job. She'd face her family. She'd forget Eduardo. She had to; otherwise the rest of her life would be bleak…

"*Querida.*"

She whirled around. Eduardo was standing in the open doorway of the master bedroom, wearing a well-cut black tuxedo. He looked so devastatingly handsome that her heart lifted to her throat.

His eyes were as black as his jacket. His dark, short, wavy hair set off his handsome, chiseled face to perfection. As he came into the bedroom, the muscles of his powerful body seemed barely constrained by the civilized, sophisticated tuxedo.

He slowly looked her up and down, and his eyes seemed to devour her in the floor-length silver dress. "You look ridiculously beautiful," he said huskily. "Every man will envy me tonight."

"Oh," she said in shock, and blushed. She had no idea how to react. He'd never said such a thing to her before. On this, the last night of their marriage, she suddenly felt as awkward and self-conscious as if they were on a first date. "Thank you. Um. You, too."

He smiled. "I brought you a gift."

Pulling a black velvet box from his tuxedo pocket, he opened it in front of her. Her jaw dropped when she saw the priceless emerald and diamond necklace sparkling inside.

She looked up with a gasp. "That's—that's for me? Why?"

He gave a low laugh. "Do you really need to ask?"

She bit her lip. "Is it like—a going-away present?"

"No." He shook his head then gave her a charming, crooked grin. "Think of it as an early Christmas present." Setting down the box on the bed, he pulled the necklace from the black velvet setting. "May I?"

Nervously she held up her long brown hair and allowed him to place the necklace's heavy weight around her neck and latch it in the back, shivering as she felt his strong, warm hands brush against her nape. It was the first time he'd touched her in months, and it caused a tremble to rise from deep inside her. Moving away, she glanced at herself in the mirror. She put her hand over the green jewels sparkling in the light from the black wrought-iron chandelier.

"It's beautiful," she said over the lump in her throat.

Their eyes met in the mirror. The smile left his face.

"Not half as beautiful as you," he said in a low voice. "No other woman can compare."

He was standing behind her, so close their bodies could almost touch. Sensual need suddenly poured through her, so intense and deep that it made her knees weak. She closed her eyes.

"Why are you being nice to me?" she choked out. "Why now? When it's the end?"

Coming behind her, he put his hands on her bare shoulders. "Who says it's the end?"

She felt the weight of his hands on her skin and breathed, "The prenuptial agreement."

Eduardo turned her around, and she opened her eyes. She could feel the heat radiating from his body. Feel its answering, unwilling fire in her own.

Nervously she licked her lips. His gaze fell hungrily to her mouth. "You have to know what I want," he said softly.

His freedom, she thought unhappily. While as for her... The time of their marriage had only taught her to crave him again. To yearn. To want.

"Of course I know," she said, and tried to laugh. "It must have felt like the longest three months of your life."

He stroked her cheek. "It has."

She swallowed. "Three months of waiting, and waiting..."

"Three months of hell," he agreed.

She exhaled, blinking back tears as all her worst fears were proven true. "Well, tonight it will end."

His dark eyes tracing her face, her cheeks, her lips. "Yes," he said softly. "It will."

Shaking, she turned away, picking up her satin clutch off the bed. "I'm ready."

"Good." His sensual mouth curved as he held out his arm. "Mrs. Cruz."

Breathlessly she took his arm. He led her downstairs to the penthouse foyer, where they bid farewell to Mrs. McAuliffe, who would watch their sleeping baby. Eduardo pulled Callie's white fur wrap from the closet and placed it gently around her. She felt the weight of his hands against her shoulders and shivered, remembering last night's dream that had felt so real, when she'd imagined his naked body over hers. With a tremble, she glanced down at his thick fingers spread across the white faux fur. Heat flashed across her body as she remembered the sensation of his fingertips against her skin. Shuddering, she pulled away as they took the elevator downstairs and went outside.

"Good evening, Mr. Cruz, Mrs. Cruz," the smiling doorman said, tipping his cap. "Have a wonderful night."

"Thank you, Bernard." Eduardo put his hand on the small of Callie's back, guiding her to the black limo waiting at the curb. Sanchez held open the door as she climbed into the backseat, exhaling as she pulled away. And yet, as they drove through the sparkling, snowy city, every inch of her body was aware of her husband beside her. She didn't relax until the car stopped, and she could escape the tight space beside him.

The Winter Ball was being held at a glamorous old hotel on the edge of Central Park. As Callie walked through the lobby on her husband's arm, her fingers barely touching his sleeve, she looked up at the soaring, frescoed ceilings in awe. Cruz Oil's Christmas party last year had been huge, but it was nothing compared to this, the most lavish social event of the season. As they entered the enormous ballroom, she saw a winter wonderland. White twinkling lights sparkled from black bare trees, in front of a white background illuminated with pale lavender light. Winter was Callie's favorite season, December her favorite month, and she gasped with wonder at the fairy forest of white.

Then the fantasy came crashing down as she saw the guests milling around them: gorgeous, skinny socialites and powerful men, the type who'd all gone to prep schools and Ivy League colleges, who'd come from the best families and summered together in Kennebunkport and Martha's Vineyard. And who was she? Nobody.

Back at the penthouse, Callie had felt pretty; but here, she felt chubby and awkward. Scrawny, tall models seemed to circle them like sharks, looking hungrily at Eduardo.

"Do you know them?" she whispered, clutching his arm as he led her past them through the crowd.

"Who?"

"Those women who are staring at you."

He glanced over at the gorgeous supermodels. "No."

"Oh." She swallowed. Was he telling the truth? Or just trying to spare her feelings? She felt an ache in her throat, wondering if he'd had affairs with any of them. If he hadn't, he was probably counting down the moments until their divorce, marking out his future sexual conquests. And who could blame him? Three months without sex would be was a long time for a man like Eduardo.

But not for her. Callie had only had one sexual experience in her whole life. And with the only man she'd ever wanted. She'd tried not to care, told herself their marriage was just a sham. But just the thought of him jumping into bed with any one of those gorgeous, hard-eyed women made her want to throw up.

But Eduardo wasn't looking at the models. He was looking at Callie. "Can I get you a drink?"

Nervously she nodded, and when Eduardo brought her a cup of punch in a crystal glass, she gulped it down.

"Be careful with that," he said, sounding amused as he sipped his own Hendrick's martini, garnished with a slice of cucumber. "It's stronger than you think."

But Callie was tired of being careful. The punch tasted fruity and tart and sweet, with a little bit of bite. It tasted like temptation. Finishing it off, she held out her glass. "Please get me another."

He shook his head, looking down at her with dark eyes. "Take care, *querida*."

"I'm tired of taking care," she whispered. "Just for this one night, I want to be reckless."

Eduardo gave her a slow grin. "As you wish."

Turning, he went toward the bar. When he returned, the intensity of his gaze flooded her with heat.

"Here," he said in a low voice, holding out her drink. Their fingers brushed as she took the glass, and she shivered.

For weeks, he'd treated her with distant civility. She might as well have been one of his staff, the nanny who cared for his child. But tonight… Tonight he was looking at her. Really *looking* at her. As if he wanted to rip off her dress, kiss every inch of her skin, and make her lose her mind with pleasure.

He left me, she reminded herself fiercely. *I mean nothing to him. He only slept with me in the first place because I was* convenient.

"Thanks," she muttered, taking the glass. "What's this drink called, anyway?"

His lips quirked. "It's called a Rudolph."

"A Rudolph? Why?"

"It'll make your nose red and you fly all night."

"Oh," she muttered. Ask a silly question. Knocking back her head, she drank deeply, aware of his gaze upon her face, her neck, her breasts. She kept drinking until the cup was empty, and she had no choice but to meet his eyes. His dark eyes caressed her face.

"Have you ever had a hangover before?"

"No."

"Want one?"

She'd never experienced a hangover, but the idea of waking up with one tomorrow sounded appealing. It would be a welcome distraction from their impending divorce. "Maybe."

Music from the orchestra swelled across the ballroom and he held out his hand. "Dance with me."

Shaking her head, she looked toward the gorgeous cluster of supermodel-types on the edge of the dance floor, who were still watching Eduardo with voracious eyes. "Why don't you ask one of them?"

He frowned at her then glanced over before setting his jaw. "Why would I?"

"They seem to know you."

"Lots of people know me."

A lump rose in her throat. "Why don't we just end the charade? You don't need to be so discreet. I know perfectly well that you've had lovers during our marriage."

His eyes turned sharp. "Who told you that?"

"No one had to tell me. We haven't been having sex, so I assumed…"

"You assumed wrong."

For a long moment, they stared at each other.

"Are you really telling me the truth?" she whispered, her heart in her throat. "But it's impossible. There must have been someone else!"

His dark eyes burned like fire. "So that is what you think of me." His voice was low and terse beneath the rising music. "That while insisting on your absolute fidelity, I would cheat on you and betray our marriage vows?"

"What else do you expect me to believe? I know you, Eduardo. There's no way you've been celibate for the last three months, especially when women throw themselves at you! No man could resist that. Especially not—"

"Especially not me?" he said with dangerous quietness.

She shook her head tearfully. "You got what you wanted. Our baby has your name. Now all your friends have seen me, they'll know you did the right thing by our baby, and they'll know why our marriage didn't last."

"Which is?"

"Just look at me!" Starting to feel dizzy from the alcohol and the heat of the ballroom, she looked down at her overflowing curves in the tight dress then gestured toward him. "And look at you!"

Eduardo's brow creased as he looked down at his tuxedo, then back at Callie in her silver gown—the gown that had made her feel so pretty at the house but that now only seemed to emphasize her overblown figure compared to the stick figures of the models. He shook his head. "I don't understand."

"Oh, forget it!" she choked out. "It doesn't matter. Not anymore!"

But as she started to leave, she felt his larger hand enfold her own. Taking the empty glass from her, he set it on the silver tray of a passing waiter and pulled her into his arms. His dark eyes searched hers. "I never betrayed you, Callie."

She licked her suddenly dry lips. "Why would you be faithful to me?"

"If you have to ask, you don't know me at all." His hand tightened on hers. "Dance with me."

Callie stared up at him, her heart in her throat. She knew she should refuse. Her mind was reeling at the thought that he'd been faithful to her. Without her anger, she was vulnerable. She had nothing to defend her. The marriage would end tomorrow. She was so close to being free. She couldn't let him any closer now. She should run, as fast and hard as she could.

But as he led her to the dance floor, she couldn't resist, any more than she could resist breathing.

"All right," she whispered. "Just once." *To say good-bye*, she told herself.

Turning to her, Eduardo pulled her against his body. All around them, pale purple shadows moved against soft lavender lights, and the white bare trees looked like lacy latticework beneath twinkling white stars. Surrounded by couples swaying to music, they began to dance. Eduardo held her tightly, nestling her against the white shirt of his tuxedo. She felt his warmth. His heat. She felt the strength of his arms around her.

Callie closed her eyes, pressing her face against his chest. She felt strangely safe. Protected. She felt as if she'd gone back in time, to that one perfect night when she'd felt he cared.

For the next two hours, they never left the dance floor, and Callie was lost in the haze of a perfect, romantic dream. As Eduardo held her, as she swayed in her silver gown, she looked up into his handsome, sensual face and everything else fell away. She barely heard the music. She and Eduardo were alone, in an enchanted winter forest.

And she realized she loved him.

She'd never stopped loving him.

Callie froze, staring up at him as unseen couples whirled around them in the violet shadows.

"What is it, *querida*?" Eduardo said softly, looking down at her.

Callie licked her lips, feeling dizzy and hot all over. She couldn't let herself love him again. She couldn't be that stupid. She couldn't.

"What are you trying to do to me?" she said hoarsely. "What are you doing?"

Eduardo stood still on the dance floor, looking down at her. A tremble went through her as a current of awareness sizzled down her veins. Her mouth felt suddenly dry as he stroked her cheek.

"What am I doing?" His dark eyes searched hers, and he whispered, "I'm kissing you."

Callie couldn't move, couldn't breathe, as he lowered his mouth to hers.

She felt the heat of his sensual lips like satin and the warmth of his breath in an embrace that swirled around her body with breathless magic. She felt his hard, hungry lips against her own. Felt the scratchy roughness of his chin, as his hands ran softly through her hair, then down the bare skin of her back.

His kiss was exactly how she remembered. Exactly how a kiss should be. His deeply passionate embrace didn't just promise pleasure—it whispered of eternity. And against her will, words filled her soul that were an incantation in her heart.

I love you, Eduardo.

I never stopped loving you.

Oh, God. Could he feel it on her lips as he kissed her? Had her own body betrayed her?

"I want you, Callie," he murmured against her skin.

She saw the blatant desire in his dark eyes and suddenly felt like crying.

"How can you torture me like this," she whispered, "when we both know in the morning you'll only toss me aside? I gave you my devotion. And you treated me like trash!"

"Callie!"

"No!" She ripped away, not wanting him to see the anguish in her eyes. She couldn't bear that final humiliation. Turning, she ran off the dance floor. Pushing through the crowd, she rushed through the ballroom, running past the coat check without stopping for her wrap. She ran blindly through the lobby and out of the hotel, into the street, where she was nearly run over. A taxi driver honked and yelled at her angrily, but she barely heard him. She crossed the street to Central Park.

The park looked almost eerie in its snowy whiteness beneath the black, bare trees, just like the illusion inside the ballroom, but dangerous and cold, the real thing.

Moonlight filled the dark sky, illuminating the small clouds around it, making them glow like pearls in black velvet. As Callie ran, she wept, and it wasn't soft, feminine weeping, but big gulping sobs. Wiping her eyes, she glanced behind her.

And saw Eduardo following, an ominous figure in black.

She gasped and started to run, tripping on her shoes as she ran deeper into the park. She raced headlong down the windswept path, knowing that if he caught up with her, he would see her shameful love for him and he'd see her pathetically broken heart.

One of the high-heeled shoes fell off her feet. Turning around, she started to go back for it, but when she saw him right behind her, she kicked off her other shoe instead and turned back to run. The frozen, snow-kissed path felt like cold knives against her bare feet, the silver dress dragged against her legs and the winter air bit against her naked shoulders.

Then Eduardo caught up with her. His powerful arms lifted her off the frozen ground.

"Go away." Crying, totally humiliated, she struggled against his hard chest. "Just leave me alone!"

"You think you're disposable to me?" he said grimly, looking down at her. The moonlight gave his black hair a silver halo, like a sensual, dark angel come to lure her to hell. "Is that what you think?"

"I know it!"

"You just had my baby," he ground out, his dark eyes glinting. "I'm not a brute. I wasn't going to force myself on you!"

She tried to kick her way free. "Of course not, when you have half the supermodels of this city queued up outside our door. How can I ever compete with that? You said it yourself—you can't wait to divorce me!"

"Oh, my God." His jaw clenched. "Do you know how much I've wanted you? How long? Do you?" he thundered.

She stared at him, shocked at his fury.

His voice dropped. "I've wanted you for a year, Callie. And I've waited for you. For a year."

"No," she whispered. "It's not true."

What she saw in his dark eyes made her shiver all over. "My God. How can you not know? How have you not seen it?"

Her heart nearly stopped in her chest. She licked her dry lips. "You haven't tried to touch me, not once. You've barely even looked at me."

"You were a new mother. You were drowning." Reaching out, he brushed long brown tendrils off her shoulders. "You didn't need me trying to seduce you, placing more demands on you when you were only getting four hours of sleep. You didn't need a lover. You needed a partner. You needed me to be a good father."

She stared at him.

"And you were," she choked out tearfully. "The best father Marisol could ever have had."

Callie heard his intake of breath, felt the way his hands tightened on her as he held her against his chest. Looking down at her, his angled face was in dark silhouette.

"Thank you," he said softly. All around them, the winter landscape glowed in the moonlight.

"You really—wanted me?" she whispered.

He gave a harsh laugh. "I tried not to. Told myself that our night together was meaningless. Reminded myself that you were a liar engaged to another man, and you'd betrayed us both when you gave me your virginity."

Ice flashed through her. "I—"

"But I couldn't forget you. No matter how I tried." He shifted her weight against his chest. "There has been no other woman since the night you were in my bed," he said roughly, looking down at her. "Do you understand what I am telling you? No other woman."

She stared at him. "But...but it's been a year."

His dark eyes looked through hers. "Yes."

Callie couldn't believe what she was hearing. She licked her lips. "But those pictures of you with that duchess in Spain..."

"She is beautiful," he whispered. He shook his head. "But she left me cold."

Tears spilled unheeded down Callie's cheeks, freezing against her skin as she looked up at her husband. "No. No, it can't be true. You can't have been celibate for a year, wanting me—"

"You don't believe me?" he said grimly. He released her, slowly letting her slide down his body to her feet. "Then believe this."

And lowering his head, he pulled her body roughly against his, and kissed her once more, hot and hard.

CHAPTER SIX

CALLIE'S mouth parted in a gasp as she felt the smooth satin of his lips, the sweet rough fire of his tongue. She felt the warm strength of his arms around her, and in the dark, cold solitude of Central Park, surrounded by snow and the bare black trees of winter, she felt an explosion of heat.

Murmuring words in Spanish, Eduardo tightened his embrace as he held her against his chest. She dimly felt the icy wind against her cheek as tendrils of her light brown hair blew all around them, but the sensation of his lips against hers felt like a thousand flickers of fire.

As he kissed her, a sigh escaped her lips and she tilted her head back to deepen the embrace. Feeling his body so strong and hard against hers, her endless longing could no longer be repressed. With a soft moan, she wrapped her arms around his neck. She no longer felt the cold air against her skin, the frigid ground beneath her feet. She barely heard the distant traffic of the city and the wind through the bare trees. The night was frozen and dark, but Callie felt hot as a summer's day, lit up from within.

Eduardo's hands stroked her back, down her bare arms. Prickles of need spiraled through her everywhere he touched. Everywhere he *didn't* touch.

His lips gentled against hers, seducing and enticing where they'd once demanded and taken. Memories of another winter night went through Callie, leaving her lost in time, as if all the grief and pain of the last year hadn't happened, and she'd teleported back into the most perfect night of her life.

She wrapped her fingers in his hair. He felt so good, so powerful and masculine. His warrior's body made her feel feminine and small, and as he kissed her, as his sensual mouth moved against hers, she was completely beneath his control....

Then, with a harsh intake of breath, Eduardo pulled away. Taking his phone from his pants pocket, he dialed. "Sanchez," he panted, never looking away from Callie. "Outside. At the corner."

Hanging up, he put the phone in his pocket and reached for her, lifting her back into his arms.

"You don't need to carry me," she whispered. "I'm not cold."

He looked down at her almost pleadingly. "Let me."

Exhaling, she relaxed into the warmth of his arms, and Eduardo carried her back down the path, stopping to pick up each of her shoes, holding Callie with one arm as if she weighed nothing at all. When they reached Central Park South, he put the high-heeled shoes on her feet and gently set her down on the sidewalk.

"Thank you," she said, shivering, but not from cold.

Without a word, he pulled off his black tuxedo jacket and wrapped it around her bare shoulders and sparkling silver dress. His eyes were dark, his voice deep. "Never thank me. It is what I want to do. Take care of you."

Callie swallowed, her mouth dry, her heart pounding as she leaned against him. Thick snowflakes, illuminated by streetlights, started to fall from the dark sky. Was it really possible that Eduardo had been celibate for a year, longing for her? That he'd known the same feelings she had… The lonely bed, the regret, and most of all: the endless craving…?

Her mind told her it was impossible, but his kiss had told her differently.

"Callie," he whispered. "You know what I'm going to do to you when we get home."

Her heartbeat went crazy, her breathing became quick and shallow and she felt a little dizzy. He wanted her. She wanted him. But the last time he'd made love to her, the joy and heartbreak had nearly killed her. Their marriage was ending in just a few hours. She was so close to being free…

But suddenly, freedom from Eduardo sounded like death. Wrapping her arms around him, she placed her cheek against his white tuxedo shirt and closed her eyes, listening to the beat of his heart. They remained there, holding each other silently, as the soft snowflakes fell in their hair and tangled in their eyelashes.

"The car's here." His voice was hoarse. She opened her eyes and he led her into the backseat of the limo. As Sanchez drove them from the curb, Eduardo didn't seem to care who might see as he turned to her. Reaching out his hands, he cupped her face. He lowered his head toward hers.

At the last instant before their lips touched, she turned her head away. "I can't."

"Can't?" he said hoarsely. "Why? Because—because you love someone else?"

She looked at him in the backseat of the car. His face was so impossibly handsome that her heart twisted in her chest. Every inch of her body was crying out to be in his arms, but lifting her chin, she forced herself to say, "I'm afraid."

He blinked. "Afraid?"

Afraid it will rip my heart apart so thoroughly that the

pieces will never be glued back together. "I'm afraid…it wasn't part of our deal." She swallowed. "Our marriage is in name only."

Eduardo's sensual lips curved. "What gave you that idea?"

"At the courthouse, when we got the marriage license, you said—"

"*You* called it a marriage of convenience. Which it is. But I never said it would be a marriage in name only. I promised to remain faithful, and I have. But I cannot suffer, wanting you, for the rest of my life."

"You don't have to. Tomorrow is our three-month anniversary. Our marriage is over." She paused, suddenly confused by the look in his eyes. "Isn't it?"

"No." His eyes glittered in the Christmas lights as they drove through the city. "There will be no divorce."

Time seemed to stop for Callie.

Behind his head, she dimly saw the bright lights illuminating the colorful displays in shop windows. "But you said three months!"

"I changed my mind." He scowled at her. "From the day I held our baby, I knew that whatever I'd once planned, our marriage would be—must be—permanent. That is the best way to raise our child. The only way. I'd hoped you would come to realize that."

"But you said you'd divorce me," she whispered. The will-o'-the-wisp Christmas lights seemed to be dancing away, disappearing along with her dreams of returning home to her family. "You promised. You said our marriage was just to make our child legitimate, to give her your name!"

His eyes had turned utterly cold, his body taut beneath his tuxedo. "You should be pleased," he said stiffly. "As my wife, you have everything you could possibly want. A fortune at your disposal, beautiful homes, servants, clothes and jewels."

"But what about…" Her throat closed and she looked away. "What about the people I love?"

"You'll love your children," he ground out.

Wide-eyed, she turned back to face him. "Children?" she stammered. "As in…more than one?"

He narrowed his eyes. "It is lonely to be an only child. Marisol needs siblings. Sisters to play with. Brothers to protect her."

Callie stared at him, remembering what she'd heard about Eduardo's poverty-stricken childhood in Spain, about his mother who'd run off with her lover, and his proud, humiliated father, who'd shot himself in the aftermath with an old World War II rifle. At ten years old, Eduardo had been shipped off to a great-aunt he'd never met in New York, and even she had died when he was eighteen. He had no one. He was alone.

She couldn't even imagine it. As much as the restrictive rules of her old-fashioned parents had chafed her, and as much as her little sister had irritated her on a regular basis, Callie couldn't imagine being an only child—and an orphan to boot, whose parents had both chosen to abandon her. Sympathy choked her, but then she hardened her heart. "So just like that, you expect me to agree? You expect us to remain married, to have more children? To plan it all in such a cold-blooded fashion?"

Glaring at her, he sat back in the car seat, folding his arms. "Marisol will be wanted. She will be safe and loved. She will have two parents and a home. There will be no divorce."

Horrified, Callie stared at him.

Stay Eduardo's wife?

Forever?

Her heart twisted in her chest. It was all like some strange dream. For a moment she was mesmerized by his certainty. Perhaps Eduardo was right. Perhaps it would be better for Marisol...better for everyone.

But how could she stay married to him, loving him as she did? He still wanted to be married to her for one reason only: to give their child a good home. How could Callie spend the rest of her life giving him her love, when all he wanted was—at most—her body?

Could she sacrifice her heart, and all hope of ever being loved? Could she spend the rest of her life feeling unloved and alone, in order to give her child the home she deserved?

Swallowing, Callie lifted her chin. "My family would have to be part of Marisol's life. And mine. I miss them. My parents and my sister and—" She cut herself off, but too late.

A sneer rose to his lips. "And Brandon McLinn, of course. His light still glows so brightly in your heart." He set his jaw, turning away. "You disappoint me."

Controlling herself with a deep breath, she didn't rise to his bait. "It was unreasonable of you to block me from seeing him. The only reason I went along with your demand was because I knew that as soon as the three months was over I could—"

"Yes." His eyes were hard as he glared at her. "I know exactly what you were planning to do."

The limousine stopped and Sanchez opened the door. Miserably she followed Eduardo out of the car. Why did he always take things so wrong? Why did he persist in being jealous of Brandon?

Eduardo didn't even look at her as they walked through the lobby of their building. The hot passion of Central Park seemed to have evaporated like smoke. He pressed the button, and they stood without touching, waiting silently in front of the private elevator.

Then he abruptly turned to face her, his hands clenched.

"I've left you alone too long," he ground out, his eyes dark. "I was trying to give you space to grieve the past and accept your new life. To embrace your future as my wife." Furiously he seized her in his arms. "But I see I took the wrong path with you. I should have staked my claim long ago."

Callie stared up at him, her eyes wide with shock. "You can't—"

Tightening his grip on her, he brought his mouth down on hers in a hard, punishing kiss. Trembling, she tried to push him away, but he was too strong for her. Especially when his lips tasted like sweet fire...

The door to the elevator opened with a *ding*, and Eduardo lifted her up into his arms. He looked down at her fiercely.

"Tonight, wife," he growled, "I'm taking back my bed."

The elevator door hadn't even closed before he was pressing her against the mirrored wall, his mouth hard and hungry against hers. Callie had given up any thought of resisting. In fact, she'd given up any thought altogether. Wrapping her arms around his neck, she returned his kiss with equal hunger. He released her, letting her body slide down his, and she felt his hard desire for her. She felt hot, wearing his tuxedo jacket, and through the thin cotton of his shirt, she felt the strength and heat of his body as he held her tight and kissed her, so long and hard and deep that she prayed he'd never let her go.

At the *ding* of the elevator, he picked her up and carried her wordlessly through their massive foyer, beneath the crystals of the shadowy chandelier above. His black eyes never left hers as he carried her up the curved, sweeping staircase. His gaze reached into her heart, taking brutal possession of her soul.

"Och, you're home early!" Downstairs, Mrs. McAuliffe came out into the foyer, her voice cheerful. "The baby's sleeping and happy and—oh."

As if from a distance, Callie heard the woman's shocked intake of breath, saw her turn and flee back down the shadowy hall toward her own rooms on the first floor. But for once in her life, Callie wasn't embarrassed. She couldn't care. All that mattered was this.

Without a word, Eduardo carried her up the last stairs and down the hall to the master bedroom. He set her down on her feet beside the king-size bed. She glanced down at the mattress, remembering how she'd slept alone for all the nights of their marriage. But she would not be alone tonight.

Her husband caressed her hair, tucking tendrils behind her ear. She shivered as his rough fingertips brushed her sensitive earlobe, and his hand slowly moved down her cheek to her throat, beneath the expensive diamond-and-emerald necklace to the sensitive corner between her neck and shoulder. His body towered over hers as he pulled his oversize tuxedo jacket off her shoulders, dropping it to the floor.

Walking around her slowly, he stroked the bare skin of her shoulders. Fire raced up and down her body as he finally faced her, cupping her face. He lowered his mouth to hers.

His lips were soft and warm, rough and hard all at once, searing through her body like lava, melting her core from within. Her full breasts ached, crushed against his muscled chest. He reached around her, and she heard, and felt, the pull of the zipper. Suddenly the weight of the silver strapless gown fell to the hardwood floor.

Stepping back, Eduardo looked at her in the moonlight. "You're beautiful," he said hoarsely. "I've waited for you so long. Too long…"

Yanking off his black tie, he tossed it to the floor. But as he started to unbutton his tuxedo shirt, his hands seemed clumsy. She looked at his fingers and realized they were shaking, just as hers were. With a low curse, he finally just ripped off his shirt, popping the buttons with brute force and kicking the expensive garment away. She nearly gasped at the beauty of his incredible upper body in the moonlight. The muscles of his chest were hard and defined, from his broad shoulders to his nipples and the dark arrow of hair that traveled down his flat, hard belly.

Wearing only trousers, he came closer, running his fingers along the curve from her waist to her hip. His gaze devoured her in the plunging strapless bra and matching panties. Beneath his gaze, she should have been acutely aware of her body's every flaw, and yet she saw the hunger in his eyes and she'd never felt more womanly or desirable.

A low growl escaped Eduardo's lips. Grabbing her hips with both his hands, he pulled her to the bed. Sitting down on the edge, he lifted her into his lap, so she straddled him.

Wrapping his hands in her hair, he pulled her head down and kissed her fiercely. She kissed him back with equal force, gasping at the sensation when her naked belly brushed against his bare chest. He cupped her breasts over her silky strapless bra. Her nipples tightened to agonizing points, her breasts heavy and tight. Reaching around her with one hand, he unhooked her bra. His first sight of her full breasts, swollen to twice their normal size from nursing, made him gasp. He slowly reached to cup her bare skin. His large, rough hands caressed her naked breasts and Callie's body went tight, as a hot current of electricity traveled from her nipples to her toes, sending spirals of hot, aching need to her deepest core.

"So beautiful," he breathed again. The bed was covered in a pool of silvery light, leaving the two of them in their own magic world as he pushed her back against the pillows.

Never taking his gaze from hers, he stood beside the wall of windows overlooking the entire Upper West Side, and removed first his trousers, giving her a glance of his powerful legs and trunklike thighs, then his silk boxers.

Callie's heart lifted to her throat as her husband stood before her, utterly naked and unashamed.

The moonlight frosted his naked chest, giving him an otherworldly appearance, like a powerful warlord from the mists of legend, a fierce barbarian king. He looked dark, handsome and powerful, illuminated by a gleam of silver. He looked like a dark knight from a fantasy. He moved toward her, and her whole body—down to her soul—trembled from within. And in the magical silvery light, his erection jutted from his body, proud and hard and every bit as huge as she'd remembered.

A spasm of fear went through her. After childbirth, what if it hurt to have him inside her? What if he was rough? What if he even tried to be gentle but was still just so big that he split her apart?

Eduardo moved over her on the bed. She sucked in her breath as he stroked her cheek, slowly kissing down her neck. She tilted back her head as she felt his lips caress her skin, gasping as she felt his hands' featherlike touch, cupping her breasts. Lowering his head, he kissed one breast, then the other, and slowly stroked down her body, down her collarbone, down the soft curve of her belly. Tension coiled low and deep inside her, and hardly knowing what she was saying, she breathed, "Yes…"

"You're mine, Callie. Only mine." He put his hand on her cheek, his eyes dark. "Tell me…"

"I'm yours," she whispered, her voice choking on a sob. *Of course* she was his. She'd been his from the moment he'd first taken her hand, when he was the CEO of a global multibillion-dollar company and she was just his secretary.

Lowering his mouth to hers, he kissed her, long and deep. His tongue teased hers, lightly at first, then plunging deeper into her mouth as their tongues intertwined, slick and hot and wet. She felt his hand stroke her, moving softly down her belly. His fingers moved along her hip, over the top edge of her panties, and she shivered, aching for him. His hand moved so slowly, so lightly. He stroked down the side of her hip, over her thigh, between her legs. As he continued kissing her, she felt his hand move with agonizing slowness up the inside of her thigh, and held her breath…

But he moved his hand away, cupping her breast. She exhaled, pulling him closer, wanting to feel his weight on her. But he wouldn't be distracted. His hand moved back to her inner thigh, traveling upward frustratingly slowly as she held her breath. Finally he stroked over her panties. He teased her. She gasped as he gently cupped the mound between her thighs.

Kneeling between her legs on the king-size bed, he pulled her silk panties down, down, down. She felt the soft fabric slide like a whisper down her skin. Suddenly naked beneath him, she felt him climb naked on top of her, lowering his head to kiss her. His tongue moved between her lips, his mouth stretched her wide. And she felt him hard and thick at the entrance to the hot center that ached between her thighs. Every inch of their bodies, her soft curves and his hard, muscled form, seemed fused together with need, sweat and fire. Only one part of them had yet to be joined. One part on fire with need. She felt him, huge and hard, nudging against her wet, hot core.

But she was afraid. She braced for him to thrust himself inside her, cleaving her tender flesh, but instead, exhaling, showing visible control, he slowly thrust a single inch inside her. She gasped. She felt so wet, enfolding his enormous shaft. He pushed further, to two inches. He was so thick it ached a little, stretching her, but as he slid inside, it felt good. So good. Just like the first time...

Then she remembered. With a sudden cry, she lifted up on her elbows and breathed, "Condom?"

His dark eyes narrowed, and then he scowled. "I forgot..." He started to reach toward his nightstand. Then he looked down at her with a sensual, slow-rising smile. "I do not need a condom, *querida*. Ever again."

"You—don't?"

"You are my wife." He pulled back his hand, and his expression turned wicked as he looked at her with heavily lidded eyes. "I want to get you pregnant. Now."

"Now?" she said, her eyes wide. It was too soon. She hadn't even had a period yet, since the birth of her baby three months ago. She shook her head. "I'm not ready..."

"We have eight bedrooms," he insisted. "I want to fill them. I want the noise and joy of many children. And I want you as their mother." As he held her wrists, holding her down to the bed, his dark eyes seared hers. "Let me fill you with my baby, *querida*."

Callie stared up at him, feeling pinned to the bed. Was she ready to make that lifelong commitment to Eduardo that he wanted? Ready to be bound to him even further? Even deeper?

He pushed himself back into her, and she closed her eyes, gasping with pleasure. He felt so good inside her. Farther and deeper sounded like all she'd ever wanted. She tried to think about the decision that had to be made but her rational mind fell away as he gripped her hips tight. His huge shaft slowly filled her, inch by inch, sliding through her tight, wet passage.

She gripped his shoulders, her fingernails digging into his skin as she arched her back, her head tilted back. Her whole body was taut and aching with need for more, just a little more. She wanted him to fill her all the way, to ram himself deeply inside her. Her breasts swayed as he penetrated her. Her nipples were taut as he lowered his head to lick one rosy peak. With his rough mouth on her, his hips took decisive action. He thrust deeply inside her, all the way to the hilt, and she nearly screamed with pleasure.

But even then, reality intruded. She'd made this mistake once. Not again. Never again. Her fingers gripped into his shoulders, and she opened her eyes, pushing him back.

"Condom," she panted.

For a long moment, he stared at her. Then his eyes narrowed. Rolling off her, he grabbed a condom from the nightstand and sheathed himself in a quick movement, rolling it down over his thick shaft in the manner of a man who'd done it many, many times. Then he climbed back on top of her. Anger seemed to seep from his body, and Callie licked her lips, wanting to repair the mood between them.

"Thank—"

He put his finger roughly on her lips. "Don't," he ground out.

Gripping her hips with his hands, he thrust himself inside her, all the way to the hilt. She gasped, forgetting their argument, forgetting everything as he rode her, hard and deep. A shudder built inside her, a tremble like an earthquake as he filled her, like an underground river bursting from the cracks of a dam. She felt tension ratchet higher and higher inside her, shaking her. Her head fell back as she held her breath, climbing higher and higher still. She closed her eyes as her lips parted in a soundless cry.

Then it was no longer silent, and she screamed, clutching his shoulders as she exploded.

A low, answering cry came from his lips. His hard, handsome face was pale, as if he'd held himself back by only the slenderest thread. But as she shook and tightened around him in ecstasy, he surrendered. He thrust inside her one last time, impaling her so hard and deep she felt split in two, and he filled her with a hoarse shout, his eyes closed, his face euphoric. Almost reverent.

Collapsing over her sweaty, exhausted body, he held her against his chest. "You will belong to me," he whispered. "You'll soon surrender."

Turning toward him, Callie pressed her cheek against his bare chest. Her own heartbeat roared in her ears. As she drowsed in his powerful arms, exhausted and protected by the warmth and strength of his naked body, she knew it was already true. It had always been true.

Her heart had surrendered long ago.

CHAPTER SEVEN

CALLIE woke up with a start. What time was it? Was that her baby crying?

She rose blearily from bed before she was even quite awake. The moonlight had moved across her bedroom, so she must have slept. With a gasp, she remembered how her husband had just made love to her. She glanced back at the bed with her heart in her throat and a smile on her lips.

The bed was empty. Eduardo was gone.

She glanced at the clock over the mantel on the bedroom's fireplace. Three in the morning. Where could he be? Why would he leave her in the middle of the night, after he'd so thoroughly reclaimed his bed?

Her cheeks grew hot at the memory of last night. He'd claimed her in a way she'd never forget.

Then her baby wailed again from the nursery, louder this time. She hurried through the adjacent door, turning on a little lamp shaped like a giraffe that gave a soft, golden light. She picked up her baby. "It's all right," she soothed. "Mommy's here. I'm here." Cradling her chubby three-month-old baby in her arms, Callie carried her to the gliding chair near the window. As she nursed her child, the baby's complaints faded. Looking down at her, Callie was lost in wonder at her baby's beauty, at the long black eyelashes she'd gotten from Eduardo brushing against her plump cheeks. One of her baby's tiny hands gripped her finger.

We have eight bedrooms. I want to fill them.

What would it be like, Callie thought, to have a whole houseful of babies like this? To have a large family? An adoring husband?

Slowly her eyes looked around the cheerful nursery. It was warm and luxurious, but she would have liked to create her baby's nursery herself, even with just a bucket of paint, a sewing machine and her own two hands—not paying someone else to do it, but doing it herself as a labor of love. Next time, she promised herself. Then stopped.

Next time.

Could she really stay married to Eduardo, knowing he would never love her? He knew how to make love...oh, yes. She shivered, closing her eyes as she remembered how he'd caressed her last night. Remembered the feel of his body against hers. The husky sound of his voice as he'd said, *You belong to me.*

He knew how to make love.

But she'd never seen him truly care for anyone. Except their baby.

Was their lust, and mutual care for their child, enough to sustain a marriage when their values were so different?

After her baby nursed back to sleep, Callie left her on her back in the oval-shaped crib, careful not to wake her. She'd likely sleep another four hours now, or maybe more. Every night, she slept a little longer. Her baby had become an excellent sleeper.

And maybe she would be now, too. Closing the nursery door softly behind her, Callie smiled. The last few hours, after falling asleep in Eduardo's arms, had been the best sleep she'd had all year.

He wanted her to be his wife forever. He wanted them

to be a family. And she'd loved him for years. Even when she'd hated him, it had been the hurt of a woman who'd been rejected from the person she loved most.

Maybe it could work. Maybe it could be enough.

Or maybe, somehow, he would grow to love her, as she loved him. She closed her eyes, hugging herself at the thought. If there was even the slightest chance of him loving her someday, she would have married him at once. Remembering, she bleakly opened her eyes. No wonder Eduardo had called her *naive* and *ridiculously sentimental*.

Where was he, anyway? She looked around her dark, empty bedroom. Where could he be at this time of the night?

Maybe he'd gone to the kitchen for a snack.

Pulling on a soft blue chenille robe, she went downstairs, but the kitchen was dark and empty. Walking past the wall of windows with its magnificent view of the city, she went down the hall to his home office, then to the theater room, then even past Mrs. McAuliffe's suite. She could hear the older woman's soft snoring muffled through the door. Puzzled, Callie finally went back upstairs.

Glancing in the empty guest rooms, she had just decided to phone their bodyguard in his separate apartment downstairs when she heard Eduardo's voice in the guest room.

"Nothing has changed." His voice was the smooth, arrogant tone she remembered. "Nothing."

With an intake of breath, she pulled back from the doorway, leaning against the wall of the dark hallway with one hand over her mouth and the other over her heart.

"Don't call here again," he growled, and hung up.

A little squeak escaped her lips. Who was Eduardo talking to? An old lover? Was that why he'd snuck out of bed to talk to someone in private, so his wife couldn't hear? Even as Callie tried to tell herself that she was overreacting, that he could be talking to anyone, her heart was gripped with fear.

There has been no other woman since the night you were in my bed. Do you understand what I am telling you? No other woman.

She exhaled as the vise grip on her heart loosened. Eduardo was not a liar. If anything, he was cruelly honest. As his secretary, she'd seen him callously dispose of one lover after another, plainly telling them to their faces that he was bored with them, or that he had absolutely no intention of being faithful. He was not a liar.

But then, he'd never had to lie. He'd never been married before.

"What are you doing awake?"

With an intake of breath, she saw him in the doorway, looking down at her with dark eyes. "Um…" Her fingers fidgeted with the belt of her blue chenille robe. "I got up to feed Marisol and you were gone."

"I didn't want to wake you." His handsome face was impassive. "I couldn't sleep."

"Oh. I'm sorry." She bit her lip, feeling guilty that she'd slept so well. "Is something wrong? Was I snoring, or…"

He gave a low laugh then shook his head soberly. "I just don't sleep well with other people in my bed. I have never managed it."

She frowned. "Never?"

"Have you ever heard of me letting a woman sleep over?"

Callie stared at him, remembering when he'd been her boss, the most heartless playboy in the city. "N-no," she said hesitantly. She gave him an awkward smile. "You were kind of famous for your one-*hour* stands, actually."

He leaned against the door frame, looking down at the floor. "It's hard to let down my guard."

"Even with me?"

He looked up. "Especially with you," he whispered.

The low lights of the hallway caused hard shadows across the angles and planes of Eduardo's face. His jawline was dark with stubble, giving him a piratical air. He looked like a pirate all over, in fact. A sexy, dangerous, hard-bodied pirate. Without thinking, she put a hand on his warm, hard, bare chest above drawstring cotton pajama pants slung low on his slender hips.

"Is there anything I could do to help you sleep?" Realizing how blatant that sounded, she blushed. "I mean, could I get you some warm milk or something?"

"No," he said abruptly then amended, "but thanks."

She looked at him. "Why didn't you kick me out?" she whispered. "Last Christmas, the night I stayed at your house?"

His eyes met hers. "You weren't just some starlet I picked up at a gala. You were important to me. I wanted you to stay."

"You did?" she breathed. "Why?"

"Don't you know?" Pulling her into his arms, he lifted her chin to meet his gaze. Then he smiled...the charming, megawatt smile that always twisted her heart in a million pieces. "I need you, Callie."

Eduardo looked at his wife in the shadows of the hallway. Her pale cheeks were rosy, her emerald eyes bright, and her light brown hair, long and wavy, fell over the shoulders of her blue robe. She was so sexy, so soft and desirable. He'd just had her, and already he wanted her again. He wanted her even more.

Callie's eyes filled up with tears.

"You need me? I thought...I thought you only wanted me here because of the baby."

He moved toward her, gently brushing her hair off her shoulders. "That's not the only reason."

Trembling, she looked up at him. Words seemed to tremble on her lips, but at the last moment, she turned away. Staring down the dark, quiet hall, she wrapped her arms around her body. The sleeves of the blue chenille robe hung long over her wrists, making her look like a kid playing dress-up.

"I want to stay with you," she said softly. "And be your wife."

Eduardo's heart rose with fierce triumph. "*Querida*—"

She held up her hand. Her green eyes were luminous. "But I will no longer neglect and ignore my friends and family just to coddle your insecurity."

Her harsh words were like a slap across the jaw. His eyes widened then narrowed. "*Coddle* my *insecurity*." His voice was low and dangerous. "You mean how I've forbidden you to talk to Brandon McLinn."

"Yes."

Jaw tight, he took a step toward her. "You should just let him go."

"No." Her eyes glittered defiantly. "He's my friend."

"Friend!" he snarled. He shook his head. "He told me you'd been engaged since high school. He said even if you'd fallen into bed with me, I meant nothing to you and that you'd soon be done with me—"

Eduardo stopped, his jaw tight, his heart pounding. He hadn't meant to say so much. Brow furrowed, Callie came closer, and the soft light from the guest room illuminated her pale, beautiful face. She gave an awkward laugh.

"Want to hear a funny story? At senior prom, we made this silly pact that if we weren't married by the time we were thirty, we would marry each other."

"You're only twenty-five."

"Yes, I know. I'm starting to wonder if perhaps Brandon was—" she licked her lips uncomfortably "—well, maybe threatened by you."

Suddenly it all made sense.

Eduardo sucked in his breath. "You weren't in love with him, were you? He was trying to get rid of me, and it worked." He clawed back his hair with his hand. "Once I was out of the way, he used your pregnancy as an excuse to move in for the kill."

Drawing back in confusion, Callie shook her head. "He loves me, yes, but like a brother!"

"I was such a fool." Pacing two steps down the hall, he could hardly believe his own stupidity. That night, that beautiful Christmas Eve night when they'd first made love, when he'd taken Callie's virginity, he'd thought their relationship might be different from all the rest. But he'd thrown away that precious connection—based on the insinuations of his rival!

"Brandon McLinn is in love with you," he ground out. "I saw it in his face."

"He must have been trying to protect me."

"You may be blind to his true feelings. I am not." His eyes narrowed. "You will never contact him again. Or your family."

"What?" Callie's mouth fell open. "What does my family have to do with anything?"

Eduardo couldn't explain, or she would find out everything he'd been keeping from her—for her own good. "I am your husband. You will trust me and obey."

"Obey?" Callie glared at him, folding her arms. "What century are you in? You might be my husband, but you are no longer my boss!"

"Am I not?" he said softly. He reached his hand to her cheek, stroking softly down her neck. She closed her eyes, and he felt her shudder beneath his touch. "I am trying to protect our family. I have my reasons. Believe me."

But Callie stiffened, stepping back, out of his reach. "No."

His eyes widened then his brows lowered. "No?"

"I want to be your wife, Eduardo. I do," she whispered. "But I have to see my family. And Brandon."

"I could take you to court. The prenuptial agreement—"

"So do it." She looked at him evenly. "Take me to court."

She was calling his bluff. He had no desire to sue his own wife, the mother of his baby. And now they both knew it. He exhaled, clenching his hands. "I will not allow you to—"

"It's not a question of you *allowing* me. I'm telling you. I need a relationship with my family—including Brandon— and so does Marisol. I'm going home to visit my family. You can divorce me. But you can't stop me."

Checkmate, he thought, almost with despair.

He still couldn't forget—or forgive—the way her parents had treated Callie when she'd called them just two hours after the birth, anxious to tell them about the baby. She'd had every reason to relax and get some rest, but instead she'd tried to share the joyous news with her mother and father. She'd been left sobbing with grief. The memory still made his jaw clench.

Eduardo had always dreamed of having a family of his own. A family that was kind and loving, not cruel or harsh as his own had been.

He wouldn't let anyone make Callie cry like that. Ever.

Staring at her, a thought took hold of his brain. Morally reprehensible—but then, he thought grimly, he was already in so deep he might as well go a little further.

It was for her own good, he repeated to himself. For her own good, and the safety of their little family.

"Have you considered, *querida*," he said in a low voice, "that perhaps they might not want to see you?"

Callie looked at him with stricken eyes. "What?"

It was cold, it was cruel, it was wrong. But he pushed aside his twinges of conscience. He had to be ruthless. "Has McLinn contacted you once in the last three months?" He tilted his head. "Has anyone in your family tried to call you back, even once?"

Her folded arms fell, and she looked uncertain. "No." Swallowing, she blinked fast. "But I can't blame them. I let them down."

"No," he said sharply. "You had a baby. You got married. And when you tried to share that news with them, they ripped you apart."

She took a deep breath. "I know it might seem that way…"

"They were cruel to you." He could still remember the rasp of her father's voice. *You'll never be a decent husband or father, and you know it. If you're even half a man, you'll send her and the baby home to people who are capable of loving them.*

"I'll make them forgive me." Callie's emerald eyes glittered suspiciously. "I have to try."

As she turned away, he grabbed her arm. "Write to them first."

She turned back to face him. "What?"

"If you show up in person, who knows how they'll react? What if they shut the door in your face? Do you really want to risk it?"

Callie looked pale, staring at him.

"Write first," he said smoothly. "It's the best way to gather your thoughts. And give them time to consider theirs."

"Well." She took a deep breath, her expression crestfallen. "Maybe you're right." She looked down at her feet. "I would die if they shut the door in my face. Or if they refused to see Marisol. I can't even imagine it. But then," she said unhappily, "I thought they would call me before now...."

He put his hands around her shoulders. "Write to them."

"You think so?"

"Absolutely."

She bit her lip. "Even Brandon?"

Exhaling, jaw tight, he gave a single nod.

She sighed. "All right."

"All right?"

She looked up. Her green eyes were bright, her cheeks flushed. "Thank you," she said haltingly, "for helping me. I don't know what I'd do without you."

Eduardo had never seen her look so beautiful. Mesmerized, he reached down to stroke her cheek then pulled her into his arms. He felt her soft breasts press against his chest, and breathed in the floral and vanilla scent of her hair. He felt the warm whisper of her breath against his bare chest, and his drawstring pajamas suddenly felt three sizes too tight. "I told you," he said hoarsely. "I don't want your thanks."

"But—"

"Don't." Especially since he had no intention of allowing her letters to reach her family—or McLinn. He put his palm against her cheek, his fingers threading through her hair. "You are my woman, Callie. I would do anything to keep you safe and happy."

Looking up at him, she suddenly blurted out, "Who were you talking to on the phone?"

He stared at her. "What?"

Looking grumpy, she folded her arms. "I wasn't going

to ask," she sighed. "I was going to be totally stoic and silent about it."

"Oh, *querida*." Smiling, Eduardo stroked her cheek. She was so transparent. He loved that about her. "You wondered if I was talking to some woman?"

"The thought crossed my mind. Every woman wants you...."

"And I want only one woman in the world." Lifting her chin, he looked straight into her eyes. "I am yours and only yours, my beautiful wife. I will never betray you, Callie."

"You won't?"

"I was just talking to a rival...who lives far away."

"Oh," she said. With a sigh of relief, she hugged him, pressing her face against his bare chest.

Stroking her back through the soft chenille robe, Eduardo exhaled at how close it had been. She must have heard the end of his phone call. If she'd heard the whole conversation, she wouldn't have been worried about some imaginary woman. No, it would have been far more dire.

"Try to contact my wife again," Eduardo had growled, "and you'll regret it."

"You can't keep me from her. We both know you're not good enough. You'll never make her happy." McLinn's voice had been angry, and with an edge of desperation that had grown over the months Eduardo had blocked the man's letters and phone calls. Yesterday, there had even been an attempted delivery of a cell phone in a padded envelope. His bodyguard had opened the package while Callie was upstairs getting ready for the Winter Ball.

An hour ago, Eduardo's anger had finally boiled over. Rising from their bed as Callie slept, he'd used the number from his investigator, and called McLinn's cell phone in the middle of the night.

The young farmer had actually threatened him, saying he was going to call the police and claim Callie was being held against her will. Against her will!

Eduardo narrowed his eyes. The police he could deal with. But McLinn had threatened to return to New York. He could not guard Callie at every moment in the city, keeping her from any unexpected meeting. Nor could he risk letting her talk to McLinn. He could only imagine what the man would tell her.

He needed a third option.

From the day they'd wed, he'd assigned the same investigator who got dirt on business competitors to keep track of his wife and all her family. Eduardo had burned the angry letters sent by her father, the pleading tearstained cards from her mother. He'd tossed her sister's bouquet of sappy flowers shaped like a pink baby carriage in the trash.

At first he'd done it because he didn't trust Callie. Then he told himself he was just trying to protect her. Sure, her father was trying to be nicer now, but even Eduardo's own parents had had their good days. He wouldn't allow them access to Callie until he knew for sure they wouldn't hurt her again.

But deep in his heart, he knew that wasn't the only reason.

You weren't even man enough to come and ask me for her hand. The memory of her father's cold words still rankled in his mind. *You might own half our town, but I know the kind of man you really are. You'll never be a decent husband or father, and you know it.*

To Walter, as to many others, Eduardo was just a selfish, demanding tyrant, the foreign CEO that his employees obeyed—but despised.

So be it. Eduardo didn't need the man's respect. But he

wouldn't let anyone insult his wife. Or cause them problems that could tear his family apart.

Stroking her back, Eduardo took a deep breath. He was starting to trust Callie again. But he didn't trust the world. Whenever he let himself care for someone, they disappeared from his life. He wouldn't let that happen. Not this time.

"Eduardo?"

Callie was looking up at him in the shadowy hallway, her brow furrowed. Her robe had fallen open slightly to reveal her plump breasts, and suddenly he knew exactly what he needed. He pulled her closer, stroking the edge of her neckline as he murmured, "You said something about helping me sleep?"

"Er." She suddenly blushed. "I just thought…"

"Yes." Grabbing her hand, he led her back to the master bedroom. Pulling the robe off her unresisting body, he pushed her back against the bed. His wife looked like an angel in the moonlight, he thought, her light brown hair silver twined with gold, her pale skin luminous. Her breasts were huge, their full rosy tips bright and vivid against her white skin.

Eduardo kissed her hard and deep. He felt her respond, kissing him back with equal fire, and wanted her as if he hadn't already been satiated that night. He wanted her even more than he did yesterday, and all the year before that. Her small hands roamed his body, stroking his naked chest, caressing his shoulders, his back. He exhaled when she ran her fingers lightly over his backside then groaned aloud as she ran her hand questingly over the hard shaft beneath his drawstring pajama pants. Her face was rapt as she stroked his hard length through the fabric. He grabbed her wrist.

"I do not know—how long I can last," he groaned.

She gave him a smile full of infinite feminine mystery. "So don't."

"*Querida*—"

She unlaced his pants and pulled them down his hips, to his thighs. His hard shaft sprung free from the fabric, and she looked down at him with awe. Reaching out, she took him fully in her hands.

"Callie," he breathed. Her touch felt too good, causing him to jerk involuntarily beneath her stroke. His heart was pounding. He wanted to bury himself deep inside her, impale her, fill her to the hilt now—now—*now*! "What are you—?"

Her eyes were dark and full of need as she pulled him over her onto the bed. "Take me," she whispered.

A low growl rose in his throat as he looked down at her, spread across the bed for his pleasure. He didn't even take the time to pull off his pajama pants. He couldn't. Leaving them across his thighs, he positioned himself and thrust inside her, filling her.

She gasped, gripping his shoulders. Her face filled with anguished ecstasy, and for a moment he thought he'd gone too far, too deep. He started to withdraw.

"No." Gripping her fingers into his flesh, she started to move beneath him. "More."

He pushed inside her again, and she moaned. He rode her, harder and faster, until the bed frame rocked loudly against the wall.

"Stop!" she whispered, looking up at him. "Don't wake the baby!"

He exhaled in a surprised laugh then, leaning forward, kissed her forehead tenderly. Gripping her hips, he slowly thrust inside her in a controlled movement. Somehow the silence just deepened the pleasure. Made it forbidden. He rode her wet and hard until she gripped his upper arms and he heard her soundless scream of pleasure. With a rush of ecstasy, he slammed into her one last time with a shuddering, silent gasp as his whole world shimmered and exploded.

He fell on top of her. It might have been minutes, or an hour, later before he was aware he might be crushing her beneath the weight of his body. He didn't know how much time had passed, which was strange. For one precious moment, it had almost felt like sleep....

He started to move away from her, but she grabbed his arm. "Stay with me."

He hesitated. He knew he wouldn't be able to sleep beside her. But in this moment, he could deny her nothing. Without a word, he rolled back and pulled her to his naked chest, spooning her smaller body with his larger one.

She turned around in his arms. "I love you."

Shocked, he stared down at her in the dark bedroom. Her beautiful, round, upturned face was glowing, tears sparkling down her cheeks in the moonlight.

"I love you, Eduardo." Closing her eyes, she pressed her cheek against his bare chest. "I never stopped loving you, and I never will."

A tremble went through his body as he stroked her hair. Hearing those words on his wife's lips—the words he'd detested and avoided hearing from any other woman—was a sudden, precious gift. Sweet beyond measure.

Poison in his heart.

Now he had even more to lose. Even more to protect. His arms tightened around her. Would she still love him if she found out what he'd done? After Brandon McLinn explained it to her in the most destructive way possible?

He said with forced cheerfulness, "What do you think about spending Christmas in the south of Spain?"

Pressing her face against his chest, she gave a contented sigh. "Spain?"

He stroked her back, keeping his voice casual. "I have a villa on the coast, not too far from my old village." *And five thousand miles from Brandon McLinn.* "What do you say?"

She smiled up at him sleepily. "I'll go anywhere with you."

Eduardo gloried in his wife's generous spirit and trusting heart. Callie knew his flaws better than anyone. And yet somehow she'd chosen to love him.

It was the most precious gift he'd ever received. And the one he least deserved.

Within minutes, she fell asleep in his arms. Eduardo stared out the windows at the dark city and the vast blackness of the Hudson River. It was cold December, when night lasted forever and spring was a distant promise. She loved him. And it was like hot summer to a half-frozen man.

He would never let her go. Ever. Even if it cost his very soul.

In the darkness, his eyes hardened.

He wouldn't lose her. Not now. Not ever.

CHAPTER EIGHT

SITTING by their pool overlooking the Mediterranean, Callie was trying—again—to convince her body to tan in the warm Spanish sun. She glanced back toward their luxurious, enormous villa, where her baby was taking her afternoon nap. Callie loved it here. All right, she was still shockingly pale, but she'd never been so happy.

Or so sad.

In the four months since they'd left New York, her handsome husband had taken their family all over the world via private jet, to all the glamorous places she'd once dreamed of as a girl. They'd spent Christmas here at the villa, decorating their enormous Christmas tree with oranges. On Christmas Eve, they'd gone to a candlelight service, then after putting the baby to bed she and Eduardo had a midnight supper by candlelight. It had been a special, sacred night between them, the one-year anniversary of the first time they'd made love.

When she woke the next morning, Eduardo was gone, as always. Getting Marisol from her crib, she'd gone downstairs to discover an obscene number of gifts beneath their Christmas tree, and beside it, a debonair Santa with twinkling black eyes, in a red suit far too large for his sleek physique and a fake white beard over his chiseled jawline. Marisol had laughed in wonder and delight, and so had

Callie. Santa had presented their baby with so many expensive toys and clothes that it could have satisfied a child army. Marisol had responded by playing with the tissue paper and then trying to chew on her own shoe.

Callie had giggled. "See what happens when you spend too much money on a baby, Santa?"

Santa turned to her. "And I have something for you, Mrs. Claus, er, Cruz."

Reaching into his big black bag, he'd pulled out a key chain that had her initials, "CC", created in what looked to be diamonds and gold. She'd taken the key chain with an incredulous laugh.

"It's beautiful…but are you crazy? People lose key chains. I'll be scared to use this."

Santa smirked. "The key chain isn't the gift. Look again."

Frowning, she looked down at the ridiculously expensive gold-and-diamond key chain and saw the key. Her mouth went dry as she looked up. "What's this?"

He gave her a sudden wicked grin. "Go outside."

Still in her red-and-green flannel pajamas, she'd lifted their baby on her hip, and gone out into the courtyard of the villa, with Santa close behind. Even on Christmas Day, the Spanish sun was warm, and the air smelled of orange groves and the ocean. She'd stopped abruptly in the dusty courtyard.

There, with a big red bow on the hood, she saw a brand-new Rolls-Royce.

"The silver reminded me of you," he murmured softly behind her. "It's the color of the dress you wore to the Winter Ball a few weeks ago. You sparkled like a diamond. You shone like a star."

Turning to face him without a word, Callie pulled down

his white beard. Eduardo's handsome face was revealed, his dark eyes glowing with admiration.

"And every day, Mrs. Cruz," he said, stroking her cheek, "you're more beautiful still."

With an intake of breath, she threw one arm around his neck and, standing on tiptoe, gave Santa the kiss of his life. It wasn't until Marisol began to squirm and complain that Callie recalled that she was squashing their baby, and that she probably shouldn't let her baby see her kissing Santa Claus anyway.

Callie drew back with tears in her eyes.

"Thank you," she whispered, then shook her head with a laugh. "But I'm afraid you're going to be very disappointed with my gift to you."

"What is it?"

"Soap-on-a-rope and a really ugly tie," she teased.

"Oh, yeah? I've been needing those."

She smiled at him. In reality it was a homemade coffee mug she and Marisol had made together, etched with her baby's tiny handprints, which she knew he'd love.

He sobered. "You give me a gift every day, Callie," he said softly. "By being my wife."

She'd looked at him, her heart in her throat. Then her smile faltered. "I just wish I'd heard from my family today."

Eduardo's eyes darkened, and he gave her a tight smile that didn't meet his eyes. "Do not worry, *querida*. I am sure you will hear from them soon."

But she hadn't, not in all the months since then. She'd sent her parents and her sister a letter every week, filled with photographs of Marisol and of their life in Europe. She'd told them how the baby was growing. She'd told them about Marisol's first tooth, the first time she'd turned over in her crib, the first time she'd sat up by herself. She'd described everything that had happened over the seven months of her baby's life. Callie had even poured out her feelings about Eduardo, her former boss, whom she'd once tried to hate but now loved. She wanted to undo the damage she'd once done, and let them see Eduardo as he really was: a good man.

In response to all her carefully written letters, she'd gotten only cold silence.

She tried not to let it bother her. When Eduardo was home, he gave her and the baby his full attention. He'd needed to take business trips again, to the Arctic and Colombia and elsewhere. But whenever he traveled to a destination he thought his family might enjoy, he brought Callie and Marisol along, traveling on the private jet with a full staff and Mrs. McAuliffe in tow. It was amazing.

They'd spent Valentine's Day in Paris, in a royal suite at a five-star hotel with a view of the *Tour Eiffel*. After the baby was asleep, Eduardo had surprised Callie with a romantic, private dinner for two in their suite. She shivered, remembering champagne, chocolate-dipped strawberries and hot kisses that had lasted for hours.

Most recently, they'd gone to Italy. In Venice, he'd rented a palace overlooking the Grand Canal and they'd shared a romantic gondola ride; in Rome, Marisol had had her first taste of lemon gelato, which she'd savored by letting it dribble down her chin.

Such adventures they'd shared as a family. Growing up on her parents' rural farm, the farthest Callie had ever traveled as a child was to the county fair. She'd never have imagined she'd someday have a life like this. International. Glamorous.

Now, the afternoon sun lowered behind the swaying palm trees as Callie sat beside the gorgeous infinity pool back at their villa. She turned her face toward the blue sky.

Taking a drink of cold, lemon-flavored water, she closed her eyes, stretching out on the lounge chair, relishing the warm Spanish sun on her cheeks.

Seven months of marriage and she still wasn't pregnant. But Eduardo never seemed to tire of trying. He wanted her pregnant. Each night, after they made love, he held her till she slept before he slipped away to the nearest guest room to sleep alone. She hated waking up alone. But that was a tiny thing, nothing really, compared to the multitude of joys in her life, with her baby and husband she loved.

But she still missed the family she'd left behind in North Dakota. It was a heartache that never quite went away.

Her letters hadn't worked, in spite of her best efforts. Her eyes flew open and she stared up at the blue sky. Maybe it was time to do something drastic.

"Callie."

She heard her husband's voice across the pool. Lifting her head, she smiled as she watched him walk toward her, wearing only swimming trunks that showed off his tanned, magnificent body. She could not look away from his hard-muscled torso, powerful arms and strong thighs. The sensual way he moved seduced her—without him even trying!

"I like seeing you by the pool," he said appreciatively. Lifting a dark eyebrow, he looked over her pale body in her tiny bikini. "You look hot, in all those clothes."

She giggled. "You always say that. You told me I looked hot when it was pouring rain in London in January. I was shivering like a drowned rat and you started taking off my clothes!"

"I'm always available to help take off your clothes." Taking her hand in his own, he said innocently, "Care for a nice refreshing swim?"

Eduardo had a look in his dark eyes that made her suspect their "nice refreshing swim" would soon lead to rampant nakedness for them both. The heat in his gaze left her breathless. Her husband didn't seem to see any flaws in her post-pregnancy figure. He called her *beautiful, gorgeous,* and *irresistible,* and once she was naked in his arms, he told her so with his body.

"All right." Smiling, Callie let him pull her to her feet and lead her into the pool. The bobbing water felt cool against her bikini and sun-warmed skin. Once in the deep end of the pool, he pulled her into his arms and kissed her.

His lips felt hot and hard against hers. She clung to him as he kissed her, relishing the feel of his hard, muscled body towering over her petite frame. She loved him so much. And though he hadn't spoken those three words back to her, she was convinced it was just a matter of time...

He pulled back with a shiver. "Oh, *querida,*" he said hoarsely. "I'm going to miss you."

"Miss me?" She blinked. "Where are you going?"

As they held each other in the pool, the water bobbing against her breasts, he stroked her cheek with a scowl. "Marrakech. To complete a business deal."

"Morocco? For how long?"

"Hard to say. The man is unpredictable. The negotiations might last a day—or a week."

"A week? A full week at the villa without you? I can't face it."

"I'll miss you, too."

She took a deep breath. "But it might be the perfect time for me to visit my parents. I'll just take the other jet while you're gone..."

He frowned. "What?"

She met his eyes. "I've been writing my family every week for four months. It's not working. I need to go see them."

Eduardo stared at her. Was it just her imagination, or did some of the color disappear behind his tan? "Absolutely not."

"Why?" She tilted her head, folding her arms. She'd expected a fight and was ready for it. "You won't exactly miss us. You'll be in Morocco."

"Maybe I'd like you and Marisol to come with me. Marrakech is beautiful in April."

"That wasn't your plan a minute ago."

"Plans change."

As the cool water of the pool bobbed around them, they glared at each other. Above them, the wind blew through the palm trees, and she could hear the roar of the distant ocean as seabirds cried out mournfully across the cloudless blue sky.

And Callie broke. "I miss them, Eduardo." She unfolded her arms, blinking back tears. "I don't know what else to do. I miss them."

He set his jaw. "I thought you were happy here—"

"I am. But I *miss* them. Every hour. Every day. It's like a hole in my heart." She put her hand over his chest. "Right here." Tears streamed down her cheeks as she looked up at him. "I can't stand the silence. I feel lost without them."

Eduardo stared at her for a long moment. Then, closing his eyes, he exhaled.

"All right," he said in a low voice.

"All right?"

He looked down at her. "Not McLinn. But your parents and your sister—yes."

"I can go see them in North Dakota?" she breathed, hardly able to believe it.

"But I don't want you and Marisol so far away from me. And I need to be in Marrakech tomorrow…"

Her heart, which had been rising, suddenly pinched. She said dully, "So I should put off my visit."

"No." Taking her in his arms, he gently lifted her chin. "I will charter a jet to collect your family. If they agree, they will meet us in Marrakech tomorrow. How about that?"

She stared at him, shocked.

"You will see them. And they will get a chance to meet me." His jaw clenched as he looked away. "Not just as the CEO who owns the oilfields outside your town, but as your husband. As Marisol's father." He looked back at her, his darkly handsome face suddenly uncertain. "Is... is that satisfactory?"

"Satisfactory!" she cried. She threw her arms around him in the pool and kissed him, over and over, kissed his cheeks, his forehead, his chin. "Oh, Eduardo, I love you so much. Thank you, my darling, thank you!"

He straightened in the pool. His hard-muscled body dazzled her. Droplets of water cascaded down his tanned skin, sparkling in the sun as he lifted her up, wrapping her legs around his waist.

"This time," he whispered, "I'll let you thank me."

And he kissed her, long and hard, beneath the waving palm trees and the hot Spanish sun.

Many hours later, Eduardo looked down at his naked wife, sleeping in his arms in the darkness of the bedroom. It was past midnight. And he wanted to sleep with her.

Not just make love to her. Making love was easy. Callie was damn beautiful. A man would have to be dead not to want her constantly. Especially when she was happy, as she'd been today.

She'd been so thrilled to speak with her parents on the phone that afternoon. She hadn't noticed how shocked her parents were to hear from her, and learn she was in Spain. But after tears on both sides, the Woodvilles had agreed to take his chartered jet and join them in Morocco, after a quick stop at the American consulate to get their very first passports.

Later that evening, as Eduardo discussed necessary travel arrangements with his assistant, Callie had bounced off the walls with excitement and joy. After dinner, they'd played with the baby, given Marisol a bath and put her to bed, and then Callie had grabbed his hand and pulled him to bed, too. Even after making love for hours, for the second time that day, it had still taken unusually long for Callie to fall asleep in his arms: a full ten minutes.

That was hours ago. Eduardo looked bleakly across the luxurious master bedroom of the villa. God knew he'd tried to make himself sleep. But it was always the same. After they made love, he would hold her, his body relaxed, his soul in perfect, blissful peace. He would cherish her in his arms, so soft and willing and warm. But the instant he closed his eyes, sleep disappeared. He tried to relax, but his muscles became tight until beads of sweat broke out on his forehead.

He'd never slept with any of the women he bedded. But he'd never wanted to. He'd thought it would be different with Callie. But even with her, he still couldn't let down his guard completely. Eduardo exhaled, knowing he wasn't going to be able to sleep tonight, either. He should get up and go to the guest room to sleep, like usual.

Yet he wanted to sleep with his wife.

He wanted to deserve her.

Since the day they'd wed, Eduardo had done everything he could to keep his family safe and happy. He'd supported Callie in every way.

Except one. None of her letters to her family had ever

left the house. And she'd never gotten any of their mail, forwarded from New York. When Sami Woodville had tried to phone his office, he'd instructed his secretary to block her calls. When she'd called his cell phone, he'd changed his number.

A cold chill went through his body. Would Callie ever forgive him when she discovered what he'd done? Would she understand that he'd done it for one reason: to protect their family?

He'd been ruthless for a reason. But when Callie had wept with grief in the pool today, something had snapped inside him, and he couldn't do it anymore—even though he knew all hell would break loose when she spoke with her parents and put two and two together. It was remotely possible for the mail service to misplace a letter, but not scores of them. Callie would soon figure out who'd had means and motive to suppress them.

Eduardo stared bleakly at the bedroom ceiling.

He should tell her himself what he'd done, rather than letting her figure it out. Rather than—say—letting Brandon McLinn be the one to tell her. His jaw tightened. He was sick of feeling the ghost of McLinn always at his back. Tired of waiting for the moment when Callie would finally be disgusted by Eduardo's flawed soul and leave. Tired of feeling Brandon McLinn always waiting in the shadows, ready to take Callie away the instant he made a mistake.

Was this that final mistake?

His arms tightened around Callie.

Her parents and sister were already somewhere over the Atlantic, but his investigator was having trouble tracking down Brandon McLinn. He believed the young farmer might be on his way, even now, to southern Spain, since he'd discovered their villa's location from Callie's family.

Eduardo allowed himself a grim smile. By the time he arrived here, Callie would be in Morocco.

The smile faded as he looked at Callie's slumbering, trusting face. He should pull his private investigator off Brandon McLinn, along with Walter, Jane and Sami Woodville. He should stop going through his wife's mail or screening her calls at the villa. He should just take a deep breath, and trust her. Trust everyone.

But he couldn't. It would mean flying blind. If Eduardo didn't know the future, how could he prevent catastrophe? How could he keep his family safe? How could he make sure she would never leave, never break his heart; never break Marisol's?

Listening to her quiet, even breathing, he squeezed his eyes shut. His whole body was tense, and sleep danced away from him, mocking him.

Wearily sitting up, Eduardo watched the gray light of dawn through the windows, and heard the faint call of morning birds above the roar of the ocean. He put his head in his hands. He wanted to deserve her. He wanted to trust her.

He wanted to love her.

"Eduardo?"

He felt a gentle hand on his back. He turned, and saw Callie looking up at him with luminous eyes. "What is it?"

He looked down at her. She was naked, and beautiful, and unafraid. He said in a low voice, "I had a dream that you left me."

Her eyes went wide. She sat up, shaking her head. "No." Reaching for him, she pulled him back into the soft comfort of her arms. "That will never happen. Never."

Reaching out, he twined his fingers in her hair. "My parents loved each other once," he said. "They wanted a child. They built a home. Then they grew apart, twisted by secrets and lies. My mother met a new man, and my father was destroyed by it. Everything ended."

Callie took both his hands in her own. "That won't happen to us."

Blinking fast, he looked out at the gray dawn. "I had a dream."

Callie stared at him, suddenly frowning.

"But you don't sleep," she said slowly. "You don't dream."

Eduardo turned to her. She was so beautiful, his wife. So gentle and kind. She believed the best of everyone, even when they didn't deserve it. He took a deep, shuddering breath.

"I do now," he whispered.

CHAPTER NINE

CALLIE'S hands and feet bounced rhythmically against the interior of their four-wheel drive as they drove from the Marrakech airport. Eduardo, who was driving beside her, reached out and stilled her knee with his hand.

"Sorry." She looked up at him with an apologetic smile. "I'm excited."

"Yes." He smiled back at her, his dark eyes warm. "I know." Then a troubled shadow crossed his expression, and he turned away to focus on the road, gripping the wheel.

Business negotiations usually didn't faze Eduardo. Callie wondered why he seemed so tense. He generally relished a good fight. Shrugging it off, she cooed at their baby in her car seat behind them. Through the back window she saw the other vehicle following with their staff and bodyguards as they drove past the twelfth-century ramparts of the medina to the vast sprawling palm desert beyond. The sky was blue above the distant, snowcapped Atlas Mountains.

She turned back to her dark, impossibly handsome husband beside her. He was wearing a business suit, but his dark coloring and black hair made him look like a sheikh. In her own long purple caftan, with the window rolled down and the warm Moroccan wind blowing through her hair, she felt like a cosseted Arabian princess at his side.

It was officially the happiest day of her life. After today, she'd have no reason to ever be sad again.

"Thank you," she said for the millionth time.

Eduardo gave her a sideways glance. "Stop."

"You don't know what this means to me—"

"I mean it." His jaw was tight as he turned off the main road to a guardhouse. Pulling up to a heavily scrolled metal gate, Eduardo spoke in French to a security guard, who with a very deep bow, swung open the gate. Eduardo drove up a long sweeping driveway with the other car behind them.

Callie looked up through the front windshield, her eyes wide when she saw the enormous Moroccan *riad*, two stories tall and surrounded by gardens. Willowy palm trees graced the edges of large swimming pool that sparkled a brilliant blue in the sun. The grand house itself was the combination of traditional Moroccan architecture and old French glamour. Craning her head, Callie looked up with awe at the home's soaring curves and the exquisitely detailed scrollwork. "What is this place?"

"In the 1920s it was a hotel. Now it belongs to Kasimir Xendzov, who loaned it for our visit."

"He's not staying here?"

"No."

She turned to Eduardo in shock. "Why would he leave a place like this?"

He shook his head. "He is in the city as little as possible. He prefers to live like a nomad in the desert." His lips curved. "Like those sheikhs, in the romance novels you love."

"But he's Russian?"

"The local people call him the Tsar of the Desert."

"Oh." The romantic phrase made her shiver. "What's he like?"

"Kasimir? As cold and heartless as his brother. You remember Vladimir Xendzov?"

She tilted her head. "Prince Vladimir? The man who stole the Yukon deal from us?"

"He's not really a prince, no matter what he says. But yes. They're brothers. They've spent the last ten years trying to destroy each other."

Callie stared at him, aghast. "That's awful!"

Eduardo smiled with satisfaction. "A fact that will help me get what I want."

"Prince Vladimir was vicious," she said, troubled. "Corrupt. Definitely unsafe."

"And not a prince."

She pressed her lips together. "Is it smart to make a deal with his brother?"

"Don't worry. We are safe here. Kasimir is our host. His honor is at stake." Pulling the car up to the front of the house, he turned off the engine. Getting out, he handed the keys to a waiting servant. Callie stepped out behind him with her seven-month-old baby in her arms, and heard the soft water of a fountain. She looked at the huge house beneath the hard blue sky of the desert, and saw a shadow move in the window.

"Are they here?" she whispered.

Eduardo gave her a single, silent nod, and an involuntary shiver went through her. She walked towards the *riad*, her baby against her hip, her husband and bodyguards following behind them.

The house seemed Moorish in design, with a flat roof and intricate tile work. They walked through the soaring arches to the door. Inside, the walls were decorated with floral and geometric motifs, intertwined flowers and vines in green, red and gold-leaf paint all the way to the ceiling. Past the foyer was a cloister, an outdoor walkway built around a lush courtyard garden. Callie took a deep breath of the fresh air, listening to the sound of a burbling fountain mingling with birdsong.

Then she heard a woman's scream.

Whirling around, Carrie instinctively held up her arm, protecting her baby from the unseen danger.

But there was no danger, just her sister, racing at her full blast!

"Sami," Callie cried then she looked behind her and saw the smiling eyes of her parents. "Mom! Dad!"

"Callie." Her mother was openly weeping as she pulled her into her arms. "And is this your baby? My grandchild?"

"Yes, it's Marisol," Callie choked out. Her mother sobbed, wrapping Marisol and Callie into a hug with Sami. Her father wrapped his large form around the whole family and she saw to her shock that he, too, was weeping— something she'd never seen in her whole life.

"I missed you all so much," Callie whispered. She glanced at Eduardo out of the corner of her eye. He was standing back, watching them from the shadows.

"It's my fault." Pulling off his John Deere cap, her father rubbed his gray head with the heel of his hand. "I never should have written that nasty letter, chewing you out. It was just your Mom kept weeping, and you know I can't think straight when she's crying. I don't blame you for the silent treatment." His voice caught. "I wouldn't have written me back, either…"

Callie had no idea what he was talking about, but it felt so good to be with her family and have them clearly happy to see her and the baby. Marisol, looking at all the crying adults around her, gave a little worried whimper, looking up at Callie for reassurance. "It's all right," she told her, smiling. "It's finally all right."

As Jane Woodville held out her arms, tears were streaming down her plump cheeks and she looked like a slightly more wrinkled version of her granddaughter. "Can I hold her?"

The baby looked uncertain at first, but within sixty seconds, Jane had won her trust. Ten minutes later, Sami and then Grandpa Walter held her, and they heard Marisol's sweet baby giggle. Callie looked at her family, and could hardly believe that she'd been apart from them for seven months. They were the best, kindest people in the world.

Except for her husband. She looked at Eduardo adoringly, but he remained back in the shadows across the room.

"Mari-Marisol?" her father asked uncertainly.

Callie turned back, smiling through her tears. "Marisol Samantha Cruz."

"You named her after me?" Sami blurted out, her face screwed up with tears. "How could you forgive me? I was so selfish. I told myself calling your old boss was the right thing to do, but the truth is I didn't want you to marry Brandon." She sniffled. "How can you stand to look at me?"

"It *was* the right thing," Callie said through her tears. "Eduardo and I were meant to be together, and thanks to you we are. We're happy. Really happy…"

Callie looked back at Eduardo. He was still standing by the door, his arms folded as he watched the family reunion. Why didn't he come over to join them? It was strange. Any normal person would have come over to be part of the group. But Eduardo chose to be standoffish, to watch from a distance.

Her mother, standing beside her, followed her gaze.

"He loves you," Jane said softly.

Callie looked at her wistfully. "How can you tell?"

Jane smiled. "I see it in the way he looks at you. Like his

heart's nigh about to break." Reaching out, she squeezed her daughter's hand. "I still can't believe we're in Morocco. I always told your father that someday we'd travel and see the world. He said he'd do it as soon as it was free." She chuckled mischievously. "Eduardo's jet was the answer to my prayer."

The two women laughed, hugging each other, and for the rest of the afternoon, the family talked and giggled as Kasimir Xendzov's well-trained servants served refreshments and drinks. Eduardo continued to remain out of the circle, out of the group, until he finally disappeared all afternoon with his assistants to work on the deal. His behavior bewildered Callie. Was he just trying to give her some space with her family? But didn't he realize that he, too, was part of the family now?

After a delicious dinner of couscous and lamb, Callie said good-night to her jet-lagged parents and sister as they turned in to their luxurious bedrooms. After giving Marisol a bottle, she tucked her into a crib next door to their own large bedroom on the other side of the *riad* from the rest of her family. For the first time all day, Callie was alone. She looked at the large bed, covered with dark blue pillows. Fading sunlight fell upon the blanket in a pattern from the carved lattice window. She touched the bed. The mattress felt soft.

She heard a noise behind her. Jumping, she turned around.

Eduardo stood in the doorway. His eyes were dark, his expression set, as if braced for bad news.

"There you are," she said, furrowing her brow. "Where have you been? Why didn't you come talk to my family?"

"I didn't want to intrude."

Callie frowned, feeling puzzled by the strangeness of

his tone. She shook her head. "But you're part of our family now."

The door closed behind him as he came toward her in the bedroom. His voice was stilted. "Your family isn't rich."

She drew back, confused at the turn in conversation. "No. Especially not these days. My parents' farm has had a rough couple years...."

He came closer, something strangely intense in his dark eyes. "But you all still love each other."

"Of course we do," she said, bewildered. "Like you said—we're family."

His jaw twitched as he rubbed his wrist. In the shadowy bedroom, she saw the flash of his platinum watch. "Growing up, I thought money made a family. That it made people actually love each other enough to stay."

Callie's breath suddenly caught in her throat. "Money has nothing to do with it. Don't you know that?"

Eduardo gave her a tight smile.

"I'm glad you spent time with your family today. I have work to do before I meet with Xendzov tomorrow. Get some rest."

As he turned away, Callie stared after him, shocked. It was the first night she could remember when he hadn't wanted to accompany her to bed at night, to make love to her, to hold her until she slept.

He stopped at the door. "We need to talk," he said heavily. "Tomorrow. Then we'll see." He took a deep breath. "Afterward, I hope you will still..."

His voice trailed off. For a long moment, he stared at her, his eyes glittering in the shadows. Then he turned away, closing the bedroom door between them.

Callie was hardly able to sleep that night without him beside her. In the morning, she hurried down for breakfast, but he never appeared. She found out he'd left at dawn with his team of administrators and lawyers to work on the business deal with their invisible host, the mysterious Kasimir Xendzov. She thought it was strange, because Eduardo had seemed so determined to talk to her. About what?

And then she knew.

Was Eduardo finally going to tell her he loved her?

Joy filled her, followed by certainty. What else could it be? She was filled with happiness, counting down the moments until she'd see him again. She spent an enjoyable morning with her baby and family, sharing breakfast in the courtyard garden, walking around the estate, swimming in the pool. After lunch, as her parents took an afternoon nap with their grandbaby, Callie and Sami decided to explore the *souks* of Marrakech.

As the two sisters wandered the narrow, mazelike streets of the medina, Callie's heart was light. They walked through the outdoor markets, investigating booth after booth of copper lanterns, terra-cotta pots, embroidered *jellabas* and coral beads. She constantly checked her new cell phone in her handbag, just to make sure Eduardo hadn't called for her, but in the meantime, she was happy. Wearing a floppy pink hat, a billowy blouse and long skirt, with her wide-eyed sister at her side, Callie felt almost like a child again, when she and Sami went on "expeditions" across the wide fields and brooks of their family farm.

She suddenly froze in the middle of the outdoor market. Feeling prickles on her neck, as if someone was watching her, she whirled around.

But she only saw her bodyguard, Sergio Garcia, following at a discreet distance through the crowded medina. Eduardo never let her go anywhere without a bodyguard, and often more than one. Still, even as the afternoon passed and the hot Moroccan sun lowered to the west, the cold prickles on her neck didn't go away.

"So you really forgive me?" Sami asked softly.

Kneeling as she looked through a selection of copper lanterns, Callie smiled up at her sister. "I forgave you long ago—the day I named my daughter."

Sami's young face was dubious. "But if you forgave me, why didn't you write back?"

Callie straightened, frowning. "You wrote? When?"

"Lots of times! I even sent flowers! But other than the day Marisol was born, when you called us, we never heard a word. Not me, not Brandon, not even Mom and Dad!"

Callie gaped at her. "I wrote you letters every week! I sent hundreds of pictures!"

"We never got anything."

A shiver of ice went down Callie's spine. "Strange," she said faintly then tried to push it away with a smile. "But it doesn't matter anymore, does it?"

"We were worried about you," Sami said softly, clawing back her hair. "I'm glad you at least called us from the hospital when Marisol was born. Brandon arrived two days later and was so upset. He made it sound as if you'd been, well—" she bit her lip "—kidnapped."

Callie looked at her. "Have you been spending a lot of time with Brandon?"

Sami's cheeks turned pink. "Yeah."

"You're in love with him." It was a statement, not a question.

Sami stared at her then burst into tears. "I'm sorry," she whispered, wiping her eyes. "I've loved him for years." She tried to smile. "All the time that he loved you."

Callie shook her head. "I keep telling people—Brandon and I are just friends!"

Sami gave a hoarse laugh. "Man, you're dumb. Just as dumb as he was."

"*Was*? Have you told Brandon how you feel?"

"Not yet." Sami looked away. "I'm scared. We've spent a lot of time together lately, ice skating, looking at the stars, running errands. Whatever." She shivered beneath the fading afternoon sun of the Marrakech market. "Once, I almost thought he was going to kiss me. Then he turned away and started talking about you."

"He did?" Guilt went through Callie. "He must hate me."

"He hates Eduardo. Not you."

"Then why didn't he ever write me?" Callie whispered.

Sami looked at her as if she were crazy. "He did. I know he did. He showed me the letters."

The strange feeling went through Callie again, a dark cloud like a shadow over the sun. How was it possible that her family hadn't gotten any of her letters? Or that Callie hadn't gotten any of theirs?

Pushing the thought away, she turned back to Sami, putting her hand on her shoulder. She said firmly, "You should tell him how you feel."

Sami's eyes lit up then faded. "But what if he's not interested? What if he just laughs at me?"

"He won't."

"Yeah, but what if he does?"

"Life is short. Don't waste another day. Call him. Call him now."

"You're right." Sami stared at her then suddenly hugged her tight. "Thank you, Callie." Pulling away, she wiped her eyes. "I'll go back to the house. And call him in private. Oh," she breathed, wiping her shaking hands on her jeans, "am I really going to do this?"

"Sergio!" Callie called, wiping tears from her own eyes as she waved the bodyguard over. "Please take my sister back to the house."

"And you, Mrs. Cruz," Sergio Garcia said, his expression a smooth mask.

"I haven't finished my shopping."

"I can't leave you alone here, *señora*."

"I'll be fine," Callie said impatiently. She motioned to the busy *souk*. "There's no danger here!"

The bodyguard lifted an eyebrow. Turning away, he used his cell phone and spoke in low, rapid Spanish. Hanging up, he turned to Sami with a broad smile. "*Sí*. I can take you home, *señorita*."

"Thank you," Callie said, surprised. He'd never been so reasonable before. "Would you mind taking these bags back with you?"

"Por supuesto, señora." Garcia took her purchases, gifts for her parents, clothes and toys for Marisol, even a silver *koumaya* dagger for Eduardo. "Stay right here, Mrs. Cruz, in the open market."

"I will." Callie hugged her sister and whispered, "I think you and Brandon are perfect for each other."

"Thank you," Sami breathed fervently. "I love you, Callie." Then she was gone.

Callie was alone. She took deep breaths of the exotic, spicy scent of the air, of the distant leather tannery, of flowers and musky oriental perfumes. No bodyguard. No baby. Not even her husband. Callie was alone in this exotic foreign market. After so many months, the sudden freedom felt both disorienting and intoxicating.

Smiling to herself, she ignored the shouts of sellers trying to get her attention and walked through the market, feeling light as a feather on air as she continued to shop for gifts. Who knew if she'd ever return to Morocco again?

Her eye fell upon a tiny star carved in wood. It reminded her of Brandon's hobby that Callie found intolerably boring—astronomy. Thinking of him, a pang went through her.

Why didn't he ever write me?

He did. I know he did. He showed me the letters.

With a ragged breath, Callie lifted her gaze to the sky, turning toward the fading warmth of the sun. Above the busy, crowded, chaotic *souk*, a bird flew toward the distant Atlas Mountains. The setting sun had turned the snow-capped peaks a deep violet-pink.

"Callie."

She sucked in her breath. Slowly she turned.

Brandon McLinn stood in front of her.

Time slowed as he came toward her, tall and thin, standing out from the rest of the crowd in his cowboy hat, plaid flannel shirt and work-worn jeans. He stopped in front of her.

"At last," Brandon breathed, his eyes wet with tears. "I've found you."

"Brandon?" she whispered, her throat choking. "Is this a dream?"

"No." Smiling through his tears, he put a skinny hand on her shoulder. "I'm here."

"But what are you doing in Morocco?"

His hand tightened. "It took a miracle, all right," he said grimly. His eyes narrowed beneath his black-framed glasses. "No thanks to that Spanish bastard."

Callie gasped. "Don't call him that!"

He blinked, frowning. "But you hate him. Don't you? You said he was a playboy, that he had coal instead of a heart…that he couldn't be loyal to anything but his own fat bank account!"

Hearing her own words thrown back at her hurt. She

closed her eyes against her own cruelty. "He's not like that," she said over the lump in her throat. "Not really. He's—changed."

"Must be Stockholm Syndrome," Brandon snorted then his voice grew serious. "I've been so worried about you, Callie. I just let him take you away. I didn't save you."

Callie opened her eyes in shock. "*You* felt guilty?"

"I swore I'd leave no stone unturned, until you and your baby were back home. Safe, and free."

Smiling through sudden tears, she put her hand over his. "But we are safe. And free. I know our marriage had a rocky start, but he's been nothing but good to us."

"Good?" Brandon's jaw hardened. "He's had me followed for months."

"Followed?" she echoed.

"When Sami told me she was leaving for Marrakech, I skipped out in the middle of the night, slipping past the man watching my house. I drove to Denver and booked a flight. I've been staying at a hotel off this square, following your movements through Sami's messages."

"You knew I'd be at the market." Callie stared at him. "It was you I felt, watching me. Following us."

"Hoping to get you alone." He looked down at her, his eyes owl-like beneath his glasses. "I tried to contact you. Letters, phone calls. I tried everything short of a singing telegram. Last December, he called me in the middle of the night, warning me off. I threatened to call the police in New York. So he spirited you overseas. For the last four months, I had no idea where you even were!"

Callie remembered the night she'd caught Eduardo talking on the phone to a rival, he'd said, who lived far away. That very same night, he'd suddenly suggested they go to Spain. Once there, he'd never let her out of his sight, or even let her drive her own car, without a bodyguard. He'd said it was to keep her safe.

But safe from whom?

"I promised myself I wouldn't abandon you," Brandon said. "I've been waiting…praying…desperate. All the time he kept you prisoner."

Prisoner. Callie stared at him with a sick feeling in her belly. She was starting to think that Eduardo's planned talk later didn't involve him taking her in his arms and declaring his eternal love.

"I always knew the man was bad news." Brandon narrowed his eyes. "From the moment I first heard you talk about him. When he leased you that apartment in the Village, I knew he wanted you." His voice became bitter. "And from the sound of your voice, I knew you would let him."

"So you told Eduardo we were engaged," she said slowly. "The night he stopped by the apartment, you said…"

"I just told him the truth," he said stubbornly. "We *were* engaged. We said, if neither of us were married by the time we were thirty…"

"That was a joke!"

"It was never a joke to me." He looked down. "But I guess it was to you."

She stared at him, her cheeks aflame, unable to speak.

"I loved you, Callie," he said gruffly. "Since we were kids, I loved you."

She felt a lump in her throat, remembering their childhood. Chasing fireflies on warm summer nights. Watching fireworks on the Fourth. Christmas dinner with her cousins, aunts and uncles, turkey and stuffing and homemade pumpkin pie, sledding with her sister down McGillicuddy's hill. Even going out with Brandon's telescope at night and looking at stars until she wanted to claw her eyes out. It had been wonderful.

Her throat hurt. "I should have known. I'm sorry. But…I don't feel that way about you."

"Yeah. I figured that out." He took a deep breath then gave her a sudden crooked smile. "I've started to think that maybe I should look for someone who can love me. Who can see me. As more than a goofy, dependable friend."

Her heart broke a little in her chest. She tilted back her floppy pink hat. "Brandon—"

"But first I'm taking you and the baby home. We'll get you a good divorce lawyer. I don't care how much money Cruz has, the courts will see that you are in the right."

"You don't understand—"

"You don't have to be scared. We'll be with you every step of the way. Me. Your family—"

"I'm in love with him, Brandon," she blurted out. At his intake of breath, she lifted her eyes miserably. "I love him so much I think I might die of it. Every day all I can think is that I would do anything, absolutely anything, to make him love me back."

Brandon stared at her, his face pale. His Adam's apple bobbed then he looked at his feet as he said in a low voice, "I remember that feeling."

"I'm so sorry." Reaching out, she pulled him into her arms as she wept. "Forgive me."

For a moment, he accepted the comfort of her arms. They held each other, like kids dodging a storm.

"How can you love a man like that?" Brandon said in a low voice. "I accept that you can't love me. All right, fine. But a man who keeps you prisoner? Of all men on earth, you choose Cruz? A cruel, selfish beast of a man?"

Her heart lifted to her throat. "You don't know him,

Brandon. He's been hurt in the past. But he's not selfish and he's not cruel. If you only knew. He has such a good heart—"

Her voice ended in a gasp as Brandon was violently wrenched from her arms.

"Don't *touch* my wife!"

Turning in shock, Callie saw Eduardo's handsome face distorted with rage. A beam of blood-red light covered his black, civilized business suit, from the sun setting fire to the west.

"No, Eduardo, no!"

But he didn't hear her. Drawing back his fist, he punched Brandon so hard across the jaw that the other man, totally unprepared, dropped like a stone into the dust.

"No!" Callie shrieked. Around the *souk*, people stared at them across the busy, crowded market, speaking in a cacophony of languages. Fist raised, Eduardo started for Brandon again.

Callie ran between them, so fast her hat fell off her head. Holding up both her arms, she cried, "Don't!"

Eduardo whirled on her, his black eyes so hot that she should have burned to ash. "You told him to meet you here!"

"No, of course I didn't!" Looking at him, all Callie could suddenly think of was how he'd been lying to her face for months. How he'd caused her family pain. Forcing herself to take a deep, calming breath, she knelt down in the dust and checked on Brandon, who was knocked out cold but seemed otherwise fine. Rising to her feet, she glared at Eduardo. "Brandon couldn't contact me. A fact you know well."

Eduardo stared at her, breathing heavily. "What did he want from you?"

She lifted her chin. "To help me go back to North Dakota and file for divorce."

"And what did you say?"

"What do you think I said?" she cried. "I said no! Because I'm married to you. I have a child with you. I love you! Of course I told him no. Are you out of your mind?"

Baring his teeth, Eduardo grabbed her arm and pulled her away from the staring eyes of the *souk* and down the warren of streets to the parked car. Pushing her inside, he started the engine. It was only after they were back on the road that he spoke to her through gritted teeth.

"I found you in his arms."

Callie whirled on him. "I was comforting him!"

"I *trusted* you," he ground out.

"Trusted me?" She looked at him, tears in her eyes. "That's a joke! You never trusted me. You kept me a virtual prisoner, locked away from my family. Did you think I wouldn't find out?"

Eduardo looked at her, his handsome face pale beneath his tan. Setting his jaw, he didn't answer.

"When I think of all the time I spent," Callie whispered. "Sending them picture after picture, letter after letter." She looked up at him fiercely. "And the whole time, you were keeping them away, and me, locked away in your own little cage!"

He turned his eyes grimly back to the road. As he drove from the fortified gates of the medina toward the sprawling palm desert, he was silent, his jaw tight.

"You're not even trying to deny it," she said, tears streaming down her face.

He changed gears with more force than necessary. "I was going to tell you about it," he retorted. "It's why I told Sanchez he could leave you there. I wanted to surprise you at the market, and take you out to dinner just the two of us, so we could talk in private. So I could try to make you understand."

"I understand, all right!"

His hands clenched on the wheel. "I was trying to protect you. To protect all of us."

"Brandon said he was followed. Did you have me watched, too? What about my family?"

Eduardo looked at her then looked away.

"Keith Johnson had the detail," he said flatly.

The hot Moroccan air blew through the car window, whirling over her skin. "Keith Johnson?" she faltered. "But you use him to gain information on your rivals. On your enemies." She looked at him. "Which one am I?"

"You're my wife," he said tightly. "I was trying to keep you safe."

Her emotions were so jumbled she felt numb. "Safe!"

He glanced at her out of the corner of his eye. "What was I supposed to do?" he said roughly. "Let another man destroy our marriage?"

Callie's throat hurt. She closed her eyes, hearing the purr of the engine and soft whirr of the tires against the road.

"No," she whispered. "You destroyed it yourself."

She looked at him, and his dark eyes burned through her. Then wordlessly, he looked back at the road as the car turned into the gatehouse and drove up the sweeping entrance to the *riad*.

"We left Brandon," she cried. "Injured in the medina..."

"I'll send someone to check on him," Eduardo said coldly, not looking at her. "I wouldn't want your *best friend in all the world* to be left abandoned and alone."

Parking the car, he turned off the ignition and got out. Callie didn't move. She stared at the beautiful tile work of the grand home, at the green gardens and swaying palm trees above the blue-water pool. This place truly was paradise.

Her hands were shaking. She felt chilled to the bone.

The car door opened.

"Come, *querida*," Eduardo said quietly, reaching for her hand. She did not resist as he pulled her from the SUV and into the house. Inside the *riad*, all was quiet. Perhaps her parents and baby were sleeping. Callie heard only the soft burble of the fountain from the courtyard garden.

She felt her husband's hand in her own, as strong and protective around hers as it had ever been. But everything had changed. Was it only that morning that she'd been so happy, feeling like all her dreams were coming true? As Eduardo led her through the cloistered walk around the interior courtyard, she felt cold in the fading light of the sun.

"Why did you do it?" she rasped. "Why?"

Eduardo stopped.

"I'm tired, Callie," he said wearily. "Tired of trying to keep you. Tired of feeling like I'm failing. Tired of knowing, whatever I do, it won't be good enough."

"I did nothing but love you."

"Love is nice." His eyes glittered like hot coals as the edges of his lips curved. "Love changes nothing."

She stared at him, her heart chilled. "Is that what you think?"

"It's what I know," he said grimly, and that was the end. Her heart frosted over.

"You were right about one thing," she said. "Brandon was in love with me. But you've been so wrong about the rest. You are a wonderful father, Eduardo. But—" she gave him a trembling smile "—a terrible husband."

Hearing the noise of servants down the hall, he pulled her into their bedroom, closing the door behind them.

Looking down at her in the shadows, he spoke in a low voice.

"I always knew that someday you would see through me."

She felt trails of ice on her cheeks and lifted her hand to discover she was weeping. She loved him. But she wouldn't be his prisoner. Not anymore.

"I loved you, Eduardo." Her voice choked. "I loved you so."

His handsome face was hard with anguish. "*Loved*?"

"I would have done anything to make you love me," she whispered. "Anything." With a deep breath, Callie looked up at him through her tears. She squared her shoulders. "But I won't be your prisoner." Pulling off her diamond ring, she held it out to him with a trembling hand. "So I can't be your wife."

CHAPTER TEN

IT WAS like a punch through Eduardo's gut, a blow so deep it reverberated against his spine.

When he'd found Callie embracing McLinn, it had been like walking into a nightmare and seeing his worst fear come to life. He'd felt fury that he'd never known. He'd wanted to kill the man with his bare hands. And he might have done it, if not for Callie.

Now, sinking down on the bed, Eduardo stared at the ten-carat diamond ring twinkling in his palm. And realized that seeing Callie with another man had only been his *second*-worst fear.

Somehow, he'd always known this day would come. It was almost a relief to get it over with, rather than always wondering when it would happen. When she would leave him. His hands tightened over the ring, feeling the hard diamond bite into his palm. He spoke over the razor blade in his throat.

"I will start divorce proceedings tomorrow."

Her lips parted. "What?"

"I'll do what I should have done a long time ago." He looked at her. "Set you free."

Tears streaked her pale, beautiful face like stardust in the fading red twilight outside the latticed window. "I just can't live with a man who doesn't trust me. Who tries to control every aspect of my life."

"I understand." He gave her a grim smile. "I told you on our wedding day that when our marriage ended, the prenuptial agreement would see us through."

His wife looked white and wan, standing beside the bed. She looked like a ghost. "I didn't think you would let me go so easily."

He tried to ignore the fierce, white-hot blade of pain that entered his body.

"I am tired," he said harshly, "of always wondering what you're thinking. What you're doing. Tired of waiting for the day you'll wise up and leave." Rising to his feet, he cupped her cheek. She shuddered a little, turning toward his touch like a flower. He said hoarsely, "It's almost easier this way."

"And Marisol..." she whispered.

The knife twisted in his chest. Dropping his hand, he stepped back. "We will always be her parents. We'll be respectful of each other, for her sake. I will pay child support. We will share custody."

"Right," she said, looking dazed. "Right."

"And if there is another child..." His lips curved humorlessly. "This time, you will tell me, *si*?"

"Yes. Yes, I will." Callie's lovely, round face looked bewildered as she swayed where she stood, like a drunk who'd lost her balance.

"You and your family can return to North America tomorrow."

She turned, walked two steps then looked back at him. He could see her shaking. "And Brandon?"

"Ah, yes." He smiled grimly. "Brandon. As you said, he is a member of your family, is he not? As I," he added lightly, "never was."

She swallowed then looked up at him pleadingly. "You won't…won't do anything to hurt him?"

Reaching out, Eduardo brushed some long wavy tendrils of light brown hair off her shoulder. Even now, saying goodbye, he was mesmerized by Callie's beauty. Now more than ever. When he was losing her forever.

"Of course I will not hurt him. I'm not the monster you seem to think." He remembered how he'd been tempted to kill the man just hours before, and shook his head with a hard laugh. "Well. I have no reason to hurt him now. Our marriage is over. We are free."

"Free…" she whispered.

McLinn's harsh words from long ago went through Eduardo's mind. *You can't keep me from her. We both know you're not good enough for her. You'll never make her happy.* And he realized that he'd always agreed. But he'd tried to keep Callie just the same. Selfish and wrong, when he knew he'd never be able to love her the way she deserved. Christ—he couldn't even sleep in the same bed.

"Yes. You're free." Eduardo turned away, making his voice deliberately casual as he said, "Marisol fell asleep in her playpen, in your parents' room. Do you want to see her?"

Callie did not answer. She just looked at him, her green eyes dark as a midnight sea. Her beautiful, grief-stricken face was more than Eduardo could bear. It had to end, he thought heavily. So let it end. Merciful and quick.

Taking his wife's limp hand, he pulled her out of their bedroom and through the deepening shadows of the courtyard. Midway through the garden, she stopped. He looked back at her in the twilight, surrounded by the shadows of palm trees and the soft cool burble of the fountain. Crystalline tears sparkled down her pale cheeks, glimmering in the fading moonlight.

"I'm sorry," she whispered, her eyes luminous. "So sorry."

Exhaling, Eduardo slowly pulled her into his arms. She pressed her face against his heart, which felt like it was breaking beneath his ribs.

Her voice was sodden, muffled against his shirt. "I didn't want it to end this way…"

His arms trembled around her. He thought of all his mistakes, everything he'd done wrong from the beginning, all the things he would have changed if he could. But the truth was he didn't know how. He couldn't trust anyone—especially not someone he loved. Because deep in his heart, he didn't believe in happy endings, only bad ones. Ones that felt like this.

"It was never your fault," he said, stroking her hair. "Just mine. All mine."

Hearing Callie sob, his throat constricted, and he wanted to cut out his ears, his eyes, rather than be faced with the pain he'd caused her. Desperately he pushed his feelings away, just as he'd done his whole life. Lifting her chin, he gave her a crooked smile. "Our marriage wasn't all bad, was it?"

"No," she whispered, searching his gaze in the shadows. "Most of it was wonderful."

"We gave our daughter a name. We will still give her a good home."

"Yes," she agreed. "But two homes. Apart."

He gave her a single unsteady nod then looked away, afraid of what she would see in his eyes. Afraid to speak and have her hear weakness in his voice. For long moments, he held her in the deepening shadows of the courtyard, listening to the water of the cool fountain as they stood in silence. Above them, palm trees waved against the deepening violet night.

Eduardo closed his eyes, breathing in the scent of her hair. Feeling the sweet softness of her body against his, knowing he was holding her for the last time.

It was best for her to leave. It was the only way to spare them both unnecessary pain. But the thought of it felt like death.

"It's all right," he said, gently brushing the tears from her cheeks, though he knew it would never be all right again. "You'll go home. You'll be happy there, just like you were."

"Yes, I will." She wept.

He heard the hoarseness of her voice, and knew what the words cost her. Emotion rushed through him, and before he could stop himself, he cupped her face in both his hands. "But before you leave, there's one thing you have to know. One important thing I've never said." He looked down at her. "I love you."

Callie sucked in her breath, her eyes wide.

"I love you as I've never loved anyone." He looked down at the flowers at his feet. "But I can't love you without hurting you. Without hurting both of us. Without being a man I don't want to be." Looking at her stricken face, he whispered over the razor blade in his throat, "That's why I'm letting you go."

In the shadows of the garden, Callie's eyes were deep emerald, like an ancient forest older than time itself. Her beauty was like an ache in his heart. Unwillingly he lifted his hand to her cheek, touching the softness of her skin as he looked into her eyes, connecting them soul to soul. Beneath the violet-tinged sky swept with stars, he heard the howl of the wind, shaking the palm trees above.

"I'm sorry I couldn't love you as you deserve," he said hoarsely. "I always knew I didn't deserve you. And I knew, from the beginning, that it was a matter of time—"

Standing on her toes, Callie cut off his words by covering his mouth with her own.

Her lips were soft and sweet, trembling against him. He felt the warmth of her body against his, and a surge of anguished need rushed through him like an overflowing river. A gasp came from the back of his throat, and he wrapped his arms around her, pulling her against him tightly as he returned her kiss hungrily. On her lips, he tasted salt with the sweet and no longer knew if they were her tears, or his own. All he knew was that he was kissing her for the last time and he had to make it last forever. He had to kiss her so deep and hard that he'd possess this memory for all time, not just on his lips, but in his heart.

Eduardo's fingers twined through her long hair as they embraced, their bodies pressing together as they clutched each other mindlessly in front of the courtyard fountain. He felt the tangled smoothness of her hair, breathed in her scent of flowers and vanilla that mingled with the exotic spices of the desert wind. He stroked down her back, marveling at her shape as he wrapped his far larger body around the small woman who'd conquered him so completely. Looking at her, touching her soft skin, feeling her breasts against his chest, he kissed her with anguished passion. Need burned away every other thought or desire of his soul, except to possess her.

With a gasp, he pulled away. Looking down at her beautiful face, he saw the shadows of the rising moon move against her skin; saw the breathless, aching need in her eyes. Without a word, he lifted her up into his arms. He carried her silently to their bedroom.

For the last time, he took Callie to bed.

Setting her down on the mattress, beneath the pattern of moonlight through the latticed window, Eduardo pulled off her blouse, kissing her neck, her shoulders, her arms.

He pulled off her skirt, stroking the length of her legs, kissing the sensitive spot behind her knees with a flick of his tongue. He pulled off her lacy white bra, cupping her breasts, suckling her until she gasped.

"Callie," he said hoarsely. "Look at me."

She obeyed, and her beautiful eyes shimmered with tears as she watched him move down her body, pulling her panties down her legs. Still fully dressed in his black suit, he kissed her naked body. Up her calves. Her inner thighs. He paused at the crux of her thighs, letting the warmth of his breath curl between her legs, inhaling the tantalizing scent of her.

Pushing her thighs apart with his hands, he bent his head and tasted her, stretching her wide. She was sweet and smooth as satin. He nestled himself between her thighs and flicked the tip of his tongue against her hard, aching core. He felt her writhe beneath him, bucking her hips to escape the intensity, so he held her hips against the bed, forcing her to accept the full rough pleasure of his tongue. He stroked her, lapped her. When she was dripping wet and trembling, he pushed three fingers a single inch inside her.

Panting for breath, she threw out her hands, gripping the soft cotton blankets as he suckled her hard pink nub, swirling his tongue in featherlight circles and pressing his fingers deeper and deeper inside her. Callie's hands tightened on the blankets, her back arching, as if only her grip kept her from flying off the bed. He heard the long gasp of her breath, felt her body lifting from the mattress, higher, higher, felt her body grow tense and tenser still. Until she exploded.

Her soft, wet walls contracted tightly around his fingers as she cried out, twisting her body from side to side, in a symphony of mindless, helpless pleasure. He watched her face. He'd given her that pleasure. He'd made her weep with grief. But at least he'd also made her scream with joy. As she opened her eyes, still panting for breath, her expression was almost bewildered as she looked up at him. "I love you," she whispered.

Cupping her face, he looked down at her. "I know."

She stroked his face, his hair, his neck, his jacket. He lowered her mouth to hers, and she kissed him back almost savagely. He felt her tongue, her teeth. He felt her need for him. He felt her heart. Fully dressed, he moved against her, his erection hard and throbbing against her thighs.

A sob come low from her throat. She flung her arms around his neck, pulling him down against her with sudden desperation. Her fingers frantically attempted to pull off his tie, to unbutton his shirt. Pulling away from her, he yanked off his coat and tie. He ripped his civilized white shirt and tailored trousers and silk boxers to the cool tile floor.

Naked, he faced her, his soul as bare as his body. Without a word, he lowered his mouth to hers, stroking her, telling her with his touch everything he could not trust himself to put into words.

Covering her body with his own, he felt her full breasts against his chest, felt her soft, feminine curves sway against his hardness. The satin-smooth skin of her inner thighs stroked the hard length of his shaft, and her wet core tantalized his aching tip alluringly. He heard her gasp with need as she twisted her body beneath him, gripping his hips with her hands, trying to pull him closer, spreading her thighs in unconscious seduction.

But he did not want to take her. No. Not yet. Beads of sweat covered his forehead as he held himself apart from everything he wanted most. This was the last time he would possess her, and he wanted to make it last forever. As long as she was in his arms, he would not have to face the heartbreak and grief that waited for him on the other side. He would not have to face the dark solitude without her...

She stroked his back, her breasts plumping against his chest. He felt the sweaty heat of her skin, heard the breathless hush of her sigh. Gripping her shoulders, he closed his eyes, trying to resist. But she knew him too well. She moved beneath him, suckling his earlobe, breathing on his neck as she ran her hands on the back of his upper thigh, below his buttocks, between his legs. She stroked him—and he felt the hot, wet core of her slide against him—pulling him inside—

With a choked gasp, he surrendered. His body took over. With a low growl, he grabbed her shoulders and plunged himself inside her in a single deep thrust. Her body tensed, then melted, parting for him, accepting him, embracing every inch of his thick length. Pulling back, he thrust again with a gasp, and again, riding her. His every muscle was taut in the exquisite precipice between agony and pleasure. Six thrusts and only the grimmest vestige of self-control kept him from exploding inside her. But he had to make it last. He had to. He could not live without her....

Rolling onto his back, he lifted her over him, impaling her. Her thighs gripped his hips as he let her control the rhythm and speed. After months of bed play, his once-virgin secretary had become a fiery seductress. He thought having her on top would slow him down, make him last. But instead, as she pushed herself against him, he filled her harder and deeper than he ever had. Her heavy breasts swayed back and forth against his face as she rode him, going deeper with each thrust, until he closed his eyes, panting beneath the brutal onslaught of pleasure. Reaching his hands behind him, he gripped the headboard of the bed.

Harder, deeper. And wet, so wet. As she slammed

against him, her walls wrapped around him, tight, so tight, pulling him into an abyss of mindless pleasure. His eyes rolled back as he gripped her hips with his hands, his whole body shaking with the agony of need. He felt her quicken and pulse around him as she flung back her head and screamed with joy. Looking up at her, seeing her beautiful face filled with ecstasy, her eyes closed as if in prayer, he could no longer resist. With one last savage thrust he exploded inside her, riding the wave with her. His hoarse cry mingled with hers as he came and came and came, never looking away from her beautiful face.

And Callie collapsed on top of him, clutching him to her hot, sweaty body, happiness pouring out of them both like radioactive light.

Afterward, Eduardo held her. For the first time, he was grateful knowing that he wouldn't be able to sleep beside her. He could hold her all night. He'd watch her gentle face slumber beneath the latticed moonlight. She felt so soft in his arms. So warm. So sweet. His eyelids became heavy as he held her. Closing his eyes, he kissed her temple, breathing in the vanilla and floral scent of her hair. He loved her so much he thought he could die of it. He would hold her all night long. He'd relish every hour. Every minute...

Eduardo woke with a gasp.

The pink light of morning poured in through the window as he realized that he'd slept beside his wife for the first time.

In panic, he looked at her side of the bed.

It was empty. For the first time, Callie had been the one to rise in the middle of the night. She'd been the one to leave. And as the first wave of anguish hit his body, he knew this was how he'd always known he would be.

Alone.

CHAPTER ELEVEN

CALLIE sat at the kitchen table of her parents' farmhouse and looked at the papers in her shaking hands. The words seem to swim in front of her eyes.

Divorce papers.

"It'll be quick and painless," her lawyer had assured her when he'd given her the file. "I marked each place for you to sign with a yellow tab. All the tough questions were already dealt with in the prenup. You'll share custody, switching visitation each week, and with Mr. Cruz's extremely generous level of alimony and child support you'll be the richest woman in Fern County." The lawyer gave her a sudden sharp grin. "Good thing every divorce case isn't so quick and painless, or else I'd be bankrupt."

Quick. Painless. Callie heard a wheel squeak as her nine-month-old daughter crossed the floor in the antique walker used by three generations of Woodville babies. Marisol giggled at the sound, and her laughter was like music. Callie smiled at her daughter through her tears.

"Pa-pa-pa?" Marisol said hopefully.

Callie's smile faded as she looked down at the papers. "Soon, sweetheart," she said over the lump in her throat. "You'll see him tomorrow." Marisol would be flown back to New York for a week with Eduardo, and Callie would have to endure seven long, aching days without her child.

Then the next week, they would switch, and it was Eduardo who would be alone.

He'd been fair. More than fair, allowing Callie to live at such a distance, using his private jet to shuttle Marisol between North Dakota and New York. Callie had no idea what they'd do when it was time for Marisol to start school, but something would surely be worked out. Money, it seemed, could solve any problem.

Except this.

Callie didn't want his money. She wanted him. She was still in love with him.

But he'd let her go.

She hadn't seen Eduardo for two months, since she'd left Marrakech with her baby, Brandon and her family. Since then, their only point of contact had been through their lawyers. Even Marisol's pickups and drop-offs each week were handled by Mrs. McAuliffe.

Callie hadn't seen him. But each night, she dreamed of him, of their last night together, when they'd kissed in the shadows by the fountain. When they'd made love so passionately and desperately the bed seemed to explode into fire. When he'd huskily spoken the words she still, against her will, held to her heart.

I love you. I love you as I've never loved anyone. But I can't love you without hurting you.

Once, she would have given ten years of her life to hear Eduardo say he loved her. Now, the words were poison. She'd cried for weeks, till there were no tears left. But there was no other answer. She couldn't live as his prisoner. And he couldn't risk giving her his heart if she wasn't.

Two teardrops fell on the divorce papers spread out across her parents' blue Formica table. When she'd come back home, part of her had hoped she might be pregnant, which would at least give her a reason to talk to her husband again. But even that hope had failed her.

"Ma-ma?" Marisol's dark eyes, exactly like her father's, looked up at her mother with concern.

"It's all right," Callie whispered, wiping her eyes and giving her daughter a tremulous smile. "Everything is fine." All she had to do was sign the papers and her lawyer would file them. She'd be Callie Woodville again. Callie Cruz would disappear.

Across the small kitchen, where it sat in a small woven basket, the gold and diamond double "CC" key chain flashed at her in the morning light. It seemed forlorn and out-of-place in the key basket, amid the clutter of pens, sticky notes and unpaid utility bills around the twenty-year-old phone. But even her keychain wasn't as out-of-place as the shipment that had arrived at their rural North Dakota farm yesterday. Picking up her steaming mug of coffee, Callie went to the kitchen window and pushed aside the red gingham curtain.

Outside, beside her father's red, slightly rusted 1966 pickup truck, her sleek silver car was now parked in front of the barley field.

Callie closed her eyes. She'd never thought she would have the strength to leave Eduardo.

But then, she never thought he'd let her go.

And he'd already moved on. She'd already seen pictures of Eduardo in a celebrity magazine, attending a charity gala in New York with the young Spanish duchess. Callie wondered if they'd marry, once his divorce to her was final. Her heart twisted with jagged pain at the thought, and for the first time, she truly understood what Eduardo must have felt when he'd thought she was in love with Brandon.

How hard it was, to set the person free that you loved most on earth. But Eduardo had done it.

Now so must she.

Callie heard an engine coming up the long driveway. Looking back out the window, she smiled. About time. Taking another sip of her coffee, Callie watched Brandon and Sami leap out of the Jeep.

Brandon's heart hadn't remained broken for long. Since their return from Morocco, now freed of his guilt and concern over Callie, he'd finally allowed himself to give his heart to the young woman who'd been his constant companion for nine months. Yesterday, he'd asked Sami to marry him.

Their parents had been cautious at first, then ecstatic. News of the engagement had rapidly spread across Fern, and thanks to Jane's eager posting, to all her internet friends, across the world. Callie swallowed, feeling a little misty-eyed. *Engaged.* Her best friend and little sister were planning to be married in September.

As the two vagabonds traipsed through the door, Callie shook her head with a wry laugh. "Engaged or not, sis, Mom and Dad are not happy you stayed out all night."

"It was totally innocent!" Brandon protested. Then his full cheeks blushed beneath his black-framed glasses as he gave Sami a sudden wicked grin. "Well, *mostly* innocent…"

"We were up at McGillicuddy's Hill," Sami said quickly, "to see the comet away from the lights. There were so many stars." She looked dreamily at her fiancé. "Brandon knows all the constellations. We just lost track of time…"

"Good luck explaining that to Dad."

"Dad knows he can trust Brandon," she protested. She turned to him. "Like I do. With my life."

Brandon looked back at Sami with love in his eyes. Taking her hand in his own, he kissed it fervently. And Callie suddenly felt like an intruder, standing in the cozy,

warm kitchen in her old purple sweatpants and ratty
T-shirt. "All right," she said awkwardly. "You should talk
to him, though."

"Where is he? Out in the fields?"

Callie nodded. "Alfalfa by the main road."

"Don't worry." Brandon clutched Sami's hand. "You
won't have to face him alone."

"I know."

As he pulled his car keys out of his pocket, they turned
toward the door. On impulse, Callie blurted out, "Wait."

They paused, staring at her questioningly. Crossing to
the key basket, Callie took the "CC" keychain and held it
out to them. "I want you to have this."

"What?" Sami exclaimed. "Your car?"

Brandon glowered. "Why?"

"It's—" Callie grasped at straws "—an engagement
gift."

"Are you kidding?" Sami blurted out.

"We don't need anything from *him*." Brandon looked
mutinous. It was possible he still nursed a grudge. "My
Jeep works just fine."

Sami turned to him. "Think of it as compensation for
him punching you," she said hopefully.

It didn't help her case. Brandon scowled.

"Please take it." Callie shook her head. "I hate looking
at it. It makes me remember…" Her voice trailed off, as
she felt overwhelmed by sweet memories of the Christmas
day Eduardo had dressed in a Santa suit and given it to
her. How happy they'd been… She gave them a tremulous
smile. "Sell it. Use the money however you like."

The young couple looked at the dangling gold-and-diamond keychain.

"We could buy land," Sami said.

"A farm of our own," Brandon breathed. He blinked
then snatched the keychain from her hand. "Very well. We

accept." He paused, tilting his head with a grin. Then he sobered. "Thanks, Callie. Thanks for being the best friend I've ever had." He turned to Sami. "Till now."

And then they were gone, racing out of the farmhouse to the car parked near the barn. Their conversation floated back to Callie on the June breeze.

"One ride before we sell it?"

"Let's go the long way, past the Coffee Stop!" Sami giggled. "I want to see Lorene Doncaster's face when she sees me in this thing…."

"Your father will forgive us for being out all night. I'll explain. It was the fault of the stars…"

The fault of the stars. Alone in the kitchen, Callie stood in the warm sunlight of her mother's cheerful kitchen. She looked back at the divorce papers. She saw the black, angular scrawl of Eduardo's signature. He'd asked for a divorce. It was the only thing to do.

Wasn't it?

She picked up the pen in her trembling hand. She looked down at the empty line beneath his black signature.

Was their marriage really nothing more than a nine-month mistake?

She exhaled, closing her eyes.

Then, an hour later, she got a call that changed everything.

"Good progress today. So, same time next week?"

Eduardo nodded, pulling on his jacket. He left the therapist's office and took a deep breath of the morning air. The June sky was bright blue over Manhattan.

"Sir?" Sanchez stood ready at the curb, waiting beside the black Mercedes sedan.

Eduardo shook his head. "Think I'll walk."

"Very well, sir."

Eduardo walked slowly down the street, feeling the sun on his face, hearing the birds sing overhead. A bunch of laughing schoolkids in identical uniforms ran by him on the sidewalk, reminding Eduardo of the *Madeline* book he'd read to his two-week-old daughter, to the great amusement of his wife.

He stopped, feeling a sudden pain in his chest.

He would see Marisol soon, he reminded himself. His jet was already gassed up and ready at a private airport outside the city. He glanced at his platinum watch. Mrs. McAuliffe was likely headed for the airport now, if she wasn't there already, preparing to make the long flight across the country and back. She would collect the baby from his soon-to-be ex-wife. From the woman who still haunted his dreams.

Blankly Eduardo stared up at the green trees above the sidewalk. The trees looked exactly like they had in early September, when he'd first shown up in the West Village demanding marriage. On the day when, in the space of a few hours, he'd gained both a wife, and a child.

His stomach clenched. He suddenly couldn't bear the thought of going back to work. All those hours of work, all those days and years, and for what? He was a billionaire, and yet he envied his chauffeur, who went home every night to a snug little home in Brooklyn with a wife who loved him and their three growing children. Eduardo had a huge penthouse on the Upper West Side filled with art and expensive furniture, but when he was alone, the hallways and rooms echoed with the laughter of his baby. Of his lost wife.

Soon to be *ex*-wife.

He clenched his hands into fists. Had Callie signed the papers yet? Why hadn't she signed them?

It had been two weeks since he'd signed the divorce

papers, and the waiting was slowly driving him mad. He wanted it done, finished. Every day he was still married to Callie was acid on his heart, making him question if he'd made a mistake, if there was still a chance she might have forgiven him—if he could have earned back her trust.

He clawed his hair back with his hand. No. No way. She was probably engaged to Brandon McLinn by now and planning their wedding. McLinn's steadfast loyalty had triumphed at last. And unlike Eduardo, McLinn fit into Callie's world as Eduardo never would. He'd remember to ask her father for permission first. No one could ever deserve Callie, but if anyone had earned her, it was Brandon McLinn.

So why hadn't she signed the papers? Why?

He didn't know. He honestly didn't know. And it was like crossing a high-wire without a net.

Since Callie had left him in Marrakech, he hadn't checked up on her once. He'd fired Keith Johnson from her case. He'd even given his lawyers strict instructions not to give him news of her. They were to contact Eduardo when her lawyer had filed the signed paperwork for the divorce, and not before.

But he still hadn't got the call. Did that mean there was hope?

Closing his eyes, Eduardo turned his face toward the sun as he thought about how he'd isolated her during their marriage. No. No hope.

"Hey!"

Looking down, Eduardo saw a little girl of about eight or nine, standing apart from five other schoolgirls. She held up a picture. "You dropped this."

Reaching out, he took the photo of Callie and Marisol, taken at the Spanish villa at Christmas. Marisol was just three and a half months old then, giggling, flashing her

single tooth. Callie was mischievously wearing the Santa
hat she'd stolen from Eduardo, smiling as he took the picture. Her green eyes glowed with love. Grief choked him,
so much his knees nearly went weak. "Thanks."

"I know how it feels to lose things," the little girl said.
"Don't be careless."

He looked up, his eyes wide.

"See ya." With a skip, the girl turned away, racing back
down the street with her friends, with the reckless joy of
childhood freedom.

And a lightning bolt hit his heart.

Eduardo had told Callie to leave. He'd been the one
who'd filed for divorce. He'd set her free, knowing she deserved better than a man who tried to control her, to spy
on her, who wouldn't trust her.

But what if he could have just chosen to be a different man?

Eduardo stared at the flow of traffic on the busy street.
What if his past didn't have to infect his future? What if
he could choose a different life?

Hope rose like a wave inside his soul, no longer to be
repressed. He'd set Callie free. But could he do the same
for himself—be the man he wanted to be? The divorce
wasn't final yet. Was there still time?

Could he ask her for a second chance?

Ask her to be his wife—not his prisoner, but his partner?

Gripping the photo, he whirled around, causing four
construction workers to spit curses as he knocked past
them on the sidewalk. Eduardo caught up with Sanchez just
as his sedan was pulling from the curb. Yanking open the
back door, Eduardo threw himself inside. "The airport!"
he panted. "I need to see my wife—now!"

Sanchez gave him an enormous smile. "Yes, sir!"

He stomped on the gas, and Eduardo pulled out his phone to call Mrs. McAuliffe about the change in plans. Before he could, his phone rang in his hand. He saw Keith Johnson's number. Scowling, he turned the sound to Mute. But after he hung up with Mrs. McAuliffe, as the car crossed the George Washington Bridge, his phone buzzed again. Looking down, he saw his lawyer's number and a chill went down his spine.

His lawyer.

Did that mean...

Could it be...

Eduardo narrowed his eyes. No. As the phone stopped, then urgently started to vibrate a second time, Eduardo rolled down the window, and tossed it into the Hudson.

It wasn't too late for him to change. He wouldn't let it be.

He made it to the airport as his jet was warming up, and took his place on the jet bound for North Dakota. Refusing his surprised flight attendant's offer of his usual martini, Eduardo paced back and forth across the cabin for hours, planning what he would say to Callie. He tried to write down his feelings then finally gave up in disgust. He would pray that once he saw her, he'd know what to say.

Sitting restlessly in the white leather seat by the window, he felt like a jangle of nerves. Wishing the jet could go faster, he looked down through the wispy clouds and watched the green rolling hills of the East Coast slowly transform to the flat, brownish landscape of the northern prairies.

When they finally landed at the tiny airport outside of Fern, his legs were shaking as he went down the steps to the tarmac. The airport was just like he remembered when he'd visited so long ago, the day Callie had come to meet him as the local office liaison. But this time, he had no staff. He was alone.

Eduardo had forgotten what it was like to exist without layers of employees and servants insulating him from the real world. He felt clumsy, trying to remember how to do things himself, with no assistants. No bodyguards. On impulse, he stopped at the airport's single shop to buy Callie some flowers and an eight-dollar box of chocolates. The place was deserted, and it took five long minutes before the salesclerk even noticed he was there, and came out from the back to ring up his order.

But Eduardo didn't chew him out. He didn't try to throw his weight around. He no longer wanted to rule this town. He wanted to fit in. He was suddenly desperate to be part of Callie's world, if only she would let him.

He didn't go completely unnoticed. At the car rental counter, the female clerk looked at his face, then his credit card. Her jaw fell open, and her gum almost fell out of her mouth.

"Eduardo Cruz?" she said faintly. "*The* Eduardo Cruz? The owner of Cruz Oil?"

"Don't hold it against me." Impatient as he was to find Callie, he gave her his best attempt at a grin. "I, um, seem to have lost my phone. Do you happen to know the way to the Woodville farm? Walter and Jane Woodville's place?"

"Of course I know it." The young woman chewed her gum thoughtfully. "At the corner of Rural Route 12 and Old County Road. I went to school with their daughter." Her eyes darkened. "I saw her driving around in the Rolls-Royce yesterday...."

"Thank you. She's the one I came to see—"

"But she's not at home," she said. "I'm sorry to tell you this if you're a friend, but she was in an accident. A car accident."

Eduardo nearly staggered back. "What?"

"That car was smashed right up," she said sadly.

Car accident. Memories went through him of when he'd heard of his mother's death in a smash-up on a treacherous road on the Costa del Sol. An icicle of stark fear went down his spine. "You are mistaken," he said faintly. "That car is very safe...."

"Some kids were riding bicycles in the middle of the road. Her fiancé swerved, and the car smashed straight into a telephone pole. She's in critical condition at County General...."

Eduardo reached across the counter, his eyes wild. "Who's her fiancé? Who is he?"

"Brandon McLinn..."

He didn't wait to hear more. He grabbed a map off the counter.

"Mr. Cruz, I really am sorry—"

Running to his rental car, he drove for the hospital, racing down the highway at a hundred miles an hour. If he got pulled over by a policeman, he knew he'd go to jail. But he didn't give a damn.

He couldn't lose her. Not now...

Anguish gripped his throat. He could have been with her all this time. He could have been chasing her the last two months, trying to make her forgive him, trying to be the man she deserved. Instead he'd let her go. Why couldn't he have just treated her right from the beginning? Why had he wasted so much time trying to control their lives? Control was the illusion, not love. There was no such thing as perfect safety. No such thing as perfect control. You couldn't make someone love you. And even if you did, you couldn't make it last forever.

People left. People died.

But love endured. He could choose to love Callie with

all his heart and strength, love her with full knowledge of both her flaws and his own; love her with every ounce of his being until the day he died. That was his choice.

He'd once told her that love changed nothing. It was wrong. It changed everything.

Clutching the steering wheel, he prayed he'd reach her in time. Callie had to be all right. His daughter couldn't grow up without a mother. He couldn't live without his wife.

The afternoon sunlight cast the waving fields in a golden glow beneath the wide blue skies. He increased his speed to a hundred and twenty, as fast as the little rental car would go along the empty highway.

Don't leave me, Eduardo begged soundlessly. *Don't leave me.*

CHAPTER TWELVE

It had been a horrible night. And a very long day.

Callie rose achingly from the chair by her sister's hospital bed. She needed coffee or fresh air. She was still wearing the same purple sweatpants and T-shirt from yesterday, with her hair pulled back in a ponytail. They'd all been awake through the night, and now, in late afternoon, everyone had collapsed with exhaustion. Brandon was curled up in a chair on the other side of Sami's bed, and Jane and Walter had fallen asleep on the couch, her mother's head on her father's shoulder, and baby Marisol snoring loudly against her grandpa's chest.

Callie quietly left the hospital room. Once she was safely in the hallway, she took a deep breath and sagged back against the door, covering her face with her hands. It was all her fault. If she hadn't given them the car they wouldn't have taken the detour through town. They wouldn't have been in the accident.

Tears burned Callie's eyes. But the crisis was past. Her sister would recover.

She was grateful beyond measure, but the tears weren't just out of gratitude. Callie had a good reason to feel an extra dose of anguish today. A private reason of her own…

She closed her eyes. She missed Eduardo so much. His handsome face. His glowing dark eyes. And his voice. She could almost hear it now, rough with an edge of Spanish accent.

"Where's my wife? Where is she, damn you?" The man's voice echoed down the hallways of the small hospital. "I want to see her *now*!"

She knew that voice. She still dreamed about it every night. Slowly Callie turned.

And saw Eduardo arguing at the nurses' station down the hall. His black hair was rumpled, and so was his suit. She'd never seen him so disheveled before, so completely out-of-place, so handsome and powerful and everything she'd ever wanted.

"Eduardo," she choked out.

At the end of the hall, he turned and saw her. With a sob, she started toward him at a run, in the same instant he started running for her.

They fell into each other's arms, and it was only when Callie actually felt him, strong and solid beneath her hands, that she knew for sure it wasn't a dream. She felt his protective, steadying arms around her and all the fear and shock of the last twenty-four hours fell away. She no longer had to be strong for her family. She burst into tears.

"Callie, Callie," he whispered fervently, kissing her forehead. "You're all right. Thank God, you're all right."

Pulling back, he looked down at her, his eyes glistening suspiciously in the hospital's fluorescent lights. Then he wrapped his powerful arms around her tightly, holding her as if he never wanted to let her go. Callie exhaled for the first time in two months, weeping with the joy of being again in his arms.

"You're safe," he breathed, stroking her hair as she pressed her face against his chest. "Safe."

Wiping her eyes, she looked at him in confusion. "But

what are you even doing here? I thought you were in New York?"

"Would you believe me if I said I was in the neighborhood?"

She smiled weakly.

"I, um, brought you some flowers and candy." Looking around, he cursed softly. "They are here somewhere…"

"Oh. Right." Her heart dropped. With all the worry about her sister's accident, she'd forgotten his week started today. She said dully, "You're here for Marisol."

Eduardo stared at her, his dark eyes infinite and deep as the ocean. "I'm here for you." He took her hands in his own. "Come back to me, Callie. Give me one more chance."

"What?" she breathed.

"Be my wife. Let me be your partner, by your side. Let me spend the rest of my life loving you. And striving to deserve your love in return."

Her voice caught in her throat. "I…"

He gave her an unsteady smile. "I'm too late, aren't I?"

"Too late?"

He looked past her ear. "You've moved on."

Turning around, she saw Brandon peeking out of her sister's door, his face questioning before he ducked back. Frowning, Callie turned back at Eduardo. "What are you talking about?"

"The girl at the car rental counter told me about your accident. She also told me that you're engaged. You and Brandon." His eyes were bleak as he tried to smile. "I guess I should offer my congratulations."

Callie nearly staggered back with shock.

"You don't know," she whispered. Sudden rising joy filled her heart, choking her with hope. "The engagement announcement was on my mom's web page days ago. It was even in the newspaper this morning. But *you don't know.*"

Eduardo shook his head, his jaw tight, his eyes forlorn. "I fired my investigator two months ago. Told my lawyers not to talk about you. I even threw away my phone."

"Your *phone*?"

"I was mad at it." He gave her a small smile. "I still do some stupid things. But my therapist says there's hope…"

"Your therapist!" she cried, nearly falling over in shock.

"Talking about the past has helped me understand the choices I've made as an adult. And why I was so afraid to love you." He took a deep breath. "Because I do love you, Callie. So much." He looked down at the green cracked tiles of the floor. "Brandon is…he is a good man. I know he'll make you happy."

Moving closer, she reached up and lifted his chin. "Brandon and I aren't together. He's engaged to my sister."

Slowly Eduardo lifted his head. Shock filled his expression, followed by savage joy. "Your sister?"

"I gave them the car yesterday and she was hurt in the crash." She pressed her lips together. "We were worried. For a few hours last night the doctors weren't sure she'd make it. She lost a lot of blood. But she came out of surgery this morning and the doctors say she'll be fine. She just needs a lot of rest."

"Thank God." He hugged her close and whispered, "So she's engaged to Brandon. I always knew I liked her."

She pressed her cheek against his shirt, and her tears made the fabric wet as she sniffled. "Ever since it happened, all I could think about was that I wished you were here. So you could hold me and tell me that everything would be all right."

"Oh, *querida.*" For a long moment, he held her tightly then he looked down at her. "I know I'm selfish and ruthless and occasionally a jerk. There will be times in the future you'll want to punch me. But give me one more chance to love you. Just say the word," he vowed, "and I will never again leave your side."

She started to speak, but he put his finger to her lips. "Before you give your answer," he whispered, "let me finish my argument…."

Lowering his mouth to hers, he kissed her in an embrace so pure and breathless and true that it left her in no doubt of his love for her, and so passionate it left her dizzy and swaying in his arms.

She looked up at him.

"Stay with me, Eduardo," she breathed, blinking back tears. "Don't ever go."

His dark eyes lit up with joy. "Callie—"

"I love you," she whispered, and he kissed her again, so long and hard that several members of the hospital staff cleared their throats and made loud comments suggesting they *get a room* before Eduardo finally pulled away.

"I wish I'd done things differently from the start," he said against her hair. "That I'd given you a real wedding, and asked your father for your hand…" He snorted, his eyes twinkling as he confessed, "Do you know I actually tried to write you a poem on the flight here?"

"You did?"

"A love poem."

"A love poem from the great Eduardo Cruz." Giggling, Callie shook her head. "Now that is something I really, really want to read."

"Not in this lifetime. You'd laugh yourself silly."

"I could do with a laugh." Callie put her hand on his hard, rough cheek, then slowly traced down his throat, to linger against his chest. "And we both know you'll give it to me sooner or later."

She felt him shiver beneath his touch. "Yes," he said huskily. "I will." He took a deep breath as he cupped her face. "I will give you everything. Everything I have. Everything I am. Both the good and bad."

"For better or for worse." Rising on her tiptoes, she kissed him again, in clear and complete defiance of the hospital staff. She felt the hard, satin strength of his lips, felt the heat of his tongue brush against her own. She wanted to kiss him forever. And she could. She was his wife....

Callie pulled back with a horrified gasp, her eyes wide. "What is it, *querida*?"

"I signed the divorce papers yesterday!" she wailed. She gave a choked sob as she threw her arms around him. "Oh, Eduardo. We're divorced!"

He blinked then slow joy lifted his handsome features, like the rise of the first spring dawn after endless cold winter. He gave a low laugh. Lifting her chin, he stroked her tears away with the pads of his thumbs. "Oh, my love. That's the best news you could have given me."

She blinked in shock. "It—is?"

"Of course it is." He smiled down at her, then leaning forward, he whispered, "This time we're going to do it right."

It was a warm evening in late July as Callie stepped out of her parents' farmhouse to the porch, where her father was waiting in the twilight.

Walter Woodville turned then gasped as he saw his eldest daughter in her wedding gown. "You look beautiful, pumpkin."

Callie looked down shyly at the 1950s-style, tea-length gown in ivory lace. "Thanks to Mom. She did the alterations from Grandma's dress."

"Your Mama always makes everything beautiful. And so do you." Tears rose to his eyes as he whispered, "I'm so proud to be your father." His voice was suspiciously rough. Clearing his throat, he held out his arm. "Are you ready?"

She walked with him the short distance across the gravel driveway. The rising moon glowed across the wide ocean of her father's barley fields. The night was quiet and magical. Fireflies glowed through the sapphire night. As they went toward the barn, she could hear the cicadas at a distance, but even their eerie singing wasn't enough to drown the loud drumbeat of her heart.

Clutching her father's arm with one hand, and a bouquet of bright pink Gerbera daisies in the other, Callie looked back at the farmhouse. Her childhood home was a little careworn, with yellow paint peeling in spots. But it was snug and warm and full of good memories. She looked at the swing on the porch, at her mother's red flowers in pots. So many memories. So much love.

"I just hope we do everything right," she whispered.

Her father smiled. "You won't."

"Then I hope we do half as well as you and Mom."

He put his hand over hers, his craggy face sparkling with tears. "You will. You two were made for each other. He's a good one," he said gruffly.

Callie resisted the urge to laugh. Her father had a new appreciation for Eduardo since their three days up at the fishing cabin in Wisconsin. Any man who could face Callie's father, her four uncles and six male cousins, and Brandon, all with guns and hunting bows, was clearly man enough to be Walter's son-in-law. The way Eduardo had humbly asked permission for his daughter's hand in marriage hadn't hurt, either.

Somehow, even Brandon and Eduardo had managed to bury the hatchet. The story she heard afterward was a bit muddled, but apparently while they were at the cabin Brandon had nearly shot Eduardo in the foot with his hunting rifle. Callie was rather dubious about how this equaled friendship, but afterward the two men had drunk beer around the campfire. "Marrying you two Woodville sisters, we realized we needed to be allies," Eduardo said with a grin, and Callie wasn't sure whether she should be offended or not.

Eduardo had won Jane's approval even more easily, simply through his vigorous appreciation for her cooking and fruit pies. "Although," her mother had said coyly, "a few more grandchildren wouldn't hurt."

Eduardo had looked at Callie with a wicked grin, even as his voice said meekly, "Yes, ma'am."

At the thought, Callie's eyes welled up. She was finally sure about a question that had distracted her for days. She could hardly wait to tell Eduardo…

"Don't cry!" her father said, aghast. He pulled a handkerchief from his coat to dab at the corner of her eye. "Your mother would never forgive me if she thought I said something that smeared your makeup."

"I'm not crying," Callie wept. Blinking back tears of his own, he patted her hand and led her past the outdoor reception area, which had a temporary dance floor lit up by torches and surrounded by coolers full of beer and the finest champagne. They reached the barn, and Callie stood in the huge open doorway in her wedding gown beside her father, who was beaming with pride.

The music on the guitar changed to an acoustic version of the Bridal March. All at once, her friends and family rose from the benches used as makeshift pews, gasping as they stared at Callie.

But she had eyes only for Eduardo.

He stood at the end of the aisle, handsome in a vintage

suit. His dark eyes lit up when he saw her, and he looked dazzled. He was flanked by the best man and maid of honor, who themselves were planning to wed in just two months' time. Sami's leg still hadn't completely healed, and she used a crutch, but she glowed with happiness. So did Brandon, every time he looked at her. He'd cheered Sami throughout her hospital stay by talking about the small farm they would buy once they wed, using the insurance check from the wrecked Rolls-Royce. Callie felt a lump in her throat as she looked at two of the people she loved most in the world, who were both happy at last.

And so was she.

Today, she would marry her best friend. But Eduardo wasn't just her best friend. He was her soul mate, her lover, the man she trusted, the father of her child. The man she wanted to sleep with every night. The man she wanted to wake up to every morning. The man she wanted to fight with, to make love to. The man she wanted to yell at and laugh with. The man she wanted to love for the rest of her life. Her partner.

"Dearly beloved," the parson began, "we are gathered here today…"

As he spoke the magical words that would make them once again man and wife, Callie looked at her once and future husband. Swaying lanterns glowed above them in vivid colors as Eduardo looked down at her. Love illuminated his chiseled, angular face. His dark eyes were deep with devotion.

"Who gives this woman to be married to this man?"

"Her mother and I do," Walter said, and Callie heard the tremble beneath his rough voice, felt the shake of his burly arm as he handed her over to Eduardo's keeping. Kissing her father's cheek, Callie smiled down at her mother in the front row, who held baby Marisol in her lap.

As the parson spoke the wedding homily, Callie listened to the soft wind against the barley. She heard the creak of the old barn around them as Eduardo spoke his wedding vows, and the low timbre of his voice reverberated through her soul. She felt the strength of his powerful, gentle hand as he slid a plain gold band on her finger, simple and special and eternal. Just like their growing family.

Callie hid a smile. She could hardly wait to tell him that he wasn't just becoming her husband again, but a father again, too. Their baby was due in February. Perhaps she would whisper the news in his ear during their first dance, while they swayed together surrounded by flickering torches, beneath a sky so wide it stretched forever. Maybe they'd spend the summer here, autumn in New York, winter in Spain. Their love crossed oceans. But when it was time for her baby to be born, she knew there was only one place she wanted to be. Home.

And as she looked up at Eduardo, that's exactly where she was. In his arms, she was home. No matter where their lives took them.

"And do you, Calliope Marlena Woodville, take this man to be your lawfully wedded husband, for better or for worse, for richer or for poorer, to love and cherish from this day forward, until death do you part?"

In the breathless hush, Callie glanced back at her baby, at her family and friends in the old barn. It was exactly like she'd always imagined it would be. Closing her eyes, Callie took a deep breath, remembering all the impossible dreams she'd had as a girl.

Then, opening her eyes, Callie turned back to Eduardo, and spoke the two words that made all those dreams come true.

* * * * *

ONE NIGHT
WITH GAEL

MAYA BLAKE

For Romy, for your invaluable help with all things South Africa.

Any mistakes are mine!

CHAPTER ONE

POR EL AMOR de todo lo que es santo! For the love of everything that's holy!

Gael Aguilar gritted his teeth and stopped short of invoking actual martyred saints as he listened to excuse after excuse roll off the tongue of the man he was talking to on the phone.

At the end of his very short tether, he cut across yet another effusive apology. 'Let me get this straight. You're supposed to be here, in New York, holding auditions, but instead you chose to go skiing, in *Switzerland*, and are now laid up in hospital?'

'It was just supposed to be a weekend thing for my wife's birthday, but... Look, believe me, no one's more sorry than I am, okay?'

Not okay. Gael jerked his head back against the car's headrest none-too-gently. 'What's the medical verdict?'

'Leg's broken in two places. It's going in a cast tomorrow. Provided there are no further complications I'll be back in New York on Thursday, to pick things up, but we can't miss the Othello Arts Institute slot today. It's been arranged for months.'

Ethan Ryland, his director, was almost pleading. Gael barely stopped himself from pointing out that he should have known better then than to indulge himself with a continental trip. He also barely stopped himself from uttering the pithy words that would have brought him immense satisfaction right then and there. But temporary relief wouldn't alter the facts facing him.

He couldn't fire the director. Somewhere in the small print of his multipage contract was the perfect excuse for what was happening now, Gael was sure. Had he not had bigger matters demanding his attention, he would have taken the time to seek out other small print, words that swung in his favour, and used them. Hell, he wouldn't even need to lift a finger himself. That was, after all, why his company had a whole firm of lawyers on retainer.

But he couldn't do that. For one thing, embroiling the Atlas Group, the staggeringly successful but still infant global conglomerate he'd birthed with his half-brother in litigation right now would be bad for business. Not only would his half-brother Alejandro take satisfaction in demanding his head on a platter, their Japanese partners the Ishikawa brothers would also have a thing or two to say about the matter.

The merger between their three companies was barely six months old—as was his personal relationship with Alejandro, following decades of their actively and conspicuously avoiding each other.

While the business side of their relationship had flourished after a few initial setbacks, personal interaction between him and his brother had taken a two-steps-forward-one-step-back approach. Their once-a-month business meetings had grown decidedly stilted in the past three months and, frankly, Gael was on the verge of deciding it was time to take a permanent step back and run his side of the business from his Silicon Valley base.

It didn't matter that he knew the reason why.

The past. Always the past. And not just *his*. His mother's. His father's—the father who'd been woefully lacking in being worthy of the name. Alejandro himself.

He pushed the recent confrontation with his mother aside, stepped back from the thoughts of torrid retribution he harboured towards his director, and forced himself to speak. 'What exactly do you wish me to do?' he snarled.

'Just sit in on a cast call. You know my work—that's

why you hired me. You also know what you want. It will be filmed, of course, so I'll see it when I get back. But nothing beats experiencing the raw, visceral performance in person. Tapping in to the emotions of acting is only potent on camera if it's saturating in real life.'

Gael exhaled and curbed the urge to roll his eyes at the melodrama of the director's speech. 'Send me the details. I will attend this meeting you've set up,' he snapped into the silence thickening in the back of his limo.

A breath of relief shot from the sleek phone console at Gael's elbow. 'Thanks, Gael. I owe you one.'

'You owe me more than one. You owe me a first-class Atlas Studios maiden movie, to be unveiled—hiccup-free—as part of my digital streaming relaunch in six months' time. Make no mistake: you only get this one free pass. Let me down again and you'll be out. Is that clear?'

'Crystal.'

Gael hung up before more useless platitudes reached his ears and instructed his driver to alter their destination. It looked as if he was staying in New York for one more night.

Activating the phone again, he dialled a familiar number in Chicago. As he waited for his brother to pick up Gael admitted to himself that he felt the tiniest sliver of relief to have avoided the Chicago trip for one more day. Because, contrary to the challenge he'd thrown down to Alejandro a year ago, about his brother acknowledging him as his blood, Gael himself had never been inclined to claim the Aguilar name. No matter that there wasn't any doubt as to his parentage, the name had never sat well on his shoulders.

After all, he was a bastard whose mother had tried to cloak his name in imagined respectability by naming him after the father who hadn't wanted him. Had his mother not pleaded with him, Gael would've changed his surname to

Vega years ago. But she'd beseeched him—out of the same bewildering devotion to the man she'd chosen to reproduce with, he was sure. And he'd relented. He'd withstood both the blatant and the silent mockery from strangers and gossipmongers from childhood into adulthood for as long as he could. Then, like his half-brother, he'd retreated to the other side of the world.

The news that their father was once again indulging in the extramarital affairs that had brought Gael into the world had turned his stomach. Alejandro, for his part, after a series of conversations with his parents, seemed a lot less bitter about the whole thing. Not so much Gael.

And, on top of that stomach-turning news, his last conversation with his mother hadn't ended well when he'd found out *she* was entertaining his father's advances again. Nor had the exchange he'd had with Alejandro lent any insight into why their respective biological parents were hell-bent on perpetuating chaos.

'Do I want to know what you're thinking?'

Alejandro's question, posed after one too many whiskies in his brother's office a few short weeks ago, slashed into Gael's brain.

'No.'

His brother's brooding gaze settled on him. 'Tell me anyway.'

'I'm wondering why polygamy was ever banned,' Gael had responded.

Low, bitter laughter had spilled from his half-brother. 'Trust me, I'm a one-woman man, but the same thought has crossed my mind many times about our parents.'

'You know what? I don't think they'd be happy with polygamy, even were it an option. They'd still find a way to make their lives—and ours—a living hell.'

Sour amusement had disappeared under the cloud that always accompanied thoughts of his father and mother.

He didn't like to lump them together as *his parents* because they'd never been that to him. Sure, Tomas Aguilar had attempted to make a mockery of a family with his mother when Gael was a child, but that had been more to do with his twisted game to hurt the wife who had worn his ring and borne his firstborn than with love for Gael or his mother.

His father, his mother...his past...had nothing to do with the issue that confronted him now. And he'd never been one to expend energy on fruitless ventures.

Gael arrived on the doorstep of the Othello Arts Institute late—courtesy of an accident on the Queensborough Bridge—and alighted from the back of the limo in a fouler mood than he'd been in two hours before.

Not because of the call with his director, or even the chaotic traffic. No, his teeth-grinding could be laid firmly at his brother's feet.

Alejandro had been nauseatingly understanding of Gael's excuses, even going as far as to put Elise, his fiancée, on the line, to reassure Gael that all was well and they would welcome him to Chicago any time he pleased.

Wondering whether his brother's brooding tone had been meant to reassure him, or to deliver a subtle message that Alejandro still maintained an arm's-length approach to their relationship, despite Gael himself wishing it so, was what had thrown him into a worse mood.

He pushed open the glass doors to the sharp-angled building and entered the world-renowned institution, clearly aware he was spoiling for a fight. He didn't bother taking a steadying breath because it would be of no use. Only two methods restored his control when he felt like this—losing himself in computer code or losing himself between the thighs of a woman. One had made him richer than his wildest dreams. The other never failed to restore equilibrium to his very male aggression.

The urge to pull out his phone and arrange his next assignation with his flavour of the month was only curbed by the reminder that this inconvenient detour was still business. And business *always*—without exception—came before pleasure.

He sought directions to the room he needed and entered to find two casting directors ready and waiting.

An hour later Gael's mood had taken a sharp dip further south. The auditions had gone worse than abysmally—and he'd arrived from the viewpoint of an outsider. Tense handshakes with the directors and a swift exit preceded his urge to go back on his word and fire his director immediately. If this was what he had in store then he was better off parting company with Ethan Ryland before the process advanced beyond salvaging.

Sí, someone most definitely needed to atone for his mood. He pulled the phone from his pocket.

And stopped.

The door to his left was only partially ajar, but he heard her clearly. Her voice, filled with pure, unadulterated emotion, carried even without being raised high.

Removing his hovering thumb from the call button, he pushed the door with his forefinger. When it started to creak he stopped and stepped back. Glancing up and down the quiet hallway, Gael saw another door farther away at the end of the auditorium. Quick strides granted him silent entry into the shadowed rear of the cavernous room in time to catch her impassioned speech.

'You won't leave me. I won't let you. You think you love her, but you don't. And, yes, I know you enough to tell you what is in your heart. I love you that much, Simon. Enough to forgive. Enough to take another chance on us. But for us to happen you need to stay. Please...take the chance.'

Gael realised he was holding his breath as he watched tears stream down her face. She raged for another minute, then collapsed onto the stage. Genuine sobs convulsed her petite body.

Against his will, he was riveted, the breath he'd scoffed at needing moments ago locked in his throat. He watched her struggle to her feet, saw a hiccup shake through her as the last of her emotion rippled free. She swiped at the tears with her wrists and walked to the edge of the stage, chest rising and falling, her gaze expectantly on the audition director—who stared at her for uncomfortably tense seconds without speaking.

A fizzle of irritation wove through Gael's body and his already black mood darkened further at the director's deliberate silence.

'Your performance was…commendable, Miss Beckett. I can tell you poured your heart into it.'

A tiny hopeful smile from the performer. 'Thank you. I did.' The response was firm, but husky, probably owing to her emotional expenditure.

The director regretfully shook his head. 'But sadly I need more than that. Heart is great, but what I need is *soul*.'

The actress frowned. 'I don't understand. That *was* my heart—*and* my soul.'

'In your opinion. But not in mine.'

Gael felt her acute disappointment from across the room. She gave a slight shake of her head, as if to refute the director's words. Then she gathered herself with admirable pride. 'I'm sorry you think so. But thank you for your time.'

She started across the stage towards a shabby-looking rucksack near the door.

'That's it?'

The smirking taunt from the director tightened the knot of anger in Gael's gut.

She paused. 'Excuse me?'

'According to your opening speech, you want this part more than you want your next meal. And yet you're walking away without so much as a fight?' the director sneered.

Her eyes widened. 'I thought you said... You mean I have a chance?'

'Everyone has a chance, Miss Beckett. What stands between you and the opportunities you receive, however, is how much you *want* it. Are you prepared to do whatever it takes?'

She nodded immediately. 'Yes, I am.'

The director crooked his finger. She retraced her steps to the middle of the stage. Impatiently he beckoned her further forward. She approached without hesitation.

The beginnings of distaste filled Gael's mouth as he watched naked hunger fill her face.

Somewhere in the middle of her performance she'd lost her shoes. Her bare toes breached the edge of the hardwood stage as she looked down at the director. He extracted a silver card from his pocket, traced it over the top of one foot down to her toes before laying it between her slightly parted feet.

'*This* is what it'll take, Miss Beckett. Pick it up and the part is yours.'

Gael had been on the receiving end of propositions for long enough to know what was going on. *Dios mio*, hadn't he had the row of all rows with his mother only two weeks ago over just such an issue?

He expelled his breath in a quietly seething rush as he watched her slowly sink down and retrieve what looked unmistakably like a hotel room key card.

The disappointment that lanced through him was strong enough to make him question why the scene unfolding in front of him was affecting him so deeply. Perhaps today of all days, when the past seemed to be dogging him with its bitter memories, he'd wanted to be pleasantly surprised by the elusive integrity of the human spirit. To experience a pure character to go along with the pure performance that had stopped him in his tracks, touched him in ways he was still grappling with.

More fool him.

As the director's hands moved to touch her feet Gael retreated as silently as he'd entered, his rigid gaze firmly averted from the sleazy scene unfolding on the stage.

He was looking for a fairy tale where none existed. Just as he'd once—futilely and childishly—prayed for a family that included a father who didn't wish him out of existence.

He should know better. No. He *had* known better—for a very long time.

Even before he exited the building he knew those dredged-up feelings would be crushed beneath the immovable titanium power of his ambition and success. Emotional needs and futile dreams were far behind him. What he'd done with his life since that time in Spain was what mattered.

Everything else came a very pale second.

CHAPTER TWO

So why was he back here mere hours later, pulling up in front of Othello? And at a time of night when there was guaranteed to be no one around?

Gael had resisted admitting it all day. But, despite the stomach-turning denouement, something about the woman's performance itself had stayed with him. Enough to make him pass a few precious hours re-reading the carefully selected script he'd searched through thousands for before settling on two years ago. Enough to convince him to put aside his personal feelings and revisit the actress's flawless performance.

And it *had* been flawless. With a true visionary's direction she would be able to pull off the project he had in mind for his movie launch without a hitch. Help him achieve the best possible premiere for what would be the world's largest independent streaming entity.

The project wasn't by any means the only thing sustaining the launch, but if done right the results and the benefit to the whole conglomerate would be incomparable. His partners were counting on him to get this right. *He* was counting on himself to make this vision come true.

That was why he was here, approaching the front desk with little more than a surname and a firm grip on his distaste.

The receptionist looked up, did a double take that would have amused him had his mood been anything but grim.

'Uh…may I help you, sir?' she asked eagerly.

'You have a student—a Miss Beckett. She was performing in room 307 this afternoon. I'd like to speak to her, *por favor.*'

The enthusiasm dimmed a touch. 'Do you have her first name?'

Gael frowned. 'No.'

The receptionist grimaced. 'I'm sorry, sir, I can't locate her without a first name.'

'You have a lot of students named Beckett?' he enquired.

'I can't give out that information, or even tell you if she's a student here or not. The thing is, she may not be. We hold outside auditions here from time to time. She may have come in with a director...' She stopped and cast a slightly uncomfortable glance at him, probably due to his increasing irritation with her babbling. 'Sorry, sir, but if you want to leave a card...or your contact details...I'll see what I can do?'

The smile was re-emerging, and the flick of her hair was transmitting signals he didn't want to acknowledge.

With reluctance, Gael extracted his card and handed it over. She glanced at it, her eyes going wider still as she gave a soft gasp. He watched, his cynicism growing, as realisation and an accompanying degree of avarice entered her eyes.

His former company, Toredo Inc., had been a serious player on the streaming media platform—a hit with students and young professionals long before he'd teamed up with Alejandro and the Ishikawa brothers to form Atlas. Since then, he and his partners had rarely left the media's attention.

He and Alejandro had only finished their world tour scouting to find satellite partners to enter into a joint venture with Atlas a few short months ago. During that time they'd conducted numerous media interviews, which meant his face had been plastered all over the news for weeks on end. Anyone with a decent search engine knew what the Aguilar brothers looked like, and how much they were worth—and, if their search had been thorough enough, their relationship status.

From her expression, the receptionist was no exception. He watched her cast an amusingly exaggerated look round the deserted reception area before clicking on the keyboard in front of her.

'I think you're looking for Goldie Beckett?' she stage-whispered.

The name brought to mind corkscrew golden curls and honey-toned skin. Surprisingly fitting. *'Sí,'* he confirmed. The chances of the name being wrong were minimal. If it was, he could always resume the search.

The receptionist nodded. 'I really shouldn't be doing this…but she was practising in the music room until five minutes ago. You just missed her.'

Gael stifled a curse. 'Did you see which way she went?'

'No, but I know she lives in Jersey, so she may be headed for the subway?'

'Thank you,' he bit out.

'Uh…you're welcome…'

She looked as if she wanted to continue the conversation. But Gael turned away, cutting short the familiar look that preceded a gentle but firm demand for something. A phone number. A favour for a friend. A *personal* favour. At any other time he would have been inclined to grant the mousy receptionist another minute of his time, even reward her for her help. He'd long accepted how things worked between him and the opposite sex. He gave when the mood took him. They took *all* the time—until he called a halt to their schemes and often naked greed.

But not tonight.

Not when an alien urgency rubbed under his skin, demanding he find the elusive Miss Goldie Beckett.

He rushed out into the street, already condemning the futility of his actions. This was New York City. Finding a single person in a throng of people on the sidewalk, even after nine at night, was insane. And yet his feet moved inexorably in the direction of the subway station. Behind him his chauffeur kept pace in the limo. Probably he was wondering what had possessed his employer, Gael mused.

He knew her name. All he had to do was pass it to his security people and let them find her. He'd witnessed her naked ambition for himself. All he needed to do to entice her was offer his name and the once-in-a-lifetime project he had in mind and she would come running. There was absolutely no need for him to pound the pavement.

He'd slowed his footsteps, thinking how idiotic he looked when he heard a scuffle in the alleyway.

Gael almost walked past. Unsavoury characters lurking in dark places were commonplace in cities such as this.

A husky cry and the flash of golden curls caught the corner of his eye. He stopped in his tracks, wondering if he was conjuring her up in his irritated desperation.

The alley was poorly lit, but not deep. His eyes narrowed as he tried to peer through the wisps of smoke pouring out of a nearby restaurant vent.

'No, damn you, let go!'

The distinctive voice coupled with the decisive sound of clothing being ripped firmly altered his course, hurrying him towards the night-shrouded scene.

'Lady, I won't say it again. Give me the bag.' A low, menacing voice sounded through the gloom.

A bold, mocking laugh. 'At least you have the good manners to call me *lady* as you attempt to steal my property.'

'It'll be more than an attempt in a second if you don't let go of the damn bag!'

The warning was followed by more sounds of a tussle. Then a muted scream, the distinctive thud of a body landing heavily and a hiss of pain.

Gael arrived at the scene in time to see a dark shadow loom at him, then rush past. The blocking move he threw out missed by a whisker, and the assailant was already rushing out of the alley. He had a split second to debate whether to go after the mugger or aid the victim. Gael chose the latter.

The vision before him scrambled upright from the grimy concrete. 'God, no! Stop him! He's got my purse!'

This time he caught the bundle that attempted to launch past him. Arms flailed in his hold. A firm, sinewy body twisted in his arms as he held her tight.

'Dammit, let me go. He's got my belongings.'

'Calm yourself. You won't catch him. He's long gone by now,' he replied, attempting to keep hold of the wriggling creature.

'Only because you're letting him get away. For God's sake, let me go.' She stopped suddenly. 'Hell, you're his accomplice, aren't you?' she accused.

Gael reeled back in amused shock. '*Perdón?* You think I'm a *thief?*'

'I don't know what the heck you are. All I know is you're stopping me from going after that piece of scum who's just stolen my purse. What am I supposed to think?'

She pulled at his hold. Gael thought it was probably wise to let her go, but his hands wouldn't co-operate.

'You're supposed to thank a person who has just come to your aid,' he suggested.

Eyes of an indeterminate colour widened in disbelief. 'He got my stuff *before* you arrived. You let him get away—and you think I should be *grateful?*' she spat with quiet fury.

She had fire—he granted her that. But it was the shaking in her voice that drew his attention.

Gael gripped her arms in a firmer hold, careful not to spook her further. Although he was still mildly amused she thought him a thief, her agitation meant she might take flight if he let her go. 'I'm not a thief, Miss Beckett. I assure you.'

She froze. And in the darkness he was beginning to become acclimatised to her gaze searched his with growing suspicion.

'How do you know my name?' she demanded, her voice husky with a different kind of emotion.

Fear.

That didn't sit well with him. He let her go and stepped back, although he made sure to keep himself between her and the exit. Now he had her before him he wasn't in the mood to go searching for her again should she bolt.

'You have nothing to fear from me.'

She laughed mockingly, but her trepidation didn't abate. 'Says the man who's keeping from leaving. Don't think I didn't notice the body-block. I'm warning you—I know Krav Maga.'

Again a tendril of amusement twitched at a corner of his lips. 'So do I, *pequeña*. Perhaps we can spar some other time, when we're both in the mood.'

'I don't spar just for the fun of it. I fight to defend myself. Now, either tell me why you're here wasting my time, and how you know my name, or get out of my way.'

'Your assailant is long gone. If you wish to report the incident I'm willing to lend you my phone.'

'No, thanks. If you want to do something useful will yourself into getting out of my way instead, why don't you?'

Gael shook his head. 'Not until we've talked.'

'I don't know who you are or what you could possibly have to talk to me about that involves us standing in a dark, smelly alley.'

She started to skirt him. He let her go until she faced the exit and her perceived freedom.

'I'm here because you're of interest to me.'

'I highly doubt that.' She took a few steps backwards. Stumbled. Her breath caught as she righted herself. 'I don't know what your problem is, but I assure you I'm not worth stalking, if that's your thing. And the sum total of my worth—which was eighty dollars—is now headed for the other side of the city, thanks to you. Anything else you want won't be given willingly.'

She retreated a couple more steps, until she stood beneath the single lit bulb gracing the mouth of the alley.

Gael inhaled sharply. He'd thought her performance captivating across the wide expanse of an auditorium. At the time he hadn't paid much attention to the woman herself. But he was looking now. And up close Goldie Beckett was…something else. Her dark honey-toned skin, even under the poor lighting, was vibrant and silky-smooth, her high cheekbones, velvety pouting lips and determined chin, a perfect enough combination to make his breath snag somewhere in his chest.

He wasn't by any means new to the art of appreciating beautiful women. His electronic contact lists were filled with more than his fair share of phone numbers from past and possible future conquests. But there was something uniquely enthralling about Goldie Beckett's face that riveted his attention.

Perhaps it was her eyes. Gael wasn't sure whether they were blue, or the violet he suspected, but the big, alluring pools, even though they currently glared at him, were nevertheless absorbing enough to keep him staring.

As for her body… She couldn't be more than five foot five, but even her lack of height—he preferred his women taller—didn't detract from her attraction. Nor did it diminish the curvy frame currently wrapped in a black sweater and denim skirt in any way.

A *torn* black sweater, which gaped wide enough at the

shoulder to reveal the strap of a lilac-coloured bra and the top of one voluptuous breast.

A thick silence ensued, during which she noticed where his gaze had landed. He admonished himself to get control in the few seconds before her hand snapped up to cover herself.

Her glare intensified even as her other hand crept around her neck and patted in a puzzled search. 'Oh, great!' she muttered eventually.

'Something wrong?' Gael asked, forcing his gaze from the hand covering her breast.

'Don't you mean something *else* wrong?' she snapped. 'Yes, something else *is* wrong. That…that lowlife didn't just take my purse, he took my scarf too.'

Again there was a thin tremble in her voice that struck him the wrong way.

She was probably no longer apprehensive of his presence, but she'd been attacked and robbed. A closer scrutiny of her showed another rip in her tights and muddy scuff marks on her skirt and boots.

'Are you hurt?'

Her mouth pursed and her eyes darkened. She regarded him, debating whether to furnish him with an answer. Slowly her free hand opened to reveal a bloodied deep welt across her palm.

A quiet fury rolled to life in his belly.

He balled his fist in his pocket to stop himself from reaching out to examine the wound more closely. He was absolutely sure she wouldn't welcome the move. 'My car is parked over there.' He indicated with a jerk of chin. 'If you come with me I'll get you cleaned up. Before we talk.'

Her laughter mocked again, deeper this time. 'I'm from New Jersey, Mr…whatever your name is, not Narnia. I don't step through cupboards or into limos, however flash they look, out of naive curiosity.'

Gael gritted his teeth, reached into his pocket and brought out his business card. 'My name is Gael Aguilar. I'm working on a project I think you might be interested in. I saw your...performance this afternoon and came back to look for you. The receptionist mentioned you'd just left. I came in this direction in the hope of finding you. Need I go on?'

She eyed him warily. 'You hesitated before you said *"performance"*. Why?'

Gael was a little surprised that she hadn't immediately jumped at the mention of his name, and that she wasn't preening at the thought of being pursued as he'd pursued her. Most women would find that a compliment. But what shocked him more was that she'd cut through everything he'd said and singled out the slight trip in his voice triggered by what he'd witnessed after her audition that afternoon.

It wasn't a flaw he wanted to dwell on. This wasn't personal. It was business.

The reminder, and the fact that he'd been in this alley too long, tautened his voice. 'It's not productive to dwell on the cadence of my speech, Miss Beckett. You have my word that I mean you no harm.' His gaze dropped to her hand. 'My advice, though, would be to see to that wound before it gets infected. I can help. Then we can talk. I don't want anything more from you.'

A slight frown marred her forehead before she looked over his shoulder at the limo. His driver stood to attention next to the back door and inclined his head at her. Her frown cleared.

Pressing home the advantage the sight his burly bodyguard and driver provided, Gael continued. 'Unless I'm mistaken, you now have no means of reaching your destination tonight or contacting anyone for help?'

'I'm far from as helpless are you're making me sound,

Mr Aguilar,' she muttered, although her voice lacked conviction.

He remained silent, gave her time to arrive at the conclusion he needed. After a minute she held out her hand.

He handed her his card and she stared down at it. If she recognised the information there she gave no indication. She looked from him to the car, then at the card, and back to him.

'You have a first aid kit in your car?' she enquired, quietly but firmly.

He probably did, but he shrugged. 'Possibly. I've never had occasion to use one. But my hotel is fifteen minutes away. We can get you cleaned up more efficiently there.'

She immediately shook her head. 'No, sorry—that won't work for me. That Narnia thing again, you know…?'

Gael stopped himself from growling his frustration. Never had he had to work this hard to get traction with a member of the opposite sex. Had he been in a better mood he would have been vastly amused. He shoved both hands into his pockets and thought fast.

'I was supposed to attend a dinner party tonight, with thirty other guests, on the Upper East Side. I pulled out because of the prospect of a business meeting with you. We will go there. Is that enough reassurance for you?'

She stared back at him, her injured fist slowly curling. Gael knew the abrasion would be causing her discomfort by now.

'Maybe…but how do I know the party is real and not some made-up fantasy?'

He compressed his lips before reaching for his phone. A few clicks and Pietro Vitale's face filled his screen.

'Gael, your presence has been missed. I've tried not to be insulted by a few of my female guests complaining that the party isn't the same without you,' his friend complained.

Gael's gaze shifted from the screen to Goldie. Her mouth was set in a firm, mildly disapproving line. He angled the screen towards her and addressed Pietro. 'I can remedy that, provided I can bring a guest?'

'Of course, *amico*. More is merrier, *si*? Also, the sooner, the better. *Arrivederci!*'

The Italian signed off.

'Will that suffice or do I need to request a police escort as well?' he drawled.

Goldie slowly shrugged. 'This is fine.'

Gael exhaled, a curious tension leaving his body as he nodded. 'Then come.'

Her eyes widened a fraction at his curt command, but she fell into step beside him. She summoned a tiny smile for his driver as he opened the back door for her. When she stooped to enter Gael forced his gaze from lingering on her rounded backside and shapely legs.

He entered after her and settled back in his seat. When she slid as far away from him as possible he experienced that mild irritation again. Considering what he'd witnessed in the auditorium this afternoon, her stand-offish behaviour was getting old.

'We've established that I'm not about to force myself on you, Miss Beckett, so perhaps you could drop the terrified lamb routine?'

'I'm not a lamb,' she snapped. 'And this isn't a routine.'

'Are you saying you're *always* this suspicious of everyone?'

'I'm suspicious of men who come out of nowhere and accost me in dark alleys—and, yes, men who are possibly wolves dressed in lambs' clothing.'

'And yet here you are,' he said.

Her expressive eyes snapped at him. 'What exactly are you saying?'

Gael stared at her as the car slid into traffic. 'I mean

your options aren't looking very good right now. So perhaps a little gratitude wouldn't go amiss. I might decide you're not worth the effort and leave you to your fate. Is that what you want?' he asked, watching her closely.

'I've just been attacked. I'm within my rights to be wary,' she replied.

'Yes, but I think you trust your instincts too—which is why you're here, *no*?'

'You think you know me?' she enquired, narrow-eyed.

'I think my assessment is right. Instinct first, then after that you let other…urges guide you.'

'What's that supposed to mean? What urges?'

His mouth twisted. 'You tell me.'

'I have no idea what you're talking about. And if this is the way our supposed business meeting is heading perhaps I'm better off cutting my losses right now.'

Gael sighed. 'While you decide on that will you allow me to put your seat belt on for you? I wouldn't want you to suffer another injury en route to what you imagine is your gruesome end.'

Her eyes narrowed. 'You're mocking me?'

He reached for the seat belt. 'I'm trying to find a way to have a conversation without getting disagreed with at every turn.'

She inhaled long and hard, her gaze going from the buckle in his hand to his face. When he cocked an eyebrow she nodded and pressed herself back against the seat. Moving closer, Gael wondered whether his offer had been a good idea. Underneath the distinctive smell of her intimate acquaintance with alley concrete he caught the scent of apples and honeysuckle. And at close quarters he saw her pulse racing at her throat, her skin flushing when he drew the belt between her breasts.

The stirring in his groin wasn't surprising—he was a red-blooded male, after all—but he cursed its presence all the same, especially when he cradled her hip for a precious few seconds before the lock slid home and his blood heated up to discomfort levels.

When he finished the task and sat back it wasn't without a modicum of relief.

He was almost glad when she cleared her throat. 'So, what do you want to talk to me about?'

He brought his mind firmly back to task. To business. 'I have a proposition for you. If you're agreeable we'll get you cleaned up first, then we'll talk, *si*?'

CHAPTER THREE

GOLDIE TRIED TO FOCUS as the sleek, luxurious car rolled down Columbus Avenue and turned on to Central Park West. She didn't think she'd hit her head when that horrid brute had wrestled her purse away from her. And yet a hazy sensation, as if she'd fallen down a rabbit hole, swirled all around her, making her wonder if her faculties were intact. Making her wonder if she'd heard him right.

What had this unfathomably riveting stranger said? A *proposition*.

She wanted to snort under her breath. Nothing good could come out of a proposition from a man like *that*. A man with the face of a fallen angel, hell-bent on practising his sorcery on unsuspecting women. A man with a voice so hypnotic she wondered if he'd practised that precise cadence and for how long before he'd attained that perfect sizzling-you-to-your-toes note that accompanied each faintly accented word.

He was the kind of man who was everything her mother had always yearned for and never achieved. The exact type of man Goldie had sworn off after witnessing time and again the way they used their God-given attributes mercilessly.

Goldie didn't hate *all* men. But she drew a particular line at playboys with enigmatic eyes and captivating faces that defied adequate description and bodies to match. Throw in the type of wealth and raw power this man next to her exuded and her warning bells clanged loud enough to be heard on the Long Island Sound.

So what was she doing in his car?

Goldie frowned, then answered her own question. Circumstances had forced her into it. But that didn't mean she wasn't still in control. Of her mental faculties *and* of her body. That zing she'd felt when he'd secured her seat belt had been a temporary aberration. The whole last hour had been a surreal sequence of events she intended to put behind her as soon as possible.

She glanced at him from the corner of her eye. When she was certain his phone had absorbed his attention, she turned and stared at his profile.

Seriously, he was like a Roman statue she'd once seen at the Museum of Natural History when she'd visited with her mother. Their trip had occurred on one of the rare times when her mother had been sober and coherent enough to make the visit. They'd stared at the statue for what had felt like an eternity, absorbing its unspeakable beauty. Her mother had sighed wistfully before her eyes had filled with tears.

Goldie had known what those tears were about. What they were *always* about. Wishes unfulfilled. A past thrown away because she'd made the wrong choices. The biggest one of which had been letting Goldie's father get away. A lump had risen to Goldie's throat as she'd watched her mother stare hard at the statue, wishing it was flesh and blood.

It had been a fruitless wish, of course.

Except Gael Aguilar was a living, breathing version of that statue.

A version who turned his head and stared straight at her in the next moment, blasting her with long-lashed light hazel eyes. Goldie attempted to look away, but for some stupid reason she couldn't drag her gaze from him.

'This proposition of yours…what's it got to do with your occupation?'

The scrape in her palm was filthy and stinging badly. Enough that it made unclenching her hand difficult. She dropped her other hand from her ripped sweater long enough to pull the business card from her pocket. It read *'CEO, Atlas Group'*. She'd made it her business to research every TV and movie production company in New York, Hollywood and Canada, just so she wouldn't miss any opportunities that might whisper past the hallowed halls of Othello. She'd never heard of Gael Aguilar's company.

'It's a new arm of my company.'

'So you were trolling the halls looking for guinea pigs?' she asked.

For some reason that amused him. Both sides of his sensual mouth lifted. Even that small action lightened his face in a way that made her breath catch. Made her wonder what it would be like to be the recipient of a full, genuine smile.

'We really need to get off the subject of animal references. I'm a man. You're a woman. Let's refer to ourselves as such, *si*?' he drawled with a raised brow.

Something in his gaze made her self-conscious. She cursed silently when heat rushed up to redden her face. Because of her chosen career she'd needed to train herself not to blush at the drop of a hat, and yet she was doing just that, simply at the droll, slightly mocking look in his eyes.

'My question still stands,' she sniped, to cover her uneasiness.

'And it will be answered in the fullness of time. I need your undivided attention for that discussion.'

'What makes you think you don't have that now?'

'You mean in between trying to hang on to your modesty and the swelling of your hand?' he enquired, his tone almost gentle.

For some reason that made something tighten in her midriff. Before she could form a disagreeable response he was leaning forward. He snagged a bottle of water from the well-stocked bar at his side of the car. Snapping the plastic top free, he wet a handful of tissues and turned to her.

'May I?' he requested, again in that gentle voice she didn't want to associate with him. Men like him weren't gentle. Men like him were predators, only intent on taking, taking, *taking* and leaving behind callously discarded husks.

Goldie wanted to refuse on principle, in solidarity with her poor mother and with the bitterness that sometimes spilled into her just from being close to it. She didn't doubt that her mother's bitterness had stained her in some way, made her wary of certain types of men. Men like the casting director from today's audition, for instance.

She silently shook her head, veering away from the subject even while admitting she was old enough to know some of the blame for her mother's current circumstances came from Gloria Beckett herself. It took two to tango, after all.

Tango.

Okay, she wasn't going to allow an image of her tangoing with this man to cloud her already dizzying thoughts. Determinedly she clenched her gut against any more fanciful thoughts and held out her right hand.

Gael Aguilar cupped her hand in his. Goldie forced herself to ignore the alarming tingling where they touched and watch clinically as he cleaned her wound as best as the meagre supplies allowed. He worked quickly and efficiently, his manner gentle but firm. When he was finished, he disposed of the tissues and eyed her with a steady look.

'Better?'

She tested the flexibility in her hand and gave a short nod. 'Yes, thank you.'

'You see, we're not above civility after all, Miss Beckett.'

Despite the amusement in his voice there was a thin veil of something else in there...something she couldn't pinpoint. Or perhaps she wasn't willing to pinpoint it?

She'd puzzled over this man for far longer than common sense dictated was wise. 'Are we there yet?' she asked instead, then cringed at the juvenile question.

His amusement increased.

Certain he was about to make another joke at her expense she hurried to add, 'I don't have all night.' She glanced at her watch, her heart lurching when she realised the time. 'In fact, I don't think I can do this thing tonight after all. I need to be somewhere else.'

Her mother needed only the smallest excuse to regress into depression and fall off the wagon. Goldie had assured her she'd be home by ten. Any later and her mother would fret. Fretting would inevitably lead to her seeking solace at the bottom of a bottle. Goldie could only pray that her mother had fallen asleep watching TV tonight.

'You need to be somewhere else? And you didn't think to mention that before you got into my car?' His amusement had vanished. Light hazel eyes narrowed incisively on her. 'Is this some sort of game?'

'Excuse me?'

'Are you wasting my time, Miss Beckett?'

Irritation rushed up her spine. 'With respect, *you* insisted on this meeting. Granted, I'm curious to find out just what this *proposition* is, but I hadn't realised how late it was—'

'And suddenly you need to be somewhere else? You have someone waiting for you, perhaps? Boyfriend?' His gaze dropped to the hand curled into her lap. *'Husband?'*

The word held a sneer that stiffened her back, and again she caught that look in his eyes. As if he held her far below his normal regard.

Puzzlement and that growing irritation made her frown. 'That really isn't your business, is it, Mr Aguilar? Are you in the habit of interrogating your potential business colleagues like this? It *is* business you intend to discuss

with me, isn't it? If not, then I suggest you let me out
right now—because I wouldn't want to waste more of your
time!'

His jaw flexed for a second before his expression turned
neutral. Eyes that had been mocking and mildly amused
became opaque. 'It *is* a business proposition. If you need
to be elsewhere, then so be it. But will you be able to live
with yourself if you don't find out whether this is an opportunity you want to miss or not?'

There was a taunt in those words. There was also a look
in his eyes as if he wasn't sure whether he wanted her to
say yes or no.

'Does that line usually work for you?'

A sculpted eyebrow went up. 'What line?'

'The "do things my way or you'll kick yourself for ever"
scam?'

He gave a half-sigh, half an irritated huff. 'I grow tired
of this vacillating. You have one minute to say yes or no.
Starting right now.'

He had the temerity to stare pointedly at his watch.

Dear God, she really *had* fallen down a rabbit hole! She
thought she'd hit bottom with the sleazy proposition from
that casting director this afternoon. It still made her skin
crawl. But had she merely fallen into another dimension?
One where the person making a proposition wasn't even
certain whether he wanted his offer accepted or not, but
went ahead and dared her to consider it anyway?

About to shake her head to clear it, she saw his eyes
sharpen.

'Make up your mind, Miss Beckett. We're here.'

Goldie looked out of her window. Sure enough, they'd
pulled up in front of one of those flashy-looking high-rises
that dotted the Manhattan skyline. This one came complete
with liveried doorman, shiny awning, and a uniformed
concierge behind an imposing reception desk.

She redirected her attention to the man whose posture held more than a whiff of impatience and arrogance. 'Twenty minutes. That's all I have.'

His mouth thinned. 'We shall see.'

About to ask him what he meant, she found her words choked off when he opened his door and alighted, then turned to hold out his hand.

She didn't want to touch him. Not after the way it had felt the last time. And because she didn't want to let go of the tear in her top that showed half her boob. She shifted along the seat, and was debating how to exit with as much dignity as she could muster when he reached in and scooped her out as if she weighed nothing.

'What are you— Put me down!' she spluttered, outrage filling her as he marched her through the double doors being held open by the doorman and into a waiting lift.

He set her down and immediately the doors slid shut. The whole thing had happened in less than two minutes, and yet Goldie felt as if she'd just experienced the headiest, longest rollercoaster ride of her life. Impressions of heat, masculine scent, tensile strength, strong capable arms and…absurdly…above all, safety, buffeted her as she stared at him in astonishment from her side of the lift space.

Once he'd pressed the button for the penthouse he stepped back with a cool look. 'You said twenty minutes. I wasn't about to have the time eaten away while you decided which leg to use to exit the car.'

'My God, you're insane!' Or maybe *she* was. She hadn't been given the chance to dissect things properly yet.

His jaw flexed and his hands were rammed into his pockets. 'Far from it, *querida*. Someone has to remain rational in what is fast turning into a farce. Tell me—do you always make a huge production out of every small decision?'

'You don't know me well enough to label me a drama queen, Mr Aguilar.'

Suddenly the air in the lift thickened. The glance he levelled at her held the heavy weight of judgement. 'I've seen enough to reach a conclusion, I think.'

'What's that supposed to mean?' she countered.

One hand emerged from his pocket long enough to wave her away. 'We will not waste time discussing inconsequential subjects.'

'Do you go out of your way to ride roughshod over *everyone* you meet, or am I the lucky recipient of your special attention?'

He shrugged, sent her a sardonic whisper of a smile and exited the lift, once again leaving Goldie looking at him askance.

She followed him out, then drew to a halt when the double doors before them were flung open to reveal a stocky Italian with twinkling brown eyes, shoulder-length hair and a wide grin.

'Gael! *Amico!* You're here. Now my night is complete.' His gaze swung to Goldie, looked her over, and his grin dimmed a touch. 'Okay, this is…interesting. My friend, do you care to tell me why your plus one is in this state? I trust you implicitly, of course, and I'm sure in a fight you'd come out the winner, but I'm not averse to attempting to kick your butt if you had something to do with the lady's um…state…'

'"The lady" is standing right in front of you,' Goldie offered with a saccharine smile. 'And trust me, she's quite capable of answering for and defending herself.'

The man's concerned look dissolved, to be replaced by the wide smile again. 'Of course. Tell me your tale, sweet one, and allow me to vanquish those that need vanquishing.'

Goldie felt a reluctant smile tug at her lips. 'I'm fine. Really. And it wasn't…your friend's fault.'

'So he was your rescuer?' the Italian asked hopefully.

'I wouldn't stretch it that far.' She looked at the man in question to see mockery and a tight little smile playing at his lips.

'*Sí*, Pietro, we're still trying to work out the finer details of our…association. But perhaps if you would be so kind as to point out the bathroom Goldie can clean up?'

Pietro nodded. 'Of course, of course. Come with me.'

He led them through the double doors and immediately turned into a bright hallway. Goldie got an impression of grey and gold decor, loud but not intrusive music, and lots of laughter coming from the living room before Gael Aguilar's presence beside her grabbed her focus. He really was imposing. And taller than she'd thought in the alley. As for those broad shoulders—

'Here you are.' Pietro turned a door handle and nudged it open to reveal a large bedroom. 'The bathroom is through there. You should have everything you need. If not, please let me know.'

Goldie found another small smile. 'Thank you.'

'*Prego.*' Pietro returned her smile, then with a nod at Gael walked away.

Gael remained, his eyes on her. Her senses began to jump and dip in that alarming way again.

'I'm fine to take it from here,' she said, when he made no move to leave.

He made an impatient sound. 'I think we've established that I'm not going to attack you, Miss Beckett. Accepting my help won't dislodge your feminine independence. Besides, trying to see to your wound with your non-dominant hand is going to eat into my twenty minutes. Unless you want to restart the clock?'

Goldie pressed her lips together, wanting to be annoyed with him for the way he made her feel a touch ridiculous. But, short of telling him she tended to refuse help from men like him on principle alone, thus probably seeming even more ridiculous despite her beliefs, she couldn't think of how to counter his assertion.

'Okay, thanks.' The words came out far too easily. Her brain knew it and her accelerating heartbeat acknowledged it as he stepped into the room and shrugged off his jacket.

His navy shirt clung to thick, sleek muscle as he flung the jacket away and moved towards the bathroom. She followed slowly, trying to hold at bay the sensation of orbiting close to a ravenous vortex.

She arrived in the spacious bathroom to find him setting out first aid materials on the double-width vanity unit. When he had finished he started to fold back his shirtsleeves.

Goldie tried to look away from strong, brawny forearms feathered with dark wispy hair as they were revealed. But the urge was hard to resist.

Her breath caught lightly as he glanced behind him and cocked his head at her.

'Come to the sink. We'll wash your wound properly before I apply some antiseptic.'

She joined him at the sink, taking care not to stand too close when his presence registered so insistently next to her. Gael Aguilar was dominating. His body seemed to vibrate with a force field that mercilessly drew every living thing into its orbit.

He turned on the taps, tested the temperature, then held out his hand. Recalling the tingling when he'd touched her in the car, Goldie wanted to refuse. But this silly dance had gone on long enough. She needed to get this over with and go back to her life. Her mother.

Thoughts of Gloria spurred her on.

She gave him her hand and once again he cupped it in his. And once again the tingling started. Only this time the sensation was twice as intense. Whether it was to do with the bright lights of the bathroom, which cast their skin to skin contact in a vivid tableau, or with the fact that he was much closer to her than he'd been in the car, she wasn't sure. All she knew was that touching Gael, having his thumbs move across her palm as he rinsed the angry gash, was like nothing else she'd ever felt.

When her breath felt strangled the sound was audible in a silence marred only by their mingled breathing. Like in the car, his movements were gentle. But the fire he created with his fingers was not. Growing alarmingly short of breath, Goldie wanted to snatch her hand from his. But then he made a sound. And she looked up. Their eyes met in the mirror. She forgot to breathe all together.

Gael's eyes had grown darker, stoked with a dark fire that made her belly clench tight. Recognising the feeling as her first ever genuine sexual attraction, Goldie gasped. His gaze dropped to her parted mouth. Stayed riveted until the almost visceral stare made her lips twitch with a need that bordered on alien.

Beneath the running tap his hands continued to caress hers. But neither of them moved their gazes except to drift them over each other's faces, returning over and over again to their mouths.

She wanted to kiss him. Be kissed by him. Now.

Her lips parted.

Gael made a sound beneath his breath. A guttural, primitive sound. And he broke his gaze from hers.

Released from the power of that rabid scrutiny, Goldie gulped greedily on the air flowing back into her lungs. Along with even more alarm at what had just happened. The thoughts she'd entertained, the want coursing through her…

Dear God… What's wrong with me?

After that sordid, grossly insulting proposition the casting director had flung her way this afternoon, sex should be the last thing on her mind. It should be buried even deeper than normal, beneath the tight, rigid focus of her ambition and her need to make something of herself. Her need not to end up like her mother—a slave to her sexual needs and emotional wellbeing, dependent on others for her happiness.

And yet here she was, letting this man touch her, trail his long fingers over her skin as if he were caressing a lover. And she…she *liked* it.

She withdrew her hand abruptly, almost knocking it against the side of the sink in her haste to dislodge the electricity his touch created.

'I… Thanks. Can we get on with it now, please?' she said, avoiding another look into those burnished gold eyes.

He muttered something beneath his breath in Spanish. But he snagged a hand towel and wrapped it around her hand before he drew her to the vanity unit.

'Sit down.'

The order was firm enough to put her back up, but she wasn't in the mood to argue any longer so she sat down where he indicated and held out her now slightly less throbbing hand.

The antiseptic stung, made her wince.

'Are you okay?' he enquired, in a deep, low voice.

Goldie wanted to look up, felt almost compelled to look into those eyes again, but she forced her gaze to remain on the clinical movements of his medical attention.

'Yes, thank you.'

He completed the cleansing, then applied a light bandage over her palm. Her hand felt a million times better by the time he was finished.

'Now for your head.'

'What?'

He held up another cotton bud. It was then that Goldie registered the slight throb at her temples. Something like relief poured through her. Then she silently grimaced at being *glad* of the minor head injury. The small gash which Gael was now cleaning didn't really explain her temporary lapse of control or the low hum through her veins. But she clung to it as the cause just the same.

Once he was done he stepped back. His gaze dropped to the hand she still had on the wide tear in her sweater. A hand growing numb from holding the torn garment in place.

'What are we going to do about this?' he enquired.

She bit her lip, recognising that she couldn't very well go out into the party with a rip in her sweater. The ripped tights she could take care of by removing and disposing of them. But the tattered sweater would stand out—and not in a good way.

'I...I couldn't impose on you to find me a sewing kit, could I?' she ventured.

His eyes widened a touch, dark gold lightening to its natural hazel colour as mockery returned. 'I sincerely doubt Pietro would have something so domestic lying about. But I will do my best.'

He balled the hand towel he'd used and threw it into the laundry bin before he left the bathroom.

His departure infused the room with a lot more oxygen and a lot more clarity.

Goldie jumped off the vanity unit and stared at herself in the mirror. Besides the notable evidence of her tussle with the mugger, she didn't look as horrid as she felt. But she had lost her phone, the little money she had and, more importantly, all the details of the casting directors and agents she'd planned to contact in the hope of landing a job.

Her last paying job had been an infomercial three weeks ago, which had paid enough to sustain her and her mother's bills for another month. Her mother's part-time job as a waitress paid very little. Things were getting more than a little tight.

She'd gone into today's audition with more hope than expectation. When it had gone well she'd allowed herself to hope even harder. Until her hopes been dashed by the slimy words rolling off the director's tongue.

'My hotel room. Nine p.m. Perform well between the sheets and I'll make your dreams come true.'

Goldie had barely managed to stop herself from being sick before she ran out of the auditorium and into the bathroom. Locking herself in a stall, she'd been ashamed of the tears she'd allowed to fall. But she was proud that she had picked herself up and returned to the music room to practise her singing. She wouldn't give up because of one casting director who gave his profession a bad name. She couldn't afford to.

Taking a deep breath, she tugged off her boots and cleaned them with tissues, then finished tidying herself up as best she could. Spotting a dressing gown hanging behind the door, she quickly took off her clothes, disposed of the ripped tights and shrugged on the gown. She was securing the belt around her waist when Gael knocked.

Self-consciousness assailed her, even though the gown draped her from shoulder to ankle. Sucking in a deep breath, she opened the door.

What Gael Aguilar held out to her was most definitely not a sewing kit. 'My assumption was correct, it seems. This will have to do instead. Courtesy of Pietro's absent niece.'

Goldie eyed the scrap of material in his hand. The black cloth had probably started life in a designer's imagination as what a dress looked like. But even without examining it too closely she could tell it would be too small. On some level she knew Gael was probably trying to help. But the man's presence aggravated her on such a raw, subliminal level that she shook her head firmly in refusal. 'No, I don't think this will work.'

His mouth firmed. 'Go against your wish to fight me on every front, Miss Beckett, and just try it on. You might be surprised. Unless you wish to join the party in that dressing gown?'

Since that was out of the question, she bit back a grimace and took the dress. Eyeing the garment, she fingered the label, her breath catching slightly when she caught sight of the exclusive designer name. 'Okay, I'll wear it.'

She'd expected her acquiescence to draw another mocking response from him. Instead a hard look settled in his eyes.

'I'm glad you find *something* agreeable. Try not to keep me waiting too long, *si*?' he drawled.

Goldie shut the door without responding. She suspected dealing with a man like Gael Aguilar would be trying enough at the best of times. Add the circumstances of their meeting, and the fierce awareness that showed no signs of abating whenever they were in close proximity... She admitted that her spinning senses weren't up to dealing further with the torrent of emotions he elicited.

Returning the gown to its hook, she stepped into the dress and tugged the inch-wide straps onto her shoulders. One look in the mirror drew a gasp. The material was luxuriously elastic enough to accommodate her curves but still give her room to breathe. Reluctantly fingering the hem that ended at mid-thigh, she admitted it looked spectacular, and it felt like heaven next to her skin. But the back...

Goldie eyed the exposure of her skin from nape to waist and swallowed deeply. No way could she carry off wearing her bra with this dress. Heat rushed into her cheeks as she took a deep breath and unclipped her bra. Stuffing it into the vanity unit drawer, she grabbed her boots and tugged them on. Their familiarity brought a touch of balance and, after combing her hands through her hair again, she turned and opened the door.

He was standing at the far side of the bedroom, his surprisingly brooding gaze focused out of the French windows onto the New York night skyline.

Goldie walked in and drew to a halt in the middle of the room, her gaze once again homing in with almost helpless intent on the man who leaned with such loose-limbed indolence against the wall.

His head turned and his gaze hooked on hers before his scrutiny dropped. His sharp inhalation echoed through the room as he took her in, the hands in his pockets visibly bunching as he straightened abruptly.

And stared.

Sexual awareness, now recognised as the potent substance it was, was unstoppable as it lanced her. Intensified just from the look in his eyes.

Beneath the expensive silk and elastic blend heat suffused her, rushing through her body in a maddening dash she had no hope of stopping. But she tried. Heaven help her, she had to. Or she'd lose her mind.

Slicking her tongue desperately over her lower lip, she cleared her throat. 'I'm ready to hear your proposition now, Mr Aguilar.'

CHAPTER FOUR

THE HEATED LOOK didn't abate in his eyes. But her words, like so many others tonight, seemed to trigger a response within him.

A negative one this time.

After a few charged seconds his expression grew shuttered, and his aura when he approached her vibrated with repressed emotions she couldn't place her finger on.

'Gael,' he clipped out as he passed her and headed for the door.

'Excuse me?'

'My name is Gael. I prefer it to Mr Aguilar. Use it.'

'That sounds curiously like an order,' she replied.

He stopped abruptly, turned to face her. A deep sustaining breath lifted his chest before he speared her with his incisive gaze. 'We've both had a trying day, Goldie. Can we attempt to make it slightly *less* trying before we part ways?'

She was sure it was the use of her name, spoken so smoothly, so sizzlingly, that drew the fight from her, made her lift one shoulder in a feeble shrug. 'Sure, I can try.'

'*Gracias,*' he intoned. Then added, 'Thank you.'

'Um…no problem.'

A tinge of amusement lit his eyes before he shook his head. '"No problem" aren't words I associate with you.' He abruptly held up one hand. 'Not that I want to test the theory right now. Come, we shall get a drink and find a place to hold our discussion, yes?'

At her nod he resumed his exit, slowing his long stride to accommodate hers.

They entered a large, rectangular living room, decorated with a severely modern and minimalist hand. The centrepiece of the room was the futuristic-looking light fixture that seemed to take up almost a quarter of the ceiling space. Beneath this gleaming white and silver masterpiece Pietro's guests laughed and mingled. The man himself was the centre of attention, surrounded by a coolly elegant circle of females.

His grin widened when he spotted them approaching, and he beckoned them with open arms.

'Ah, there you are. Confirmation of our adventures in the Andes is needed, my friend. Sadly, I don't think these fine ladies here believe a word I'm saying!' he said to Gael.

Gael's gaze drifted over the ladies in question, who sparkled and preened even harder under his attention. Although he smiled, Goldie noticed the mirth didn't touch his eyes. Not that the action didn't have the desired devastating effect. Almost without exception every woman in the group strained towards him, their gazes rabidly checking him out.

'That particular pleasure will have to wait, my friend. I have more important things to attend to right now.' He turned to the waiter who had appeared next to him and snagged two glasses of champagne.

Goldie dragged her attention from the nearest fawning woman to shake her head as he offered her one of the glasses. 'No, thank you. I don't drink.'

She caught more than one woman sniggering.

Pietro frowned, his features almost comical with alarm. 'You don't drink? You're not underage, are you?'

'No, I'm old enough to drink, but I choose not to,' she repeated.

Her mother's dependency on alcohol to get her through tough times and the depressing consequences when that crutch failed to work had taught Goldie at a very early age never to go near the stuff.

His eyes turning speculative, Gael returned both drinks to the tray and steered her outside towards a bar set up on the terrace. After taking her order for an apple spritzer and getting mineral water for himself, he led her to a quiet part of the hardwood floored space. Between two tree-sized ferns a white sofa had been set up beneath a heated lamp, which threw a lovely warm glow over the area.

'Why don't you drink alcohol?' he asked abruptly once they were seated.

'Do I have to have a specific reason?' she prevaricated.

He shrugged. 'Most people tend not to do it for two reasons—a natural aversion or an active life choice stemming from experience. I want to know which applies to you.'

Her fingers tightened around her chilled glass. 'Why?'

'Because one reason doesn't require further explanation, but the other might warrant further discussion if we're to work together.'

'So you're saying if I happen to be a recovering alcoholic it may ruin my chances at this imaginary job I'm yet to hear about?'

'I'm saying situations and flaws can be dealt with if they're known up front. I don't want to be blindsided by issues further down the line.'

'Mr Aguilar—'

His jaw tightened—a tiny movement, but she saw it nevertheless.

'Gael,' he intoned.

'Gael.' She stopped, unwillingly savouring the name on her tongue. Wanting to say it again. She cleared her throat and forced out a laugh. 'We seem to be getting way ahead of ourselves. Can we start this whole thing over? Please?' She held out her hand. 'I'm Goldie Beckett, graduate of Othello with honours in Acting and Musical Art. Currently unemployed and, yes, looking for a job.'

Gael stared at her hand. That mockery was swirling through his eyes once more.

After a beat, he took her bandaged hand in a firm but gentle hold. 'Gael Aguilar. My accolades are too numerous to name, but suffice it to say I'm in a position to make your dreams come true.'

Ice drenched her. She snatched her hand from his as words from earlier in the day, albeit without the sleazy overtones, fell into her lap.

His expression turned brooding. 'Something wrong?'

'Yes. You presume to know what my dreams are when you don't know me from a stranger in the street.'

'You just stated that you are unemployed. My response only pertains to an attempt to reverse that. Unless you wish to remain in a state of unemployment?'

She swallowed the bile of distaste the reminder of the day's earlier events had elicited and attempted to remain calm. 'I'm sorry. You mentioned before that you'd seen some of my audition this afternoon. I didn't notice you there, I must admit. Did you…did you see all of it?' She fervently prayed that he hadn't witnessed the sleazy exchange with the casting director immediately following the audition.

'I saw enough to make up my mind. Enough to make me return to find you.'

She lifted her glass and took a sip of her drink, her mind frantically ticking over. If he'd seen enough of her performance to make him hunt her down, then did she dare think he'd only seen the acting part, not the unsavoury denouement?

'You have a part you want me to play?' she queried, making sure to bleed her voice of hope.

It was that vulnerable hope that the casting director had exploited this afternoon, to make that demand of her. She planned not to let this man even close to the feverish hope burning in her heart.

'I have a part I *potentially* want you to play,' he amended. 'Subject to a few stipulations. And the usual auditions, of course.'

'Stipulations?'

He nodded, the light bouncing off his jet-black wavy hair. 'Very rigorous stipulations.'

'Such as?'

'We will discuss them later. Right now the broader questions concern your availability and your commitment to a long-term film project.'

Her heart skipped a beat, despite her promise to herself not to let hope take over. 'What's the role and how long are we talking about?'

'Female lead in a psychosexual thriller. Three to four months, travelling all over the world.'

Excitement fizzed through her blood. 'I'll need to read the script.'

'You'll be given a full synopsis to familiarise yourself with the story. But first you need to tell me whether you're free.'

About to say yes, she stopped when her mind veered to her mother. Despite the fierce ambition burning in her heart, the thought of leaving her mother on her own for four months made her heart lurch. But at the same time she knew this was what her mother wanted for her.

Goldie just hoped that pride in her daughter would make Gloria stick to the straight and narrow.

She returned her attention to Gael's face and experienced a slight chill at his expression. 'I'm sure I can work something out.'

One side of his mouth ticked with a hard twitch. 'Time to put your cards on the table, Goldie. Are you married?' he asked in a clipped voice.

She frowned. 'What? No.'

'Do you have a lover or a partner who will be displeased at your long absence from home?'

'I...no.'

His eyes narrowed. 'That hesitation doesn't fill me with confidence. I prefer *not* to start any association with lies.'

Affront stiffened her jaw. 'I'm not lying. The person I'm concerned about is my mother. I still live at home. With her. And she's...'

'She's what?'

She swallowed. 'Fragile.'

'In what way?'

'In ways I prefer not to divulge until something—if anything—comes out of this discussion. But I'll make sure, if it comes to it, that my home life doesn't interfere with my job.'

Silence ticked by as he stared at her. 'You're ambitious,' he drawled, with a touch of censure that grated over her skin.

'You say that like it's a bad thing. Did you not get where you are today by pursuing *your* ambition?'

He nodded. '*Sí,* but I've come to learn there are various types of ambition.'

She opened her mouth to answer, but a church clock nearby chimed, reminding her of the lateness of the hour. Whatever Gael's views on her ambitions were, they'd have to wait to be discussed some other time.

She placed her glass on a nearby table and stood up. He rose up before her, effectively blocking her from leaving.

'Where are you going? We haven't finished talking.'

She dragged her gaze from his broad shoulders and imposing body to meet his gaze. 'I can prolong our meeting, but first I'll need to call my mother. I was just going to ask Pietro if I could use his phone.'

His mouth compressed for a second, then he reached

into his pocket and brought out a sleek, ultra-modern-look-ing phone. One she hadn't yet seen on the market. Not that she paid much attention to such trendy luxuries.

'Use mine.'

He placed the phone in her hand. She swiped her hand across the screen. Nothing happened. He cupped her hand and performed something magical with his fingers. The phone buzzed to life.

'How may I help you, Gael?' a sultry voice queried.

Goldie's eyes widened as he sent her a sly smile. 'Guest call coming up,' he said into the phone. Then he held it up to her.

'Speak the number into it and you'll be connected. When you're done with your call come and find me.'

He left her alone on the terrace and headed back inside as she recited the number of her next-door neighbour. The time on the phone read just gone ten p.m. If by some mir-acle her mother was asleep, the last thing Goldie wanted to do was wake her.

Mrs Robinson, on the other hand, rarely slept, and was always glued to her TV screen, watching her favourite shows. Sure enough, the old woman answered her phone on the third ring.

'Mrs Robinson, it's Goldie. Do you mind checking in on my mother for me, please? I don't want to wake her if she's asleep, but I don't want her to worry—'

'Of course I will, dear. I took her a slice of peach cob-bler earlier, and she said she'd be heading to bed early. I'll go and peek in on her now. If she's up I'll stay with her until you get home. If she's asleep I'll call and let you know.'

Goldie bit her lip. 'Um…you won't be able to reach me, Mrs Robinson. I lost my phone earlier tonight. My phone *and* my purse.'

'Oh, no—are you okay?'

The old woman's concern touched her heart.

'I'm fine, thanks. I'm so sorry, but do you mind checking on her now, while I'm on the phone, please?'

'Of course. Hold on.'

Goldie breathed a sigh of relief as she heard the sprightly woman head for the door. Goldie had given her a key to their apartment years ago, when Mrs Robinson had offered to keep an eye on Gloria whenever Goldie was away. The arrangement had helped Goldie maintain peace of mind when she was at college, then later when she was out at auditions and at work.

She heard Mrs Robinson let herself in. After a minute she heard the soft snick of a door shutting.

'She's sleeping, dear. Don't worry about her. I'll keep watch. Now, what about you? Will you be okay to get home?'

Goldie hadn't quite worked it out, but she wasn't about to add to the kind old woman's burden. She looked towards the living room, where the party guests milled around, some spilling out onto the terrace to enjoy the view. Gael Aguilar wasn't one of them. When she found herself searching harder for him, she abruptly averted her gaze.

Crossing her fingers, she told a little white lie. 'I'm with a friend at the moment. I'll be fine.'

'All right. I'll see you later, honey.'

Goldie pulled the phone from her ear, not sure how to hang up. When the phone went dark she assumed it had shut itself off. She looked up to find one of the women who'd been in Pietro's circle smiling at her from the bar.

Only her smile held a whole lot of speculation. The green-eyed kind.

'So, *you're* with Gael, are you?' The slight slur, figurative and literal, was hard to miss.

Goldie forced herself not to bristle. 'No, not really.'

The blonde took her answer as an invitation to stroll

closer. Expensive perfume and the faint traces of alcoholic over-indulgence reached Goldie's nostrils.

'No? If you're not together then why hasn't he been inside with us?' she demanded.

Goldie glanced towards the living room and shrugged. 'He's in there now, if you want to go talk to him.'

The blonde laughed—a brittle sound that spoke of more than just a passing interest in Gael Aguilar. 'This may be a time of equality and all that, but a woman still likes to be chased by a man.'

'Right. Okay.'

Wanting an end to the conversation, Goldie searched for her glass, only to find it had disappeared—probably taken by one of the super-attentive waiters dotted around the place. Sure enough, one of them saw her drinkless state and darted towards her with an eager smile and a tray full of drinks.

Goldie started to shake her head. 'No, thanks. I don't—'

'She doesn't drink,' the blonde stage-whispered to the waiter. When he started to turn away she stopped him with a hand on his arm. 'Wait, this is fruit punch, isn't it?' She indicated a pink drink with a gaily coloured umbrella and a straw sticking out of it.

The waiter nodded. 'Yes, ma'am.'

The blonde snagged the glass and held it out to Goldie. 'Here you go. Problem solved.'

Goldie took the drink, having no intention of drinking it. Her smile grew stiffer as the blonde examined her critically from head to toe.

'Interesting boots.'

Again, the observation came with a smile that was meant to take some of the sting out of her words.

'Interesting…dress,' Goldie replied.

Her unwanted companion laughed. 'You have a spine. I'm Heidi, by the way. And if you weren't here with the man who broke my heart last year—the man who now looks at me like we've never even met before, never mind *dated*—I'd almost like you.'

Something tiny but sharp lodged itself in Goldie's side. 'You and Gael were an item?' she asked, even though she told herself she didn't care about the answer.

Heidi's nose wrinkled, but Goldie saw the dart of pain in her eyes.

'An *item*? How quaint. We were *lovers*. I shared his bed for six glorious weeks. Then I hit my inevitable use-by date and was bade, *Hasta la vista, baby.*'

'Inevitable?'

Her laugh held more of the pain that was slowly emerging from the bottom of her champagne glass. 'As regular as clockwork. No one, to date, has exceeded Gael Aguilar's famous month-and-a-half dating limit. So don't get your hopes up.'

Goldie frowned at the umbrella and the straw. 'You've got things completely wrong. I only met him tonight.'

Heidi's eyebrows went up. 'And he already looks at you like *that*?'

'Like what?' she asked, growing a little hot under the blonde's scrutiny.

'Are you *serious*?'

Uncomfortable with where the conversation was going, she lifted the drink to her mouth and took a long sip.

When Heidi continued to stare at her as if she was dim, Goldie shrugged with more than a hint of irritation. 'I really don't know what you're talking about. And I don't think you have anything to worry over...you know...if you want to...um...rekindle things?'

This time the laughter was pure white-hot bitterness. 'Second rule of dating Gael Aguilar. There is no second chance. Once he's done with you, you're finished for good.'

She took another drink, then hiccupped. Then grimaced as if she was in actual pain.

Goldie wanted to tell her to stop. That she really didn't need to know any more unsavoury details about the man who'd come to her aid—the man who seemed taken enough by a fraction of the ten-minute performance he'd seen today to pursue her.

But Heidi was on a roll.

Goldie sipped at her drink and racked her brain for a convenient excuse even while she kept one eye on the living room doorway. Now she was sure her mother was safely asleep there was no need for her to rush back home, but she still needed to come up with a way to get home that wouldn't mean tapping into the emergency money she kept in her closet at home. She'd already used too much of it earlier this month, when her mother had been too depressed to go to work.

With each minute that passed Goldie saw her choices dwindling. It was too late to make her way back to Othello to ask to stay with one of her friends there. Just as with each passing minute she was learning way too much about Gael Aguilar. His preference in women— sleek, tall blondes. How many homes he owned—eight at Heidi's last count. His love of fast cars—immeasurable. His favourite food—authentic Spanish-made *paella*. His bedroom skills—

Um...no!

'I think I'm going to head back in now,' Goldie interrupted, before she could be made privy to gossip she didn't want to hear. 'Will you be all right?'

Heidi waved her empty glass at her. 'Of course! Go get my... I mean *your* man. Enjoy your six weeks!'

The statement ended with another hiccup that sounded uncomfortably close to tears.

Her heart went out to the woman. She started to reach out, wondering why her arm felt so heavy. 'Heidi—'

'Is everything okay here?' Gael's deep voice enquired.

They were both startled, and both swayed on their feet as they turned to face the source of their conversation. Gael reached out for her arm and Goldie gasped with surprise at the dizziness that assailed her.

But even in her confounding state she saw how he completely ignored Heidi.

'I...yes. I'm fine—'

'I thought you said you didn't drink?' came the sharp, cold query.

Goldie frowned. Or at least she attempted to. Her face suddenly felt funny. 'I don't. This is fruit punch.'

He calmly took his phone from her, then her glass, eyeing her with deep censure. 'It is fruit punch. Laced with rum and vodka.'

'Wh-*what*?' She turned her head with growing difficulty, met Heidi's unrepentant gaze. 'But you said it was...'

Too late, she realised what had happened.

Gael turned to his ex. 'Are *you* responsible for this, Heidi?' he gritted, his voice filled with black ice.

'Oh, so you *do* remember my name,' Heidi retorted waspishly.

'*Santo cielo!* Word of advice: playing stupid games like this with me is guaranteed to put you even lower in my regard. Grow up!'

Tears welled in her eyes. 'Damn it, Gael. Do you *have* to be so cruel?'

'Only when you pull stunts like this. I suggest you find a quiet place and get yourself together. Goldie—we're leaving.'

Goldie, beyond stunned at how easily and gullibly she'd fallen into such a dangerous situation, could only nod. She couldn't even summon pity or anger for the other woman as Gael led her past the avidly gossiping guests, a protesting Pietro, and back into the lift.

The buzzing in her ears and the thumping of her heart prevented her from speaking as she walked, plastered to Gael's side, to the limo. He helped her in, secured her seat belt as her mind reeled.

'Oh, God, I can't believe I was so… That she just…' She started to shake her head, then stopped abruptly when her vision swam.

'Believe it. Some people tend to regress into childish behaviour when they feel slighted. Heidi has perfected the art.'

She wanted to ask then what he'd seen in the woman to make him date her, but the question was redundant. The blonde was a goddess. And, according to her, just the type of woman Gael favoured.

The car started to move, turned a corner. Goldie slapped a hand to her mouth as her stomach roiled. When he passed her a white paper bag she grasped it gratefully.

When the car had steadied, she risked a glance at his wavering figure. 'I'm sure you think me…naive and gullible.'

She wasn't sure whether he'd shrugged or not, but his voice held a distinct bite. 'For someone who claims not to drink, I'm surprised you didn't recognise the peculiar taste straight away.'

'I wasn't…I didn't…I've never tasted vodka before. Or rum.' She grimaced. 'Does this mean I've lost my chance with you? I mean with the audition?' she ventured, feeling her tongue slurring her speech.

God, how many times had she heard her mother sound like this? And how many times had Goldie's spirits dropped with disappointment and pity?

Hard hazel eyes sliced into her. 'Just as you claimed earlier, I too have to be elsewhere tomorrow. And since I can't have a conversation with you now, in this state, I'll have to see when my schedule opens up again.'

Her fingers curled around the lowered paper bag. 'Just give it to me straight, Gael. Tell me whether I've blown it or not so we can say our goodbyes.'

'What difference will it make?'

She licked her lips, desperation beginning to claw through her. 'If I haven't blown it completely I'd like the opportunity to fix it. I…I need this job. I need *a* job!'

His nostrils flared slightly. 'And how would you propose to go about *fixing* it?'

She shook her head, then groaned. 'I don't know. Maybe you can tell me what I can do…how I can—?'

His pithy curse dried up her words.

Goldie knew then that she was digging herself deeper into the hole she'd unwittingly found herself in. It was too late. She'd messed up a shining opportunity. Through ignorance and gullibility.

She snorted, her insides shredding with disappointment and chagrin. How *could* she have fallen into the same trap she'd condemned her mother for for so many years?

'What's your address?'

'My…address?'

'My driver will deliver you home,' he stated, his voice neither gentle nor harsh.

It was almost as if he'd become indifferent to her.

Goldie fought to dismiss the slight pang that thought brought and focused on a much more troubling problem.

'I can't go home,' she muttered, the words filling her with even more distress.

'Excuse me?' His voice was filled with chilly cynicism.

She grimaced, her hand shaking as she lifted it to her numb cheek. 'I can't go home in this state.'

Gael's gaze sharpened on her face. 'Why not?'

Shame dredged deep inside her. 'I… My mother is a recovering alcoholic. I can't… She can't see me like this.'

He regarded her for several charged seconds before his jaw clenched. *'Dios mio.'*

'I know how this looks, okay?' she pre-empted, before he could voice the condemnation bristling over his frame. 'But I can't do this to her! After everything she's been through, I can't—'

'Calm yourself, Goldie. I was merely going to say I'm not blameless in all this. I should've suspected Heidi would try something like this. I shouldn't have left you on your own for so long.'

She heaved in a breath and fought the clogging in her throat. 'I… Thanks.' She clenched her unhurt hand, ashamed at how low she felt. 'I know you probably think I'm pathetic right now, but I'm responsible for my mother. If she sees me like this it'll destroy her. In many ways I've been the adult for a long time. Every choice I make…she's my number one priority.'

His mouth tightened. 'Even when the choices you make aren't sound?'

She shrugged. 'I'm not perfect. I make mistakes like everyone else. That doesn't mean I should rub her nose in it. She has enough to deal with.'

'I see.'

'*Do* you?'

'Let's not enter another debate, hmm…?'

Her eyes widened when he shoved his door open. She stared around her, not sure when the car had stopped.

'Where are we?' she asked.

'My hotel. Since you don't want to go home, you can stay here tonight,' he said.

A different emotion, separate from the ones she was already battling, fizzed through her. 'I'm not sure—'

'I'm staying in the presidential suite. Besides the master suite there are two more bedrooms. With locks. You're invited to use either one of them. If you don't feel safe enough with that, tell my driver where you'd like to go and he will deliver you to whatever destination you require,' he stated in implacable tones.

The same instinct that had told her she could trust him enough to get into his limo after the mugging told her she could trust his offer. But suddenly Goldie wasn't sure she could trust *herself*.

She'd let herself down spectacularly once tonight. Did she dare trust that she wouldn't make another mistake on this surreal night?

But what alternative did she have that didn't involve wandering the streets in an intoxicated state, with a bulls-eye on her back for every creep out there?

She swallowed hard and accepted that this was the best possible, safest choice on the table.

'I accept your offer. Thank you.'

Twenty minutes later Goldie was in the most comfortable bed she'd ever slept in, the double doors to the princess suite locked after a solicitous Gael had brought her a glass of water and turned down the bed.

Now, stripped to her underwear, Goldie sighed and drifted off to sleep among the dreamiest of pillows.

CHAPTER FIVE

SHE WASN'T SURE what made her jerk awake. Perhaps it was the muted sounds of the city, when she was used to her quieter neighbourhood just outside Trenton, New Jersey. Whatever it was, once her racing heart slowed she became aware of another raging need. Thirst.

The glass Gael had left her with was empty, although she didn't recall drinking the water. She grimaced at the hazy, alcohol-distorted memories and got out of bed. She hated it that she hadn't made it home, but after what had happened Goldie knew this option was best. Her mother wouldn't have been just disappointed, she would also have blamed herself. Didn't studies show that alcoholism was sometimes hereditary? And Gloria blaming herself would only bring about one result—depression.

For the past few months her mother had been doing well. Goldie couldn't stomach being the cause of any form of regression in her mother's wellbeing.

Rising from the bed, she looked down at her scantily clad body. The thought of putting on that clingy dress again just to go and fetch a glass of water brought another grimace. Going to the adjoining bathroom, she shrugged into a dressing gown bearing a distinctive exclusive designer's monogrammed label, belted it, and left the suite with the empty glass.

Her bare feet moved silently over marbled floors as she walked along the ornately decorated hallway and into the vast living room. Styled in white, gold and royal blue, the presidential suite was the last word in elegance, right down to the hand-scrolled stationery and the monogrammed cushions that graced the brocade sofas and antique claw-footed chairs. Also dotted around the room were gilt and mother-of-pearl framed mirrors, and expensive paintings reflected perfection and elegance at each turn.

On the far side of the living room, set back from a second grouping of blue and gold-striped settees, a black baby grand piano gleamed under the lamps left on to illuminate the space. Next to it was a tiny kitchenette, housing a fridge and a collection of expensive drinks.

It was there that Goldie went to fetch bottled water. And there she remained frozen after, having taken a large gulp, she heard the heated sound of Gael's voice as he paced the private terrace outside.

She didn't want to eavesdrop, and really she didn't understand a word of the bullet-fast Spanish he spoke into the phone, but that didn't matter. She saw his pacing grow hurried as the conversation gained intensity. His fingers spiked through his hair and Goldie's breath caught as he swore beneath his breath.

She eyed the semi-dark living room.

Leaving the small alcove would reveal her presence. But staying where she was, witnessing what appeared to be an argument—although she wasn't absolutely certain— would be a worse violation of his privacy.

Taking a deep breath, she slid her glass onto the counter and stepped out of the alcove. Just in time to hear him snarl before he ended the conversation.

Like a magnet, her gaze swung to him.

He stood frozen between the French doors, the phone tight in his grip, his eyes locked on her.

'I don't speak Spanish, so I didn't understand any of what you were saying,' she blurted.

One corner of his mouth twisted, although tightly packed anger still seethed from his tall, imposing frame. Moving forward into the room, he shut the door behind him and tossed his phone onto the counter without taking his eyes off her.

'You don't need linguistic understanding to know what's going on.'

'I guess not,' Goldie replied, her skin jumping at the sparks still lurking in his eyes. She stared at him until the breath locked in her lungs. Then she dragged her gaze away. 'Um…goodnight.'

'Are you feeling better?' he asked, and his voice contained a bite. She couldn't determine whether it was aimed at her or was residual from his phone call.

She stopped her retreat. Nodded. 'Yes, thanks.'

'Then stay. Join me for a nightcap. Yours will be water, of course.'

For some reason she felt a little bit better that a trace of mockery was back in his voice. Retracing her steps to the counter, she picked up her half-empty glass and waited for him to pour an expensive-looking cognac before she joined him on the sofa.

She noted that he still wore his shirt and trousers from earlier, although a few more buttons had been undone on his shirt, giving her a glimpse of a firm, bronze contoured chest and a strong throat.

Averting her gaze from the arresting sight, she stared around, painstakingly counting the pieces of furniture in the room as a distraction tactic.

Fifteen.

Her eyes swung back to him.

Gael was watching her. He didn't seem inclined to speak, appeared just content to sip his drink, preferring to keep his thoughts internal. Goldie licked her lips, knowing this wasn't the time to pursue the business conversation they'd begun before her inadvertent trip into Liquor Land. When his stare got too much, she glanced around again, her gaze landing on a small ornate clock on top of an antique console table.

Two o'clock in the morning. 'So, do you conduct *all* your business meetings in the early hours of the morning?'

His gaze shifted from her to the contents of his glass. 'That wasn't business. It was family,' he said, confirming her earlier suspicion.

'Family?' she intoned faintly.

'*Sí.*' That crack of a smile was at his lips again. 'You're not the only one with maternal challenges.'

'You were arguing with your *mother*?'

His mouth twisted. 'You could say that.'

'Why?'

'Because there's a problem. Isn't that why people argue?' he snapped.

She frowned. 'Well, yes, but...'

'I don't wish to talk about that, Goldie.' His voice was a low, raw command.

Knowing how *she* felt about the subject of her own mother, she nodded. 'Okay. What *do* you wish to talk about?'

'You. Why acting?' he asked, his voice cold and abrupt.

'Because I'm good at it,' she stated without arrogance.

His breath huffed in a short laugh. '*Sí,* that you are.'

He raised his glass in a toast that felt wrong. And not in the mocking way she was getting used to.

She stared at him, but couldn't read his expression. 'Gael—'

'How many auditions have you given like the one you performed today?' He cut across her.

'This was my second. The first was for a workshop in the East Village a month ago.'

'And the script? What play is it from?' he pressed.

She hesitated, unsure where he was coming from. Unwilling to have her work mocked. 'It's my own work. I wrote it last year.'

'Tell me about it.'

Goldie shrugged. 'It's a story about…resilience, dependency, trust. About two people who care for each other but can't be together because of perceived insurmountable obstacles.'

He took a sip. Swallowed. His eyes locked on her. 'What obstacles?'

She toyed with the ends of the gown's belt. 'Alcoholism. Infidelity…' she murmured.

'And the piece you performed today? Which of those two things did it deal with?'

'Both. Her alcoholism. His infidelity. He wants to give up. She wants to stay and fight.'

He stiffened, his eyes slowly narrowing. 'It sounds like they're toxic together. Don't you think they're better off apart? As far from each other as they can get?'

'Maybe they are—maybe they're not. But surely it's better to find a way through the conflict than to give up at the first hurdle? Stick it out for a while for the sake of the love that might be buried beneath all that? Surely they owe it to themselves to root through the toxicity and find it? Maybe that's what will heal them?'

She forced her voice past the lump threatening to rise in her throat.

'What if their so-called love is toxic too? And how long is "a while"? How much is enough when everyone around you has to bear the brunt of the toxicity?' he demanded.

His voice had grown ragged, raw with a frustration and anger that she knew instinctively stemmed from that phone call.

'I don't have the answers. But I know I'd never give up something that important that easily,' she said.

He stared at her, his gaze probing deep. Deeper.

'Do it,' he said, in a low, rumbling voice just a shade above a whisper.

Her breath caught. Strangled her. 'Do…what?'

'The piece. Perform it for me.'

Shock sent her rigid for a second. *'Now?'*

'We're both awake. We're here. You asked me in the car what you could do. *This* is what you can do. Show me what I want to see.'

It was clear that Gael was still affected by whatever had happened during that phone call. Talking to his mother had disturbed him badly. Enough to make Goldie consider saying no…consider questioning his objectivity.

Because this no longer felt like business. This had become something else. Something emotional. Something hot and heavy and dangerous. Perhaps even deeply personal.

But, on the flipside, it was just what she needed. She needed her audience to be emotionally invested, not clinically detached. Even if he didn't believe what she was selling, he would feel strongly about it somehow. And wasn't that a good thing?

Reaching out, she offered him the glass in her hand. His gaze went from it to her face and back again before he took it. Set it to one side.

The moment his gaze returned to her face she spoke the first lines.

'You won't leave me. I won't let you.'

'Maybe it's the best thing for me to leave.'

His raw, unexpected response made her heart race faster.

'You think you love her, but you don't.'

'Perhaps I'm not capable of loving anyone. Not even myself.'

The words were spoken with a quiet, strong conviction that made her eyes widen. Made her certain she was glimpsing something Gael Aguilar might not want her to had circumstances been different. Had he not been caught up in whatever emotions held him prisoner right now.

'I don't believe that. Besides, I know you enough to tell you what is in your heart. I love you that much, Simon. Enough to forgive. Enough to take another chance on us. But for us to happen you need to stay. Please...take the chance.'

'Even if staying is perpetuating the cycle? Destroying us and everyone else who comes into our orbit?' he rasped, his eyes fixed firmly on her.

Tears prickled her own eyes.

Slowly she reached out and laid a hand on his. *'We'll find a way, but we'll only find a way if we're together. Don't leave. Please...take the chance on us. I love you. Fight with me. Fight for us.'*

The powerful exposing words, spoken from a place in her own personal pain—the pain of suffering a broken family—rumbled through the room, moved through her as she blinked and raised her gaze to Gael.

The look on his face made her breath catch. It was a mixture of pain, regret and frustration. There was also hunger. A visceral need for connection that lanced her from the short distance between them.

'*Dios mio*, you're good. So very good...' he muttered, his tone gravel-gruff.

Between one second and the next the hand beneath hers moved, turned and captured hers. He drained his glass and tossed it aside. Then he used their meshed hold to drag her close.

Goldie ended up in his lap, the air knocked from her. Before she could take a needed breath Gael's mouth was on hers. Hot and sizzling and cognac-laced.

He brought every emotion bubbling beneath the surface of his skin to the kiss.

Goldie had been kissed before, either through her work or through casual acquaintance dates that had never gone anywhere. No past experience came close to what she was feeling now as Gael's lips devoured hers, slipped past her stunned senses to breach them deeper. Her hands curled into his shirt, fisted, held on tight as his tongue licked her lower lip, her upper lip, then charged inside, his intense savouring of her drawing fire through her veins, drenching her from head to toe in white-hot sensation. Need slammed hard into her, making her moan and strain closer to his tensile strength, to the heat of sleek muscles moving beneath the cotton shirt.

She slid her hands higher, closer to the exposed skin of his chest, his throat. At her first touch they both groaned. Gael dragged her closer still, his hand moving to her hips and positioning her more firmly in his lap until the bottom of her robe fell open, her legs moved to either side of him. When she was situated to his liking he speared one hand through her hair, using his hold to angle her head, fusing their mouths closer together.

The kiss was like nothing and everything she'd ever dreamed of. Goldie felt as if she was flying and drowning at the same time. Her lungs screamed with the need for oxygen. She wanted to deny their request, to just keep experiencing the incredible sensation of kissing Gael Aguilar.

Only the pressure of his hand in her hair finally broke her free. But it was only so he could set her back a scant few inches, stare up at her with a face masked in raw, edgy lust.

'I want you, Goldie. I want to have you. Right here, right now,' he rasped, low and deep, his eyes dark with ravaging hunger and fierce intent.

Beneath her, his hips flexed, his powerful erection nestling deeper between her thighs, ramming home to her the strength of his desire.

Need pounded with relentless force through her. A need she knew she should fight. But for the life of her she couldn't summon the willpower. All the same, she tried.

'Gael—'

He closed the gap between them, forcing her answer back down her throat as he kissed her again, showed her with his mouth how feeble any protest she wanted to attempt would be. Groaning, she slid her hands up his strong neck, noting the raging pulse beneath her touch, glorying in it for a second before her fingers spiked into his hair.

His guttural groan was one of encouragement. Of ferocious need. They stayed like that for endless minutes, her on top of him, kissing him as if her life depended on it.

All too soon, he forced her head back again.

'Don't deny me, Goldie. Don't deny us both,' he rasped.

His accent was more pronounced, his voice curling around the words, burning them into her skin the way his eyes burned for her.

At twenty-four, Goldie knew she was an anomaly in the virgin stakes, and would probably draw mockery from Gael if he knew the depth of her innocence. But it was an innocence she was proud of—an innocence she'd fought to retain simply because she knew what throwing it away on the wrong person would make her feel further down the line. She'd watched her mother throw her body and her emotions away on the wrong men for far longer than she wanted to dwell on.

She'd already made a mistake that might have had disastrous consequences tonight. Was she risking making another?

She sucked in a deep breath—which emerged in a rush when Gael leaned up and slowly licked her lower lip. Her whole body shook with the headiness of that bold claiming. The fingers she had locked in his hair tightened, encouraged him as he kissed the corner of her mouth, her cheek, her jaw, her earlobe.

'Let me have you, Goldie *mia. Por favor*,' he whispered

in her ear. 'Let's turn this unfortunate night into a better one. A memorable one. I can make it so good for you.'

She groaned beneath the weight of his torrid, tempting words even as she fought to rationalise what was happening. Could she do it? Could she give herself to him for just one memorable night?

The answer burned hot and urgent beneath her skin. But Goldie ignored it for a moment, pulled her dwindling faculties together for long enough to separate what was happening here from the history she knew and had fought hard to prevent repeating.

Where her mother had fallen down had been when she'd imagined herself in love with the men who had ultimately used and betrayed her. Nothing so fanciful was happening here tonight. Gael wanted her body. She wanted his. Their needs were mutual. The only emotion present here was the hunger that demanded to be answered.

'Say yes, *mi dulce*.' He kissed her cheek one more time, then drew back to spear her with flaming eyes. 'Say *yes*.'

The word, eating her alive, burst free. 'Yes.'

His harsh exhalation preceded his forceful rise from the sofa. The moment he was upright he urged her legs around his waist. Then, with one hand banded around her, the other fisted in her hair, he made his way unerringly down the hall and into the master suite.

The room, like the rest of the penthouse, was luxury personified. Tasteful and expensive antique furniture mixed with contemporary designs to produce a breath-taking setting fit for a king.

Or for an impossibly sexy, arrogant, ravenous Spaniard, whose sole attention was fixed on her with a feverish intensity that made every single one of her senses jump in mingled excitement and trepidation.

Burnished eyes trapped her in place as he set her down and started to undo the remaining buttons of his shirt. With each further expanse of golden skin revealed her mouth and fingers tingled with the need to touch, to taste.

'Take off your robe, Goldie,' he commanded gruffly as he shrugged off his shirt and tossed it aside.

Her fingers twitched, but for the life of her she couldn't move. Because he was perfect. Not a spare ounce of flesh resided on the upper half of his body. She'd been so right to compare him to that Roman statue. His musculature was streamlined, a true work of art that filled her with awe. And with a great, demanding need.

Between her thighs her flesh pulsed with an unfamiliar urgency. An urgency so great she wondered how she was still standing.

'Goldie.' His voice was a furnace-hot warning. 'Are you deliberately keeping me waiting?'

Her head moved in a slow shake and her hand reached for the belt. 'No. I just…wanted to look at you.'

His breath was expelled harshly, almost as if she'd surprised him. Colour slashed high on his cheekbones and he closed the gap between them, speared his fingers into her hair. He angled her face up but didn't kiss her, merely traced that hot gaze over her face.

'You can look at me all you want later. Right now I want you naked and beneath me. So the robe, *bellezza* Goldie. *Take it off.*'

With quick, jerky movements she pulled the belt loose and shrugged the robe off her shoulders, leaving only her cotton panties on.

His gaze stayed on hers for a long, absorbing moment before he slowly stepped back. His exhalation was half a groan, half an expression of wonder. The fingers of one hand traced her pulse, her collarbone, then moved down to the delicate space between her breasts. Then he moved behind her, fingers still on her skin, tracing over her shoulders to the top of her spine.

A shudder rushed over her—the beginning of many that rolled in a never-ending reaction to Gael's touch on her body. His fingers drifted down her spine, then back up again, eliciting a deep moan she was helpless to stop. In the next instant his nails were dragged lightly down her body and he groaned at her deep shudder. She swayed beneath the onslaught of fierce desire. It triggered a frenzied response and suddenly he was back in front of her, his fiery gaze moving down her body, savouring her anew.

'*Santo cielo*, you're exquisite,' he murmured huskily.

Catching her around the waist, his movements a touch uncoordinated, he tossed her onto the bed and tugged at his belt.

Goldie brushed her hair out of her eyes, the better to see him, and then almost wished she'd averted her gaze when his body was revealed in all its manly, almost intimidating glory. She swallowed hard when she took in the fullness of his manhood.

Heavens.

A trace of that arrogant smile touched his lips as he moved towards her. 'Your beautiful eyes stare a little too hard, *guapa*. Do you wish to unman me before we even begin?'

She blushed, hot and fierce, drawing a low laugh from him. She dragged her gaze up with monumental effort. 'You're laughing, which tells me you don't think my unmanning you is a possibility.'

His laughter drifted away, replaced by deep, stark hunger. He stalked to the bed, prowled to loom over her. One finger traced over her nose to her mouth, testing the suppleness of her lower lip before he demanded entry. When she took his digit into her mouth, he groaned.

'With a woman as intoxicating as you, everything is possible.'

His kiss this time was ten times more carnal, devastatingly brutal in its hunger. Luckily Goldie was equally ravenous for this new, dizzying sensation that threatened to drown her. But she hung on, clung to Gael's broad shoulders as he took her on a frighteningly exciting journey.

Even after he broke away and started to trail his mouth down her body she was still lost in that intoxicating kiss. It was only when he reached her breasts, tweaked and sucked on the stiff, needy peaks, then dropped lower to kiss the sensitive skin below her navel, teasing her panty line with his teeth and lips, that she fell into a different but equally exhilarating dimension of pleasure.

Her panties were tugged off in quick, expert movements. Then he was parting her legs, kissing his way up her inner thighs.

Goldie didn't even attempt to halt what was coming. She wanted it all. Was greedy enough to raise herself onto her elbows, stare in wonder as he drew inexorably closer to the bundle of need between her thighs.

His gaze locked on hers in that final second before he tasted her, his nostrils flaring one last time as he drew in her essence. He muttered something hard and pithy under his breath. Then he swiped his tongue boldly across her flesh.

Her hips jerked as sensation pounded her in a merciless wave. She collapsed back against the pillows, her breath emerging in shameless pants as pleasure surged through her. When Gael found the bundle of nerves that screamed for attention she cried out, her eyes squeezing shut to savour the sensations she knew instinctively would blow her away. The pressure between her thighs increased, and his tongue flicked urgently against her flesh as he groaned through his own pleasure.

Between one breath and the next she was flung into nirvana, her mind and body no longer her own as pure bliss buffeted her. Her moan fused into one long, earthy sound, and her convulsions were endlessly thrilling.

The moment her pulse began to slow she felt him move, heard him reach across her body. She opened her eyes to see him tearing open a condom, rolling it over his impressive girth.

Goldie debated then whether to tell him that she was a virgin, that he was about to be her first. But she knew then that two things might happen.

Firstly, he might not believe her. She hadn't forgotten the occasional glimpses of censure he'd sent her way a few times since they'd met. Men like Gael had cynicism bred into their DNA. She couldn't explain any other reason for those looks.

Secondly, he might believe her and think she had an agenda in all this—a motive for giving herself to him. It couldn't be further from the truth. Theirs was to be a coupling bred solely of attraction and need. Nothing more.

So she bit her lip and forced herself to meet his gaze. Whatever he saw in her face satisfied him enough to make him lower his body to hers, to free her lip from her teeth and take her mouth in a possessive, incandescent kiss.

After an age, he lifted his head.

'Touch me, Goldie. Hold on to me when I take you. I want you to know who it is that possesses you tonight.'

The raw demand robbed her of her already short breath. 'Gael—'

'*Sí*, say my name like that. Just like that...' he commanded gruffly as he positioned himself between her legs. One hand gripped her thigh, and the other fisted in her hair. The easy strength with which he held himself poised above her was testament to his powerfully honed physique, which was a beautiful sight to behold.

His fierce arousal spoke of a different power altogether—one that made her heart palpitate with trepidation even as her senses flared in anticipation.

Remembering his instruction to hold on to him, she slid her arms around his waist, caressing the corded muscles in his lower back.

Hazel eyes darkened as they met hers. His head dropped and his mouth fused with hers as he penetrated her with one sure, focused thrust.

Her muted scream rose and died between their kiss. But not the pain. God, not the pain. That held her rigid for a few endless seconds.

Above her, Gael's eyes flared, probed. He raised his head and stared at her. 'Goldie...?'

She wasn't sure whether it was a question or an observation. She registered her lost innocence and held on to him, unable to form words as the pain lingered, then faded to leave behind new, breath-catching sensations.

'Gael...' she murmured.

He shook his head, perhaps answering his own question. Perhaps caught in the burgeoning rapture of their union. He moved. He groaned. His head went back as he withdrew and thrust again.

'*Dios mio*, you feel sensational,' he muttered roughly.

'Gael...'

He withdrew and thrust again, his mouth dropping to hers for a searing, groan-laced kiss. 'Yes, Goldie. My name on your lips. Don't stop. I want to hear it.'

And she wanted to say it, she realised. So she did.

He set the pace—slow at first, then faster, building a conflagration within and between them that soon raged out of control. With it came a feverish need to touch, to kiss, to taste, to bite. Her nails raked and dug in as he took her higher. His fingers fisted in her hair, and he devoured her mouth as pleasure overtook them.

When the bough broke her cries mingled with his unfettered roar. Guttural words in Spanish poured from his lips as his climax pulled him under. Then Gael half collapsed on top of her, catching himself at the last moment to roll them over.

Hearts racing, they gulped air into their starving lungs, their hands unable to stop moving over each other's sweat-coated flesh.

But eventually their heartbeats calmed. Hands stilled. Breath was restored.

Gael pulled himself free, unable to find adequate words to sum up what had happened in the last hour. He left the bed and entered the bathroom without looking at the woman whose body he'd just shamelessly gorged himself on. He wasn't usually so lacking in after-sex small talk, but for the life of him he couldn't seem to locate his tongue.

Entering the bathroom, he shut the door behind him, then leaned weakly against it. His body still thrummed with what he could only describe as the most sensational sex he'd ever had in his life. But already tendrils of regret burrowed beneath his skin.

This shouldn't have happened. Not like this. Not when the phone call with his mother and her blatant confirmation that she was once again embroiled in an affair with Tomas Aguilar had set him on the finest, most dangerous edge.

Because the mere mention of his father's name had triggered more memories. Memories that had left him deeply puzzled as to why his mother—who should know better—was once again taking this degrading path.

For Tomas Aguilar, Katerina Vega had been a salacious means to a calculated end the first time round. Tomas had admitted as much when Gael had confronted him on his twenty-first birthday. Just as he'd admitted what Gael had always been too afraid to learn—that he'd been an unfortunate consequence of that game of emotional roulette.

Personally, his illegitimacy had long ceased to distress

him—simply because he didn't give it much cerebral capacity. It was a buried burr, cemented over with time and distance, and he'd learned to live with it. The taunts from his childhood were in the past, as was the village where he and his mother had been relentlessly stigmatised as outsiders and homewreckers. Even his inability to sustain a relationship past a month or two had worked out for him in the long run by diverting his focus to empire-building.

And yet all these years later he'd yet to succeed in getting that last damning statement out of his head.

'Tú estás un error...'

'You are a mistake.'

Gael knew it was partly that voiced statement that made him feel relief each time he left Alejandro's presence. His half-brother was a lot of things, but Gael knew he was not a mistake to the parents who'd created him. And while Alejandro had preceded Gael in leaving Spain, for reasons similar to his own, witnessing him taking steps to confront his past...and succeeding...left Gael still feeling an annihilating bitterness every time he thought of Tomas Aguilar.

So he'd chosen not to think of his father at all.

But now, with his mother's actions—which he was growing more convinced were of her own volition this time—he couldn't think of anything *but*!

He'd let his emotions get the better of him tonight. Perhaps even taken advantage of Goldie because of it.

Cursing, he moved from the door to the sink. About to remove the condom, he looked down. Froze. And cursed some more.

No. It couldn't be. She was in her twenties. She couldn't be a virgin. And yet the evidence of blood, the confirmation of his suspicion when he'd taken her, was glaring and unmistakable.

Dios mio.

Shock morphed into a different sensation. Had this been a trap? A way to secure a surer payday?

Disposing of the condom, he washed himself and stalked back into the bedroom, ready to confront her.

Except Goldie was curled on her side, fast asleep.

For ten minutes he paced the room, unaccustomed indecision plaguing him. Then, once he knew there was only one way to play this, he turned and headed for his dressing room.

CHAPTER SIX

THE WORST POSSIBLE CHOICE in a sea of bad choices.

She'd gone to sleep dreading those words were true but they were the first to slam across her mind the moment Goldie woke up. Because even before she opened her eyes she knew things wouldn't look better in the bright light of day.

Not after Gael had hurried away after making love to her as if hell's demons snapped at his heels.

Not after being left alone with nothing but her thoughts to occupy her.

The beginnings of doubt and disappointment at what she'd done crowded her every thought process.

The bottom line was that she'd found a neat argument to give herself permission to sleep with Gael. But in the cold light of day those arguments rang disturbingly hollow. She'd indulged herself simply because she'd been too weak to resist the temptation of the most compelling man she'd ever met.

Sure, she could forgive herself for it—eventually—but in succumbing to momentary madness had she given up more than her virginity? Had she also burned bridges in the career she'd fought tooth and nail to succeed in forging for herself? She didn't need the internet to confirm to her that Gael Aguilar had power and clout. Nor was she naive enough to think she could escape unscathed from her one mistake should he be indiscreet enough to whisper about what had happened between them.

She only had one choice. She had to talk to him—make it clear that they were to treat what had happened between them last night as the transient indulgence it was and nothing else. She wasn't above begging for his discretion if it came to that. She had too much to lose.

Turning over, she opened her eyes.

To see an empty space next to her.

She wasn't surprised to find him gone. After all he'd left her wide awake, seconds after they'd made love, and locked himself into the bathroom. Had she not been completely shattered, she would have dragged herself off to the other bedroom to avoid what must have been an even more humiliating sight for Gael when he'd emerged from the bathroom.

Had he even slept in the same bed with her? Or had he availed himself of one of the unoccupied bedrooms so he wouldn't have to look at her or deal with her? Had she been so disappointing that she hadn't merited six minutes, never mind his customary six weeks? Not that she'd intended to have that long a time with him!

Her face heated as humiliation mounted. She didn't want to acknowledge the dull pain in her chest, but Goldie was a believer in facing problems head-on. Yes, she'd given her virginity to a man who hadn't even acknowledged it. A part of her was glad of that. But another small part mourned her lost innocence because, while the experience had been phenomenal, she couldn't think about it without thinking about what had come after. Without thinking about why her chest felt tight with unsettling emotions she was too anxious to examine.

Dragging herself upright, she looked around her. The dressing gown was draped over a chair, her underwear laid on top of it. More heat surged into her face at the thought of Gael touching her things. Pushing the disturbing thought away, she rose, then gasped as her body's discomfort registered. The enormity of what she'd done grew as she gathered the clothes and made her way back to her room.

If she'd still kept the diary she'd used to as a teenager,

the events of the last twenty-four hours would have been
emblazoned in red ink across her trusted leather-bound
notebook. But, alas, they were to be confined in a secret
vault in her mind, only to be examined on the rarest of occasions at some remote point in the future, when humiliation didn't burn this bright or this painfully.

She was debating in her mind exactly when that occasion would be when she entered the other bedroom suite.

The note propped up against her pillow was hard to
miss, with the hotel's distinctive burgundy and cream stationery standing out against the white sheets, and the bold
black scrawl across the paper.

Trepidation eating at her, she walked across the room
and plucked up the folded paper.

Goldie,
I've decided to go a different way with the discussed
role. The driver will be waiting when you're ready
to take you wherever you need to go. Take as much
time as you need.
The contents of the envelope are a token of my
gratitude for your time.
G

Even before her numb fingers had located and opened
the envelope, which had been propped up behind the note,
sheets of icy rage were bucketing down on her.

Yesterday Goldie had thought that casting director asking her to go to his hotel suite for sex if she wanted the
role she'd auditioned for was bad enough. Now she knew
the depths of true humiliation.

She wasn't even sure why she took out the sheaf of dollar bills and counted them. Perhaps she wanted to know
just how much her degradation was worth to Gael Agui-

lar. It certainly wasn't because she intended to use a single cent of it.

Ten thousand dollars.

Hot, humiliating tears filled her eyes. When they dripped down her cheeks she angrily swiped them away. Was this how her mother had felt each time she was used and discarded?

Goldie wasn't proud that she'd inadvertently walked in her mother's shoes. But she hadn't done it through choice. She didn't deserve this!

Her anger wiping away the last of her humiliation, she dressed in last night's clothes, uncaring of how she'd look walking across the famous hotel's lobby. Her rage would insulate her just fine.

She stopped in the bathroom long enough to wash her face and tidy her hair before she exited the suite, the note and the envelope full of cash clutched tight in her fist.

A butler of indeterminate age emerged as she entered the lavish living room. 'Good morning, miss. Would you like some breakfast?' he asked in cultured tones.

Putting on her best acting skills, she smiled and shook her head. 'No, thank you. Is it possible to summon the driver?'

'Of course, miss. Would you like me to tell him the destination or would you prefer to relay it yourself?'

'I'll take care of it. Thank you.'

The butler nodded and crossed over to a nearby phone. After a short conversation he returned. 'He's pulling up now, miss. If you'd allow me to escort you…?'

He led her out to the private marble-floored foyer and into the lift that solely served the presidential suite. Stepping in with her, he swiped a gold access card and pressed the button for the ground floor. Goldie was thankful for his discretion as they exited onto a side street that led to Fifth Avenue, but she couldn't stop herself from wondering how many times this butler-driver scene had been staged to facilitate Gael's predilection for one-night stands.

The very thought filled her with even more distaste and anger, darkening her mood as she emerged into the sunlight.

The limo was parked only steps from the revolving doors, its driver standing attentively at the back door. He tipped his hat when he saw her, his face politely neutral.

Goldie hated herself for the lie she was about to tell, but she would never be able to live with herself if she let this go unchallenged. She couldn't bear the thought that Gael Aguilar would reside in his lofty kingdom, content that he'd bought and paid for her and was therefore free of wrongdoing. So she waited until the butler had retreated before she faced the driver and waved the scribbled note.

'Gael left me a message that you were to take me wherever I wanted to go?'

'Yes, miss,' the driver responded.

'Well, I'd like to go home, but now the silly man wants me to have breakfast with him before I do. And after my unfortunate mugging last night I don't have a phone to call and tell him I can't. Can you take me to where he is, please?' she pleaded.

The driver started to frown.

Goldie hurriedly continued. 'It'd serve him right for me to just let you take me home, but I don't want to get into another fight with Gael. Not for another twenty-four hours, at least! So help a girl out—please?' She put on her best smile.

After the briefest hesitation, he nodded. 'Of course, miss. He's not too far away.'

'Thank you.' Goldie expelled a secret sigh of relief as he opened the back door and helped her in. The moment the door shut she unclenched her fists and closed her eyes as a deep shudder of unexpended adrenaline rushed through her.

The limo started to move and she was thrown back to last night. She should have walked away, found the nearest police station and taken her chances with the men in blue rather than the man in a black suit.

Pursing her lips, she squashed down might-have-beens and caught the driver's eye in the rearview mirror. 'Is he... is he in a meeting?'

Now she was doing this, the thought of an audience made her cringe—but not enough to alter her decision.

'Yes, miss. The production meeting should be done in half an hour.'

She fought back slight trepidation, nodded and murmured her thanks. Trying to calm her nerves was no use. Her heart was thrumming loud enough to block out the busy sounds of New York traffic as they traversed Midtown.

When the driver pulled up in front of a sheer glass office tower Goldie almost lost her nerve. The bundle of cash clutched in her fist—the representation of the grossest insult she'd ever suffered—spurred her on.

She exited the car and nodded her thanks.

The driver said, 'He's on the tenth floor, I believe. I've called the receptionist. She'll let you in. And, miss...?'

Goldie paused. 'Yes?'

'He probably deserves what's coming to him, but go easy on him.'

Her eyes widened. The tall, heavyset man, who might easily double as a bodyguard, doffed his cap with a discreet smile before getting back into the car. Bemused, she walked into the building, wondering why the driver was giving her access to confront his boss if he'd seen through her ruse.

Maybe he felt Gael deserved it? On account of having done it before?

Her bewilderment increased as the lift rushed to the tenth floor. But by the time she exited and was shown to the conference room her anger was firmly in place. She shoved open the double doors and entered.

Gael sat at the head of a large table, flanked by executives on either side. She didn't bother to stop and count how many people were in the room, but she knew all eyes had turned to train on her.

He saw her, froze mid-speech, his eyes widening, wary and watchful. On a screen to the side of him a vaguely familiar man also stopped talking and glanced her way.

'Goldie—'

'This is how you operate, is it?' She waved the envelope at him from the opposite end of the oval table. Her voice shook with anger, but she didn't care. 'What's the twenty-first-century version of *wham-bam, thank you, ma'am*? And, seriously, after *that* mind-blowing night I would've thought I'd warrant at least fifty thousand! Are you sure you don't want to revise the sum? After all, sleeping with a big, bad boss like you would gain me upwards of few *hundred* thousand if I should take it to the press, hmm?' she sliced at him.

He surged to his feet, planting his hands on top of the table as his cold eyes glared dire warning at her. 'Goldie, this isn't the time—'

'Or the place? I beg to differ. I think this is *exactly* the time to show you what I can do. Isn't that what you asked for last night? For me to show you what I can do? And weren't your exact words something along the lines of, "*You're good. So very good*"? So what changed your mind between last night and this morning? I think I deserve to know that at the very least, don't you?'

His jaw clenched for one heart-stopping second. 'If you know what's good for you—'

She laughed—a bitter, spiky sound that didn't feel one little bit natural. 'What's *good* for me? I think we both know I made one gross misjudgement after another when I chose to trust a single word you said. I may be an actress, Gael, but you were very good at pretending too. Maybe you should try your hand at acting. But I need two small favours from you, if you'd be so kind?'

His jaw clenched. *'Sí?'* he said through gritted teeth.

'First of all, the next time you come across me being mugged, do me a favour and keep walking. I'm absolutely sure I don't need your brand of chivalry. And secondly…'

Darkened hazel eyes glared at her across the gleaming table. 'Yes?'

She ripped open the envelope, pinched the dollar bills between her fingers and flung the whole lot across the table. 'Take your sleazy money and shove it where the sun doesn't shine!'

Beneath the flying bills, stunned silence gripped the whole room. Gael's eyes blazed with incandescent rage.

Knowing she'd struck her mark, Goldie dramatically brushed her hands clean, then began to walk backwards, her eyes still connected with his, a triumphant smile curving her mouth. She'd clawed back some of her dignity. She might have cratered her career in the process, but that was a problem to be tackled another day. Her immediate problem for now was to find a way to get home. It looked as if she'd have to plough deeper into her meagre savings for a taxi ride after all—

The sound of applause froze her thoughts and her feet. Her mouth dropped open as more hands joined in with the clapping. On the screen, the man she now recognised as a famous director pumped his fist, his face split into a wide grin as he pointed an accusing finger at Gael.

'Gael, you sly, brilliant man! You spend twenty minutes laying into me for the delay to the production when all along you had *this* up your sleeve?' The man barked out another laugh, before turning his gaze to Goldie. 'You— Goldie Whoever-you-are—just made my day! I can already see the headlines…not that I court them of course. The media will lap you right up. Nothing captures the movie-going public's imagination more than a newbie blowing their socks off. I don't think it's too premature to say welcome to the team—'

'Ethan, shut up for a moment,' Gael bit out, his gaze still locked on her.

He hadn't so much as moved a muscle since she'd flung his money in his face. And with each moment that passed she feared the look in his eyes would erupt into actual flames.

She'd made her point. She needed to get out of here. *Fast.* Despite the crazy talk spewing from the mouth of the award-winning director. Another step back brought her to the double doors.

'Come on. You trusted me with this project, Gael. Gave me carte blanche to find the best actress for the lead character. I know my broken leg hasn't helped matters, but—' he tipped his head towards Goldie, another smile splitting his face '—with this gem you've discovered we can start production almost immediately.'

Goldie frowned. 'I… What…? I don't know what you're talking—'

'Gentlemen, ladies—excuse me for a few minutes, *por favor*?' Gael interrupted once more.

He was rounding the table in quick, purposeful strides, his eyes cutting into her, silencing any further speech she could muster. Galvanised by the look in his eyes, she turned sharply, slammed her hands against the door in her rush to escape. When it opened she rushed through with fast, skin-saving strides towards the lift.

She'd poked the dragon in his den. Woken it. No need to stick around and watch the resulting inferno.

She reached the lift doors just as hands closed over her arms. Turned her firmly around.

Burnished eyes blazed down at her. 'You think you can create a spectacle like that and get away scot-free?' he seethed.

'It was nothing short of what you deserved,' she launched back, her hands going to the hands holding her prisoner in a bid to prise them off her. 'Let me go.'

He dragged her close and fired under his breath, 'Not until you're made to understand the consequences of what you did back there.'

'Whatever they are, they were worth it,' she returned defiantly.

A dark cloud descended on his face. 'Are you sure?'

'Yes, I'm one hundred per cent sure! Let me go, Gael.'

Behind her the lift door pinged open.

'Take a minute, Goldie. Think about what you're doing. Any hint that what you have just done *wasn't* an audacious audition could spell the end of your career. Are you prepared to take the risk?'

'To make my point that I'm not a whore you leave money on the bed for when you're done? *Absolutely.*'

His nostrils flared and a look passed through his eyes. Regret, maybe? Or surprise? She gritted her teeth.

'I don't think of you like that.'

'Oh, good—I'm so glad we've got that established. What about your note? You've "*decided to go a different route*"? The only difference between you actively pursuing me last night and leaving me that poor excuse of a *Dear Jane* note this morning is the fact that we slept together. So pardon me if my powers of deduction are right on point!'

His jaw visibly tightened. 'Calm down, Goldie.'

'No—and stop saying my name like that.'

'Like what?'

'Like I'm a recalcitrant child you're trying to manage. I'm done talking to you. I want nothing to do with you. Let me go and I'll try to forget we ever met.'

'*Santo cielo.* You should stop pursuing a career in acting and form an international debate team. You'd absolutely excel at it.'

Without waiting for an answer to his damning of her character, he dropped his hand from her arm to her wrist and dragged her towards another set of doors.

Shoving them open, he led her into an empty conference room, making sure to block her exit.

She didn't want to look at him—didn't want to be close enough to him to breathe in his unique scent, to watch the beauty of his square-jawed face and be reminded of how she'd explored his body last night, how he'd moved so powerfully inside her. So she stalked as far away from him as possible and stared out of the window at the Midtown traffic.

'Ignoring me isn't going to make this conversation conclude any faster,' he delivered.

She placed her hands on the window ledge to steady herself. She wanted to drop her forehead to the window too, but that would be one weak gesture too far. 'I told you, I have nothing further to say to you. Nor do I imagine you have anything to say to me. Your little note and the deplorable cash buy-off said it all for you. But I'm prepared to grant you two minutes. Say what you dragged me in here to say, then I'm leaving. And don't even *think* about trying to stop me.'

She sensed him prowling behind her for a full minute before he spoke. 'The money wasn't supposed to be taken the way you took it.'

What her laughter lacked in humour it more than made up for in scorn. 'Right. And I was born yesterday.'

'*Dios...*'

She heard his deep inhalation.

'I'm good at reading people, Goldie. Reading between the lines. Deny it all you want, but you're in a fix. Otherwise you wouldn't have fought for dear life to hang on to that tattered bag last night. And you wouldn't have chosen not to call a cab to take you home if you'd been able to afford it. Unemployment means different things to different people. I suspect in your case it means near destitution.'

Shame dredged her, sending prickles of tears to her eyes. She blinked it away rapidly. 'Bravo for that incisive dissection of my life.'

He sighed. 'Hate me all you want for pointing out the obvious. But you also mentioned that you needed a job quickly. The money was my gesture of assistance—'

Pride and anger made her whirl around. He was standing a few feet behind her. Tall and imposing and altogether too much for her roiling senses. 'I'm not a charity case!'

'No, you're not. And I didn't think you were.'

He paced a few steps before shoving his hands in his pockets. She was beginning to notice it was his self-calming gesture.

She supposed he needed calming after her calling him out and making a spectacle of him at his meeting.

'Are we done?'

He shook his head in a decisive movement. 'No, we're not done. You'll accept my apologies if I didn't make it clear that the money had nothing to do with what happened between us last night. It was a gesture of generosity, not payment for services rendered.'

A large dose of the hurt that lingered in her chest abated, but she wasn't about to show her relief. 'Fine, apology accepted, but you can keep your money.'

She started to walk past him. One hand shot out of his pocket and slid over her hip. Goldie jerked out of the way, in no way wanting to be reminded of what it felt like to be in his arms.

'Please don't touch me.'

His jaw tightened but his hand balled and dropped back to his side. 'As you wish. But before you walk out the door and demolish the chance you've created for yourself, stop and think for a moment.'

'What do you mean, the chance I've created?'

One sardonic eyebrow went up. 'Are you really so blind that you can't see the bigger picture?' He stabbed a thumb in the direction of the adjacent conference room. 'In your burning need to make a point you've turned an unfortunate event into an opportunity. Are you going to cut off your nose to spite your face by walking away now?' He was almost taunting her.

She folded her arms. 'Whatever was going on in there is none of my business. If they've mistaken me for the actress you wanted to cast then you can explain their error to them. I'm leaving.'

He laughed. 'After going to all this effort to create a buzz for yourself?'

'Careful, there, or that apology you uttered a few minutes ago will seem like something out of a past lifetime and I'll resume detesting you.'

He shrugged. 'I state things as I see them. You came here to make a point. You've made it. Don't let the effort you've put in go to waste.'

'Are you seriously trying to tell me to capitalise on you treating me like a prostitute?'

A look crossed his face. 'Don't make this emotional, Goldie.'

'Wow. I'm sorry if I'm not as cut-throat as you.' She shook her head. 'Why are you even pursuing this? Your note was quite clear. You woke up this morning and decided you didn't want me after all.' She thought it best to ignore the telling gleam that reflected briefly in his eyes. 'So what's changed?'

The jaw already clenched tight hardened. Silence ticked by until she was sure he wouldn't answer.

Leave, her hammering heart urged. *Before things get any weirder.*

'Are you going to answer me, Gael?' she blurted.

Eyes raked her from head to toe before meeting hers full-on. 'You were a virgin. And you didn't think to tell me.'

Goldie swallowed. Fought the heat and trembling that had begun in her lower limbs. Suddenly she wished she'd stayed by the window, not been standing on her own two legs for this unexpected turn in the conversation. Thankfully, her legs held her up. And her chin rose when she commanded.

'I don't remember any instance during the night when we were obliged to exchange sexual histories. Perhaps you thought we'd be there all night while you recounted yours?'

The barb struck home, made his nostrils flare in pure Latin temper before he reined it in. 'Are you saying being divested of your innocence meant nothing to you?'

The harsh, condemning tone was back. But she wasn't about to stand for it any longer.

'What I choose to do with my virginity is my business. Tell me the experience was ruined for you because of it and I'll apologise.'

His eyes gleamed with pure carnal memory before he blinked, but that look singed her very skin.

'It wasn't ruined. Far from it,' he returned gutturally.

That blush she was fighting won the round. Heat surged into her face and she averted her gaze for a second. 'So what was the problem?'

'The problem is *why me*? Why now? Innocence at your age is rare. I can't help but draw certain conclusions.'

She stared at him, her brain firing wildly at her. It took a heartbeat or three for her to realise where he was coming from. Horror made her hand fly to her mouth. 'You think I hung on to my virgin status just in case a guy like you came along so I could hawk it for a huge payday?' Shock made her voice squeak.

He had the grace to look momentarily confused before his inscrutable expression returned. 'That scenario isn't a foreign concept and I'm sure you're aware of that.'

'I'm aware of no such thing! I'm not sure what circles you move in… Wait—scratch that. After my run-in with your conscience-free ex I can hazard a guess as to the depths your ilk are prepared to sink to for your sick pleasures. But think about this for a second. *If* I were that avaricious, don't you think I'd have negotiated my price *before* I slept with you?' she demanded.

He levelled a hard gaze at her, in no way swayed by her argument. 'That sort of innocence isn't always easy to prove before the event.'

Her mouth dropped open for several heartbeats before she managed to shake her head. 'My God, why…? How did you get like this?' she whispered, sheets of ice dredging her stomach at his blatant accusation.

His face closed completely and his every feature was devoid of emotion. 'I'm a bastard, *literally*—and, I'm told, figuratively. I've learned to accept that nothing that feels that good comes without a price.'

Goldie held her breath, unwilling to admit in any way that the newest emotion which had risen to join the riot of feelings inside her was sympathy for him. He was the bad guy here. He was the one causing her pain.

'Please take it from me that what I gave last night had no strings attached whatsoever. And then please let me go.'

Again a touch of confusion clouded his forehead. 'I don't think you understand why I brought you in here. Regardless of what I thought last night—and I'm prepared to concede that I may have got the wrong end of the stick with you—your performance in there has guaranteed you the part.'

There was zero pleasure in hearing that. She shook her head again. 'Why?'

'Because, believe it or not, that scene you just enacted is uncannily similar to one from the script. You weren't acting, but they thought you were. And you've won them over—especially my director.'

'Right. And you?'

He cast her an inscrutable look before he shrugged. 'What I think is no longer relevant. The only question now is, do you want the part or not?'

CHAPTER SEVEN

GOLDIE EYED HERSELF in the mirror as the make-up artist applied the final touches to her make-up. Her character, Elena Milton, was the same age as her, so there wasn't much to be done in the way of make-up for the early scenes—especially since the scene they were about to shoot was one that required her to be makeup-less.

The director, Ethan Ryland, was waiting for the sun to begin setting on the plains of the KwaZulu-Natal game park, where the next scene of *Soul's Triumph* was being shot.

In her hand she clutched the script, which she always kept close by even though she knew her part by heart and could recite every other part in the script too.

When the make-up artist pronounced her ready, Goldie jumped off the stool and headed outside. While most of the cast and crew chose to stay in the cool confines of their air-conditioned trailers and chalet when they weren't shooting, she preferred to absorb the stunning beauty of South Africa's south-eastern province every chance she got.

Probably because she still couldn't believe she was there.

The experience so far had been surreal, and Goldie couldn't believe they were already halfway to being done with the movie. She had certainly learned a lot in the last five weeks. And to think she'd never imagined she would be here at all…

After Gael had thrown his gauntlet at her feet that morning, just over a month ago, she'd spent a torn, frantic twenty-four hours weighing the pros and cons of accepting the less than wholesome opportunity he had dangled once again within reach.

At her mother's urging to do as much research as possible, she'd succumbed and looked up the man she'd given her virginity to on the internet. She'd come away stunned, albeit with a half-hearted understanding of why Gael Aguilar reacted with suspicion to everyone around him. The trait wasn't admirable by any stretch, and nor was it forgivable when it pertained to her. But it was clear that the sheer prestige and power he wielded along with his half-brother, Alejandro Aguilar, through their company, was enough to draw an army of sycophants and other unsavoury characters.

Even those who sacrificed their virginities in the hope of a pot of gold…

Whatever.

Had she believed in that sort of thing, Goldie would have toyed with the notion that destiny was hell-bent on giving her this role. Even after Ethan's repeated assurances that he was going to stop auditioning because he believed he'd found his actress she hadn't been convinced.

She didn't doubt for a second that Gael's involvement in the project was what had made her initially reticent about taking the part. Gael might have accepted that he'd got her motives wrong, but the hurt hadn't quite gone away. Probably because neither had the cynicism she glimpsed in his eyes whenever he looked at her.

It had only been after her second meeting with Ethan and his team—minus Gael—two days later that Goldie had started to entertain the idea that the opportunity *was* one she could grasp and launch a career out of.

Before that, though, there'd been her mother to contend with.

Gloria Beckett had been beyond ecstatic that her daughter had landed the plum role in a big production movie.

But even as they'd celebrated with a trip to her mother's favourite restaurant, at Gloria's insistence, she'd worried about being absent from home for the long weeks shooting the movie would take.

She'd eventually divulged her worry to Ethan, only to find out Gael had lined up a list of sober companions for her to interview for her mother. Her mother had resisted at first, but once Goldie had made it a condition of her acceptance or rejection of the role Gloria had relented and let her hire Patience, the middle-aged companion.

In the week before she'd flown to Vancouver, where the other half of the film had been shot, Goldie had been able to rest easy when she'd seen how well Patience and Gloria got along.

Now, as she watched a family of elephants foraging, from the porch of the timber chalet which housed their on-location skeleton crew, she allowed herself a peaceful sigh and a small smile.

Ethan and the crew were a dream to work with. And as for the story...

She glanced down at the script of *Soul's Triumph*. The story of Elena Milton and Alfonso Veron was unbelievably powerful, at times disturbingly heartbreaking, but utterly sublime. A tale of triumph against adversity, it charted the lives of two unlikely souls each tied to a different destiny from the moment they met. But while common sense and inevitable heartache dictated they take different paths, they were continually drawn, for better or worse, back to each other, in an often shocking and volatile relationship that spanned decades and brought untold hardship to their families.

Today's shoot was the first meeting between Elena and Alfonso. Goldie had already met her Spanish lead, an actor in his mid-twenties who spoke very little English. Although he delivered his lines perfectly, conversation off-camera was minimal—a fact for which Goldie was secretly glad.

Even now, weeks later, she was still grappling with the tumultuous twelve hours she'd spent with Gael and wasn't in the mood to deal with much else, even friendly banter between co-actors. The crew for the most part also left her alone. Sure, they'd invited her along on their free day excursions, and she'd partaken of a few, and for dinner and drinks, of which she'd accepted none. She didn't think she would be able to accept a social invitation from anyone for a while after the Heidi debacle.

'Goldie, we're heading out in five minutes. You ready?'

She nodded and smiled, gave a thumbs-up to Ethan as he joined her on the porch. He returned the gesture with the tip of the crutch he still had to use, then turned to supervise the crew loading equipment into a Jeep in the car park.

Ten minutes later they set off, and Goldie found herself smiling again as the stunning landscape unfolded before her.

Ethan caught her smile. 'Is this your first time in Africa?' he asked.

'No, but it's my first to this part of Africa, and my first time when I know I'll keep a vivid recollection of it,' she answered.

He frowned. 'You've lost me.'

She laughed, although the sound was tinged with a deep-rooted sadness. 'I'm half-Ghanaian, but my last visit to my father's homeland was when I was a child. I don't remember much of it, and I haven't had a chance to visit since then, for various reasons.'

'Oh, right…' There was a note of sympathy in Ethan's voice but he didn't probe further, for which she was grateful.

They arrived at the location of the shoot and were greeted by the animal handler who would be keeping an eye on the cheetah needed for this scene. None of the animals in the private game reserve were tame, but one or two had been hand-reared due to injury. One in particular, a gorgeous, graceful cheetah named Asha, had won a part in the movie.

Goldie kept a respectful distance from the animal as she was readied. When she got her cue she made sure her running shoes were laced properly and waited for Ethan's signal.

Being chased by a semi-tame cheetah was in equal parts terrifying and exhilarating. Doing it three times, until Ethan was happy and before the sun dipped into the horizon, was a touch nerve-racking. But she managed it, and delivered her lines alongside the actor playing Alfonso, then smiled widely when she got a fist-pump of approval from Ethan.

'Scene Three is officially in the bag. Although I would *never* recommend getting chased by a wild animal in the savannah as a way to meet the love of your life for the first time.'

Amid the laughter and high fives for a job well done, Goldie looked up. And saw Gael lounging against the hood of the four-wheel drive furthest away from the cluster of crew vehicles.

Gael watched her eyes widen as she spotted him. Shock was swiftly replaced by deep wariness as she stared at him. The wide smile on her face from a moment ago faded to nothing.

He ignored the tiny spurt of regret that look elicited and shoved his hands into his pockets. It was only a matter of time before the rest of the cast and crew noted his presence. Gael had wanted a quiet moment before he was interrupted. He'd had his quiet moment, but he'd used it to question why he was here at all.

Sure, Alejandro and the Ishikawa brothers—his partners—had questioned him extensively on how the project was going, and he had promised them an update. But he could easily have video-conferenced with Ethan for a full report, as he'd done in the weeks since the project had got underway. He hadn't needed to fly for almost a day to inspect proceedings for himself.

But, hell, he was here now. And he didn't want to examine why, for the first time since he'd reached adulthood, he'd gone for a long stretch without taking a woman to his bed. He didn't want to examine why the only woman who seemed to stir his senses was the woman he'd shared a stunningly memorable night with. One who wanted nothing to do with him. One he knew deep in his gut he needed to stay away from.

And yet here he was…

He watched Goldie glance around her, as if she was debating whether to acknowledge or ignore his presence. Gael smiled to himself. *He'd* give himself a wide berth too if he could—especially after the few weeks he'd had.

It had started with his visit to Chicago three weeks ago, and Alejandro asking him to be his best man. It had gone downhill from there.

Every aspect of the Atlas Group's business was running like a well-oiled machine. And yet he couldn't focus—couldn't get past the thought that the past seemed to be on a collision course with his future: namely in the form of the father he'd put out of his life and his mind a very long time ago.

When, at the end of a fraught business meeting, Alejandro had suggested Gael return to his home base in Silicon Valley to get his head straight he'd wholeheartedly agreed, jumped on his plane—and headed to South Africa instead.

And now the woman who'd taken up more of his

thoughts than he was even marginally happy with was trying to pretend he didn't exist.

The crew were beginning to pack up. Ethan spotted him and waved, but Gael's cool nod as he approached Goldie thankfully kept the other man away.

He reached her. Stared down at her. Her nostrils quivered slightly as she stared boldly up at him. The African sun had lent her skin an even more vibrant tone, which made her stunning violet eyes more vivid and alluring. Recalling how silky her skin was, how warm and enthralling it had felt to touch her, he was glad his hands were deep in his pockets. His senses were poised on the edge as it was. He didn't want to add touching where it wasn't wanted to his list of things to deal with. But not touching didn't mean he couldn't look his fill.

His gaze raked the khaki-coloured dress she wore with a tightly cinched belt that emphasised her small waist, then her bare legs and the ankle boots adorning her feet. She looked capable and utilitarian—as her part demanded. But with the shoot over she'd let her hair loose, and dark gold corkscrew curls bounced over her shoulders. Again the memory of having his fist locked in those waves tore through him, powerful and fierce. He clenched his gut against the sensation.

'It's good to see you, Goldie.'

'*Is* it?' She stopped, pursed her lips and shook her head. 'No. Sorry—I promised myself the next time I saw you I'd make an extra effort to be civil, so here goes.' She took a deep breath. 'Thank you for sorting out the sober companion for my mother. You didn't have to, but I really appreciate you doing that…so, thanks.'

He allowed the smile that tugged at his lips—the smile that had been nearly non-existent these last few weeks— to filter through. 'You're welcome. I wanted to give you peace of mind. I trust everything's going well in that department?'

She nodded, her eyes rising from where they had settled on his chest to meet his. She even deigned to offer a tiny smile. 'Yes, they're getting on like a house on fire, or so I'm told.'

'I'm glad to hear it.' He didn't want to begrudge her the peace of mind that was sorely lacking in his own life.

Her eyes searched his. Gael wasn't sure what she found, but her face lost a little of its tightness. He exhaled, realised he was breathing a little easier, and then turned when he sensed they were no longer alone.

Ethan approached on his crutches. 'The crew are about to head out, and the cast and I are heading for the airstrip. Goldie, do you want to join us? Or...?' he paused, his eyebrows lifted.

Gael shook his head. 'There's no need. I have my plane here. We can all fly back to Durban on my jet.' He nodded to Ethan's plaster cast. 'I'm sure you'll be much more comfortable on my plane than on the turboprop.'

Ethan laughed. 'Now, there's an offer I'm not about to refuse. We'll meet you at the plane?'

Gael nodded. Waited until his director hobbled off before he turned to find Goldie regarding him with a steady look.

'Without inciting an argument, can I ask why you're here?' she asked.

He shrugged. 'My partners wanted an update. So did I. And Durban is great at this time of year, I'm told.'

'So you're here on a working vacation?' she probed.

The inkling that he wasn't wanted deepened a pang he didn't want to acknowledge. About to tell her he hadn't taken a vacation in a decade and wasn't about to take one now, Gael paused. 'Why not? I've been told I'm "grumpy

and insufferable" lately. So maybe a timeout is just what
I need.'

That minuscule smile reappeared. 'Did whoever dared
to make that observation get away with their lives?' she
teased, and fell into step beside him as he headed for the
last remaining vehicle left in the deserted dirt car park of
the game reserve.

'Sadly I had to rule out homicide. Doing away with
my future sister-in-law before she becomes my brother's
wife—or even at any time after that—will *not* end well
for me. My only choice was to remove my grumpiness
from her presence.'

Her smile widened, turned into a laugh.

Something twitched in Gael's chest at the sound—a
feeling of wanting to join in, to revel in her warm amusement at his own expense.

Her cute nose wrinkled when he stopped beside the
truck and stared at him. 'So you're here to foist your
grumpiness on us instead?'

He opened the door and saw her into the passenger seat.
Shutting the door, he leaned an elbow on the open window.
'I'm in the land of cheetahs, fireflies and stunning sunsets,
amongst a thousand other pleasures. I'm certain I'll find a
useful outlet for my mood,' he murmured.

The sparkle in her eyes didn't dim, but her amusement
altered as a different sensation arced between them. Gael
recognised it. Waited for her to recognise it too. He didn't
exactly plan on doing anything about it—she'd made
her feelings abundantly clear that day in his conference
room—but the moment felt too visceral to dismiss. So he
stood there, with her breathtaking face and body mere
inches away, and watched her eyes darken as sexual awareness zapped the air between them.

Abruptly, she averted her gaze from his. 'Can we go,
please?'

'Of course,' he murmured.

Despite his intimation otherwise, he *was* here solely on business. Although in hindsight he accepted that he might have handled their morning-after differently, he stood by his decision to keep his hands off Goldie Beckett.

For one thing, she was now effectively his employee—and mixing business with pleasure never boded well in the long run. His brother and Elise might have proved the exception to the rule, but statistics weren't in favour of such occurrences ending well.

For another, he hadn't forgotten what he'd witnessed in that auditorium at Othello. Her virginity might have proved that she hadn't gone through with the director's proposal, but Gael had seen her allow the director's touch. Had seen her take the keycard, watched her consider the proposal. As much as he wanted to explain that away, he couldn't.

Especially as since then Goldie had as much as admitted that her career was her top priority. That she would do anything to further it. Who knows what would have happened had Gael not come along? Hell, her immediate reaction to being drunk for the first time in her life had been to enquire whether her actions had affected the opportunity he'd been offering her.

On some level Gael admired her dedication, and it was undeniable that she had the talent to back the ambition. But the thought of her doing *whatever it took* left a bitter taste in his mouth, reminding him too much of the issues he was dealing with when it came to his mother. Rightly or wrongly, he couldn't think of one without thinking of the other. They both struck a little too close to home and, despite her attempting to explain herself to the contrary, he hadn't been able to erase Goldie's last performance with that director in the auditorium from his mind.

As a tool for enabling him to keep his hands off her it

was effective, he mused as he slid behind the wheel and turned on the ignition.

The ride to the private airstrip where his plane was parked was conducted in silence, and took less than ten minutes.

On the plane, he let Goldie wander off to take a seat next to Ethan. As much as it struck an unpleasant chord within Gael, he ignored the feeling and struck up a conversation with the actor playing Alfonso, who was glad to connect with a fellow Spaniard, even though Gael only half paid attention to their discourse.

His gaze was drawn inexorably to the woman chatting in low tones to Ethan. Her occasional husky laugh bounced across the space between them and sizzled along Gael's nerve-endings.

He was almost relieved when the plane landed in Durban forty minutes later. This time an appointed driver chauffeured them to Umhlanga and the Oyster Box Hotel, where the cast and crew were staying. After agreeing to have a proper meeting with Ethan the next morning, he trailed after the departing Goldie. She was standing in front of the private lift that served his suite when he joined her.

Her eyes landed on him and widened. 'You're staying in the presidential suite too?'

'According to the bookings manager it's the only suite with a spare bedroom not already taken up by the cast and crew. I hope you don't mind sharing?'

A frown clenched her forehead for a few seconds, before a resolute look slid across her face. 'Of course not. She mentioned that the other room might be used by other people. I just didn't think...'

'That I would be your first room-mate?' he finished.

She eyed him a touch warily as he stepped into the lift beside her. 'Yes. But it's not a problem. The bedrooms are on different floors, so hopefully I won't disturb you too much.'

Her smile was less natural than it had been on their ride back from the game reserve. Gael experienced another bite of regret.

'I will let you know if I'm planning any wild parties.'

This conversation was ridiculous. He wanted her at ease, but he was aware that he himself wasn't at ease. So he let silence rule for the remainder of the short lift journey and their walk to the entrance into the suite.

'Have dinner with me,' he invited.

The offer had been delivered without much forethought when she'd started to beat a hasty retreat towards the stairs that led to the suite upstairs.

She paused. Her sumptuous lips parted. 'I don't think...'

'In the interest of fresh starts and civil leaf-turning, I also wish to make an attempt. You haven't eaten yet, have you?'

Gael wasn't bothered by the knowledge that he was pushing. He was known for remaining civil with the women he'd had liaisons with—Heidi being the only exception—so why not Goldie?

Slowly, she shook her head. 'No, I haven't.'

He nodded, a welling of satisfaction moving through him. 'Do you want to eat out or in?'

'I had planned on taking a shower, then ordering in...'

He crossed to the dining room and returned with a lavish menu, which he held out to her. 'Decide what you want and I'll have it delivered here for us by the time you're done with your shower.'

He saw a look of refusal cross her face before whatever resolution she was striving to achieve forced a nod from her.

'Okay.' She took the menu and scanned it quickly. 'I'll

have the lobster bisque to start, the chicken *involtini* and the lemon cheesecake, please.'

He took the menu from her with a wry smile. 'Nothing local for you? I can recommend something if you prefer?'

She grimaced. 'I tried a selection of dishes a couple of nights ago. They were heavenly, but sadly they didn't agree with me.' She rubbed a hand across her midriff. 'Turns out my constitution isn't as adventurous as my spirit.'

Gael frowned, his gaze following her hand. 'Are you okay?'

'Yes, I'm fine now,' she replied. 'But I think I'll stick to food that I know for now. I'll see you in half an hour?'

He nodded, watched her shapely legs stride up the stairs and then resolutely turned away. They were being civil, sharing a suite like reasonable room-mates—not two people who'd shared a sizzling, passionate few hours in bed a few short weeks ago.

So he *wouldn't* imagine her undressing, stepping into the shower, rubbing shower gel all over her incredibly responsive body...

A low curse flamed from his lips. The libido that hadn't so much as twitched around any other woman he'd come into contact with since he'd slept with Goldie was now threatening to rage out of control.

He crossed to the phone and relayed their dinner order. Then he went into his own room and showered.

She was back downstairs when he emerged, wearing a flowing *boubou* gown in a distinct African print, with her hair brushed loose and wavy. The bold oranges and reds complemented her dark colouring, making her look even more striking.

His gaze travelled from her exquisite face and down her body. When she caught his eyes on her bare feet, she grimaced and wrinkled her toes.

'I hope you don't mind? My feet have been in hot and

sweaty boots all day. I can't bear the thought of confining them again.'

For some absurd reason he couldn't pull his attention from her peach-painted toenails, nor stop himself from stepping closer to breathe in the unique scent he was sure didn't come out of a tube of luxury product. Goldie's scent was one he hadn't been able to get out of his mind.

'Of course not,' he replied, his voice curiously gruff.

Her smile dragged his eyes up. Gael found himself absorbing it, wanting to bask in it. To perpetuate it long into the night.

Dios, what was wrong with him?

'Would you like a drink?' he asked abruptly.

Her smile dimmed.

Do better. He needed to do better. As much as he enjoyed sparring with an argumentative Goldie, he admitted he liked this 'new leaf' version better. She still had the fire he was drawn to, but in this place and time he could almost forget that there was a facet of her character he quietly despised. It was a naked ambition she was willing to do just about anything to achieve, and he knew he wouldn't be able to abide it into the future.

The future? What future?

He had no plans of reinitiating or prolonging anything.

He'd built an empire.

He'd dated beautiful women.

And he'd vowed never to marry any of them because, inevitably, each and every one of them showed their true gold-digging and opportunistic characters eventually.

On top of that he had known from an early age that he would never produce a child who might feel a trace of the sting of rejection he'd suffered.

Nothing would change that particular vow. Not even Alejandro's engagement and the subtle hints about revisiting old ground that he kept tossing Gael's way. That, most of all, was a grenade he intended to keep tossing back into his brother's lap.

'An apple spritzer?' he tried again, careful to keep his voice even.

Her nod was a touch wary. 'Yes, thank you.'

Although there was a drinks console nearby, Gael crossed the room to the well-stocked bar, to give himself—and her—time to adjust, regroup.

He heard her pad over to the large rectangular windows that opened onto the wide patio and the stunning view of the Indian Ocean beyond. After fixing her drink he poured a glass of burgundy for himself and joined her outside, where the table had been laid by the private butler.

They sipped their drinks and watched the rolling waves hit the shore on the beach down below for a few minutes before their food arrived.

Halfway through their first course she raised her gaze from her plate. 'How long are you planning to stay?' she asked in an even voice, but he detected the thin nerves behind it.

'Until I can no longer avoid my duties as my brother's best man.'

Her eyes widened. 'Your brother's getting married that soon?'

'In ten days,' he answered, aware that the tension he'd hoped to dispel was still very much present.

'Why is it that he's getting married but you're the one who has the jitters?' she asked, and her acuity was a touch disturbing.

'I wish him well, of course, but the inescapable truth is that a lifelong commitment like marriage more often than not fails eventually.'

She frowned. 'You think your brother's marriage is going to fail?'

He shrugged. 'We don't come from admirable stock

when it comes to the sanctity of marriage. He's…brave to want to give it a try, nevertheless.'

Troubled violet eyes connected with his. 'I… What you said back in New York about being—'

'A bastard?' His jaw clenched. He thought about evading the suddenly abrading question, thought about how they'd ended up here in the first place. 'I'm the product of an affair my mother had with Alejandro's *still married* father.'

Her mouth dropped open. 'Oh.'

He took a large sip of wine. '*Sí.* Oh.'

She shook her head. 'I didn't mean *oh* like that. I mean, I'm the last person who should be shocked…' She stopped and frowned. 'If Alejandro's asked you to be his best man, then your relationship with him must be good—so your past circumstances can't matter that much to him?'

Gael recalled their last fraught meeting. Recognised that this time all the tension had been his alone. Although Alejandro had resisted at first, lately he'd been much more open—most likely thanks to the influence of his fiancée, who was open-hearted and open-armed about embracing new family, seeing as her own family situation was lacking.

'The relationship isn't without its challenges, but it's… progressive.'

'So it's progressive now, but you think that relationship will fail too?' she pressed.

He frowned. 'There are always adverse factors at play.'

'And you intend to take those adverse factors lying down, just like you do with your businesses?' she asked lightly as she cut into a piece of chicken.

'I have never failed at a business venture,' he quipped.

'So why are you prepared to write off a sound relationship and watch it fail without putting in as much effort as you would into a business venture?' she parried.

His smile felt as cynical as his soul. 'Because business is conducted and thrives without the single detrimental component that damns us all.'

'And what's that?'

'Useless emotion.'

Her fork stilled and her eyes widened. 'You think emotions are useless?'

'They're more harmful than useless. They cloud judgement and ruin lives.'

Gael knew he'd been unable to hold back the bitterness ravaging him when her face clouded with something close to sympathy.

Goldie shook her head. 'How do you…? I don't understand.'

He gritted his teeth, tried to stem the words that seemed determined to spill. And failed. 'You recall your little story about infidelity and alcoholism?'

'Of course,' she said.

'The former has been the story of my life—what my building blocks are based on. I left Seville over ten years ago and thought I was free of it. Turns out I'm not.'

'Your mother?' she queried cautiously.

A vice tightened around his chest. 'And Alejandro's married father. Version two point zero.'

Anxiety darted across her face at his tone. Her fingers toyed with her water glass before she asked, 'Does Alejandro know? Does his mother know?'

He laughed harshly. 'Alejandro knows. He seems to have found a way to accept it, but I haven't been so fortunate. As for his mother—yes, she knows. Most likely she enjoys the chaos associated with it. They all seem to thrive on it, in fact.'

Enlightenment whispered over her face. 'That's what you were talking about that night? What you meant when you referred to—?'

'Toxic relationships? *Sí,* Goldie *mia.* When it comes to those types of relationships I am vastly knowledgeable.'

Her expressive eyes shadowed. 'I'm so sorry.'

Gael frowned, wondering why those two words sank deep inside him, attempted to soothe a place he'd believed was too mauled by past pain to be still alive. The sensation was so alien it robbed him of breath and speech.

Thankfully the butler arrived with their dessert course. Gael refused the sweet platter in favour of an espresso, hoping the caffeine would clear his head and put a stay on his runaway tongue.

Goldie's cheesecake was set before her with a flourish that drew a small smile from her. He nodded his thanks when his drink was handed to him.

About to gulp down the hot beverage, he looked up, frowning, as Goldie turned green.

She bolted from the table before he could utter a single word. Gael rushed after her—only to hear the bathroom door slam shut before the sound of violent retching sounded from within.

His gut tightened in alarm. 'Goldie?'

More retching, followed by a low, miserable moan. He knocked on the door, turned the handle. It was locked.

'Open the door, Goldie.'

A grunt filled with discomfort, then a cough. 'Um… no, I'm fine. I'll be out in a second.'

He gritted his teeth. 'You're not fine. You're vomiting.'

He absently wondered why that observation filled him with alarm, why the helplessness assailing him grew with each futile second.

A half-laugh sounded. 'Yeah, I think I'm aware of that little fact—' Speech ended and retching restarted.

He resisted the urge to ball his fist and pound the door open. '*Dios,* why did you lock the damned door?'

No answer. More vomiting.

He had to satisfy himself with waiting for her to finish emptying the contents of her stomach before she answered.

'Because I didn't want you to see me.'

'Modesty is the last thing you should be concerned about if you're sick. Can you open the door—*por favor*?' He tried his most reasonable voice.

'No. I...I'm feeling better. I'll be out in a minute.'

Argumentative Goldie was back. Short of breaking down the door, Gael could only grit his teeth and resign himself to pacing the hallway until he heard the sound of the lavatory flushing and a running tap.

When she didn't emerge for another five minutes his anxiety swelled higher. 'Damn it. Open the door!'

'Sir? Can I help with anything?' The solicitous butler had appeared behind him.

Gael curbed the urge to demand the spare keys to the bathroom, accepting that perhaps he was overreacting. Goldie had mentioned having a stomach upset after some food two days ago. He could still hear movement and the occasional splash of water, so she hadn't passed out—or worse.

'No, we're fine. If I need anything I'll call.'

He waited until the butler had left, then returned to the bathroom door. 'You have two minutes to come out, *guapa*. Then I'm coming in.'

'Okay, fine.'

He hesitated for a second, then returned to the patio. He poured a glass of water and downed it, then poured one for her in case she needed it.

He knew less than a minute had passed, so he forced himself to the balustrade to stare unseeingly at the view. He *was* overreacting. Goldie being sick might disrupt the movie's shoot, but it wasn't something they couldn't overcome.

But if it was more than a stomach bug...if she was falling ill with something else...

When his practised deep breathing barely calmed his flailing control, he cursed under his breath.

'Gael?'

He whirled away from the view, his relief at seeing her standing there more welcome than he knew it should be. Her hair looked tumbled and a touch wild, as if she'd run her hand through it several times without a single care about the way she looked—which put her firmly in a unique category far from most of the women he'd dated.

Framed in the light spilling from the living room, she was a gorgeous sight, despite the paleness of her face. A sight he wanted to see more of. Much more, he realised. And accepted. Perhaps he'd been too hasty to consign them to being just temporary room-mates. The chemistry between them was beyond electric. It was unique enough to warrant further investigation. Exploration of the best, carnal kind.

Prising himself off the low wall, he walked towards her. Saw the mixture of horror and acute trepidation in her eyes. And froze.

'Goldie! What's wrong? Do I need to call a doctor?' he demanded, his voice turning harsh with barely curbed concern.

'No, I don't think so.'

'You don't *think* so?'

'I…I think I know…' She stopped and swallowed, then a charged little tremble shook her frame. 'Gael, I think I'm pregnant.'

CHAPTER EIGHT

THE LIFE-CHANGING WORDS uttered out loud locked something deep into place inside her. Goldie had no explanation for it, but she knew she wouldn't need a pregnancy testing kit or a blood test to confirm the truth burning in her heart.

She was pregnant.

From her single night in Gael Aguilar's bed she'd fallen pregnant.

And he...he looked as if he'd been hit by a giant wrecking ball.

She turned around, stumbled back into the living room, sank down onto the sofa. Despite the juggernaut of emotions tumbling through her she heard him approach, take up residence in front of her. A glance upwards showed him with crossed arms, the skin around his mouth pinched tight as eyes turned dark and turbulent pierced her.

'You're pregnant.'

The words were devoid of emotion. But they demanded confirmation.

'You don't just *think*? You're sure?' he grated out in an icily controlled voice.

She licked dry lips, went over the dates she'd spent the last ten minutes in the bathroom desperately calculating. When they fell a good fourteen days short—*again*—she nodded.

'I'm late. I'm never late. I just thought... God, I don't know *what* I thought. I know it sounds naive, but I thought having sex and...and getting ready for this job may have disturbed my cycle.' She met his gaze, saw the frigid disbelief there and closed her eyes. 'Trust me, I know how that sounds. But with everything that's happened these past few weeks...' She stopped and stared at him. 'Are you going to stand there glaring at me all night?' Her voice shook, and, oh, how she hated herself for it.

'What else is there to say? Except maybe congratulations?'

Her stomach threatened to roll again. She placed a soothing hand over it. 'I don't know about that. I haven't taken it in yet.'

'*Haven't* you?'

His voice was a stiletto, cutting through the noise in her head.

She glanced up, and her heart dropped to her feet at the look on his face. 'What are you implying, Gael? What exactly do you mean by *congratulations*? On the pregnancy or on something else?'

'You need clarification?'

'Yes!' She surged to her feet, swayed, and sat down again. 'Please don't tell me you think I did this *deliberately*?'

Light, cold eyes stared unflinchingly back at her. 'Perhaps not the failure of the condom, but I'm afraid the "naive" argument doesn't fly. You're an intelligent woman, Goldie. I don't believe you ignored your hitherto *regular* cycle at all. You knew you were pregnant but chose not to say anything.'

'Why would I *do* that? Why would I be so—?'

'Calculating? I can think of a few reasons.'

Horror clenched her heart in a vice. 'Enlighten me, then, please.' Her hands began to tremble with the force of her chagrin and the shock that was rocking through her. She curled them into her lap and fought the prickle of tears that burned her eyes.

'You're already on the fast track to stardom—thanks to a few well-placed circumstances. But this pregnancy guarantees you the fastest possible route to achieve your aims.'

'My *aims*?' she whispered.

'You want to be a successful actress, do you not?'

She shook her head in confusion. 'Yes, of course I do— the same way you strive to be successful at what *you* do. I love what I do and I'm good at it. But I've also worked hard for it. There's nothing wrong with that and I won't apologise for it.'

'Of course not. Just as there's nothing wrong with the few hundred thousand starlets who want the same thing you do. Except you saw an opportunity for a fast track and you took it.'

'An opportunity *you* told me I'd be a fool to refuse, if I remember… Oh, you're still talking about the pregnancy? You think—' She stopped, too horrified to put what she suspected he meant into words immediately.

He raised a mocking eyebrow, dared her to continue.

'You think that just because you own a production company I deliberately kept this a secret, so I'd be set career-wise and security-wise for life?'

'*Sì*. Exactly.'

She shook her head again, unable to fathom how he could read her so wrong. How could he be so twisted about her motives? Or complete lack thereof. Had his past circumstances really done such a damaging number on him that he truly believed that?

'Gael, let me make one thing clear. I didn't want to lose the opportunity you presented me with, once you yourself talked me into it. But, please believe me, I would never put my career before the welfare of an innocent child,' she stated, her heart dredged with a hurt whose depths she couldn't quite touch.

'Sadly I have no proof of that besides the words falling from your mouth. *Will* have no proof of that until the child is born,' he rasped icily.

'How…? What did I do to make you think this of me? We barely know each other—'

'I know enough.'

'To condemn me like this?' she rasped, feeling her voice, like everything inside her, threatening to go numb at the flaying condemnation she saw in his eyes.

'On the way back from that dinner party in New York did you not plead with me? Tell me that you'd do *anything* to get the part?'

'Anything within reason. Like an audition. Or a screen test. Even an initial interview to see if my credentials were what you needed. Something *within* my profession. Not… not *this*!'

His eyes followed the hand she slid low over her stomach, then his gaze rose to hers, icier, more soul-shredding than before.

'*This?* The baby is a mere *thing* to you?'

'Oh, please—why are you trying so hard to twist my every word?' she cried, blinking back the further tears that threatened. 'I didn't trick you, or keep this baby a secret from you. I've only just worked it out myself. I'm not out to get my hands on your billions, or use the baby as leverage for my career. I haven't even been able to absorb the news and you're already labelling me a heartless gold-digger who would trade her unborn child for fame and fortune!'

'You wouldn't be the first,' he drawled, the same way he had that day in New York.'

Pain, raw and bracing, ripped through her. 'You know what? Go to hell, Gael. And stay there!'

This time when she stood her feet felt more inclined to support her.

He took one step forward.

She countered by taking several away from him.

He halted. 'Where do you think you're going?' he demanded, his voice quiet but grating.

'Anywhere I don't have to continue this ludicrous, demeaning conversation with you. I'm not one of the women you've dated in the past who came with a portfolio of agendas. Hell, we're not even dating. So leave me alone.'

'Goldie—'

'No! If you have something else to say to me that *doesn't* involve you shredding my character, talk to me in the morning. Otherwise I'll thank you to stay away from me.'

He laughed. 'Stay away from you? When you're carrying my child? Believe me when I say that will not happen in a million years. We *will* talk in the morning, Goldie, whether you wish to hear what I have to say or not.'

'Don't count on it.'

'Goldie—'

'Goodnight. I'd say sleep well, but I hope you spend the rest of the night thinking about your unfounded accusations and stewing over them.'

Her words, his warning—*everything* rang in her ears long after she'd brushed her teeth and slipped between the covers.

The shocking reality that history had well and truly repeated itself for another Beckett was so visceral it brought tears to her eyes. Goldie herself was the product of a one-night stand, conceived when her mother had been part of a charity's volunteer group in Ghana and had fallen for the charms of a local businessman. But, unlike the men who'd followed, her father had tried to make it work, even moving continents to be with her mother.

Sadly, her mother had been unwilling to settle for being a wife and mother in a picket-fenced house. Gloria had believed there were bigger and better things out there for her. Her reluctance to give their relationship a chance had eventually driven her father back to his homeland, leaving her mother to fall prey to dreams that had never been fulfilled and a lifetime of being taken advantage of by unscrupulous men.

Goldie had always known in her heart that the lessons she'd learnt via her mother's experience wouldn't lead her down the same path. But one night's wrong decision *had* led her here. Only this time she was the one being called unscrupulous. Avaricious.

She hated the tears that welled up in her eyes. Hated Gael in that moment for making her feel lower than she already felt. Because what had they created together other than a child who would hate her, and possibly its father too, for bringing it into a world where there was no chance of its parents ever being together?

Goldie knew how lonely and frightening things could get. Already she feared for her child. In light of Gael's revelations about how he felt about his family, how could she not?

Her hand slid over her stomach as weariness and inevitability washed over her in equal measures. She didn't have all the answers for how she was going to deal with what was happening to her. Far from it. But Goldie knew without a doubt that she would fight to her very last breath to make sure her child didn't suffer an ounce of preventable pain or rejection. Just as she knew that if that involved battling with Gael Aguilar she would bring the same fervour to the task.

With that resolution burning bright in her chest, she closed her eyes and willed healing sleep.

Her sleep was relatively peaceful. But twice she got up in the night to throw up. Twice she heard Gael prowling through the suite. Clearly her curse had worked, but she couldn't take any joy in that. She shut her mind to it, concentrated only on making it to the bathroom and back to bed both times.

It was almost as if now her mind had caught up with

what was happening in her body her baby was determined to make its presence felt one way or another.

She fell asleep just before dawn, her hand on her stomach, her mind whirling with a million thoughts.

Less than an hour later she was up. Determined to stick to some sort of routine, she donned the aqua-coloured bikini she'd used since coming to Durban, and threw a light matching sarong over it. Slipping her feet into gaily coloured sandals, she settled a wide-brimmed hat on her head and drew back the sliding doors to step out onto the private patio fronting her bedroom. Steps led down to the beach and the dramatic shoreline.

Pausing to breathe in the fresh air, she let her gaze drift past the iconic red and white Umhlanga lighthouse to the gleaming waters of the Indian Ocean. Seagulls flew overhead in the early-morning sun, and Goldie blanked her mind as she struck out for the quarter-mile walk along the shoreline.

Pregnant. She was *pregnant*.

She would buy a pregnancy test to confirm it as soon as she could, but even without the visual proof with each pulse of the word in her brain her breath caught. She reached the end of her walk and stopped to face the ocean, her mind spinning.

How would a child fit into her world? Where would they live? *How* would they live? How would her mother feel about being a grandmother?

How did Gael feel about being a father?

That question stood out above all the myriad hurtling through her head. It was also a question whose answer she knew she'd discover soon.

Swallowing, she raised her face to the warming sun's rays for a minute, before shedding the sarong, hat and sandals and walking into the sea.

Swimming was blissful, as usual, but already she worried about what such active exercise would do to her baby, and gave up halfway through her normal lengthy swim. Collecting her things, she strolled back towards the side of the hotel. The first thing she needed to do, once she'd had a talk with Gael, was to dig up as much information as she could on how to keep healthy during pregnancy.

Once again she was assailed with a frightening but growing thrill over her impending future.

No matter what. She'd fight to her last breath.

Discarding her things on a lounger next to the private pool that served the presidential suite, she turned on the outside shower to wash off the salt water. She was washing sand from between her toes when she heard the hurried slap of bare feet.

'Where the hell have you been?' Gael demanded forcefully. 'I was about to send out a damned search party.'

She turned, her gaze momentarily obscured by the water running down her face. Sluicing it away, she tilted her head back from the spray. He was livid, the chest beneath his white polo shirt rising and falling as if he'd run a marathon.

'I went for a walk on the beach, followed by a swim,' she said, fighting to keep her voice on an even keel. She needed to keep calm. For her baby's sake.

'Without bothering to tell me?'

'I went for a swim yesterday too. In fact I've walked and swum every day since I got here. I do it before breakfast and before we go on location. Should I have reported to you then too?'

Fury blazed across his face as he stepped closer. 'Don't be flippant, Goldie. You know what I mean.'

'Do I? A few things have changed, granted, but are you seriously expecting me to turn my life upside down because—?'

His hand slashing through the air chopped off her words.

'*Everything* has changed, Goldie. Accept that now, before we exchange further words.'

About to contradict him, she stopped. Because he was right. *So* right.

For one thing, once their child was born this man who stood brimming with fury and power before her would be connected with her for ever. And if he chose to take an interest—and judging by the look on his face he already was—he would have a say in her child's welfare.

The thought sent a shiver through her. Weirdly, it wasn't a shiver of terror. More a dread of the unknown. Because suddenly another factor loomed large in her brain. This child wasn't hers and hers alone. It also belonged to Gael Aguilar.

The thought was unsettling enough to make her words tumble out. 'Gael...I... It was just a walk. A swim.'

'And what if something had happened to you?' he rasped.

'The beach is safe. Nothing would have happened.'

He gritted his teeth for a few tense seconds, before his gaze flicked to the torrent of water cascading down her body. 'Are you done?'

She nodded and turned off the shower. 'Yes.'

Glancing round, he spotted a pile of towels and grabbed the largest one. Goldie reached up to smooth back her wet hair, then froze when she caught his eyes on her.

Slowly, Gael advanced, his hot scrutiny rushing down her body and returning on a slower trajectory. 'How could you not have known you were pregnant?' he scythed in a heated voice barely above a guttural whisper.

Her breath knotted in her lungs. 'Excuse me?'

Light hazel eyes reached her breasts, lingered for a long

moment. 'Your body is already changing. How do you expect me to believe you didn't know?'

'There was so much going on. I...I wasn't paying attention. Gael, I didn't know—I swear.'

His mouth tightened, but he handed over the towel without acknowledging her words. 'Come inside when you're done here. We need to have that talk.'

She watched him walk away, his strong, shorts-clad legs taking him from her view in seconds. She took her time to dab the excess moisture from her body, even though it didn't buy her any more time to formulate her thoughts.

Simple reason was, she had no idea what was coming with regard to Gael.

When she walked into the living room he was pacing, the phone pressed to his ear. He stopped, his gaze fixated on her as he spoke. 'Work it out, Ethan, and let me know.'

The hairs on her nape prickled as she watched him hang up and toss the phone onto the dining table. 'What was that about?'

He gave a tight, mirthless smile. 'Setting out contingencies.'

'What does that mean?'

He prowled to where she stood. Scrutinised her face and body one more time. 'First things first, *guapa*. How do you feel?'

The question was solicitous, caring. The emotions bristling from his body and eyes told a different story.

She sidestepped. 'Why are you asking?'

'You were up during the night. I have a doctor on standby—'

'I don't need a doctor. I feel fine.'

A tic manifested at his temple. 'You found out you're pregnant last night. Don't you want to know immediately how best to take care of yourself?'

She frowned, knowing she'd walked into that. 'I… Of course.'

He nodded, and strolled back to the table. Grabbing a white paper bag, he handed it to her. 'Before the doctor comes let's make absolutely sure of your state, shall we?'

Still frowning, she took the bag, looked inside. 'A pregnancy test…' She wasn't sure why the band tightened around her chest. She'd planned on getting one anyway. But Gael doing so seemed…*hurtful*.

'We need to be equipped with as much information as possible going forward, do we not?'

The explanation dissolved a little of her hurt, but not all of it she noted as she nodded and headed for the bathroom.

Gael was standing at the wide rectangular windows staring out at the view when she emerged from the bathroom. He turned immediately when she walked into the room, his narrowed eyes piercing hers before dropping to the two sticks clutched in her fist. Quick strides forward brought him unapologetically into her personal space.

'Well?' he breathed, his eyes gleaming with a feverish look.

Goldie swallowed. 'Yes.' She handed him both sticks.

He stared down at the tests, his gaze riveted on the writing displayed on the tiny screen.

Pregnant. 3+ Weeks

After an age, he tossed both tests onto the console table behind her. Closing the gap between them, he speared his fingers into her hair, angled her head up so she couldn't look away from him.

'You're carrying my child.'

The primal claim in those four words was unmistakable. Her breath shook as she nodded.

The palms cupping her cheeks firmed, as if he was focusing her attention ready for his next words. He pulled her close until their faces were inches from each other's.

'Do you accept that this fundamentally changes your life, Goldie?'

The depth of his belief in the words almost shook her enough to frighten her. But she'd worked too hard for the life she'd chiselled out for herself to cower beneath anyone's will.

'No, I don't. I'm sorry, Gael, but it doesn't.'

CHAPTER NINE

IT DOESN'T.

For a few seconds Gael was sure he'd misheard. Then he remembered exactly who he was dealing with. A woman with an iron will almost as strong as his own.

The woman carrying his child.

Surprisingly, his senses had stopped reeling somewhere in the middle of the night—between Goldie's first and second vomiting sessions. The test he'd procured first thing, when he'd thought she was still sleeping had merely been the instrument to slide that last one per cent of doubt from red to green.

The one and only time a woman had tried to trick him into fatherhood before, her quest had been tentative and ultimately bungled. Heidi had hinted at pregnancy towards the end of their time together—most likely to test the waters and her chances in the marital stakes. Gael's firm shutdown had resulted in a firm retraction of her fictional state.

Not so with Goldie. Her conviction had been firm, which in turn had cemented his.

She was carrying his child.

He was going to be a father.

But she didn't think it was a life-changing situation for her. What did *that* mean?

'Perdón?' Realising he'd lapsed into his mother tongue, he shook his head. 'What do you mean, *it doesn't?*'

She licked her lower lip, triggering a wave of heat through his groin. Nothing that had happened in the last twelve hours had changed the red-hot chemistry between them. If anything, the changes in her body had lent her skin a deeper glow, made her even more voluptuous and unbelievably stunning and heightened the awareness between them. A fact his body was reacting to in the most primal way.

'I mean *some* things will change, of course. I'm not debating that. But I'm not changing who I am because of my baby.'

His fingers wanted to tighten, to draw a more satisfactory answer straight from her mind. He cautioned himself to relax, breathe deep. '*Some* things? Tell me what you think those things are. Then tell me what you think *won't* change.'

Her mouth firmed for a second. 'I haven't laid it all out in a spreadsheet, if that's what you mean—'

'But clearly you've given it some thought, Goldie. So let's have it. Bullet-point the big things for me.'

She exhaled. 'Well, the first thing is to make sure the baby is healthy.'

'*Si*—agreed,' he said.

'Then, once he or she is born, we'll have to discuss your visitation rights and how to work around our career schedules.'

His gut tightened, disbelief flashing through his system. 'Visitation rights? *Schedules?*'

She nodded.

He dropped his hands and fought the terrible rush of dark fury and the memories of being discarded when it suited his mother that surged high. 'And where will you be living while these rights are being discussed?'

She frowned, as if his question was absurd. 'In New Jersey, with my mother—hopefully in a place that better suits us.'

'Of course. So I'm to remain in California, where I'm based, only seeing my child when a court order stipulates, hmm? Presumably you intend to pursue your career?'

'I...yes.'

'So our child will be left in the care of minders, or your mother and her sober companion, perhaps, while you're off on location around the world? Or do you intend to drag him or her with you?'

Her violet eyes grew wide, probably at his seemingly calm tone. 'Gael, I told you I don't have all the answers yet—'

'That is exactly right. You do *not*. But I do. Before I tell you, though, I have a little tale to tell you. Are you ready to hear it?'

She blinked, then raised an eyebrow. 'Do I have a choice? Aren't you going to tell me anyway, whether I want to hear it or not?'

Gael took another step back—because right in that moment he wasn't sure whether he yearned to kiss her sensual lips in an attempt to force down the memories surging, or condemn her for making those volatile emotions rise to the fore in the first place.

She shifted in reaction to the invisible fireworks sparking round the room, drawing his attention to her body, barely covered by the wispy sarong.

He whirled, slashing his fingers through his hair, and tried to seek a little clarity from the wide expanse of the ocean beyond the window. When it remained elusive, he took a deep breath and turned around again. Facing this thing head-on was the only viable option.

'I've told you a little bit about my past…my parentage, *si*?'

'Yes…' she responded warily, her gaze tracking him as he began to pace.

'What you *don't* know is that every few years when I was growing up my father would leave his wife for a few weeks and convince my mother to go away with him. Every time it was supposed to be *the* time—the moment when he left Alejandro's mother and made a life with my mother, the woman he supposedly truly loved. At those times I was parcelled off to the local orphanage or left with casual acquaintances who were paid to mind me.'

She inhaled sharply. 'Gael—'

He held up his hand. 'I'm not telling you this to gain sympathy. This is a fact of my childhood. It's behind me now, but it's not forgotten. I have accepted that I didn't even have a broken home to call my own—that my day-to-day existence was at the whim of a father who confirmed explicitly that I was an unwanted mistake when I dared to confront him.'

She gasped, her hand flying to mouth as if to cover the sound, the pain.

'I have had no interest in becoming a father simply because it's not a role I ever foresaw for myself.'

'But—'

'But now I am faced with the prospect of bringing my child into the world, things are not as clear-cut. However, there is one thing I intend to ensure will *never* happen where this child is concerned.'

She stared, unblinking, the pulse in her throat hammering wildly. 'Wh-what is that?'

'Comparing the circumstances I've just described to you with what you proposed a short while ago, do you think a man in my position, and with my power, having gone through what I went through as child, will be willing to stand idly by while my child is shuffled between minders, planes, movie locations and court-ordered visitation rights?' he gritted out.

Her mouth trembled for a second before she caught hold of herself. 'Gael, please be reasonable—'

He broke off mid-pace and planted himself firmly in front of her. He needed her to see the intent emblazoned in his heart and mind.

'Let me answer for you, Goldie. The scenario you pro-pose will happen *over my dead body*.'

The words sank in.

Her mouth dropped open in disbelief. 'So we're not even going to discuss it?'

'We just have.'

'No, we didn't. You're just trying to lay down the law.'

'I have told you what I intend *not* to happen with my child. We can now go on to discuss what *will*.'

'*Our* child.'

'What?'

'*Our* child. Equal parenting. Equal responsibility.'

'Yes—agreed. And that most definitely does *not* involve split homes on either side of the continent.'

'You can't just rule things out, Gael. We need to agree a compromise.'

'Why compromise when I have the solution?' he asked.

Her smooth forehead clenched in a frown. 'We con-firmed the pregnancy less than ten minutes ago. How can you have a solution already?'

'Very easily when what's at stake is this important.'

She gave a slight shake of her head, but her gaze didn't leave his. She blinked, her expression turning wary with trepidation. 'I think we need to talk about this some more.'

'I'm finished with talking, Goldie. The soundest so-lution to the situation we find ourselves in is for you to marry me.'

Even though her senses had screamed at her that whatever Gael was about to propose would most likely push all her alarm buttons, the words still hit Goldie square in the chest with shocking and relentless force.

She swayed on her feet.

Gael cursed, caught her by the elbow and tugged her to the sofa. 'Sit down, Goldie.'

'I'm fine.'

'I didn't say you weren't. I would still like you to sit. You were up half the night, throwing up, and you've been standing for far too long.'

She rolled her eyes, earning herself a dark frown. 'Women have been giving birth for thousands of years without turning into wilting flowers for the duration of their pregnancy, Gael.'

'*Sí*, but none of them have had the privilege of carrying my child,' he bit out.

Her mouth quirked in a parody of a smile, which vanished a second later. 'Do you have *any* idea how pompous that sounds?'

'You ask the question as if I care. You're still standing, Goldie.'

She plunked herself on a seat. Then rubbed her temple as his words attacked her once more. 'You just... You just asked me...'

'To marry me, yes,' he confirmed, his voice brimming with unequivocal power and certainty.

'But...why?'

'Because my child won't be living in New Jersey. It will be living with me.'

Cold dredged through her. 'And the only way I will have access to our baby is to marry you? Is that what you're threatening me with?'

He didn't answer immediately. Silence ticked by as he paced in front of her. Then he stopped and propped his hands on his lean hips.

'Tell me a little bit about your background, Goldie.'

Her gaze flicked up to meet his. 'Why?'

'Because I want to understand why you're fighting this, when all signs indicate that you would think this a perfect solution if other factors weren't an issue. So make me un-

derstand why our child can't be with *us*, full-time, wherever that may be.'

'I don't have to *make* you understand. Just because you
suddenly think marriage is a perfect solution, when only
last night you were dead against it for your own brother,
it doesn't mean I agree.'

'I don't think it's a perfect solution. I think it's the most
viable one.'

She batted the answer away. 'I would really like not
to talk about our child as if it's a commodity you're bro-
kering.'

His head went back as if she'd struck him. 'Trust me,
pequeña, a commodity is the last label I'd hang on our
child.'

The words were soft but deadly. Too late, she remembered what his parents had done to him as a child. Gael
might deny it, but that period in his life had left scars. Deep
scars that still dictated his motives.

'Sorry,' she muttered. 'I didn't mean to… It's just that
you speak CEO all the time.'

He lifted one eyebrow. '*All* the time?'

A fiery blush flashed into her cheeks at the blatant reference to their night together. Recollection surged into
her mind, making her breath shorten. Unable to drag her
gaze from his, she watched, fascinated, as his eyes turned
dark and stormy. Despite the brightness of the room she
suddenly felt as if they were cocooned in a dark, decadent
piece of heaven.

Which was absolutely the last thing she needed to be
thinking about now.

He seemed to arrive at the same conclusion. He blinked
and gritted his jaw. 'I'm all ears, Goldie. You grew up in
a broken home, correct?'

She winced. 'Eventually, yes.'

'And your father? Is he in the picture?'

'Long-distance.'

He pursed his lips. 'Given the choice, is that what you *wanted* to happen when you were growing up?'

She closed her eyes. Swallowed. 'Okay, you've made your point, but I still think we can make an alternative arrangement—'

'No.'

She glared at him. 'Let's explore another option. Couples live together full-time without marrying. Why do we need to be married?'

'You don't think our child's conception from a one-night affair is more than enough for it to have to deal with? You want to add to the long line of illegitimacy in his history? When you can prevent it? What have you got against marriage?'

'I… Nothing. But that doesn't mean I want to be knee-jerked into it.'

'The welfare of our child should be nothing like a knee-jerk response. It should be *everything* to you.'

Her mouth dried at the enormity of what he was saying. While she'd been lost in dreamless sleep, it was clear Gael had spent hours thinking about the situation they found themselves in. He had a brilliant mind, but she didn't think he'd put together this presentation on the fly.

Still, what he was suggesting was so…*absolute.*

'Speak up, Goldie. What's the problem?'

She laughed, unable to believe he was expecting an immediate answer from her on so monumental a subject. '*If* I decide to do this, I want a few stipulations of my own.'

His brow clamped in a frown. Then he gave a tight nod. 'Let's hear it.'

'You…you can't want to be saddled with me for the rest of our lives, nor I with you, so can we agree to a more temporary solution?'

He froze. 'You want to enter marriage with a clause that ends it on a particular date?'

'Please don't make it sound so clinical. Until ten minutes ago you were a man who didn't date the same woman for longer than six weeks! Now you expect me to believe you're willing to give up the rest of your life?'

'For the right reason—why not?'

The right reason. The baby. Not them.

'I think you're missing the point, Gael. You automatically assume that putting a ring on my finger will make this baby's life stable. I'm not denying it will, but don't you think he or she will be happier with parents who are content?'

'Are you saying marrying me sentences you to a life of discontent?'

'Don't put words in my mouth. I just want us to take a step back, think about this—'

'Five years.'

'I… What?'

'You want a fixed term? We'll give it a try for five years. After that we'll reassess the marriage. Whatever the outcome then, one thing will remain non-negotiable. We'll live in the same city and do everything to provide a smooth home-life for our child. So—five years. Do you think you can give up your independence for that long?' he bit out.

'Gael—'

'And in that time, provided you make our child's happiness your number one priority, you will receive ten million dollars per year and five guaranteed box office smash movie roles courtesy of Atlas. You say your career is important to you? This way you can rest assured it will not be unduly interrupted.'

Shock held Goldie rigid for so long she wondered whether she was in danger of turning into a fossil. When she managed to speak again, her voice shook with effort. 'And…and if I don't agree to what you're suggesting?'

Goldie was almost afraid to ask, because the purpose she'd sensed in him when he'd confronted her outside seemed to have magnified a thousandfold. She didn't need to be a genius to work out that Gael had just given her the 'either' scenario. There was a very big 'or' coming her way.

'If you don't agree, then I'll take steps to remove our child from you—completely—the moment he or she is born. I'm sorry, *amante*, this is too important for me to beat round the bush. So those are your only options. What's it going to be, Goldie? Yes or no?'

Two days.

She'd argued for time to think about Gael's proposal. He'd grudgingly given her the remainder of their time in South Africa.

So she had two days to come up with a different solution, one that *didn't* involve marrying a man she barely knew, or fighting him in court for custody of their child. And so far, a day later and with twenty-four hours' worth of filming a beach scene between Elena and Alfonso completed, she'd drawn a blank.

To fight Gael she needed far deeper pockets than she currently had. This was her first movie role, and the pay was more than she'd dreamed of, but it was nowhere near enough to take care of her child while fighting for its rights in a court of law—especially against a powerful man like Gael Aguilar. And part of her contract with Atlas involved exclusive work that might extend for almost half a year after filming, which meant that even if she wanted to be pounding the pavements on job-hunts while being heavily pregnant she couldn't.

Which brought her to the option Gael preferred. Marriage.

Her heart caught every time she thought of that, but after a few times Goldie admitted that the idea wasn't as stomach-clenching as it had first seemed.

Both their backgrounds had proved conclusively that coming from a broken home could damage a child. For the longest time Goldie had felt bitterness and anger towards her mother for not being strong enough, for pushing her father away and breaking up their family. And, although she loved and supported her mother now, she couldn't help but feel bruised inside from the times when she'd lived in constant fear that her mother would never be strong enough to make the right decisions about the men she'd let emotionally abuse her.

In her darkest moments, Goldie had wondered whether she was potentially equally fallible. It was one of the reasons why she'd hung on to her virginity for so long. She'd been afraid to find out the depths of her strengths and weaknesses.

She didn't plan on being alone for the rest of her life. And did she not owe it to her child to try and give it the best possible start in life? Even if it meant marriage, temporarily, to its father?

She didn't know everything there was to know about Gael, but he'd laid the cards that were important to him on the table. The most commendable of which involved making their child's wellbeing his number one priority. Despite the flipside being his threat to fight her for custody of their child, her rational and emotional sides felt satisfied that he was committed to his unborn child.

Enough to decide to turn his private life upside down for it within hours of finding out about its existence.

That quiet but powerful truth made her turn her head now to look at the man in question, who sat next to her as the helicopter flying them to Table Mountain soared over the breathtaking landscape.

The crew had left Umhlanga early this morning. Because of tourism restrictions, they had only a small window to shoot a scene on the mountain—which, ironically, was the scene in which Elena was proposed to by Alfonso. A scene which ended with her saying yes, and then spending the rest of her fictional life fighting to save her marriage.

Dread whispered over her skin. As if he sensed her inner battle, Gael turned narrowed hazel eyes on her. He watched her silently for a few seconds before he reached across the bench seat to take her hand.

The action was unexpected, throwing her thoughts and emotions further into conflict. Provided she kept their child as their main focus, *could* they make a go of a five-year emotionless marriage? Because she wasn't about to delude herself into thinking there were any emotions involved here. Gael was acting purely on a primal instinct to protect what was his. Much as he would in a business venture.

Whereas she…

Goldie stopped her chaotic thoughts as the helicopter landed. She honestly didn't know *what* she felt. All she knew was the pledge she'd made to protect her child.

So, although she didn't attempt to remove her hand from Gael's once they alighted and were seen into the cable car that would take them to the top of the mountain, she turned her thoughts to work and the scene in front of her.

The view from the top was unlike anything Goldie had ever seen. Enough to rob her of breath for a full minute. Enough to make her feel like a small cog in the great, unrelenting circle of life. Enough to lend her the gravity she needed to utter her lines in a way that saw the scene completed in one continuous take and Ethan give yet another pleased fist-pump the moment he yelled, *'Cut!'* But while the crew celebrated she moved off to a quiet corner of the section of the plateau, her thoughts turning inward as she drank in the spectacular view of Cape Town and the ocean beyond.

She sensed Gael before his body heat arrived behind her. Strong arms bared to the African sun came around either side of her to rest on the railing.

'Do you really need another day to think about this, *cara*? You know deep inside what needs to be done, Goldie,' he rasped in her ear.

'Do I?'

'*Sí*, you do. Don't drag this out unnecessarily.'

'I don't want to. But…*marriage*…'

He moved closer, his body caging her in tighter. She angled her head, looked up at him. Eagle-sharp eyes stared down at her, their focus unwavering.

'Don't overthink it or confuse the issue. We're not fictional characters. We can have a marriage without the melodramatic chaos.'

She gave a tiny anxiety-filled laugh. 'How can you be so certain?'

'Because we don't believe in the fairy tale. We're going into this with our eyes wide open. There is only one purpose here. We're doing this for the sake of our child. For the chance to give it the stability we were both denied. Say yes, Goldie. You stand to gain far more than you stand to lose.'

His voice was hard, almost merciless.

She swallowed hard. Slid her hands over her flat stomach, her thoughts churning.

Gael's hand sliding over hers, warming her hands, cradling their child, alarmed her almost as much as it settled her. He was claiming. But he was also protecting.

She would deal with the former if it threatened her at any point. The latter, she couldn't fault.

Taking a deep breath, affirming her pledge, she gave her answer. 'Yes.'

CHAPTER TEN

THEY LANDED IN SPAIN three days later. Once she'd given her answer things had moved at lightning speed. Papers had been drawn up, witnessed and signed, granting her unimaginable wealth and the type of acting roles that should have made her ecstatic but instead had left a faintly bitter taste in her mouth.

Somewhere along the line Gael had managed to weave her into agreeing to attend his brother's wedding. If she recalled correctly, his answer when she'd expressed reservations at attending had been a tightly voiced, 'You're about to become my wife. Who else am I supposed to go with?'

The suggestion that perhaps he might go alone had been met with a frown and a firm refusal.

'You will have to meet my family, as dysfunctional as they are, at some point. Best to get it over and done with. Besides, for once I would like to enjoy an event without Kenzo Ishikawa getting on my case about my marital status.'

'Kenzo Ishikawa…one of your business partners?'

He'd snorted, his jaw going tight before he'd replied. 'He seems to take pleasure in pointing out that I'm less of a man because I'm unattached. Our first attempt at a merger fell apart partly because of it.'

'And this is your chance to rub your attachment in his face?' Goldie hadn't been sure whether to be offended or amused. She'd chosen to be neither.

But Gael had sent her a tight smile. 'Exactly so. There is also the added bonus of beating Andro in the nuptials stakes, even if only by a few days,' he'd added with surprising relish, before absenting himself from her presence.

Now, Goldie rose from the lounger and padded to the edge of the Olympic-sized pool.

Before that wedding happened there was the small matter of *her* wedding. Special licences had been arranged. Ethan had agreed to shoot a few of the scenes that didn't involve her, then give the whole cast and crew a four-day break before they resumed filming again at the end of next week. And Gael was having her mother and Patience flown over tomorrow, for the wedding that would take place here on his estate just outside Barcelona.

The place was quintessential Spanish architecture at its best. A rambling two-storey villa, the property sat in the middle of acres of rich green valley dotted with orange and lemon trees. The villa itself, originally a Catalan manor house, modernised and extended, was made of stone, with grand arches and a vast courtyard decorated with trellises and carefully groomed vines. The house was stunning and yet homely—a place she wouldn't have immediately associated with Gael Aguilar, the ruthless and ambitious CEO who wrote computer code as a hobby.

But then a few things were beginning to surprise her about Gael—not least being this marriage he was hell-bent on in order to protect his unborn child.

In the last twenty-four hours private doctors had visited her, taken blood samples and delivered enough pre-natal advice and vitamins to stun a horse. It was too early for an ultrasound scan, but Gael had readily agreed to a suggestion to listen to the baby's heartbeat on a foetal Doppler. The loud sound echoing through the guest bedroom where she slept had brought a look of almost shocking determination to his face.

It was that determination that strengthened her belief that she was doing the right thing too.

So when Gael's housekeeper walked out a few minutes later, to announce the arrival of the stylists and the gown designer contracted to ready her for her wedding, she took a deep breath, turned around and headed for her destiny.

Goldie climbed the small hill towards the tiny chapel that sat half a mile from the villa. A tiny part of her was glad for her mother's fussing around her, because it took her mind off what was waiting for her beneath the ancient steeple. She also knew it was her mother's way of accepting what was happening.

Despite Goldie's reassurances that she was doing the right thing, her mother had voiced her worry from the moment she'd landed. Eventually she'd accepted Goldie's assurances, but it hadn't taken away the veil of concern in her mother's eyes.

Goldie's worry as to whether that concern might trigger a deeper reaction in her mother had been allayed by Patience, and the companion's brief but buoying report of her mother's progress had settled Goldie's own anxiety.

So she let her mother fuss now, because it meant *she* didn't have to do any fussing. She hadn't seen Gael in the past twenty-four hours—a surprising turn-up since she hadn't expected him to observe tradition. In his absence, questions had loomed—one in particular taking up most of her thoughts.

It was the question of sex—horrifyingly triggered by her mother's observation of the vast amounts of bedrooms in Gael's villa and how she was looking forward to seeing it filled with grandchildren.

Of course that had also brought on the question of how much of their agreement they would be sharing with others.

All those questions beat hard like butterflies' wings in her belly as she reached the doorway of the chapel. Technically, her mother was to walk her down the aisle, but Gloria wanted to walk a step behind, her hoarse insistence that this was Goldie's day, not to be spoiled by a mother who'd let her down, having brought tears to her eyes.

There'd been no time to utter words of comfort, or to take in her mother's new, more hopeful outlook on life, but something had settled in Goldie's heart upon seeing her mother again. For now, though, she needed to head up the aisle and join her life with Gael Aguilar's.

The man in question turned his tall, imperious frame and speared her with a fierce, possessive look as she walked slowly up the aisle.

He was impeccably dressed in a dark navy suit and snow-white shirt, his hair tamed and gleaming beneath the dozens of candles glowing from the cast-iron holders that hung from the ceiling, and his magnificence seriously threatened her breathing.

As his gaze raked her body she derived quiet satisfaction from the fact that she'd chosen a dress she loved, which gave her a much needed boost of confidence. The short-sleeved, cream silk lace gown that framed her figure to end in a short train behind her prohibited long strides. She'd forgone a veil in favour of a tiny tiara that held her pinned up hair in place. She wore only light make-up, and simple pearl earrings belonging to her mother adorned her ears to complete the subtly elegant ensemble.

Halfway to the altar, with her eyesight better adjusted from the almost blinding sunlight to the candlelit interior, she caught a better glimpse of Gael's face. And her breath caught.

Beneath the possessiveness, that hard look she'd never been able to fathom lurked in his eyes. A feeling of having been tried and found guilty for a crime she had no inkling of committing assailed her, causing her to stumble slightly.

She stopped to right her footing. Gael's nostrils flared as he took in her hesitation. Goldie started to shake her head, but he was already striding down the aisle.

Catching her hand firmly in his, he escorted her up to the altar. Murmurs went up in the small wedding party comprising her mother, Patience, Teresa—his house-keeper—and her husband, and the driver/bodyguard who gave her a small smile as she passed him.

They had barely stopped before the priest when Gael nodded at the tall, thin man to proceed.

The bilingual ceremony passed in a blurred rush from one moment to the next.

Her mother stepped forward to relieve Goldie of the small bouquet clutched in her fist. Then Goldie was lis-tening to Gael's deep, firm tones as he said his vows. Her eyes widened when his driver stepped forward with two rings laid out on a small velvet pillow. Gael's was a simple broad gold band, hers a platinum double circle with yellow diamond studs holding the two rings together.

Her fingers shook as she held his ring poised over his knuckle and repeated her own vows. A furtive glance at Gael showed his complete attention on her as she uttered the binding words. When she had finished an unfathom-able look crossed his face.

In that moment Goldie was certain she'd crossed a threshold she would never be able to step back from.

Gael had experienced a well of satisfaction as he slid the wedding band onto her finger and repeated the words that had made Goldie Beckett his wife. He'd secured his child's future. Ensured it would never suffer the stings of illegiti-macy and rejection he'd suffered. Would never be made to feel like an obstacle or an unwanted possession, either through emotional neglect or in the face of its mother's ambition.

He forced aside the rush of bitterness that stormed him. So far he'd been able to keep his feelings under control—had been able to contain the knowledge that Goldie's *yes* had come after his offer of compensation and a promise of a flourishing career.

He wanted to keep his emotions out of it—much as he kept his emotions out of his business transactions. And yet the boulder that had lodged itself in his chest since her acceptance of his deal wouldn't shift.

It shouldn't matter. Ultimately, he'd done what needed to be done for the sake of his child.

And yet it did matter.

He knew it mattered when he was invited to kiss his bride and sealed his mouth to hers and felt her brief hesitancy before her response kicked in.

It mattered when her gaze wouldn't meet his as they acknowledged the applause and smiles of their small group of guests once the ceremony was officially over.

He had married her to secure his child's wellbeing.

So why did his own suddenly feel precarious?

'Gael?'

He shut off his thoughts and glanced at his bride. They'd returned home from the chapel to an alfresco lunch set up on a banquet-like bench beneath two orange trees in his garden. He'd invited the rest of his staff to join them, and had endured the endless toasts with an ever-stiffening smile.

'Yes?' he responded.

'Are you okay?'

His mouth twisted. 'Of course. What could possibly be wrong on a day like this?'

She frowned. 'Please don't patronise me. Have I done something wrong?'

His jaw gritted. 'Goldie—'

'You've barely said two words to me since we left the church. In fact we've barely had a conversation since we arrived here. I know we're only doing this for the baby—'

'I would prefer it if you *don't* share our private agreement with the world.'

'That's just it. Why are we pretending to everyone that this is some sort of…love-match?' she demanded in a hushed tone.

'For the same reason we are entering into the marriage. To protect our child.'

'But…'

'Enough, Goldie. If you want to discuss this further we will—but not right now, *si*?'

Another member of staff—the head of Gael's vast stables—rose just then, to make a speech, effectively stopping her from speaking. Then there followed more speeches, mostly in Spanish, which meant she was left in the dark as to what was being said. But raucous laughter gave her a general hint.

She ate selectively, having eventually worked out which foods triggered her nausea and which would mostly likely stay down.

At one point, she caught her mother's speculative gaze swinging from her to Gael and back again. Although Goldie smiled, she wasn't sure it had been convincing enough.

She waited until Gael was occupied with entertaining a couple she'd been told were vintners from two estates away before excusing herself and returning to the villa. Accompanied by a smiling Teresa, who had insisted it was tradition that she help her dress for her wedding night, and her mother, who continued to cast curious glances at her, Goldie was forced to keep the starchy smile pinned on her face.

The moment Teresa departed, her mother faced her.

'You're pregnant, aren't you?' Gloria declared, her gaze running searchingly over her daughter's negligee-and-dressing-gown-clad body.

Her damning blush was all the confirmation her mother needed.

'Oh, Goldie…' The words were softly spoken, partly in regret, partly in tearful acceptance.

'I was going to tell you when the time was right.'

Her mother nodded, but her eyes remained troubled. 'Is that why you married him so quickly?'

It's why I married him at all. But she knew she couldn't say that. 'It's the right thing to do, Mom.'

'For you or the baby?'

For some reason that softly voiced question tightened a vice around her heart. She watched her mother's eyes fill with tears again as she sank down onto the bed. 'This is my fault. I'm so sorry, Goldie.'

She shook her head. 'No, it's not. Stop crying, please.'

Her mother's smile was sad and a touch weary. 'You can stop trying to be the adult, here, sweetheart. I know I haven't been the best role model for you. If I'd tried to make a better life for you, instead of selfishly wanting things I couldn't have, you wouldn't have rushed into this—'

'I made the decision with my eyes wide open, Mom. I…I don't regret it.'

She firmed her voice against the tiny white lie. The truth was that things had seemed so clear-cut on top of Table Mountain when Gael had whispered in her ear that this was the only viable option. But as she'd made her vows in that ancient chapel there'd been a terrible moment when she'd tried to imagine saying another set of vows, at another time and place, to someone else. The stunning realisation had come that she couldn't imagine such a time, couldn't picture another man. That she wanted this time and place to be the only occasion when she said those words.

Goldie still hadn't been able to wrap her mind around that.

'Are you sure, sweetheart? Because—'

'I'm sure, Mom.' She placed her hands over her mother's and held her gaze, repeating the words to herself in the hope that they would begin to ring true.

Her mother nodded and rose. Thinking she was about to head for the door, Goldie's breath caught when her mother wrapped her in a firm embrace, laying her cheek on top of Goldie's head.

'I should've done better. I should've been a better mother, fought harder to make us happy. I'm sorry, Goldie. I hope you forgive me some day.'

Tears filled her eyes, choking her response. 'Mom…'

'Shh, it's okay, honey. You'll do much better than me—I know you will. But if you ever need me please give me the chance to be there for you, okay?'

Unable to speak, Goldie nodded, then sat in silence as her mother left. She was still perched on the bed when a knock came on the door to the adjoining master suite.

The door opened to reveal Gael, minus his jacket and tie. He prowled into the room, power and glory falling from his impressive frame. 'Should I take it as a personal affront that my bride deserts me before the wedding banquet is over?' he drawled.

Her insides tightened. 'We're alone now, Gael. You can drop the pretence.'

He kept coming, not stopping until he reached the bottom of the bed, where he leaned his long-legged frame against the post, crossed his ankles. 'Where is the pretence, *amante*? You *are* my bride, and I *did* feel deserted.'

'So what is this? A yearning to have my fawning act reprised behind closed doors?'

His eyes narrowed as he stiffened. 'Act?'

'You don't wish anyone else to know this marriage is a sham, but do *we* have to pretend that there's more to this union than there really is?'

'Correct me if I'm wrong, but isn't this our wedding night?' he demanded bluntly.

Alarm and more than a touch of breathlessness stabbed her. 'In theory, I guess…'

His harsh laugh made her wince. 'No, Goldie, not in theory. In *fact*.'

Her stomach flipped. 'What are you implying?'

His mouth twisted. 'You were a virgin the last time we were together, but surely you don't need me to draw you a picture of what happens on the night following a wedding?'

She flushed, but boldly met his gaze. 'Of course not. Except I'm certain that picture doesn't apply to us.'

He slowly straightened, his chest rising and falling in measured breathing as he closed the gap between them. Goldie willed herself to stay still and not bolt the way her senses were screaming at her to.

'Explain to me how you arrived at this interesting conclusion?' he invited, his tone deceptively casual.

The dark gleam in his eyes said he was very much interested in her answer. And that it had better be to his liking. Or else.

She licked suddenly dry lips and searched for clarifying words. 'We're doing this for the baby, aren't we? And sex…sex will just cloud the issue. Blur the lines.'

He gave a hard, short laugh. 'So let me get this straight. You're perfectly content to condemn yourself to a nun-like existence for the next five years, and presumably you expect me to willingly subject myself to the same sexless fate?' he asked, his voice reflecting how ludicrous the idea was.

Goldie opened her mouth, shut it, then shook her head, confusion and exasperation filling her. 'This is why I wanted more time before we jumped into marriage. These are things we should've discussed beforehand—'

'So we could waste hours or days arguing it to death before you saw reason and gave in?'

Hurt and anger firmed her mouth. 'I'm not a shrew, Gael. I'd thank you not to make me out as one.'

'Very well. Tell me in simple terms that your assumption is ridiculous and we can progress with our wedding night.'

'There isn't going to *be* a wedding night! We have a deal. Sex isn't part of it.'

His nostrils flared and his eyes blazed with quiet fury. 'Only because I didn't think I needed to spell out so obvious and fundamental a point.'

'I'm sorry it's such an important thing for you. It's not to me.'

He rocked back on his heels, his features freezing like ice. 'I see. You get what *you* want out of the deal and to hell with the rest—is that it?'

'What are you talking about? I said yes because we both wanted—'

His hand slashed through the air. 'Save it, *cara*. We both know that fifty million dollars and a guaranteed five box office hit movies had a big hand in you eventually saying yes.'

Raw ice doused her. *'What did you say?'*

'Your hearing is perfect, Goldie,' he drawled. 'And I'm finished with talking.'

Her mouth was still gaping open when he took the last step and untied the belt of her dressing gown. The silk slid off her shoulders without much effort, leaving her in an emerald-green negligee.

Before Goldie could protest, one firm hand slid over her nape. He pushed her back onto the bed and prowled over her to plant his knees on either side of her hips. In the next instant his mouth plunged, hot and heavy and demanding, over hers, his tongue stabbing between her lips to take and ravage hers.

Her shock dissipated under the flames of his arrogant,

unstinting caress. Despite a large part of her brain reeling under the accusation he'd flung at her, she couldn't help but moan when one hand boldly cupped her engorged, sensitive breast. Her breasts seemed to have grown a size bigger almost overnight, their tips super-sensitive as pregnancy hormones ran riot through her. Gael was clearly appreciative of her new size, and his moans grew more guttural as impatient fingers brushed aside the straps and yanked the top part of the negligee down her arms.

He broke the kiss to stare down at her full breasts. Eyes firing a burnished gold, he took the globes in his palms and toyed mercilessly with the nerve-engorged peaks.

Her head went back as she arched under the exquisite assault. Goldie knew she shouldn't be enjoying herself this much, that what he'd said to her needed to be addressed immediately, but the sensations zinging through her body, arrowing demandingly between her thighs, were too thrilling to stop.

She cried out as his mouth closed over one stiff nipple. Several expert flicks had her hips twitching, her breath shooting out in shameless pants as liquid heat ploughed through her. Back and forth he alternated his attention between the stiff peaks. Sent her right to the edge of bliss.

And then it *did* stop.

The loss of sensation was so acute she whimpered. The sound shamed her even as she launched her fingers up to stay him, and eyes she didn't remember shutting flew open.

'Gael…?'

'*This* is why I didn't think I needed to point things out to you. The chemistry between us is as natural and vital as breathing. But if you need to be told, then hear this. Unspoken or not, sex *is* part of the deal. You may have a ring on your finger, but—trust me—this isn't a point I'm prepared to concede. So argue with yourself all you want to as long as you come back with a yes. Because tomorrow night the only bed you'll be sleeping in is mine.'

He stepped off the bed with the grace of a jungle cat and stood for a moment, staring down at her.

Words stumbled through her dazed senses—begging, pleading words that had no shame under the heavy weight of her thwarted need. With super-human effort Goldie bit them back. He'd dealt her the gravest of insults, attacked her integrity. Even if she risked expiring from the gut-clenching desire clamouring through her she wouldn't give in. Not when she knew his true feelings towards her.

Raising her chin, she firmed her mouth and returned his stare in silence.

Gael's mouth twisted with mocking bitterness. Leaning down, he traced a forefinger from her clavicle to her cleavage. 'That's how it is to be, hmm? Well…good luck, *cara*,' he murmured in a soft, deadly voice.

Then, turning on his heel, he walked away from her.

CHAPTER ELEVEN

FOR THE NEXT four days they remained locked in silent, seething battle. But they made almost comical efforts to be civil to one another in front of her mother, Patience and the staff. And Gael was an exceptional host on the occasions when they took her mother to a private gallery viewing in Barcelona and then to an open park showing of *Tosca*, both of which her mother lapped up with almost childlike joy.

But the moment they were alone his charming smile and drawling banter evaporated. He barely glanced at her as he busied himself with his newspaper or whatever meal he was consuming. The moment he deemed it acceptable he left the room, either to pound relentless laps in the swimming pool or to lock himself in his study.

Goldie had no such escape. On long walks over the estate her mother was growing to love, she endured probing questions and concerned looks. The only upside of the effort it took to maintain a happy face was that she fell into bed exhausted at the end of the day, with her sleep only disturbed at the crack of dawn by relentless morning sickness.

The day before Gael's brother's wedding—the last day of her mother's visit—she entered the dining room to find Gael pouring hot water into a fine bone china teacup. Adding two slices of lemon and a cube of sugar, he stirred it briefly before setting it down in front of her, along with a small plate of dry crackers.

'Drink this. Teresa swears by it for morning sickness,' he said gruffly.

Her surprised glance swung to his, but he was walking away to get himself an espresso. Expecting him to leave the room, since there was no one to entertain, she gulped at a hot mouthful when he sat down at the head of the table.

'Am I to assume that we're talking to each other now?' she asked, after a few minutes had passed and she'd drunk half the sweetened hot water. She was aware that her tone was a touch waspish, but she'd been unable to stem the hurt of the past few days.

'Talking has never been a problem for me. Arguing without purpose, on the other hand, bores me.'

Her breath shuddered out. 'So you either want to hear only what suits you or silence?'

He tossed back his espresso and set the cup down with a heavy hand. 'No, Goldie, the only subject I'm not prepared to argue about or compromise on is the subject of sex. And since that subject appears to be a ticking time bomb between us, I suggest you tread carefully.'

The cup trembled in her hand so she set it down. 'I know your mind isn't one-track like that—'

His harsh laugh fractured her words. 'Do you? I'm a red-blooded male, Goldie. One with a healthy sexual appetite and stringent views on fidelity. You're the woman who's taken my name and my ring but is refusing to share my bed. Since I don't intend to break my vows, I'm left with a huge, potentially insurmountable problem. So do you *really* think I'm overreacting?' he grated at her.

Her blush was fierce and all-encompassing. But then so was the ache that wouldn't budge from her heart. 'Do *you* expect *me* to have sex with you when you've accused me of marrying you just so I'll get my hands on your money?'

'Come off it, Goldie. Sex was off the table even before you signed on the dotted line. You just decided to keep it to yourself. You were biding your time before you dropped your little bombshell.'

'No, I wasn't—because I wasn't even thinking about it then. You left me in bed the first time we made love without a word. I woke up to a note that was tantamount to you telling me you'd made a mistake. And you think the natural progression from that, when we agreed to marry for the sake of our baby, automatically includes sex?'

A faint dull red tinged his cheekbones, but his expression remained rigid. 'I wasn't expecting you to be a virgin so, *sí*, I was a little…thrown. But I did return to you. Only you were asleep. I took the unselfish way of not waking you and chose to sleep in the spare bedroom. But my question still stands. You knew my views on fidelity before you married me, so what did you *think* was going to happen?'

'I expected we would talk about it. We never got the chance to discuss it so neither of us knew where we stood.'

'What about now? Where *do* we stand?' he countered.

She shook her head. 'Right now we stand with me wondering why on earth you'd want to sleep with a shameless gold-digger who would barter her child for fifty million dollars!'

He shrugged, his eyes feverishly raking her face. 'The money means nothing to me, *guapa*,' he drawled softly. 'Having your body beneath mine again in bed would be worth more than twice that to me.'

'I do *not* want to sleep with you for money!'

'Too late—you have already signed the documents, remember?'

Her hands shook so hard she clenched them in her lap before he saw. 'Why are you so determined to think the worst of me, Gael?'

'I'm merely going by the evidence before me.'

'*What* evidence? My deplorable timing because I said yes right after you threw in your supposed sweetener?'

'You signed the document,' he sliced at her again.

'Yes, I signed it. So what? Was it some sort of test that I failed? Is there no room for the benefit of the doubt in your world?'

'That is up to you, Goldie.'

'How?'

His gaze moved past her face, down her throat, to the two-button opening of her white sleeveless sundress. 'Find a way.'

He left the dining room shortly after that.

On shaky feet she got up and went to the sideboard to replenish her cup with hot water. Her mother and Patience entered as she was heading back to her seat. Greetings were exchanged. And then she went back to avoiding her mother's probing stares.

After eating a piece of toast and half a banana without incident, she begged off when her mother invited her to the local market to shop for the souvenirs Gloria wanted to take back to the US. Feeling bad, she promised a mother-daughter lunch before her mother and Patience were taken to the airport for their evening flight.

Escaping to her room, Goldie paced, her mind darting over her conversation with Gael. How could something so seemingly straightforward have become such a jumbled mess?

Was she naive not to have considered that Gael would want a wife in *every* sense of the word after he'd gone out of his way to avoid her after the first time they'd made love? He claimed he'd returned after disappearing into the bathroom for longer than was normal. But his note the next morning had left very little doubt as to his feelings.

And he'd tried to fob her off with money then too!

She paused mid-stride. It was clear that money was the issue. Gael Aguilar was used to dealing with gold-diggers and scheming women. By signing the prenuptial agreement as it stood, she'd all but drawn a bullseye on her back.

Crossing to the bed, she grabbed her purse and searched for the document. There were pages and pages of it, all wrapped up in legalese. But she eventually found the clause she was looking for. Her heart leapt as she read and re-read it. Grabbing her phone, she did a quick search for local attorneys—those who practised in English as well as Spanish.

After making an appointment, she jumped off the bed and went in search of her mother. She breathed in relief when she caught her and Patience as they headed out.

'Is it too late to join you?'

Her mother turned around and smiled. 'Of course not!'

Asking Teresa to let Gael know she'd gone out with her mother, she joined them in the SUV.

The Friday market in Villa de Gracia was bustling, with exquisite trinkets and to-die-for souvenirs at every turn. It was easy for Goldie to leave her mother happily browsing and keep her appointment with the attorney. It took a good few minutes to explain to the ageing lawyer just what she wanted, and he seemed genuinely puzzled by her request. But eventually he called in his son, who agreed to draw up the requisite documents.

Twenty-five minutes later Goldie emerged from the attorney's office with a smile on her face.

'Find a way,' Gael had dared her.

She just had.

Gael was waiting on the front steps of the villa when they returned. The three women glanced at his face as the driver braked the SUV to a stop and the easy laughter in the vehicle died.

'Well, looks like someone's headed for the doghouse,' Patience quipped under her breath. 'Goldie, honey, what did you *do* to the poor man?' the plump companion, originally from New Orleans, stage-whispered.

Goldie snorted. 'Sometimes I just need to breathe the wrong way.'

Muffled laughter ensued, quickly cut off as Gael strode to the car and opened the door.

'Everything okay, son?' her mother asked sweetly.

Gael jerked out a nod. '*Sí*, everything's fine, Gloria,' he responded, without taking his eyes off Goldie. 'Can I talk to you, *cara*?'

She could tell he was trying to keep his tone even, but the flames raging through his eyes and the white lines bracketing his mouth told a different story.

She pasted a smile on her face. 'Sure.'

He took her hand and led her into the house. Once inside, he crossed the large rotunda-shaped foyer and took the right set of sweeping wood and iron stairs that led to the second level.

'Gael—'

He stopped suddenly in the middle of the staircase and stared down at her. One hand reached out and brushed her lower lip. His fingers were shaking.

'You've been itching for an argument, *guapa*. And I'm about to give you the mother of them all. Just hang tight,' he snarled, low and deadly.

He resumed climbing, his steps quickening as they crested the stairs. It was all she could do to keep up with him as he moved to the west wing and entered his bedroom.

Goldie had only caught glimpses of Gael's suite, which was connected to hers. She'd seen it when he'd come into her room on the night of their wedding.

Seeing it in all its glory for the first time, she stopped in the middle of the room. A rich, pale wood theme was everywhere, blended from ceiling to bed to floor, interspersed with a dark marble Goldie wanted to run her fingers over just to see if it was as warm and luxurious as it looked.

Of course all that passed through her mind in a split second before the man…her husband…shut the door with a decidedly repressed click and planted himself in front of her.

For several heartbeats he just stared at her. 'You went into town with your mother?'

Goldie blinked. 'Uh…yes?'

He breathed in, long and deep. 'You went into town with your mother, and then *went to see a divorce attorney*?' he seethed with white-hot fury.

Oh, hell. Her heart lurched. 'What? No—!'

'You were seen, Goldie! The attorney's office confirmed it. So did my driver.'

He started to whirl away, one hand spiking viciously through his hair. He stopped both actions halfway through and launched himself back in front of her. He looked paler than before, a vein jumping frantically at his temple as he glared at her.

'Is this your answer when things don't go your way? Is this your way of trying to get my attention, to bend me to your will?'

She shook her head. 'You've got it wrong. Just let me ex—'

He pointed a finger at her. 'I *won't* grant you a divorce. We agreed to five years. You're going to give me those five years, and not a day less. You *do* understand that, don't you, Goldie? You *do* get that anything less and I'll make sure you're locked in a court battle you'll have no hope of emerging from for another five years after that.'

She exhaled, exasperation eating her alive. 'Well, no, I *don't* get that. *If* I want a divorce you'll have to give me one when the five years are up. That's the agreement. But—'

'But nothing! *Santa Maria*, we've been married less than a week and one argument sends you running to a— Wait… *If*?'

She tried to resist rolling her eyes. She failed. 'I'm going to explain myself to you now, Gael. Are you ready to listen?'

His brow was thunderous. 'I'm not a child, Goldie. Tell me what I need to know.'

She bit her tongue against a curt answer. 'I've told you I don't want your money.'

His nostrils flared but he remained silent.

'So I went to see an attorney to give it away.'

His eyes widened. 'What?'

'The agreement says that on each wedding anniversary I get the sum you promised wired to my account. I got the attorney to divide that money five ways—two-fifths will go to charities here in Barcelona and two-fifths to charities in the States. The fifth portion will go to a local performing arts community near where I live in Trenton.' She reached into her purse, withdrew the document and held it out to him. 'Here—see for yourself.'

Mild shock blanketing his face, he took the document from her, read it with lightning speed.

Then he frowned at her. 'You're giving away all the money?'

'All of it.'

'And did you happen to discuss divorce with this attorney while you were getting this done?' he demanded, his eyes still a touch wild.

'No, Gael. I didn't. The D-word didn't once pass my lips. You said to find a way. I found a way.'

He exhaled, his breath decidedly shaky as he bunched up the document and flung it over his shoulder. 'Why the hell didn't you say that?'

'You were on a roll. I tried to stop you, but you seemed intent on flattening me.'

He paced in a tight circle without once taking his eyes off her. '*Dios mio.* Why do I you let you drive me so crazy?' he seethed quietly.

She shrugged. 'You drive *yourself* crazy. You don't need my help.'

He gave a deep, vicious growl before he lunged for her. Fingers spiked into her hair, angled her head, a nanosecond before his mouth smashed down on hers. He kissed her hungrily, deeply, then ripped his mouth from hers a minute later.

'You found a way?' he whispered roughly.

'I found a way.'

He leaned his forehead against hers, his eyes boring into her own. 'Does that mean you want to be with me, Goldie?' he demanded, his voice hoarse with need. 'Truly be mine?'

'Yes,' she replied simply.

Because her need for him *was* that simple. She'd been a fool to imagine that she could erase it out of the equation—that she would be content to sleep next door to him for five long years. Even if it were true that Gael would tire of her after six short weeks, she was still going to take that time with him.

The kiss he delivered after her answer in the affirmative was bliss-inducing. Her purse fell off her shoulder and was forgotten. The hem of her sundress was gripped in a tight hold, pulled over her head and dropped to the floor, leaving her in the white bikini set she'd planned to wear for lounging by the poolside that morning.

Gael caressed his way down her jaw, her throat and shoulders. Cupping those, he turned her around and groaned, low and deep.

'*Amante*, you're so beautiful.'

The throaty words drew a delicious shiver from her, making her tremble in his arms. His fingers catching the long ties of her bikini top, he pulled them free and turned her around. Eyes turned burnished gold devoured her seconds before his hands resumed their caress. A deeper tremble seized her as he cupped her breasts and squeezed. Her hand rose to grip his waist.

She needed to hold on to him. It was a desire and a necessity. Her gaze rose to meet his and her breath caught at the ferocious hunger in his eyes. Unable to resist, she stood on tiptoe and pressed her mouth to his. His hands left her breasts to gather her close. He groaned when her chest pressed into his. Clever fingers made short work of the bottom half of the bikini. Then, naked, she was once again caught in his arms.

After an age of glorious kissing, Gael picked her up and carried her to his king-sized bed. Quick and efficient movements relieved him of his clothes and then he prowled onto the bed, sleek and magnificent next to her.

From cheek to neck, cleavage to midriff, every inch of her skin was covered in open-mouthed kisses, while over and over his fingers drifted over her abdomen where their baby nestled.

Suddenly he snapped his head up, eyes narrowed. 'Did you take your prenatal vitamins this morning?' he asked.

Goldie curbed the need to smile. 'Yes.'

A brisk nod. 'Did you have a good breakfast?'

'Yes.'

He completed another circling caress over her belly. 'Are you hungry now? The pregnancy book says you should eat little and often. Can I get you anything?'

She suppressed a groan of frustration, sliding her hands over his shoulders, glorying in the muscles that bunched at her touch. 'I'm fine, Gael. I don't need anything. No— actually, scratch that. I need *you*. Only you.'

His grin was full and unfettered, snagging a tight string around her heart. Bending his head, he placed a deep, reverent kiss on her belly before he began to kiss his way lower.

Goldie tried and failed to stop the hot blushes that rolled over her at the expert attention he delivered between her legs. Much too soon she was crying out and soaring high.

Still buzzing, she moaned as he rose over her, kissed her lips and caught her hands together above her head.

'Open your legs for me, *querida*,' he commanded throatily.

She obeyed wholeheartedly.

'Now, look at me. Show me your beautiful eyes.'

Her breath still unsteady from the aftershocks of her climax, she lifted her gaze. He caught it easily, his eyes pinning her as effectively as his body pinned hers.

One hand holding hers captive, he used the other to guide himself into her. They both groaned as pleasure surged, pure and dizzying. Without the restriction of a condom the pleasure was more intense—a fact Gael gutturally attested to a minute after the sensational thought flew across her brain.

'I want it like this from now on. Always. I can never go back.'

'Yes...' she readily agreed, already on a set course to flame-hot bliss.

He increased his tempo, need dictating the pace as he thrust deeper inside her. On another thick groan he lowered his head and fused her mouth with his. Tongues melding, breath mingling, they celebrated their coming together with unfettered passion, then collapsed into each other's arms as ecstasy flung them into nirvana.

Once their breaths quietened he speared his fingers through her hair and angled her face to his.

'This time when I go to the bathroom be assured that I will return,' he mock growled.

Goldie laughed, her heart lifting with a sensation she didn't want to name just yet. 'Okay.'

He left her for a minute, returned with a warmed towel. After seeing to her, he returned it to the bathroom. Her breath caught all over again as she watched his gladiator-like body move towards her. She might not be in this position for the whole of the five years they'd committed to one another but, boy, she intended to enjoy every minute of the time she did have.

'Dare I ask what's going on in that brain of yours?' he drawled.

She grimaced. 'I'm thinking we need to get up soon, before Mom comes knocking. It's almost time for them to head to the airport.'

'Right. Nothing like the thought of my mother-in-law catching me defiling her daughter to kill my buzz.'

She laughed. He joined in.

She felt another life-defining twinge of her heart.

By the time they got up to get dressed, ten minutes later, Goldie was beginning to fear the changes her emotions were going through...

CHAPTER TWELVE

GAEL ADJUSTED THE SLEEVES of his morning suit and resisted the urge to glance at his watch for the third time in as many minutes.

'Goldie, we're going to be late.'

They were expected at Alejandro's villa at noon—an hour before the ceremony started.

'I...I'm almost there.'

He frowned. He didn't understand her need to keep a separate bedroom now she was sharing his bed. Granted, it had only been one night, but her half-hearted agreement when he'd suggested this morning that she move her things into his suite had irritated him.

Now, with the added tension of the impending ceremony and the inevitable face-to-face with his father, his nape felt tight. Hell, his whole body was on a knife-edge.

He whirled from the window.

And was confronted with a vision.

Dios mio, she was breathtaking! With the time she'd spent in the sun, her *café-au-lait* skin was almost as dark as his own, making her violet eyes stunning luminous pools. But the flush of pregnancy had added a glow that made it impossible for him to take his eyes off her. With her carefully styled but already a little wild corkscrew curls, and her body draped in a shoulder-baring, floor-length dress, she looked as divine as an angel. She wore the pearl earrings she'd worn on their wedding day, but her throat was bare. She was radiant enough—didn't need further adornment.

Gael wasn't sure why the memory had chosen that moment to return, but his insides snagged hard as he recalled how he'd felt when he'd received the call from his driver about her visit to the attorney's office. The hour he'd paced until her return had felt like the blackest of his life.

Which puzzled and disturbed the hell out of him.

Telling himself it was just because she carried his child rang a little hollow. Now that he'd accepted he was to be a father, it was a position he was looking forward to. If nothing else, he wanted to conquer the demons that howled at him that the seed he came from was poisoned. He didn't believe that any more. He would be better. Their child would be cared for and cherished.

What he'd felt yesterday had been something different altogether. He'd been afraid of losing *Goldie*, not the child she carried. And if that wasn't unnerving enough, the sharp swing of his mood in the opposite direction when she'd revealed the reason for her visit had been so acute he'd been almost dizzy with it.

That latter feeling had continued to cascade through him all through the night and to this moment. For the first time in his life Gael didn't know whether he wanted to face the problem head-on, as usual, or back away from it.

'Um…say something? *Anything?*'

He chose to back away. 'It's way past time to go.'

She grimaced. 'Right. Fine.'

He smiled. 'And you look magnificent, *querida*.'

When she reached him she punched him lightly in the arm. He responded by catching her offending hand and trailing his lips across the back of it. And as he was rewarded with a smile as luminescent as her eyes Gael felt himself swing towards that unknown high. Felt himself lose the solid ground beneath his feet.

Shaking his head, he took a deep breath and escorted her outside.

They just needed to get today over and done with. Then

he could make the time to examine these *feelings* that had taken hold of him.

The limo ride to Alejandro's adjoining estate took fifteen minutes, and he welcomed the time to answer Goldie's subtle questions about his relationship with his brother. As he answered her he realised it was another first. He didn't find talking about Alejandro as difficult as he once had, and the half-brother he'd once believed he would never willingly accept had become more of a family symbol in his mind than his own mother.

His jaw tightened as he thought of his mother and her threatened visit. Gael hadn't gone out of his way to keep Goldie's pregnancy a secret—he'd told Alejandro and Elise—but he knew his mother kept tabs on him through his household staff. So he hadn't been surprised when she'd called yesterday and dropped subtle hints until he'd divulged the news.

Her immediate announcement that she intended to visit had rubbed him the wrong way. But, no matter how disappointed and bitter he felt over her behaviour, he'd never rejected any overtures from her.

'Gael, if you clench your jaw any harder it'll snap,' Goldie said gently from beside him. 'Same goes for my hand.'

He exhaled sharply, released the tight grip he'd unconsciously placed on her hand and kissed it better. '*Lo siento*. I should warn you—my father will most likely be at the wedding.'

She nodded, her sexy curls bounced. 'And…?'

'And I haven't seen him for over ten years.' He shrugged. 'I can't say how things will go.'

'Okay.' She frowned. 'Your mother won't be there, will she?'

He gave a bitter laugh and shook his head. 'No, but she's coming to the villa tomorrow.'

Her eyes widened. 'Does she know about the baby?'

'Yes, but not about us being married.'

'Do the rest of your family know?'

'I told Andro and Elise last week. As much as I relish being a pain in Alejandro's backside, I didn't want our news to take over their day.'

Her smile warmed him, made him feel less edgy. It felt like the most natural thing in the world to slide his hand around her shoulders and pull her close. Her face turned up to his immediately, and he lost himself in the sensation of kissing her.

His driver's throat-clearing announced their arrival and Gael pulled back reluctantly.

'You owe me another dozen of those when we get home.'

She rolled her eyes, but her smile widened as she slid her hand into his and let him help her out.

Alejandro's villa was almost a carbon copy of his, bar a few minor details—like the absence of a climbing vine in the courtyard and the presence of an art studio built for Elise. His soon-to-be sister-in-law had become an overnight Manga-writing sensation when she'd sold her thirty-story collection for a fortune last year. Now retired from her previous work as a PR consultant, she was pursuing a flourishing full-time Manga-creating career.

Alejandro was descending the stairs when they entered. Gael locked eyes with his half-brother and noted that the acrimony he'd spent years nursing was almost non-existent. In their own stilted way they'd managed to forge a bond—one Gael suddenly hoped would grow stronger.

He eyed his older brother's state of semi-undress with a mocking smirk. 'Are you sure you're getting married in an hour? You look like you've just escaped a drunken sailor's bachelor party.'

Alejandro's mouth quirked in a half-smile. 'This is the

result when I'm not allowed to see my fiancée for almost twenty-four hours. Whoever came up with that idiotic tradition deserves to hang.'

His dark hazel eyes shifted to Goldie. Lingered.

Although Gael knew the depth of feeling between his half-brother and his almost-wife, something very much like jealousy shifted inside him. 'Goldie, this is Alejandro, my bear of a brother. Andro—meet Goldie.'

'Pleased to meet you. And congratulations on both accounts,' Andro drawled.

Goldie smiled and held out her hand. Alejandro's eyes widened infinitesimally before he took her hand and brushed his lips over the back of it.

Gael bristled.

Andro sent him a *payback's a bitch* wink.

He laughed, knowing he deserved the payback for flirting with Elise the first time they'd met.

'Okay. Well played,' he replied.

Goldie looked from him to Andro. 'Am I missing something?'

Gael shook his head. 'Nothing worth mentioning.'

Alejandro laughed under his breath, then his expression sobered. When he glanced at a nearby clock Gael was sure he growled under his breath.

'Do you need my help with anything, or shall we leave you to your growling and staff-frightening?' he mocked.

'If I wasn't absolutely certain Elise would have my hide, I'd sink a double shot of bourbon right about now.' He cast another look at the clock.

Gael laughed. 'Good luck with that. I'll see you at the altar.'

Alejandro nodded, started to walk away and then stopped. '*Mi hermano*, I should warn you—our father is here. He arrived early. You can avoid him if you want, but if you're headed for the salon he'll be in there.'

His eyes narrowed and Gael saw the same ruthlessness that coursed through his veins reflected in his brother's eyes.

'For Elise's sake I would prefer it if you kept your reunion brawl-free—*entiendes*?'

Everything inside Gael tightened, but he managed a nod before his brother walked away. Gael remained where he stood, his senses once more on the finest of edges.

'We don't have to go in there if you don't want to.'

He started, having momentarily forgotten his wife's presence. Resolutely, he shook his head. 'This meeting has been inevitable and it's long overdue. Besides, I have a couple of things to get off my chest,' he said.

He saw the trepidation in her face, wished he could soothe it. But the strides carrying him into the salon demanded all his attention.

Gael's eyes zeroed in on him immediately—saw the moment his father sensed his presence. He stood next to his wife, Alejandro's mother, who was seated with a coffee in her hand.

Tomas Aguilar's gaze sharpened, then widened with a mixture of shock and shame before his expression was neutralised. Gael wished that evidence of shame soothed the part of him he'd for a long time denied was still hurting. Perhaps a few months ago—before Tomas had struck up his illicit affair with his mother once more—it *would* have gone some way to soothe the rejection.

But not now.

He strolled forward until he reached the two of them.

Evita Aguilar glanced up at him, her face reflecting neither acceptance nor rejection. For a moment he felt sorry for her, having tied her destiny to a man with such low scruples. But she averted her gaze and her opinion ceased to matter.

His eyes reconnected with Tomas Aguilar's and again

he saw that momentary flash of shame, this time accompanied by regret.

'It's good to see you…son,' his father said in his native tongue.

Shock held Gael rigid, then he replied tersely, 'English, please. My wife doesn't speak Spanish.'

Both Tomas and Evita started.

'Your *wife*?' His father recovered first, his gaze swinging to Goldie.

'*Si,'* Gael responded.

After observing her for a few charged seconds, he inclined his head. 'I'm Tomas, and this is my wife, Evita.'

Goldie's smile was a little guarded, but sincere. 'Hello, I'm Goldie.'

Gael's smile felt tight. 'Now that we have the pleasantries over and done with, enjoy the rest of your day.'

His father opened his mouth as if he wanted to say something. Then he glanced down at his wife and shut it again.

More bitterness dredged through Gael. Tightening his hold on Goldie, he led her away.

'I thought you were going to talk to him?'

'So did I, but I find that even that isn't worth doing any more.'

They walked through the salon's French doors and out onto a wide terrace. Beyond the large white columns rolled a sea of green grass, and in the centre was displayed the wedding arch where the ceremony was to be held. Fifty white-linen-draped chairs were divided on either side of the arch for the guests, the first of whom were appearing in limos and luxury cars at the bottom of the long driveway.

'Are you sure?'

Gael was certain the answer was yes until he opened his mouth. 'Maybe not.'

'He looked like he wanted to say something. So maybe let *him* do the talking?'

He glanced down at her with a slight frown. 'Only a short while ago he loomed large over my life, dictated my choices without me realising it.' He shrugged. 'But not so much any more.'

Gael suspected the feeling had something to do with the woman in front of him. Yet another thing to be examined later.

'All the same, you have a chance to get rid of the toxin once and for all. Do you want to look back and wonder if it would've been better to reconnect, to find some answers for yourself?'

Gael remembered hinting at something similar to Alejandro last year. At the time he'd blithely dropped a suggestion that his brother reconnect with the parents he'd walked away from. He knew Alejandro's visit to Seville hadn't been easy. Just as the contemplation of today hadn't been easy for Gael.

Slowly, he nodded. 'Maybe. Now, enough about this. You owe me a dozen kisses. Make good on one of them now, please.'

He was seconds from losing his mind from a kiss alone when footsteps pulled them apart.

Alejandro, followed by his parents, had stepped out onto the terrace, followed by the first of the guests. Waiters were serving mimosas and champagne to keep the guests refreshed until the organ struck up.

When it did, Gael led Goldie to the front row and stepped beside his brother.

The ceremony went without a hitch. Elise smiled widely when Gael welcomed her into the family. Then he watched as his new sister-in-law and his wife fell into instant friendship.

All through the ceremony he'd caught his father's eyes

on him. And after countless trips to the dance floor with
Goldie—because he didn't want to miss any opportunity
to hold her in his arms—she pushed him towards Tomas.

'It's time, Gael. Come and find me when you're done.'

He caught her before she could walk away. 'No, you
come and find *me* in ten minutes. I'm guessing that's about
how long I'll be able to stand it before things head south.'

She nodded. 'Okay—deal.'

He watched her sway off the dance floor and immediately be accosted by Elise.

His father was looking his way when he turned.

Gael snagged a whisky from a passing waiter before
stepping out of the giant marquee onto the green grass.
Above him the night sky twinkled with a thousand stars.
But he was too on edge to appreciate the view.

Tomas joined him a minute later.

Gael turned his head and met eyes the same colour as
his own. 'I hated you for a very long time.'

He didn't see any reason to mince his words. A second later he realised that he'd spoken in the past tense
and spoken in English, because he wasn't ready to have
another thing in common with the man whose blood ran
through his veins.

A wave of pain and regret passed over Tomas's face. 'I
know. And I deserved all of it. For what I did to you, and
to your brother, you have every right to hate me.'

'But you're still doing it, aren't you? With my mother?'
he accused, and a deep cloying emotion he recognised as
pain roughened his voice.

Tomas shook his head. 'No, I'm not.'

Gael snorted. 'I spoke to my mother two weeks ago.
She was going to see you.'

'Yes, I met with her to end it.'

Gael stared hard at his father, wondering whether to
believe him or not.

'I should never have started things with your mother again. It was selfish. But after Andro came to see me last year I thought you and I might reconnect too…I couldn't summon the courage to reach out directly to you. So I called Katerina.'

Gael cursed under his breath.

Tomas shrugged. 'I think you know that I'm far from perfect. I would go so far as to call myself unworthy of being a father to both my sons. But you and Alejandro have grown into exceptional men, and I remain selfish enough to want to be a part of your lives. I would be honoured to be in your life at some point beyond today, but if you don't think that's a possibility let me tell you now that I'm proud of you.'

Something tugged in his chest. Gael fought to resist it.

'You're *proud*? You told me I was a *mistake*—that I should never have been born! Because of you I don't trust anyone… I don't know how to *love* anyone. I'm a bastard who shouldn't exist.'

Tomas paled, his eyes anguished as he stared at Gael. 'But your relationship with your brother is thriving, and you have a beautiful wife who clearly worsh—'

His laughter cut off his father's words. 'A wife I'm incapable of loving because I don't know how. A wife I've paid for. Because on the night I found out you were still sniffing around my mother I was so angry that I slaked my anger and lust on an innocent woman. After that she fell pregnant with my child, and now I'm tied to her for life—'

The ragged gasp behind him tore through to his very soul.

Even before he turned around Gael knew the landscape of his life had changed irrevocably.

Because six feet behind him Goldie stood, ghost-pale and pain-ravaged, her eyes lost pools as she shook her head slowly.

'*Dios mio*... Goldie.' He started towards her.

Her hands flew out. 'No. Stay away from me!'

He couldn't fathom ever doing that. So he took another step. She stumbled back, her heel catching on the grass.

It was Tomas who went to her aid. Tomas who helped her to her feet with a gentle touch that turned Gael's stomach.

Get your hands off her! he wanted to scream. But the words wouldn't come. His life was too busy flashing before his eyes.

But he had to act. He couldn't lose her.

Unable to believe what was happening, he tried again. 'Please, *querida. Por favor*, let me ex—'

'I swear, if you take one more step towards me I'll scream the place down. And I'll leave you to explain to your brother what went down here.'

They stood frozen, the three of them, in a twisted tableau.

After a handful of seconds Tomas turned to him. 'Let her go, Gael,' his father said to him in Spanish. 'Emotions are too high right now. You can try and repair things later.'

Every instinct screamed against his taking his father's advice. But Goldie's raised chin and her aggressive stance spelled a no-go zone he would find impossible to breach. Still, his chest felt on fire with the idea of letting her go.

'*Amante*, please...' he tried again.

'I'm leaving, Gael, and I don't want you to come with me.'

He glanced at his father. Saw a tiny nod from Tomas.

His ragged sigh felt like a gasp of death. 'I'll tell the driver to take you home. I'll be there in an hour, maybe two. Will...will that be enough time?'

Dios, please let her say yes. He couldn't stand to be away longer than that.

Her mouth twisted. 'More than enough.'

With those two words his wife turned on her spiky heels and walked away.

And with each step she took Gael's senses screamed at him that he was making the biggest mistake of his life.

CHAPTER THIRTEEN

GOLDIE HAD NO RECOLLECTION of what she'd packed or how long it had taken for the driver to deliver her to the airport. But somehow she'd managed to talk to a ticket agent and buy a ticket home.

She still had a couple of days before the last leg of filming commenced for *Soul's Triumph*, for which she thanked God. Because the way she felt right now—the way her heart screamed as if it was being ripped out with each breath she took—she didn't think she could utter one line, never mind a few hundred.

She needed the comfort of home, of her mother, even though she would need to turn around and come right back to Spain in two days to join the cast and crew. Even though Gael would most likely still be here.

She just couldn't bear to be here right now. Because somewhere between his threats and his mockery and his smiles and his exceptional lovemaking she'd fallen in love with the man whose child she carried.

Goldie was too weary to pinpoint when exactly it had happened. It had happened. And even before she'd dared to hope that her fragile feelings might be returned he'd dashed hope in the most devastating way possible.

She only had herself to blame. Everything that had happened from the moment Gael had stepped into that alley six weeks ago had been her fault.

He'd made her no promises, save for telling her that he desired her and wanted the child she carried, and she'd foolishly chosen to let her heart loose in the frantic hope for love.

Squeezing her eyes shut and turning her head away

from the curious passenger next to her, she pressed her fist to her mouth as tears fell.

Maybe the newness of her love meant she could salvage her heart?

Dream on, her shattered heart mocked.

She'd fallen hook, line and sinker.

There was no going back.

Gael tried to outstare his mother-in-law as she bodily barred her front door.

'Sorry, son. She doesn't want to see you.'

There was nothing remotely remorseful in her tone. In fact her body bristled with enough quiet fury for him to realise where Goldie got her strength from.

'Gloria, I just want to talk to her for five minutes.' He used his most reasonable negotiating tone, despite wanting to roar and plead and beg.

Gloria Beckett folded her arms. 'She flew six thousand miles to get away from you. Hoping that a five-minute conversation will fix things is a touch foolish, don't you think?' she challenged.

Suitably chastised, he nodded. 'I'm willing to do whatever it takes, however long it takes. Can you please tell her that?'

He received a shrug in return, and the light violet eyes narrowed on him as he fought the urge to pace. A few times he opened his mouth to speak. Every time, Gloria's chin went up higher, daring him to utter more damning words.

Gael bit his tongue against cursing and tried to see past the woman's shoulder into the house that harboured the woman he loved—the woman he couldn't bear to be apart from for one more second. Gloria's subtle shifting told him he was pushing it.

He shoved his fingers through his hair and tried one more time. 'Is everything okay with her?'

Gloria tossed her blonde head. 'Are you asking about my daughter or about the baby?'

'I'm asking about my *wife*. About *our child*.'

'You should have thought about them before you messed up.'

Spikes of anguish ripped wounds through his heart. 'You're right. I messed up. Badly. But I want…I *need* the chance to fix it. *Por favor?*' he added gruffly when she remained intransigent.

Her stare bored into him for depressingly long seconds before she sighed. 'I'll tell her what you said, son. But don't hold your breath. My daughter is made of strong stuff. She may be bent a little out of shape right now, but she's not broken. If she learns to stand again without you, then you'll have missed your chance.'

His heart dropped to his feet as she stepped back and slammed the door in his face.

He raised his hand to knock again, then froze when he heard the ragged sobs coming from within.

He'd spent the last twenty-four hours in hell. But the woman crying inside the house—the woman his heart yearned for more than it wanted to beat—was hurting. And it was his fault. His being here was hurting her even more.

And yet Gael couldn't leave. Staggering away from the door, he stumbled down the front step and sank onto it. Time ticked by, marched on. He couldn't move.

A light rain began to fall. He watched the droplets form on his arms and drip down his fingers. His numbness kept him insulated. Gael looked up when his driver stepped from the limo and started walking towards him with a blanket. He shook his head once, fiercely, sending the man backtracking. He didn't deserve to feel warm. Besides, compared to the chill in his heart the rain was nothing.

Midnight slowly ticked by. He knew because a clock chimed inside the house.

When he heard a noise behind him he wondered if someone's house pet had chosen to join him in misery.

'Are you trying to make some sort of point by freezing to death on my doorstep?'

Gael stood and jerked round. One lunge up the steps and he was standing in front of her.

'Goldie...*mi amor*...please give me a chance to explain.' He wanted to touch her but he didn't dare—didn't want to risk her bolting back inside.

'I think what I heard was clear enough. You bought me and you don't think you can love me.'

He shook his head, spreading a few raindrops.

She wiped a drop from her cheek, her movements jerky.

'No...I mean, yes, that's what I said. But I didn't mean it. Not like that.'

He stopped and inhaled. How could words fail him, today of all days, when his life depended on it?

'What I meant was, I knew you were leaning towards a yes to my proposal even before I offered you the money and the movie roles. I tagged them on because I wanted to be able to tell myself you'd chosen to marry me because of money.'

Her brows clamped in a frown. 'Why?' she asked, bewildered.

'Hearing that you weren't wanted, that you're a mistake, even once, isn't something you can brush under the carpet and forget easily. Alejandro and I are true brothers now, but there was a time when I thought he was the same as our father in his contempt of me. Having two out of your three closest blood relations reject you as a child is...painful. I convinced myself I was okay with it, but it wasn't until lately—until *you*—that I realised I'd let it cloud a lot of my life's decisions.'

He stopped and took a deep breath.

'I have a confession to make.'

Her eyes grew more wary. 'Yes?'

'I was at Othello on another audition hunt when I heard you performing. I was stunned by you. But then I heard that casting director proposition you.'

She gasped. 'That's why you were so nasty to me when we met? Why you would look at me sometimes with that judgemental look in your eyes?'

He sighed and nodded. 'I saw him touch you, thought you were agreeable to what he'd proposed, but I know now I must have misheard.'

'I didn't understand what he was asking me at first. When I did, I told him to go to hell.'

'I guessed as much. But much later. I'm sorry, Goldie.'

Her lips pursed. 'You were saying about your past clouding your judgement...?'

He nodded. 'When you wouldn't share my bed I thought it was because I wasn't good enough for you, so I lashed out at you. I'm sorry, *mi amor*. I didn't buy you. I threw money at you so I could make myself feel better, tell myself that yearning for you the way I did was okay because I had controlled your entry into my life. It was wrong, Goldie, and I'd give anything to turn back time and unsay what I said about you to my father.'

He watched, cursed as tears slowly filled her eyes.

'*Dios mio*, please don't cry.'

'I won't lie to you, Gael. You hurt me.'

Pain sliced his insides. 'I'll fix it, Goldie. I swear with everything I am I'll spend the rest of my life undoing this hurt.'

Her mouth trembled. 'How?' she croaked.

'Let me love you. Let me earn the right to worship you. You and our child. I'll do whatever you want.'

She licked her lips. 'What if what I want...what I *need*... is you?'

A tremble seized him that had nothing to do with the

chilled wet shirt clinging to his back. 'Then take me. I'm yours.'

'Not until I know…until I'm sure how you feel.'

'How I…? *I love you.* I adore you.'

Her breath caught. 'Please say that again, Gael.'

He closed his eyes, dared to take her hands, bring them to his lips in a reverent kiss. 'I love you, Goldie Aguilar. It may be a new love, but I promise you it's strong, it's yours, and it *will* stand the test of time.'

She freed her hands to cup his face. 'Oh, Gael. I love you too.'

His eyes sprang open. 'You *love* me?'

'Yes. And my love is just as new as yours. I love you, and I'm willing to take a chance on us nurturing each other's love, if you want.'

'*Sí!* I most definitely want.'

She smiled. His heart threatened to burst out of his chest.

She threw her arms around him and stood on tiptoe. 'Kiss me, Gael.'

It was his turn to smile. '*Dios*, you don't need to ask twice. If I remember correctly, you owe me ten kisses.'

'And I would've delivered if you hadn't thrown a spanner in the works.'

His face sobered. '*Lo siento, mi amor.* Forgive me.'

'All is forgiven.'

She fell into his arms again. When they finally parted their eyes were misted with tears.

'Take me home, Gael. Please.'

He nodded solemnly. 'It would be my honour, *mi mujer.*' He swung her up in his arms and started off the porch. About to step off, he paused. 'What about your mother?'

'She knows where my heart is…that I belong where you are.'

His head dropped until their foreheads touched. 'Goldie, I promise I will never make you regret that.'

She settled one hand over his heart, the other over her stomach, where their baby grew.

'And we promise to love and cherish you. For ever.'

EPILOGUE

By UNANIMOUS AGREEMENT, voted on by their entire family, they held the wedding of their hearts two weeks after their daughter was born. Melina Aguilar lay nestled lovingly in her parents' arms as they renewed their vows in front of a much bigger, much happier congregation at the cathedral in Barcelona. Beneath centuries of history and stained-glass windows, they repeated the vows they'd uttered in that small chapel on Gael's estate.

Alejandro acted as his best man, and took delight in ribbing his brother mercilessly. And they stepped out into the late December evening to the sound of church bells and Christmas carols being sung in Spanish and English.

At the kerb, a vintage car stood waiting, beyond which a police cordon had been set up to keep back the screaming fans who shouted Goldie's name.

Soul's Triumph had been released to huge box office success three months before, and Goldie had become an overnight sensation. She'd been inundated with roles, but had elected to make only one movie a year, to free her to spend the rest of her time being a wife and mother—the two roles she cherished above all else.

She stopped long enough to wave to her fans before she got into the car, which was festooned not just with wedding decorations but also with holly and dozens of sprigs of mistletoe, some of which were also strung along the inside roof. Not that the couple needed any excuse to kiss on the long ride back to the villa once their daughter had fallen into a dreamy nap.

Goldie wrinkled her nose when Gael released her after another long, heady kiss, and indicated the mistletoe. 'Sorry about this. I tried to discourage my mother from doing it.'

Gael laughed. 'So did I with *my* mother—but I think we knew the moment those two got together that we didn't stand a chance.' He flicked a finger at the mistletoe. 'Although I'm not sure whether to be concerned that they believe I need a reason to kiss my wife, or to thank them for supplying me with so many opportunities to do so.'

He pulled her close once more and thoroughly explored her mouth.

They'd chosen to keep their reception small, for family and close friends only. And they arrived back at the house and alighted to join Alejandro and a very pregnant Elise. She was just over seven months, due on Valentine's Day—a fact which was a source of endless mocking ammunition for Gael against his brother.

The brothers had grown closer in the months following their respective marriages, and Goldie counted Elise not just as a sister-in-law but as a friend.

Goldie smiled at her now, as Elise joined her in the hallway and held out her arms for Melina.

Elise waited until the men were headed for the salon before she leaned in close. 'I think Gael has another role up his sleeve for you.' She winked.

Goldie laughed. 'Oh, really?'

Elise nodded. 'I heard him talking. He was asking Alejandro when it would be best to start trying for baby number two.'

Goldie rolled her eyes. 'And do I need two guesses as to what Andro's response was?'

Elise grinned. 'He said, "Immediately, of course."'

Both women laughed, causing their husbands to turn back and stare.

'What's going on?' Gael asked, making his way back to slide both arms around her.

Goldie smiled and kissed him. 'Nothing you need to worry about. Just yet.'

Both Alejandro and Gael groaned. Elise grinned unrepentantly and joined her husband. Goldie watched him tenderly touch Melina's cheek before he caressed his wife's rounded belly.

Gael's arms tightened around her, snagging her attention. She looked up into her husband's eyes. 'I love you. Thank you for marrying me again.'

'I'd marry you every day if I could.'

They kissed until their respective mothers walked past, clearing their throats loudly.

Gael and his mother had found their way back to each other after the end of her short affair with Tomas Aguilar. There was still a little tension all round, but hearts and souls were slowly healing.

Grinning now, Gael and Goldie joined the rest of their family and their closest friends in the large salon for traditional Spanish Christmas tapas and drinks.

As toasts were given and presents exchanged, Goldie saw a look pass between Gael and Alejandro—powerful and visceral and filled with the affection they'd been denied as children but had found in abundance as husbands and brothers.

* * * * *

ONE NIGHT TO
WEDDING VOWS

KIM LAWRENCE

CHAPTER ONE

THE PLACE DIDN'T fall silent as Sergio Di Vittorio walked through the casino but there was a discernible hush in the room, an air of expectancy as the elderly aristocrat walked in ahead of two tall, dark, suited figures. The heavier set of the two stayed by the entrance while the other followed his employer, remaining a respectful pace behind the older man as he continued his regal progress.

From where he was standing, one shoulder propped against a marble pillar, Raoul's sensually designed lips curved in a cynical smile from which affection was not totally absent as he watched his grandfather's stately arrival. In the periphery of his vision he remained aware of the middle-aged guy, eyes glazed with febrile excitement, who continued to throw good money after bad on the roulette wheel. It had been like watching a car crash, now only a matter of how many innocent victims he'd take with him…a wife, a kid…?

The reckless gleam in Raoul's own deep-set dark eyes owed more to the brandy in his hand than the spin of a wheel. Each to his own drug of choice, Raoul thought, with a lazy tolerance. He turned, a faint ironic smile of self-mockery curving his lips as he found himself automatically straightening his spine as his grandfather got closer. *Old habits die hard*, he thought to himself, and his grandfather had strong views on good posture.

The autocratic head of the diverse family businesses and guardian of the family name had strong views on most things. Gambling, for one. Not really surprising considering his only son, Raoul and Jamie's father, had blown his brains out when the full extent of his gambling debts became public.

Sergio could have hushed up the scandal and covered his son's debts—the amount involved was small change to him—but instead he had chosen to tell his son to stand on his own two feet and be a man.

Did he regret it?

Did he blame himself?

Raoul doubted it. Sergio's self-belief did not allow for doubts. Raoul's youthful anger had been reserved for the father who had taken the easy way out and left them. It was hard for a kid to comprehend that level of self-destructive desperation, or to get his head around the fact that addicts were inherently selfish. Even the years of adult understanding did not take away the bitterness or the memories of a lonely child, but Jamie had always been there for him, the older brother who had fought his battles until Raoul had got big and tough enough to hold his own.

The long fingers of the hand Raoul dug into the pocket of his tailored dark trousers flexed as his mind drifted back. He could almost feel his brother's warm fingers tightening around his own as their grandfather broke the news. The moment was etched in his memory: the single tear rolling, in what had seemed like slow motion, down his older brother's face; the metronomic tick of a clock on the wall; his grandfather's deep voice explaining that they would be living with him now.

Confusion and fear had clutched at his stomach, the heavy ache of a sob in his throat held there by the desperate need to please his grandfather. He'd saved his tears for the privacy of his pillow.

Raoul pulled his drifting thoughts back to the present, his mouth a hard line as his heavy-lidded, cynical stare drifted to the glass he lifted in a silent salute: *absent friends!* As the years went on, the pillow had given way to brandy. Or maybe he had simply lost the ability to cry altogether. Maybe he'd lost the ability to feel as normal people did.

Tears would not bring his brother back. Jamie was gone.

He lowered his gaze, his chest lifting as the dark mesh of his lashes shut out the grief. He refused to acknowledge the buffeting of a fresh wave of despair that no amount of brandy could numb.

'You were missed at the wake.' Sergio tilted his head to the spinning roulette wheel. 'So, you have decided to follow in your father's footsteps?'

With a jerk Raoul's head came up. 'It is always an option, I suppose,' he drawled. 'And you know what they say…an addictive personality is hereditary.'

Sergio responded to the remark with one of his inimitable shrugs. 'I considered the possibility.'

The frank admission wrenched a hard, cracked laugh from Raoul's throat. 'Of course you did.'

'No, you both escaped the taint but you are an adrenaline junkie, just like Ja—' The old man stopped and swallowed hard several times before continuing. 'Your brother always said that— He… Jam…'

Unable to watch his grandfather struggle for control, Raoul cut across him, throwing out harshly, 'That if I didn't kill myself climbing it would be behind the wheel of one of my cars.'

For a moment his brother's voice sounded so real that he almost turned expecting to see the familiar smiling face—*you're an adrenaline junkie, little brother, and one of these days you'll kill yourself…* The irony was like a punch to the gut.

But Jamie had been the one to die young, not because he had taken a corner too fast but because life was just not fair.

Raoul took a deep swallow of the brandy swirling in

his glass as anger circled in his head. It took a few jaw-
clenching seconds before he trusted his voice to continue.

'I never expected to see you slumming it in a place like
this, but I have to admit you do know how to make an entrance.' It was true. Even in his eighties Sergio Di Vittorio
made an imposing figure, dressed as always in black, the
abundant silver-streaked, collar-length hair catching the
light cast by the glittering chandeliers overhead.

If his emotions hadn't flatlined he might be curious
about why his grandfather was here but Raoul continued to
feel nothing. He took a swallow of brandy and checked—
yes, nothing.

*This lying to himself was actually something he might
be quite good at.*

'People were asking after you.'

Raoul tipped his head down. Sergio was a tall man, six
feet, deep chested and broad of shoulder, but Raoul had
been four inches taller than his grandfather since he was
fifteen. It still felt somehow not quite right, almost disre-
spectful, to look down on him.

'Good party, was it?' He slumped back against the col-
umn, the lazy posture giving him less height advantage.
He raised his glass to his lips, the gesture going some way
to hiding his expression as he thought, *When did you get
so damned old?*

There was nothing like a funeral to make a person
aware of their own mortality and that of those they loved…
precious few of whom were left.

He pushed away the dark thought and took another slug
of the brandy. It slid down his throat, settling in his stomach with a warmth that did nothing to alleviate the coldness that permeated his entire body, a *coldness* that had
nothing to do with the temperature in the room.

Sergio impatiently waved away a suited figure who

started to approach, and his bodyguard made sure no more attempts were made.

'We need to talk.'

Raoul had never reacted well to orders. But this was his grandfather so he ignored how the command chafed, allowing his attention to be drawn by the cry of the middle-aged guy at the roulette wheel. It was hard to tell if it was jubilance or misery, but the distraction had served its purpose.

'Raoul...!'

Raoul gave himself a mental shake and turned back to his grandfather. 'We *are* talking.'

Sergio's lips thinned in predictable annoyance. 'In private.' He made a sharp stabbing gesture with his leonine head indicating that Raoul should follow and walked off.

After a pause Raoul levered himself off the cold surface, flexed his shoulder blades, and did so.

Once the door of the panelled, private room was closed Sergio wasted no time.

'Your brother is dead.'

Any number of bitter, sarcastic responses occurred to Raoul but he clamped his lips tight on them. He had been the one who had discovered his brother's lifeless body on the floor of his kitchen and the image still wouldn't let go. An aneurysm the post mortem said. It seemed his brother had been walking around with a ticking time bomb in his chest for years and he hadn't even known it was there.

'You here to tell me life goes on?' He'd read up on it and discovered that what had killed Jamie wasn't that uncommon. Now he found himself walking down the street looking into faces of strangers and wondering who would be next.

'Not for everyone. I'm dying.'

Raoul, who had walked over to the velvet-draped window, spun back, fighting off the childish desire to cover his ears. After a moment's silence he shrugged and dropped his long, lean length into one of the leather sofas.

'We are all dying.'

Or was it only the people he loved?

He closed his eyes and did a silent body count…the mother he barely remembered, his father, his brother, his wife… No! She didn't count. He hadn't loved Lucy by the end. In fact, he had loathed her, but she was gone and they all had one thing in common: *him.*

Perhaps I should come with a government health warning?

The black humour of the thought drew a harsh laugh from his stiff lips while in his head the scornful voice retorted, *Perhaps you should stop feeling so bloody sorry for yourself?*

'It's cancer,' his grandfather said, at Raoul's response. 'Inoperable. Their best bet is that I have six months.' The older man delivered the information without emotion. 'Though I've never trusted quacks.'

Raoul surged to his feet, denial in every muscle of his taut, powerful body. 'That isn't possible.' Their eyes, both pairs dark and shot with silver flecks, connected and after a moment of contact Raoul swallowed.

'Sorry.' His teeth clenched at the laughable inadequacy of the word.

But Sergio simply brushed away the comment with a gesture of his hand. 'Continuity is important to me—you know what I'm talking about.'

Raoul exhaled a long, slow, measured breath and thought, *Hell, not* this, *not* now!

'Your brother was never going to provide an heir.'

Raoul said nothing. This was the closest the older man had ever come to acknowledging his brother's sexuality. He'd never called Jamie's long-term partner, Roberto, anything other than his *friend*. Raoul felt a stab of guilt. He should have stayed for Rob at least—the man had been utterly devastated at the funeral service.

'Jamie is barely cold…' But his skin had been like marble when… Raoul cleared his throat. 'Can't this wait?'

'Time is not a luxury I have.' Sergio saw his grandson wince and took a step forward, adopting the stare that made powerful men sweat, and laid his hands on his grandson's shoulders. 'I made allowances for you after… Lucy died.' Raoul's hooded gaze dropped, a nerve along his jaw clenched. 'But you have to move on.'

'I have moved on.'

A sound of distaste escaped the old man's lips before he turned away. 'I'm not talking about screwing around.'

The uncharacteristic crudeness from his grandfather's lips wiped the last shreds of alcohol-induced haze from Raoul's brain. 'There is no doubt about the diagnosis?'

'None.'

'Sorry,' he said again, knowing that any more tactile or emotional gestures would not be appreciated. His grandfather had a volcanic temperament but he had never encouraged physical displays of emotion in either of his grandsons. It hadn't stopped Jamie, but he… It hadn't come naturally to Raoul. He had learned the advantages of not showing his feelings—his *robot face*, Lucy had called it. Half her twisted pleasure had been seeing her victims suffer.

The older man tipped his head in acknowledgement. 'It will all come to you now. Whether,' he added before the flare of anger in his grandson's dark eyes could spark into flame, 'you want it or not. You will be a powerful man.'

The last man standing.

Whether I want it or not…and I don't!

'That power brings responsibility,' Sergio warned.

It wasn't the time to point out that many considered Raoul a powerful man already. While Jamie had chosen to

work for his grandfather, after Harvard Raoul had joined
a New York law firm, refused the opportunity to become
the youngest partner in the history of that prestigious firm
and had instead struck out on his own, ignoring all the
voices that said he'd regret it.

No voices now, when just a few years later he had offices in several global capitals with a client list of some of
the richest companies and private individuals in the world.

The perfect life, but without the rush of the court-
room he was bored out of his mind! At some point he had
stopped being a litigator and become a glorified manager.
But his brother was the only person Raoul had confided
his frustration to. *Damn you! Why did you have to go?*

'And wealth, of course, but more importantly you will
carry on the name. And don't launch into one of your
egalitarian rants—'

Raoul cut across him. 'Is this where you say something that begins with, if you want to make a dying old
man happy…?'

'Yes.'

'So, moral blackmail.' He spoke without resentment; he
could see the logic in his grandfather's approach.

'I may never see my grandchildren.'

He lowered his gaze, though not before Raoul had seen
a sheen form in the old man's eyes. But when he looked
up again the only thing in those deep-set eyes was a familiar ruthless determination. Raoul dropped the hand he
had stretched out and rubbed it along his thigh, his square
fingertips white as he pressed into muscle. He sighed.

'But I have time enough to see you married to a woman
who will give you children. You can't recapture what you
had with Lucy and it's about time you accepted it.'

An image floated into Raoul's head, a laughing face,
perfect and beautiful, the way the world had seen his
wife… *Recapture…?* Only an insane person would want

to recapture the life of undiluted hell he had lived with his blackmailing, toxic wife.

Raoul was not insane!

His marriage had not left him a woman hater. He liked women; women were gorgeous! The problem was *him*. It was a fact painfully proven that when he allowed himself to be emotionally involved with a woman, he simply couldn't trust his own judgement. It was fatally flawed.

So when his grandfather had accused him of screwing around he had not been wrong, nor had it been an accident. Casual sex satisfied a basic need, and if occasionally he was conscious—regardless of how great the sex—of a nebulous *something* missing, it was something that he was willing to live without.

'Anyone in mind?'

His grandfather ignored the sarcastic tone. 'Obviously the choice is yours.'

'Generous of you.'

'This is not a joke. Our family name is not a joke. I do not want to die with a playboy grandson as my sole legacy in life. It's time you faced up to your responsibilities.'

Raoul bit back a retort that hovered over his tongue, hands digging deep in his pockets as he walked towards the ornate marble fireplace. 'So what do you suggest— should I draw up a job spec and work my way through a shortlist of applicants? Or are you, God forbid, suggesting I follow my heart?' The sarcasm spilled over, but Raoul didn't care. The day couldn't get any worse now.

Again his tone fell on infertile ground; instead his grandfather looked thoughtful.

'That is actually not such a bad idea.'

'What, following my heart?' His experience with Lucy had cured Raoul of any trust in following his heart. The fact that there had been clues with Lucy only rubbed salt in the wound, clues that in any other situation he would not have ignored, but he had been in love and seen only what he had wanted. 'Or advertising?'

The older man flashed him a look. 'Sometimes putting things down in writing focuses the mind. After all, your wife will require certain q...qualities...' Without warning Sergio reached out for support, a sound close to a groan escaping his clamped teeth.

It was all so unexpected that for a moment Raoul froze. Then as the old man staggered the paralysis broke. The resentment of moments earlier evaporated as he sprinted to his grandfather's side, reaching him before he crumpled.

A supportive arm across Sergio's back helped lift him into the nearest chair. Raoul was shocked to feel through the tailored suit, not the solidity and strength that had always been there, but sharp ribs.

This was real. It was happening.

For the first time the reality hit him. His grandfather had been the one constant in his life and now he was dying and nothing Raoul could do would stop it.

The same way he hadn't been able to stop his mother being just another statistic in a flu epidemic, his father shooting out his brains or his brother's big heart bursting. It seemed like a lot of death and loss for one person to take. A curling wave of anger and helplessness washed over him.

He really was the last man standing. He could get drunk and feel sorry for himself or he could... He looked at his grandfather and felt an overwhelming wave of love for the tough, proud old man.

He *could* do something. His grandfather had just told him what he could do, not to stop him dying but to make him die content. He wouldn't have thought twice if it were bone marrow or a kidney he was being asked for, so why hesitate now?

Because losing his right hand would be easy compared to what his grandfather was asking. Marriage had taught him that he could not trust his own judgement when his heart was engaged. And that you could never really know another person, never trust them. So gambling your future and giving up your freedom was insane.

There had to be an alternative and when he sobered up it would be obvious…

'I'll get an ambulance.'

'No…' The hand that covered his was shaking but the voice was stronger now and emphatic as he repeated the prohibition. 'No, no hospitals. It's passed.' The hand that still grasped his grandson's tightened. 'I can't make you do this…today of all days… Jamie would have called me a selfish old—'

'Jamie loved you,' Raoul cut in roughly.

'Your brother loved life.'

Raoul nodded and pretended not to see the tears on the old man's cheeks. 'And you're not saying anything I haven't considered myself.' The expression on his grandfather's grey-tinged face made Raoul glad of the lie.

'You have?'

'I'm not getting any younger.'

'And you want a family?'

Raoul tipped his head, recalling a time when that had been true.

'It is a natural instinct.'

Any instincts he might have possessed had not survived his short marriage to Lucy. Lucy, who'd had a talent and a no-holds-barred policy when it came to inflicting pain in retribution for perceived slights and insults. A year must have passed before, in one of her rages, she had revealed the abortion she had had during the early months of their marriage.

'You think I'd get fat and ugly just to give you a brat!' she'd screamed.

He pushed away the echo in his mind and the image of

the lovely face twisted in spite and malice. It was an image he could escape temporarily in the beds of warm, willing women. But it was a good thing that it would never really leave his mind—that way he knew he was never going to risk losing his heart. He visualised that organ safely enclosed in steel; there wasn't a woman alive who could put a dent in his armour.

'Are you sure I can't…?'

'Carlo…' dabbing a hand to the sweat beading his upper lip, Sergio nodded towards the closed door '…knows what to do. You…' Dark eyes sought those of his grandson. 'You know,' he continued huskily, 'what you can do for me. No matter what, you and your brother have given my life a meaning, a richness that it would otherwise have lacked.' The dark eyes clouded as he shook his head. 'I was a bad father.'

Raoul looked into the face of the man who had struggled to show affection, but had always been there for his grandsons. A surge of emotion left an aching occlusion in his throat. A lie was a little thing to pay back the debt he owed this man. He was never going to marry, to fall in love, but what was the harm letting him think…?

'Then I must learn by your mistakes?'

'I'm sure you'll make your own.' A thoughtful expression crossed his heavily lined face. 'Is there anyone?'

Raoul forced a laugh, his dark brows lifting as he responded. 'You will be the first to know and that is a promise.'

'You probably don't want my advice, but I'll give it anyway. Don't make your final selection on looks alone. Obviously no one would expect you to marry someone you didn't find attractive…'

'That's a relief.'

'It may seem cold-blooded but—'

'Shall I take notes?' This conversation would have

been one to share with his brother. Jamie would have appreciated it; he and his brother shared the same sense of humour—*had* shared. The flicker of ironic amusement faded from his eyes.

'Practicality is not a dirty word. You shouldn't leave the important things in life to blind luck. Oh, I know you struck lucky once but you can't rely on that happening again.'

Not on my watch, Raoul thought grimly.

'Marriage should be approached like any other contract.'

Sergio's voice was stronger but his skin was still cast with a worrying greyish tinge. 'I'm sure you're right,' Raoul conceded, then, seeing the suspicious light in his grandparent's eyes, realised he'd agreed too easily. 'Shall I call Carlo now?'

Without waiting for a reply he opened the door and spoke to the man stationed outside.

Before his grandfather had time to relaunch his campaign for a grandchild, a maid who had obviously been waiting in the wings for a nod from the bodyguard appeared carrying a tea tray. Carlo followed her in.

The maid vanished and the big protective figure poured tea, slipping something from a blister pack into his employer's hand before he nodded and left.

'Man of few words.'

The tea seemed to have restored his grandfather, who snorted. 'Coming from you that is amusing, but then your brother was always the talker, I remember—'

Raoul had heard the stories many times before. Some he'd experienced firsthand, but he let his grandfather talk. He seemed to find relating Jamie's exploits cathartic, the boy he had been and the man he had become, a man Sergio had been proud of. Well, in a professional capacity, at least. By the time he got up from his chair—under his own steam—he looked more himself.

On the point of leaving the room Raoul paused and turned back, his expression intense. Bracing himself to lie through his teeth about his readiness to marry and procreate, Raoul was surprised and relieved when his grandfather asked his opinion on a very different subject.

'I would value your input on something. I was thinking of donating a new wing in your brother's name to the university hospital. Do you think he would have liked that?'

'I think he would have liked that very much, but surely Roberto would be a better person to speak to about it?' His brother's partner was a consultant neurologist at the hospital.

His grandfather looked thoughtful for a moment before nodding. 'He spoke well at the funeral.'

Raoul agreed.

'I might do that. Come walk with me to the car.'

Glad to hear the familiar note of imperious command back in the old man's voice, Raoul followed his grandfather out of the room and through the brightly lit casino.

Out of the air-conditioned cool Raoul barely registered the warmth of the evening but within seconds his grandfather's skin was filmed with moisture. Nevertheless, he rejected the arm Raoul offered with a grunt, moving towards the limo that drew up.

'I'll call tomorrow?'

His grandfather shook his head. 'Next week, as planned. I'm not dying yet.'

Watching the car pull away, Raoul found himself wondering if lying to a dying man could ever be considered the right thing to do.

The question was academic—it was done and he doubted it would be the first lie he told. But how many more would he have to tell, and how far down this road would he need to go to allow his grandfather to die happy?

With an impatient click of his long fingers he started to walk. There was no harm in humouring his grandfather, and Raoul was sure he could string it out until… He didn't want to think about another death today, another loss.

'Dio!' he murmured under his breath as he locked away the memories. To think about the children he might have had, the life he might have led was pointless, that future was lost to him.

He had a new future. Thinking of it stretching out ahead of him, he was conscious of an empty feeling in his chest. He might not have auditioned for the role, but it was his. He *was* the last man standing, or at least the last Di Vittorio standing, which to his grandfather meant the same thing.

CHAPTER TWO

'FINE. I'LL SLEEP with the first man I see!'

It was really hard to maintain any dignity, having just issued a threat worthy of a teenager having a tantrum, thought Lara. Mark's laugh in response only made her madder, so she slammed the door as hard as she could. Lara was slim but she was tall and athletic so the door rattled in its frame.

The first man she saw was the balding middle-aged proprietor of the hotel they had booked into for their *romantic* weekend.

He looked at Lara with concern as she rushed past him into the street, tears coursing down her cheeks.

The blurb had claimed the small hotel was within walking distance of all the main tourist sites, clearly a gross exaggeration. But it hadn't mattered to Lara, who had never had any intention of doing a lot of sightseeing!

How could she have been such a fool?

She had thought Mark was different. *Maybe I'm meant to be alone*, she thought. The prospect wrenched a sob from her throat.

Self-pity, said the voice in her head, *is very unattractive.* She ignored it and sniffed loudly and angrily.

This would never have happened to Lily, but then no man who took her twin away for a romantic weekend would have acted as though he'd been lured there under false pretences if he discovered she was a virgin.

Was her twin a virgin...?

A thoughtful expression flickered across her face as Lara considered the question. Her twin didn't talk to her much about that sort of thing, but then they hadn't talked about that sort of thing since the boy she'd known Lily had fancied had taken Lara to the Christmas party the year they were sixteen. It was years ago now, and a joke, but Lil hadn't see it that way at the time… What had his name been?

How ironic if Lily was not a virgin, while she, who people assumed had had more lovers than handbags, most definitely was. But then that was people for you—they always assumed the worst. So Lara had decided a long time ago that life was simpler if you just let them.

People did so love their boxes—Lily was the sensible twin while Lara was the wild child. She liked to party ergo she slept around. Right now she wished she had!

She bit her lip, feeling a fresh rush of tears.

'I hate men, all men and especially Mark Randall!'

For about thirty seconds the outburst made her feel empowered, then like all pointless gestures it left a sense of anticlimax and the knowledge this was her own fault.

It could have been worse—she could have slept with him and *then* discovered he was a pathetic loser. What was it about him that she'd been attracted to in the first place?

Smooth brow pleated, she pondered the question. True, he'd seemed like a considerate boss and he'd noticed her. Everyone noticed her, but Mark had noticed her for her work. He'd said she had potential, and she hadn't minded doing extra work, work way beyond her pay grade, because he appreciated it and he was one of the few men in the building who hadn't tried it on… *Hmm, big clue there, Lara.*

She had decided that there was sensitivity gleaming behind his horn-rimmed spectacles and kindness in his eyes. She'd felt safe around him and love, or the sort *she* wanted, was about feeling safe and secure.

Lara did not want the sort of love that would leave her feeling utterly bereft if she found out her lover or husband was cheating. *Had Dad been a cheat?* Lara didn't know for certain if the charming, charismatic father she had adored had been unfaithful. The clues had all been there, but she had never asked her mum for confirmation. She didn't think she could bear to hear the answer.

Lara never intended to feel *that* way about any man, so while her friends looked for men who made them lose control Lara looked for quite different qualities.

Qualities her new boss had seemed to epitomise. For the first time she was being treated as an equal by someone who saw her as a person and not a sex object, and she had found the combination irresistible.

He was too nice and too professional, she reasoned, to make the first move, which was sweet but a bit frustrating. Not being someone who thought patience or unrequited love were good things, Lara had set about making him notice that she could do more than file.

It hadn't been easy and she had even started to wonder if he was gay, but then right out of the blue he had asked her: a weekend in Rome. She'd been waiting for the right man and the right time and it had finally arrived—or so she'd thought.

True love. It existed, she was sure of it. You could get sent home from school for wearing your skirt too short and still be a romantic. You could party and still want a family and a home.

She was prepared to wait for the right man, but she saw no reason why the wait had to be boring! Lara was gregarious and she had always enjoyed an active social life; men liked her and she enjoyed their company.

She was aware that her lifestyle made many assume that she enjoyed casual sex, but she never strung men along and if some chose to boast of a non-existent conquest she lost no sleep over it or over those who couldn't handle the fact she wasn't into one-night stands.

The only question had been whether to tell Mark or not. In the end she'd decided she would—no relationship should start with secrets. The perfect opportunity had arisen earlier that night when he'd been scrolling through his phone and discovered a recent interview with his uncle, the CEO of the firm where they both worked.

'This is what I have to deal with, but no point offending the guy. Look, listen to this…no, this is the part where he rambles on about family values,' he sneered. 'And this is the bit when he says one-night stands are—'

'Mark?' He looked up, seeming to notice for the first time that she was standing there wearing the matching silk bra and pants she had spent so long choosing.

I'm competing with a smartphone.

'Actually, Mark.' Her self-esteem was pretty robust and the fact that he wasn't jumping on her was what made Mark different, special, someone who liked her for more than her looks, she reminded herself as she resisted the urge to throw his phone out of the window. 'I'm not really into one-night stands.'

'Sweet, but I wouldn't judge you, darling, and this isn't one night—we're here for the whole weekend.'

'I mean I've never had a one-night stand.'

He put down his phone. 'You've got a boyfriend?'

'Would I be here with you if I had a boyfriend?'

He pushed his glasses back on his nose, a habit that she'd always found endearing but that left her cold at that moment. 'I don't know, you know, I don't like the idea of stepping on some guy's toes… What does he do?'

'There is no guy. I don't have a boyfriend. You're my first.'

'One weekend doesn't mean we're engaged, sweetheart.'

'You're my first lover!'

He laughed at the joke, then, when she didn't join in, stopped. 'Not seriously.'

'Totally seriously.'

'But you can't be…you're a…you've always been…'

'Easy?' She read the expression in his eyes before he looked away and the cold ache in her chest intensified.

At her sides her fingers flexed as she fought the urge to bring her arms up in a protective gesture across her chest. It was pride that kept her chin at a challenging angle while inside she had shrivelled up in shame and embarrassment.

'No. It's just, you have to admit, you came on to me like—and Ben in Marketing…he says…'

'What does Ben in Marketing say?'

It finally dawned on him that she was serious and he looked sick. 'Oh, God, Lara, I don't do virgins, hell, no! It's such a responsibility. This is just a bit of fun, and when Carol had to cancel I couldn't get a refund.'

'Carol?'

'You wouldn't know her. She doesn't have to work, she's my, my…well, we're not actually engaged yet but—'

'So when your fiancée couldn't make it you looked around for someone who everyone knows is an easy lay…'

His sulky pout vanished as he cut across her. 'Well, you weren't supposed to be a bloody virgin!'

'So sorry, my mistake, but that's the problem with small print, isn't it?' she commiserated. 'How about if I go away, get some scalps under my belt, and come back? Will that change things?'

'We-e-ell…'

Unbelievable! He was actually considering it! She edged her voice with ice as she ground out, 'I wouldn't sleep with you if you came with a seat on the board.'

If they were handing out awards for sheer blind stupidity, I, Lara reflected grimly, would have had a clean sweep.

'Oh, and I doubt that rich, doesn't-have-to-work Carol would have been impressed by the room.' *A cheater and a cheapskate, Lara, you know how to pick them!*

* * *

As she went over the scene yet again, wincing at her exit line, her tears dried and she realised that, not only did she have no idea where she was, but when she had made her dramatic exit she had taken nothing with her, not her purse, her phone…nothing.

She paused and looked around her, debating her options. She could continue to wander aimlessly feeling sorry for herself, try to retrace her steps or find someone and ask for directions back to the hotel. Option three made the most sense, but the street was deserted.

A moment later, she wished the street had stayed deserted as out of a side alley a group of young men appeared, five or six of them making enough noise for twenty. There was some good-natured banter and a bit of pushing and shoving. It was hard to tell the mood and quite honestly she didn't fancy staying around to find out.

Alcohol, testosterone, peer pressure—not a good combination.

Hampered by her high spiky heels, she only got a few steps before one of the group spotted her.

Lara didn't react to him or to the cacophony of calls and whistles, and instead just carried on walking. *Do not show fear! Do not show fear!*

Any minute now someone would walk round that corner, a figure of authority, someone who would say… 'Ouch!'

By some miracle she managed not to fall when one of her heels came clear off, but her recovery was not elegant and the pain that shot through her ankle was agonising. She registered the laughter behind and this time it was her temper, not her heel, that snapped.

In the grip of a red-mist moment, she slipped off the broken shoe and, with it in her hand, turned to face the group. Her chest lifted in tune with her angry inhalations, her green eyes flashing contempt and fury, her mind clear of the fear she had felt just moments ago. The group of young men became the focus of all her accumulated anger and the humiliation seething inside her.

She was so focused on them that the fact that someone *had* come around the corner didn't register on Lara's radar.

Her red hair swirled around her like a silken curtain as she allowed her eyes to travel disdainfully over their collective heads.

Wrath swelled inside her, mingled with self-disgust. She had been running from them, and they were just kids... Well, teenagers really. Although this did not entirely remove the potential threat they represented, Lara was too mad to care. This was the real Lara, the one who stood her ground, not the one who'd run off crying because her dream lover had turned out to be a totally useless louse.

She took several limping steps towards them. Nobody was laughing now, the victim having taken them all by surprise, or perhaps they were just stunned by her beauty.

The scene's new onlooker could identify with that!

Dio, but she was utterly stunning! She managed by some miracle to be graceful, even minus one heel. The red dress she wore clung lovingly to every inch of her sinuous curves and clashed with the glorious cloud of hair she tossed back. She brandished the shoe in one hand while delivering a killer glare at her persecutors like some glorious Valkyrie descended from the heavens. And then Raoul got his first full look at her face.

The purity of her features had been visible in profile— she had a little chin, high forehead, smooth sculpted cheeks, and straight little nose. But what he hadn't been able to appreciate fully was the liquid flash of incredible long-lashed eyes set beneath curved, feathery, dark brows or the miracle of her mouth, the firm bottom lip softened by the lush fullness of the upper.

If the first stroke of heat had nailed him to the spot, this subsequent one shut down his brain, though the absence of his higher functions did not prevent other parts of his body continuing to act and react with painful independence.

'Your idea of a good night out, is it?'

English, her voice pitched low even in anger; it had a sexy huskiness as she rounded on the gang who probably didn't understand a word she was saying.

One laughed and she pounced on him with the verbal punch of a spitting cat. 'Big man, aren't you, with your friends around you?' she jeered, swinging her stabbing finger around the group. 'Alone would you or any of your friends here be so brave? You're a bunch of pathetic losers who should be ashamed of themselves…' She focused on the ringleader and pointed the finger at him. 'If I was your mother I'd be ashamed!'

Under the battering tirade, several of the boys started to back away and one even lifted his hand and said, 'Sorry, beautiful lady.'

Raoul agreed with the description but would have added gutsy to the description. He couldn't think of another woman he knew who would have handled the situation in the same way. It had been a risky move, but you couldn't help admire her bloody-minded bravery.

Who was she, this brave, slightly crazy redhead? She bent to rub her ankle, causing the red dress to pull tight across her hips and behind.

He thought that must be the trigger, her lovely bottom, and raging teenage hormones. Whatever the cause, the effect was an immediate and complete change of atmosphere. One second it looked as though the situation had been defused, but then one boy—that was all it ever took—who clearly wanted to show off in front of his friends, took a swaggering step forward. He yelled out a mocking taunt at his retreating comrades and advanced towards the redhead with leering intent.

As he watched, Raoul's jaw tightened, though he could tell the girl didn't understand a word of the filth the kid flung at her, but his attitude needed no translation. She stood poised in a flight-or-fight mode, watching him like a lamb watching a fox.

The situation, he decided, had gone on long enough. Raoul stepped out of the shadows, fists clenched. He found there was a smile on his face, now he finally had a legitimate target for the anger that still swirled around inside him.

Lara's energising burst of angry adrenaline had exploded like a courageous firework, but now that it had smouldered and faded away she felt scared and terrifyingly vulnerable as the boy moved towards her.

She wanted to run but her feet seemed nailed to the ground. In the periphery of her vision she was aware that the others had stopped walking away, a couple had turned back and they were all watching…waiting…?

Weirdly her brain carried on functioning regardless of the paralysing dread. Then as the paralysis lifted instinct took over and she moved towards one of the street lights. An illusion of safety was better than nothing.

She lifted her hand to her ear and began to speak, her clear voice floating across to the young men, confusing them for a moment. But then one noticed that she had no phone in her hand and the yells began again.

Do not show fear.

A bit late for that, Lara thought. The group had slowly moved until she was surrounded. *You should have run when you had the chance*, said the voice in her head. Too late now! One tormentor might not have been so bad. She could have dealt with one, talked her way out perhaps, but with several, all egging each other on…?

Aware that her options had been reduced to calling for help and hoping someone would come to her aid, Lara opened her mouth to shout. Only a strangled squeak emerged, but it was drowned out by a new voice, a voice that held an edge of bored irritation.

'Where have you been? I said outside the casino!'

The youths stopped and swivelled towards him. Raoul raised a sardonic brow and allowed his disdainful glance to drift over them, satisfied they were not going to present a problem. He ignored the flicker of something close to regret—now was not the time to get his knuckles bloody—and instead turned his scrutiny to the luscious redhead. As their glances connected he saw comprehension supplant the shock in her wide-spaced eyes—could that colour possibly be real?—and she didn't miss a beat before replying, 'Casino...?' She shook her head. 'No, you said we'd go on there afterwards.'

And *that* smile...!

He'd never understood dedicated enthusiasts who waited for hours in often uncomfortable positions to catch a glimpse of a rare bird. But he would wait for ever to see that smile again, especially as it deepened, revealing a dimple in her smooth cheek. Raoul couldn't think of a reason in the world not to respond to the challenge in her emerald eyes.

'And I'm not late, you're early.'

He watched as she pulled off her other shoe, giving another excellent view of her delicious bottom, and strolled with a sexy sway of her hips towards him. 'Luckily for you,' she breathed, 'I'm very understanding.' *What are you doing, Lara?*

God knows! came the answer, but it felt...what? Actually it was hard to put a label on the fizz in her blood. The nearest she could liken it to was champagne bubbles bursting, vastly preferable to feeling like some silly little girl who had run away.

No, you're just a silly girl who is jumping from the

frying pan into the fire! It seems you're not content with laughing at the face of danger—you have to set a collision course with it!

The racing thoughts slid through her head in the time it took her to fully absorb the man who had decided to be her guardian angel. Not that there was anything angelic about him, unless you were talking the dark, fallen and supremely sexy variety! Her first glance had told her that and even with several feet separating them she had felt the impact on her senses of the sensuality he projected, raw and primal.

A little shudder traced a path down her spine as she realised this wasn't a case of someone trying to be something— he *was* something. There was nothing contrived about the maleness, it was simply an integral part of him.

The powerful sexual charge he oozed made it almost irrelevant that he was the best-looking man she had ever seen. Well, not *quite* irrelevant, she admitted as her eyes travelled the long, lean length of him.

He was tall, *very* tall with the broad-of-shoulder, lean-of-hip sort of muscular frame usually associated with athletes. He was dressed expensively in a black suit, and a tie of the same colour was looped around his open-necked shirt; the vee of skin it revealed showed the same glowing golden tone as his face, minus the stubble that dusted his jaw and lean cheeks.

The stubble was the same black as his brows, which were straight and thick, one angled in at a sardonic slant above the narrow, heavy-lidded, thickly lashed eyes they framed. His strong-boned face was a miraculous arrangement of planes and angles, razor-edged high cheekbones, high forehead, aquiline nose and a strong jaw.

The only thing that alleviated the overwhelming masculinity was his mouth and the sensual fullness of his lower lip, though any suggestion of softness was counterbalanced by his firm upper lip, which had a hint of cruelty about it.

Her rescuer was doing some looking himself, his expression shielded by his heavy eyelids, but when he reached her bare feet one dark brow hitched higher.

Lara felt a giggle well up in her throat.

Up to that point he'd been making an effort to retain what grip on reality he had left, but the seductive sound she made precluded any return of common sense. He felt as hot as the glorious waves of her hair looked, and it was all he could do not to reach out and touch the flames.

'Long story.' She lowered her voice and leaned in closer, placing her hands on his forearms to steady herself. As her fingers pressed through the fabric she could feel the hard, sinewy strength beneath, and her stomach muscles quivered. 'Would thank you be premature? Are they still there?' she whispered.

'A couple.'

Lara wanted to ask how he knew when he'd not taken his eyes off her face, but she couldn't. Her throat was full, not with tears, but with something else, the same something that was sending intermittent tremors through her body.

They were standing close enough to be taken for lovers, close enough for his nostrils to quiver in response to the scent of her hair. He fought the primitive compulsion to pull her into him, let her feel what she was doing to him.

'You saved me.'

'It was a pleasure,' he said, breathing in that scent.

The corners of her mouth lifted in a rueful grimace. 'I didn't handle it very well.'

He watched her smooth brow furrow. There was something quite fascinating about the expressions that flickered across her vivid little face.

'I lost my temper.' She bit her lip and tilted her head

downwards, looking up at him through the mesh of her lashes. 'It's been a…not good day.'

'I've had one of those too.'

It was a connection. The silence could have been companionable, but it wasn't. The air was charged with a sexual tension so thick that Lara struggled to breathe. She'd never experienced anything like this before.

'Have I said thank you?'

His dark eyes smiled, the crinkles at the corners deepening. 'My money was on you.'

'I was scared stiff.' She gave a tiny shudder. 'Well, thank you anyway…?'

'Raoul. Raoul Di Vittorio.'

'Thank you, Raoul. I'm Lara—Lara Gray.' Ignoring the voice in her head that warned she was playing with fire, she tipped her head back; hooking one hand behind his head and stretching up, she brushed his mouth with her soft, pouting lips.

She was about to pull back when his mouth began to move slowly and sensuously over her lips. She kissed him back, not teasingly now, but with a hungry longing she hadn't felt before. A moan drifted up from her throat as his tongue slid deeper. Afraid she would fall, even more afraid that this would stop, she clutched at his jacket and hung on.

When they broke apart the street was empty.

Lara stood there, gasping for air like someone who'd just run a marathon.

There were so many alarm bells ringing in his head that Raoul could barely hear himself think. What the hell was he doing?

He was forgetting.

He took hold of her hands, releasing the lapels of his jacket from her death grip. As she let go and stepped away from him her face lifted. Her lips, swollen from his kisses, quivered as she ran the tip of her tongue over them and blinked like a sleepwalker on waking somewhere unexpected.

'Oh, my!' she whispered.

The visceral stab of lust that lanced through him took Raoul's breath away. *Dio*, but she was beautiful, and he wanted to taste her again, he wanted to do a lot more than taste her.

Lara stared up at him wanting him to kiss her again, willing him to kiss her again. It was hard to escape the bold, sensual glittering in his deep-set eyes, but Lara didn't even try.

The warm, heavy, dreamy sensation that held her rooted to the spot was now being supplanted by a heart-racing excitement that left her dizzy. Her stomach muscles quivered as her eyes lingered on his mouth. She couldn't tear her eyes clear of the sensually sculpted outline, nor forget the taste of brandy in his kiss.

'Are you drunk?' she asked, struggling to think through the sexual fog in her brain as she tilted her head to one side. She'd have liked to think it would matter if he was, but she'd never run full tilt into a solid wall of lust before, so the whole experience was new for her.

His mouth quirked, one corner lifting in a way she found utterly fascinating. Actually, everything about him fascinated her. She had no idea what it was she was feeling. It was visceral in a way that went beyond anything she had ever felt before.

'Not strictly sober, but not drunk.' It was, he realised, true. 'How about you?'

She shook her head, the excitement fizzing through her blood more intoxicating than champagne. 'Are you married?'

His expression didn't change but she saw something unidentifiable move in his eyes before he responded, 'Not any more.'

She reacted to his comment with a small grunt of satisfaction as the tiny furrow between her brows smoothed out. 'That's good.'

He smiled again and Lara's knees started to shake. None of this made any sense. She had planned on being seduced tonight but at no stage had she planned on not being in charge of the process. Or of being seduced by a total stranger!

'You're very beautiful.'

The faint rasp in the smooth, dark-chocolate purr of his voice made her shiver; the touch of his finger on her cheek made her insides dissolve.

'So they tell me.' His stare was hypnotic; the sensory overload was making her light-headed. She turned her head, not enough to break the connection. 'This is quite mad.'

'Mad can be good.'

'Can it?'

His dark eyes gleamed. 'Oh, yes.' The furrow between his dark brows deepened. 'Where did you come from?' he asked, continuing to stroke her cheek.

'I'm not sure.'

'You just dropped from heaven.' No angel had a mouth like hers. He focused on her lips and the pain in his groin, not the deeper pain that cut up his insides. She was an oasis to escape that pain, to lose it and himself inside.

His thumb touched the pouting curve of her lower lip and his hand stilled. 'Boyfriend?'

Her chin lifted a notch, her nostrils flaring as her green eyes sparked. 'Not any more,' she rebutted firmly.

'Where are you going?'

She closed a door in her head, blotting out Mark's rejection and her stupidity.

'With you, I hope.' She heard the words, the supremely confident tone, even though inside she was anything but.

Inside, she was holding her breath. She'd only just picked herself up and now she'd set herself up for another fall.

Head thrown back, she fixed him with an emerald stare that sent a fresh flash of heat through his already primed body. He could feel the hairs on the nape of his neck tingle as his body hardened in anticipation. Another time he might have blocked out his primitive response to this woman, might have heard the alarm bells, but tonight he didn't think beyond it, instead he embraced the mindlessness of it.

For the first time since he'd discovered Jamie's body he wasn't hearing Rob's broken voice in his head sobbing, 'What am I going to do without him? He's gone *for ever*. He's gone…gone…*gone*…for ever…for *ever*, Raoul.'

That was what he had kept repeating over and over until Raoul could feel nothing but pain, his, Rob's, just a universe of pain that went on and on.

Now he was feeling something that wasn't pain and regret, and it didn't matter that it was shallow or transient. He needed breathing space—not that he could *breathe* when he looked at this woman.

Did the ability to think of sex while in the depths of grief make him shallow? If Jamie had been burying him, would his brother have been able to escape so easily? Would he have wanted to?

He pushed away the speculation, the grief, the anger, the loss and lost himself to the moment of this intoxicatingly beautiful woman in his arms. He looked down into her sensual face and released a slow sigh. If he'd believed in fate, if he'd believed there was actually some grand plan, he'd have thought fate had sent her there at that moment.

He didn't believe in fate but he did believe in embracing opportunities when they appeared, and the thought of shutting out the blackness in this woman's arms just for an hour or two was irresistible.

'That works for me, *cara*.'

She felt a rush of relief—for a moment she'd thought he'd been going to say thanks but no, thanks. Her confidence had already taken a battering today.

'Good.'

He laughed, the sound sending a fresh tingle of excitement through her.

'I've never met anyone quite like you.'

'I have an identical twin sister.'

He slung a teasing look over his shoulder. 'Is she around?'

If she were she wouldn't be doing this with you. The thought came with an unbidden image of their headmistress berating her for some minor infringement 'People will not respect you, Lara, unless you respect yourself. Your sister would never—'

'No, she isn't.'

Her flat response drew a sardonic look. 'I was joking.'

For a split second as their eyes locked, Raoul thought he glimpsed a vulnerability that did not belong to the self-possessed, sensual creature who stood in front of him. But a moment later it was gone.

It had probably never been there.

Hell, he was *not* going to talk himself out of this. From the corner of his eye he saw a taxi and lifted his hand. His place was within walking distance but prolonging this agony was not on his agenda.

It was happening so quickly, she had no time to think; was this a good thing or a bad thing? She didn't know and didn't want to—the answer might make her walk away.

And she didn't want to…she *really* didn't want to.

Her senses were strangely heightened and yet she felt distanced from what was happening as a taxi stopped and then with the snap of the door she was inside, the jarring noise introducing a sense of reality to her dreamlike state.

But this was no dream.

CHAPTER THREE

'IS SOMETHING WRONG?'

Lara shook her head and her spurt of panic subsided. Instead, desire, warm and fluid, spread through her body as his iron-hard thigh nudged hers, then a second later drew away.

'Is it your ankle?'

'My ankle?' It took her a moment to recall turning it earlier. The pain had been sharp but it had subsided now. 'No, it's fine, see?' Proving her point, she hitched the long skirt of her dress slightly to expose her calf and foot, stretching them out as far as the confined space allowed. 'I just turned it, but it's fine now.'

She turned her head and found his eyes on her leg. She could see a nerve relaxing and tensing like a ticking bomb in his lean cheek as he stared.

He turned his head, his eyes only brushing hers for a moment before he leaned forward to give the driver directions in Italian. But one glimpse of the devouring heat in them was enough to pull her back in her seat shaking, frightened not by the intent she had seen written in his face but the response it had awoken in her.

She sat there, thinking of the taste of his cool, firm mouth, her hand pressed tight to her quivering stomach.

Raoul didn't move any closer or attempt to put his arm around her. As the car drew away from the kerb they could have been strangers forced to share a space on crowded public transport…except for the air thick with possibility between them.

Lara's head was spinning as she sat there, and her

thoughts began racing to keep pace with the turbulent thud of her heart.

What are you doing, Lara? You have no idea where you are, let alone where you are going. You just got into a car with a total stranger, and the plan is to have sex with him?

Mark thought you were easy—how is this different?

What does it matter? Lara asked herself. She was just using him. It would be liberating; she wouldn't have to pretend. So far her wild-child reputation had been window dressing. This was real.

A conversation with her recently engaged friend, Jane, surfaced in her head. A crowd of them had been sitting in a bar drinking shots, except for Lara, the designated driver with a zero tolerance to alcohol, while Jane showed off her ring.

'It was magic, guys, the moment I saw him I was dizzy with longing—you know what I mean?'

Because it was expected Lara had smiled and nodded her agreement along with everyone else, but she hadn't known what Jane meant. Not really. And she had actually been happy in her ignorance. Losing your balance, not to mention your grip on reality—Jane's dream man was not exactly what you'd call irresistible—was not something she envied anyone.

Had she lost her grip on reality now? It wasn't too late to change her mind.

She halted the inner dialogue and turned her head. Raoul was sitting back, both hands rested on his thighs, as he looked straight ahead. She sensed a darkness in him, and in profile the austere beauty of his face brought a lump of emotion to her throat.

He's not a sunset, or an ocean view, she reminded herself. *He's a man, a stranger. And you're in the back of a taxi with him.*

'I can take you to your hotel, if you prefer.'

The offer made her relax. The option was there, although she knew it was one she had no intention of taking. 'No, I don't want that. I want you.'

She heard a sharp intake of breath but his only response was a jerky movement of his dark head.

Raoul didn't trust himself to touch her, because he knew that when he did he wouldn't be able to let her go. The scent of her, the warmth where their thighs were almost touching, were driving him insane. A woman had not made him feel this way in a long time.

He had never been so relieved for a journey to end.

'We're here.'

Standing beside him on the pavement, watching him pay off the cab, Lara wondered where *here* was. There were no names, numbers or signs on any of the anonymous buildings this side of the street, though she could just make out a plaque on a building opposite. Squinting, she read *Embassy*, then before she could read the rest of the inscription a big set of gates slid silently open.

He gestured for her to go through, which after a tiny pause she did.

Nothing in the street suggested that this place existed.

'It's beautiful.'

Her apprehension gave way to appreciation as the tall gates closed, cutting them off from the street again. The softly lit courtyard they stood in was stone cobbled, uneven and old. The plants that spilled from the massed stone troughs in the central section filled the air with the heady scents of jasmine and lavender, and water spilled from a stone lion's head set in the wall out into an ornamental pool.

She tilted her head back. The building that enclosed the space on three sides was tall, the first-floor windows arranged symmetrically with wrought-iron Juliet balconies.

'Is it a hotel?'

He shook his head. 'No, I live here.'

'Alone?' The possibility seemed extraordinary to Lara. It was a massive place for one person...had he got the marital home after the divorce? Assuming there had been a divorce—really she knew nothing about him. She exhaled a measured sigh, starting slightly when he placed a hand between her shoulder blades. The touch of his fingers on her bare skin made her gasp.

'This way.'

Quivering inside with anticipation that she struggled to hide beneath an air of cheerful insouciance, she let him guide her up a small flight of shallow stone steps, as though she were in the habit of doing this sort of thing every day of the week.

He leaned across her to put a key in the lock of the heavy metal-banded door that was dark with age. Given the traditional, almost historical, external appearance of the building, the inside caused her to gasp in surprise.

Internally it had been opened up—presumably walls had been knocked down to create this one massive ground-floor space, bisected by a staircase that seemed to float in mid-air. The end wall had been taken out and was now glass; several sections of internal wall were exposed stone while others were pale limewashed.

The furniture was eclectic. Big, comfortable-looking sofas, a long, highly polished antique trestle table, and one entire wall lined with floor-to-ceiling bookshelves.

They had entered the kitchen area, which boasted every modern appliance set in pale ash units with polished stone work surfaces.

'This is not what I expected.' But then, nothing about their encounter had been.

Raoul gave the space a dismissive glance. He felt no emotional connection to it; he'd simply given the architect free rein. The place said nothing about him or his taste in books, except that he liked big spaces. It wasn't the soundest of financial investments he'd ever made—he'd bought it for its location and size, only to discover it was falling down.

'The place was riddled with wet rot, dry rot, deathwatch beetle, I could go on... A lesson in the danger of buying without a structural survey. Once the building was made safe I had to decide whether to reinstate the original period features or not.' His shoulders lifted.

'And you chose not.'

He nodded.

'It's spectacular.' She clamped her lips together to prevent a gushing response.

He took a step closer and the room got smaller, her heartbeat got faster, and there seemed a strong possibility her shaking knees were going to fold.

'I always talk a lot when I'm nervous.' Should she tell him before...?

Oh, yeah, because that worked so well last time.

'You're nervous?'

'Well, this might surprise you,' she said, forcing a laugh, 'but this isn't something I do every day.'

His dark brows lifted. 'No, it doesn't surprise me. Why should it?'

'It's just—'

'You don't have to explain.'

She felt hot as embarrassed colour flew to her cheeks. 'No...no, of course not.' *The man doesn't want your life history, Lara, he wants sex.*

He watched the blush and recognised the vulnerability it exposed. His jaw clenched. He didn't want vulnerable, he wanted hot, mind-numbing sex with a beautiful, bold, confident woman who could fearlessly face down a gang of thugs.

Where had she gone?

He heaved a resigned sigh and swallowed his growing frustration. The hot-cold thing was killing him and the prospect of a night of cold showers did not appeal, but in such a matter acceptance was the only recourse.

'Would you like a coffee…?'

Lara swallowed but didn't dodge his stare. There was probably something playful she should say but the emotions in her throat made even the basic truth hard to utter.

'We both know I don't want a coffee.'

'I *thought* I did. What do you want?' He lifted a strand of her shining hair with one finger and let it fall. 'Is that real?'

'Everything about me is real.' *Good line, Lara. Means nothing, but good line!* 'And I want you.'

She didn't attempt to escape his gleaming stare. She quivered as he cupped her face with one hand, her eyelashes lowered and falling in a dark filigree against her cheek. They lifted a moment later when his free hand curved possessively around her bottom.

A soft moan left her parted lips as with barely leashed violence he pulled her in hard against him.

'*That* is real,' he ground out, his breath warm on her face as he caught the soft flesh of her lower lip between his teeth. 'What you do to me is real. Everything about you,' he slurred, bending his head to move his lips over the pulse spot at the base of her throat, 'is real.'

When was the last time that he had experienced anything close to the primitive need to possess that was pounding through him at that moment? It was madness!

But madness had never felt so sweet and as the passion between them escalated definitions became irrelevant.

The kiss seemed to go on for ever. Lara gave herself up to it and the dormant passion deep inside her that he had awoken. Her head was spinning and instinctively she wound her slim arms tight around his neck, and met the repeated probing thrust of his tongue with an eagerness that masked her inexperience.

She gave a little gasp of shock as his hand moved up to cover one breast, his thumb brushing the swollen peak through the red silky fabric, causing the gasp to slide seamlessly into a low guttural moan of pleasure.

He lifted his head to look into her passion-glazed eyes, then he moved his hips against her. He watched her eyes darken in instant response, then slid his hand up and down the long smooth lines of her thigh. He heard her breath quicken before, with a muffled cry, she jumped into him, wrapping her long legs around his waist.

Raoul caught her, and brushed the hair from her face to expose one side of her neck before spreading his hands supportively under her bottom and kissing the smooth swanlike curve he had revealed. He began to carry her towards the staircase.

'I never knew that anything could feel this good, this *right.*'

She didn't know that she had voiced her thoughts out loud until his fingers slid around her jaw, forcing her face up to him.

'Don't stop!'

The fierce intentness of his dark stare did not soften as he gave a short, hard laugh. It was all he could do not to back her against the wall and take her there and then, but this was too good to hurry, much too good. 'I have no intention of stopping, *cara*,' he admitted thickly.

The need to define or analyse what was happening had passed. She tasted sweet as again he drove his tongue with sensual precision between her plump, parted lips.

Like a drowning man he kissed her as he walked with her in his arms towards the bedroom door.

Lara had a hazy impression of cool as he carried her across the room to the low platform bed set centre stage.

But the pulse of need inside her left little room for anything else. It was a need she couldn't explain even if she'd wanted to—all she wanted was him.

'I want you so much it hurts.'

He growled a response in Italian, the urgency of that language making more sense to Lara than his words as he laid her down on the bed, sweeping the pillows out of the way as he did so.

He was above her, his face a dark blur as he lowered himself. The hard press of his arousal, as it ground into her belly for a moment before he rolled them both to one side, drew a low, feral-sounding groan from Lara's lips. The erotic contact offered deep pleasure, but no release for the ache of her own arousal, the throbbing need between her legs.

As they lay thigh to thigh there was a tremor in the big hand he lifted to curve around her face, turning it up to him until their eyes caught. Hungrily he took in the details of her passion-flushed skin.

He felt something tighten in his chest as he stared into her luminous green eyes, which were glazed with passion; her plump lips were soft, trembling, almost vulnerable. His gaze remained locked on to hers as he kissed her cheeks, his warm breath moving over the downy softness until he found her mouth and possessed it before he levered himself away and began to rip off his clothes.

Watching him through half-closed eyes, Lara wondered if she ought to be undressing too. The question was academic, as her body was infiltrated by a heavy languor that seemed to pin her to the bed. She watched him, her breathing getting ragged, until finally he stood there naked, like a tall, aroused god.

Her breath caught, hot excitement flooded her body and a scalding wave of heat tinged her skin with a delicate pink.

He was beautiful, and aroused—*very* aroused—a fact that was hard to escape!

Looking at his arousal made her very aware of her own. The idea of her hands framing him, her body holding him, made her ache in a way she had never experienced. He strode back to the bed and dropped down on his knees beside it.

'I love your mouth.' An expression of rapt fascination on her face, she reached up and trailed her fingers down his stubbled cheek.

Raoul caught her wrist; turning her hand palm up towards his mouth, he felt her shiver as he pressed a fierce, damp kiss to her wrist. He ran his fingers down the smooth skin of her shoulder, hooking the shoestring strap of her dress down as he did so. Then, sliding his finger under the folds of red silk that were cut to form a soft cowl neckline, he exposed one perfect breast. Raoul reached out, his touch almost reverent as he cupped the quivering mound, weighing it for a moment, then with a groan he bent his head.

The sensation of his mouth on her skin was a sharp, searing pleasure; her body arched in response. She barely registered him peeling the second strap from her shoulders as she held his dark head, her fingers deep in his thick hair.

When he lifted his head he looked at her with eyes that seemed to burn from within. The rigid control he exerted drew the skin taut across the bones of his face, emphasising the dramatic bone structure.

His kiss, when it came, was deep and plundering, the seething emotions inside her burning hotter as she kissed him back, making tiny mewling noises of pleasure in her throat as he came to lie beside her.

The first skin-to-skin contact as he pulled her against him made her gasp, her nerve endings quivering as her breasts were crushed against his chest.

She ran her hands over the hard muscles of his shoulders, pulling back a little as she moved down his chest. His skin was warm, slightly damp, and, when she bent her head to taste, it was salty. She pulled herself half over him, running her hands over his body, getting bolder as she drew moans and gasps from him.

She bent her face to his belly and followed the line her finger had just traced with her tongue. 'Mmm…' Her murmur turned into a soft squeal as he tugged her dress down over her hips.

A couple of wriggles and a moment later she was lying there in just a pair of silky, French-cut pants. No longer lying on top of him, she was on her back, one leg anchored to the bed by his muscular, hair-roughened thigh.

Her nerve endings reacted to the brush of his eyes as they would his touch.

But then, the unexpected gentleness as he kissed her lips softly made her chest tighten with emotion.

She touched his face and whispered his name. Raoul's nostrils flared as he bent his head, but this time the kiss was not soft. It was hard and demanding, bruising in its intensity. He kissed her as if he'd drain her, and everything he wanted to take, Lara wanted to give, and more.

Her fingertips dug into the golden skin of his back as they kissed, her body felt fluid and on fire, but when she felt his fingers slide under the lacy edge of her panties she tensed. Feeling his eyes on her face through her closed lids, she blinked them open.

'Relax.'

She smiled faintly, then breathed a tremulous sigh that was lost in the moisture of his mouth.

She moved against his hand as he touched her through the silk, and closed her eyes, focusing on the sensation. Then as his fingers moved under the silk across the damp folds of sensitised skin Lara forgot to breathe, forgot her name; the pleasure was mindless and all-consuming. She dug her teeth into her lower lip as he slid her panties down her legs with what felt like tantalising slowness.

When he nudged her thighs with his knee she parted them with a sigh of relief.

'I can't stand it.'

Her agonised whisper drew a deep groan from Raoul, who caught her wrists onto the pillow either side of her face. His chest heaved as he lowered himself down, fighting the almost overwhelming compulsion to possess her fully in one thrust.

The strain of fighting himself showed in his glistening face as he entered her, the knowledge that he had never wanted a woman this much before locked away for another time.

Lara had been expecting some discomfort. What she hadn't expected was to be overcome by a climax almost before her body had adjusted to the sensation of him inside her.

It rocked her as every muscle clenched around him. A low keening cry was wrenched from her throat, and the waves of intense, mind-blowing pleasure just went on and on. She was so focused on what was happening to her that she didn't immediately realise it wasn't happening for him. Before she could come back down to earth he was moving again, pushing deeper into her with each thrust.

Lara's hips arched up to meet him, she could feel all of him and all of her, and the cell-deep awareness was almost painful, like some bright, beautiful light. Eyes squeezed tight in an effort to fully appreciate each individual sensation, Lara clung on because she didn't know what else to do. Everything that was happening was new and wonderful. Her focus narrowed until her entire world consisted of just moving with him, flowing into him.

The heat between them became a furnace as he reached deep into her. Just as Lara began to feel that she could not bear it, the invisible wall melted and it happened again, only this time it was even more intense—her body convulsed by a series of deep contractions until every nerve ending vibrated with pleasure. She actually saw starbursts through the paper-thin skin of her eyelids, and then as the tensions left her body in a series of juddering jolts she heard him groan and felt the heat of his release.

'You're beautiful.' His voice cracked as he bent his head down to her, his nose brushing hers as he angled a kiss across her lips, before rolling away.

CHAPTER FOUR

STILL FLOATING, Lara opened her eyes. His bedroom was a monochrome blur, pale walls, dark furniture, a painting on one wall that appeared to be just a splash of red. She turned her head towards the breeze blowing in through three windows that reached the floor, the transparent drapes fluttering and billowing in the breeze.

If she turned her head the other way she'd see Raoul. She could hear him breathing hard, almost as hard as she was.

She turned her head the other way.

Raoul's eyes were closed, and his chest was lifting as he breathed in and out, the golden skin glistening under a layer of moisture. In profile his face had an austere quality, like a statue. His passion-sated body continued to exert a strong fascination for Lara; the strength, the hardness, the contrast between them was part of that fascination. He was in every way a physical male ideal—*her* ideal certainly— from his lean musculature to his long limbs.

She had experienced so much with him. For a time they had been two parts of one whole and yet now they were separate—worlds apart.

Lara suddenly felt sad, and she didn't know why.

He was lying with one arm curved above his head, and without opening his eyes he lowered it. She wanted to hang on to the perfect golden moment but all the questions she didn't want to think about popped into her head.

What would he say?

What should she say?

The sheet lay in a tangled heap between them. She

hooked her toe in it and pulled, and had managed to drag a section halfway up her legs when she realised he was watching her.

'Are you cold?' Without waiting for a reply he reached for her, pulling her into his arms.

She lay stiff for a moment and then relaxed against him, tucking her head against his shoulder. Raoul stroked a hand down the smooth curve of her back, enjoying the satiny texture.

He had enjoyed her.

He'd enjoyed many women, he enjoyed sex, but it had been the most erotic experience in his life and she'd been a virgin.

Should he feel bad about that?

If he was honest, the knowledge, when he had realised, had obviously been staggering but had also been a massive turn-on. He supposed it was programmed into male genes, a hangover from less enlightened times, primitive man claiming his mate.

The theory did offer an explanation for the explosive surge of possessiveness he'd experienced when she'd nestled in his arms.

Bleakness filtered into his dark eyes. It would pass—most things did.

Before the dark thought claimed him she moved, snuggling in deeper, a slim arm snaking across his middle to anchor herself. She was half asleep already. Once more he felt a tightening in his chest, something breaking free that came perilously close to tenderness. He watched her eyelids, heavy with lashes that lay on her cheek like butterfly wings—she was sound asleep.

Another situation that he was not used to. Raoul could not remember the last time he'd slept with a woman in his own bed, and as for actually sleeping…that was easy. Never, not once, since the early months of his marriage.

Raoul closed his eyes. He had been functioning on a couple of hours a night since Jamie's death. It had reached the point where he didn't want to fall asleep, knowing that he'd relive the moment he found Jamie in his dreams, the images twisted and warped. He'd jerk awake in a cold sweat, the panic in his belly trying to claw its way out.

Tonight he didn't dream at all, so it was a shock to be woken so abruptly.

Raoul was jolted into wakefulness by an ear-piercing scream. Beside him, Lara was sitting upright, her eyes wide, staring and unfocused. As he raised himself up on his elbow she turned her head and blinked several times.

'You had a nightmare.'

'Did I?' She gave him a wide-eyed-kitten look.

'You don't remember?' He slid an arm over her warm, bare shoulder and pulled her back down.

Raoul looked into the face inches away from his, her glorious hair a wild halo, wide luminous eyes looking back at him, and he experienced a wave of fierce protectiveness that was on several levels more shocking than her scream.

'You *really* don't remember?'

'No, I never do, it's a night terror. I thought I'd grown out of them.'

'Not tonight.'

'I suppose I should have told you.'

She might have meant the night terrors but he knew she didn't.

'It might,' he agreed, 'have been an idea.'

'You…it was…thank you.' She was back on earth, not floating two feet above it, but Lara couldn't help wonder if it was the same earth…or she the same person.

There you go again, Lara—dramatising. It was sex, not an entry into an alternative dimension. People did it every day.

Of their own volition her eyes slid down his body; the

light duvet that now covered them both reached his narrow hips, revealing the golden-toned skin of his flat, ridged belly and broad, powerful chest and shoulders.

The earthy image made her shudder. Her stomach muscles clenched, a stronger version of the delicious little aftershocks that had come in the wake of the crashing release.

'I know a good cure for insomnia.' And the darkness in his heart, which he felt receding.

She flashed a mock-innocent smile while inside her heart was hammering wildly. For the first time in her life she understood why people did crazy things for sex. 'A glass of milk?'

Her smile made him hot. 'You taste more of strawberries and cream.' His mouth remaining a fraction of an inch from hers, he whispered throatily, 'I want to touch you all over this time.' He feathered a kiss across her parted lips. 'Taste you.'

She gave a little whimper and whispered, 'Please.'

It was a plea she made several times during the next hour, as he took her to the brink several times before he finally let her fall over the edge with him.

Utterly drained, but more at peace than he had felt in a week, no, a lot, *lot* longer, he barely had the strength to roll off her before sleep claimed him. It took Lara a long time to come down from the high she was floating on, and when she did her sleep was shallow and disturbed.

He woke up to the sound of the shower in the adjoining bathroom. He had barely managed to groggily lever himself into a sitting position and drag a hand through his hair when she appeared. Her freshly scrubbed, shiny face and wet curling hair looking incongruous against the indecently sexy red dress.

'Sorry I woke you.' The chirpy voice belonged to the red dress. 'Hope you don't mind, but I used your toothbrush.'

'You can use anything you like but keep the volume down,' he pleaded, holding his head.

'Are you hung over?' Did he even remember making love? She smiled her way through a stab of totally irrational bitterness. For her this one-night stand had been memorable, her first, but that didn't mean it had any significance for him.

'No, but I'm human,' he retorted. 'Being that cheerful in the morning,' he concluded positively, 'is not.'

'So you're not a morning person.'

The scowling lines of his staggeringly handsome face melted without warning into a wicked grin as he leaned back against the pillows, hands behind his head, and raised a mocking brow. 'There are those that might dispute that...'

Her cheeks burning, Lara lifted her chin. 'I'll take your word on that one,' she said, wondering whether he could be any more smugly self-satisfied. Even if his smugness was justified, it was an unattractive trait, and discovering a flaw in this perfect specimen made her feel slightly more cheerful as she moved across the room towards a mirror, combing her fingers through her wet curls.

Watching the gentle sway of her breasts against the red silk as she walked across the room, he felt his lust stir lazily. Actually, not so lazily.

'I have never slept with a virgin before.' And it had not been on any list of things to do in the near future.

She swivelled gracefully around, the expression on her beautiful face wary.

'You've clearly got no sexual hang-ups...' Though she did possess a delicious ability to blush. 'It's none of my business,' he conceded, 'but why?'

She stood there, poised, he suspected, on the point of telling him to go to hell, when she shrugged and pulled out a stool, sinking with a sigh and a rustle of silk onto it.

'You know, I've been asking myself just that,' she admitted with disarming candour. 'I planned to lose my virginity last night, just not with you. I never really thought that casual sex would work for me without the emotional stuff, you know—liking, a connection...but it did quite beautifully, thank you.'

'*Liking*...not love?'

Her candid gaze slid away as she got to her feet. 'I think we communicate on more of a lust level.'

'I'm assuming there is a man somewhere that came with the *emotional stuff* wondering where the hell you are.'

If it had been him, he'd have died a thousand deaths through the night imagining all the things that could have happened to her. 'What were you thinking?' he growled. 'You could have met anyone!'

'I expect Mark is asleep still.'

He reined in the surge of emotion. Sharing casual sex did not entitle him to bad-mouth a guy he didn't know, although the confirmation that he existed at all had not improved his mood, and he could think of no circumstance that excused a man allowing a woman to wander around a strange city alone at night.

'Poor guy,' he said in a voice laden with insincerity.

Lara missed the insincerity but heard the words, and saw a red mist.

She turned slowly, rounding on him with eyes shooting green flames.

'Poor guy,' she echoed. '*Poor guy!* He's a...' Her mouth closed over a word her mum would have been shocked her daughter even knew, and, teeth clenched, she stalked towards the bathroom.

'So you're not planning a kiss-and-make-up session.' The relief he felt was on her behalf, he told himself. Lara deserved something better.

Lara's anger faded as quickly as it had sparked into life. 'I overreacted, didn't I?' She covered her face with her hands and shook her head. 'Mark is a total and utter louse, but the situation is as much my fault as his. If I hadn't been walking around thinking I'd found my soulmate I'd have seen this coming a mile off.'

'Your hero fell off his pedestal.' It seemed suddenly sad that she would learn all too soon there were no heroes. 'So what did he do?'

She gave a laugh that rang with self-mockery and shook her head. 'Oh, why not? It's a bit of a cliché really. I came here with my boss—he asked and I said yes.

'What I *didn't* know was that I was a last-minute stand-in for his girlfriend who couldn't come, and he'd paid for the room, and he is a bit tight with money.'

It was a fault she'd been prepared to accept when he had still seemed the sensitive man of her dreams.

'It turns out he asked because he thinks I'm basically easy, actually I think he's not the only one, not that I care what people think.'

Hearing her fall back on a defence that was only used by people who *did* care, Raoul was forced to subdue a surge of protective tenderness.

'And the virgin thing,' she continued. 'I think he thought he'd been sold a…what do they call it…?'

'False bill of goods?'

She nodded. 'I said I was going to sleep with the first man I saw. I was *almost* right.'

'This boss of yours sounds like a total loser.'

'I don't know why I'm even telling you this.'

He raised a sardonic brow. 'Because I asked.' Which in itself was not just unusual and totally out of character, it was completely unheard of.

A few murmured nothings that constituted post-coital conversation were normally the precursor to him rolling out of bed and making a practised exit.

Except it was never his bed he was exiting.

From every angle this was a weird situation, almost as weird as finding he wanted to prolong this. He didn't even have a major objection to hearing her open up more, talk nonsense…maybe even contribute to that nonsense himself…?

He didn't read anything significant into it, recognising that it was not an emotional connection that was making him behave so out of character, but the knowledge that the world he had escaped from in her body last night would come rushing back the moment she vanished.

'Look, I should be going before anyone…'

He looked up and saw she was looking at a framed photo on the wall.

'That's my mother.'

'Oh!' Had she really been that obvious? 'She doesn't look Italian.' Everything about him epitomised Lara's own version of an idealised Latin male but his English was perfect and she couldn't detect any accent.

'I'm Italian on my father's side. My mother was American with a Spanish mother.' *And you are sharing this information why exactly, Raoul?* Maybe the opening-up thing was contagious?

'Your mother's dead?'

He nodded. The memory of his mother was influenced by snapshots like that one and a couple of formal portraits, which didn't match the laugh he remembered or the warm lemony scent he associated with her.

'A flu epidemic. She ought to have been safe—she wasn't an infant or elderly, she was fit and young. I was just a kid.'

An image drifted before her eyes of a boy with scratched, long brown legs and big dark eyes. Her eyes drifted of their own accord to his face, their eyes connected and something seemed to pass between them. She found the sensation so uncomfortable that she looked away quickly and changed the subject.

'Do you have such a thing as a hairdryer?' She lifted a water-darkened strand of hair. 'It takes hours to dry on its own.'

'Bottom drawer,' he said, pointing to the bathroom.

Inside the room she closed the door and, sighing, leaned back against it. Now that she didn't have to hold it together and act a version of cool, the images she had fought to banish from her head while in the room with Raoul crowded in. Remembering the exquisite sweetness of their lovemaking was agony.

She took a deep breath and straightened her shoulders. She had been prepared for remote and maybe irritated, but not for him to be so... She shook her head. What did she know? Absolutely nothing when it came to the morning after the night before.

And this might feel awkward but she was leaving here with a lot of positives. Her first time had been with a great lover, and she had not disgraced herself by saying anything terminally stupid like, *Last night was special—it must mean something to you.*

When Lara emerged from the bathroom, her hair dried to a smooth gloss, the bedroom was filled with the aroma of fresh coffee. She followed the scent downstairs.

Raoul was standing there, coffee cup in hand, wearing a black robe loosely tied around his hips. It showed a wide vee of hard, golden, hair-roughened chest. Lara struggled to keep her eyes on his strong, angular face, which, with its dark shading of stubble, was only fractionally less disturbing.

Hauntingly beautiful. From some corner of her head the description of a hero in a novel she had read recently flashed into her head. At the time she had rolled her eyes and given up on the story midway, unable to imagine a real-life man who could be described this way, and unable to connect with the book's heroine who had walked away from a perfectly good husband to be with him.

'I cried at the end,' the friend who had recommended it had confided.

Lara hadn't cried. She'd lost patience with the heroine long before. She'd thought, *Who walks away from everything for an orgasm, no matter how bone-meltingly incredible?*

Lara hadn't known a lot about orgasms at the time, but she couldn't imagine anything that would make her give up a stable home.

And then Raoul had come into her life.

And soon he would be out again, which was good. Clean breaks were good when it came to uncomplicated sex. Actually, they were probably essential.

He put down the mug in his hand, his eyes making a sweep up from her feet to the glossy, smooth curls on her head. 'You found it, then.'

She touched her face, now clear of the last remnants of make-up from the night before. She felt naked without even a smear of lip gloss to protect her from his dark, bone-stripping stare. 'Thanks, yes.'

'Help yourself to coffee. I won't be long.'

'Thanks but I should be going.' Last night now seemed like a lifetime ago, and the rejection from Mark was a distant dream.

'I'll take you back to your hotel.'

Move on...never, ever see this man again...never touch him...never... 'No, that's—'

His voice cut across her. 'Have you got money for a taxi?'

She flushed and, gnawing on the soft fullness of her under lip, brought her lashes down in a concealing sweep.

'Exactly.'

With a flash of defiance she lifted her head, tossing back her red curls. 'I could walk.'

'And that worked out so well the last time...'

Recognising that this was a battle she wasn't about to win, Lara managed a superficial attitude of amusement as she arched a brow and asked, 'Do all your one-night stands rate taxi service?'

She was trying so hard and her pretence was painfully transparent. Raoul hid his reaction to the vulnerability he didn't want to see under an attitude of brusque impatience, and reminded himself that Lucy had once seemed sweet and vulnerable to him too.

'They do if they don't mind hanging around...' He arched a brow. 'Five minutes.'

It was only when she got in the car that she realised she'd forgotten the hotel name.

'I think it begins with a C or maybe a T and I think there was a coffee shop on the corner, no, there was definitely a coffee shop.'

'Oh, well, that makes it much easier.'

'There's no need to be sarcastic. I'm sure the name will come to me.'

When? he wondered fifteen minutes later when, naming another hotel, he got the same negative shake of her head.

'You're just confusing me now,' she accused. Bad enough that even with the top of the low-slung sports car up, in the skin-tight red dress her appearance had still elicited a lot of unwanted attention.

Raoul had advised her to ignore the horn blares and the calls from pedestrians—the Latin male seemed to have a *very* extensive non-verbal vocabulary—and then gone on to ignore his own advice, rolling down his window to react with hand signals that had never found a place into the highway code!

'I'm sure now it begins with an A…'

He audibly ground his teeth. 'I thought you'd decided it began with a T.'

'Well, a T or maybe…wait, that place there.' She hit his arm and began to bounce in her seat as she turned to look behind them. 'I remember that bar with the potted palms outside and the blue squiggly writing on the sign. Turn around…turn around…'

'We're in the middle of a one-way system. Do you mind sitting still? I'm trying to focus.' To focus on the road and not the way her breasts were trying to fight their way out of the bodice of her dress. 'Do you want me to cause a crash?'

'I don't suppose this is how you planned to spend your day.'

'*Dio mio*, do not go all humble and apologetic on me.' He found unreasonable and wilfully awkward much easier to deal with.

'It's not this way,' she said as he swung the car down an alley where the walls of the tall buildings almost touched the car on either side. To make things worse he didn't reduce his speed.

'So how well do you know Rome, then?'

She flashed him a killer look and compressed her lips.

'It was a shortcut,' she said in a quiet voice as he drew up outside the hotel.

Raoul grunted and turned his attention to the building. Like most in the area, it could have done with some TLC; he was not a person who found peeling paint picturesque. 'You're sure this is the right place?'

She nodded.

'Your boyfriend really knows how to treat a lady, doesn't he?'

'He's not my boyfriend,' she gritted.

'Has it occurred to you he might have called the police?' Her wide eyes said it hadn't.

She was thinking.

'I hope not! Well, thank you and last night…you were…kind.' With a swish of silk she left the car, her comment making him feel like a total bastard.

And maybe he was, Raoul mused as watched her walk up the steps, the sinuous sway of her body in that wicked dress causing several turned heads before she vanished inside the clapped-out-looking building.

How was the man who'd brought her here and then rejected her going to react when she appeared? Raoul knew how he'd have reacted in that position. He wasn't a possessive man, but if she'd left him and spent the night with another man he'd have throttled her, or maybe just thrown her on the bed and made love to her.

And would Lara forgive him? You never knew with women. Some were drawn like magnets to men who treated them badly.

While he was grimly contemplating make-up sex and wondering if that was what was happening, Raoul was suddenly struck by how *extreme* his reactions to this woman were. There was no middle ground. Much like her, he reflected grimly, either spitting disdain or melting in submission.

With a curse he put the car into gear and pulled away from the kerb with a rubber-burning squeal. The last thing he needed at this point was a redhead to distract him.

CHAPTER FIVE

THE HOTEL FOYER was also the dining room and actually the décor inside was much nicer than the façade suggested. About half the tables were occupied when Lara walked in, causing a few brows to rise. She walked straight over to Mark.

'I was worried.' He put down his newspaper.

It might have been more convincing without the petulant pout. *What did I ever see in him?*

'Really.' Her glance moved to the buffet breakfast he was tucking into. She struggled to imagine him spending his morning driving around the city to see that the woman he'd spent the night with was safe.

'As you see, I'm fine.' She spread her arms wide and hid her irrational hurt behind a flippant façade, trying to ignore the stares she was receiving from the other diners.

'So how do you feel about the Coliseum?' His glance slid down her dress. 'After you've changed, obviously.'

Lara shook her head and stared, not believing what she was hearing. 'What?'

'I worked out an itinerary. A weekend isn't long enough to see everything Rome has to offer, but—'

She moved closer to the table and lowered her voice to an incredulous whisper. 'You expect me to go sightseeing?'

'Look, this doesn't have to be a total disaster.'

His attitude made Lara want to hit his fat face. Actually, it wasn't fat. She held on to her temper with both hands and made herself look objectively at the man she had decided would be a safe bet.

Because that was what it boiled down to. In her determination to find a man who would see beyond her face and body she'd ignored other warning signs. One major flaw in her plan had been assuming a man capable of seeing her as more than a sex object would automatically be sensitive and caring, someone worthy of loving.

No one would have looked at Raoul and thought he was sensitive and caring, she mused, heat accompanying the image of the man she had spent the night with flashing into her head.

If she could have written a list of all the things she had been consciously avoiding in a lover he would have ticked more boxes than she knew existed.

He was all the things, the breathing epitome, of what she had been avoiding in the man destined to be her first lover. Yet his raw, elemental sexuality had been matched by a gentleness and sensitivity... The only flickers of fear had been a fear of the strength of her own response, and that had quickly faded as she had embraced the passion that had blazed between them.

One of life's little jokes! It turned out she had wanted a man who would rip her clothes off and make her forget where she ended and he began.

With a sigh she tuned back into what a red-faced Mark was saying. 'The room is paid for.'

'Don't be ridiculous. I couldn't possibly stay here with you.'

Folding his napkin with irritating precision, he looked at her over the dark rim of his glasses and sounded annoyed as he asked, 'What's the alternative?'

Pushed into a corner, she bit her quivering lip. 'I want to go home.' She was embarrassed before she had closed her mouth over the unguarded words; his reaction turned her humiliation to anger.

'I thought I'd brought a woman away, not some little kid.' The defensive aggression that she had sensed beneath the surface was now overt as he added, 'I wasn't funding a school outing for virgins.'

'You weren't funding anything.' She had paid for her own flight. 'I'll leave the cash for my share of the hotel room on the dressing table before I leave.'

Turning, she stalked from the room and stomped her way up the stairs to the bedroom; not a room with a view—that was extra. Walking to the wardrobe, she pulled her clothes off the hangers and flung them in a heap on the bed before transferring them to her case. Next came the toiletries out of the bathroom. It might well be a record, she decided, turning the key on the padlock, for packing and stupidity.

She'd wanted to go away with safe and responsible and she'd got selfish and boring.

'You know, you're overreacting.'

She didn't bother to turn around but sighed and said in a flat little voice, 'Well, that's me, isn't it? A drama queen.'

'Not the best trait in a PA.'

He threw it in casually, didn't say outright that she'd be looking for another job as soon as she got home, but she'd need to have been stupid not to get the message. Lara's stomach went into a nosedive. So this was why office romances were frowned on. When they went sour bad things happened for the person who *wasn't* the nephew of the company owner.

'Don't worry. I've been thinking of moving on...' Her pride made her say it, but in reality she needed the pay cheque. Without it...she didn't want to go there! The only place she'd be going was back home with her tail between her legs.

Mark didn't immediately react. He crossed the room, picked up a tourist guide from the dressing table and shoved it into his pocket. When he finally looked at her she could see the relief on his face.

'That might be the best idea. Don't worry, I'll give you a good reference.'

She lost her struggle to hide her feelings. 'Don't make it sound like you're doing me a favour. I'm damned good at my job.'

'Yours, mine and everyone else's. Not everyone likes being told what to do by a secretary.'

Pride alone kept her chin up, *another* of her life choices coming back to bite her.

It was strange, but last night had not been a decision in her head, more a collision, one of those celestial events that nothing could stop…and if she could have, would she? The answer should have depressed her, but, in the face of Mark's unremitting nastiness, the fact it had happened made her feel not less in control, but more. She would never regret last night.

No, weirdly it had not been one of her bad life choices. University…? Lara had laughed at the idea—three years out of her life that gave her zero experience of *real* life and left her with a pile of debt hanging around her neck. Back then she'd had this crazy idea that talent and enthusiasm would make her rise through the ranks. Maybe true in some firms, but not in the one she worked for. Her glass ceiling had been set very low and her lack of paper qualifications meant she was never going to push through it.

There were no glittering prospects on the horizon, and until now she hadn't admitted it even to herself, because doing so would mean she'd have to admit she'd made the wrong decision.

'You know, sometimes it's better to admit you made a mistake,' she said.

'But if you fly back without me, people—'

She suddenly got it. 'You mean the guys in the office you told will think you're not up to it?'

'I didn't tell anyone,' he lied, red-faced. 'If *I'm* willing to make the best of this I don't see why you can't…'

Arms folded across her chest, she looked at him, not seeing sensitivity shining out from behind his horn-rimmed spectacles but a pretty boring, unimaginative and selfish guy.

'I'm really not your type, am I?' Part of his attraction, if she was honest—and that was long overdue—was the fact that Mark had never made a pass. She'd never had to fight off advances or ignore smutty innuendo.

It really ought to have occurred to her that he simply didn't find her attractive. She huffed out a laugh of self-mockery and thought, *That'll teach you, Lara, for assuming you're irresistible.* As for being the strong, quiet, heroic type—well, he hadn't even asked her where she'd been last night let alone made any attempt to find her.

Mark gave an uncomfortable shrug. 'You're beautiful, I was flattered, but—'

Suddenly Lara did not want to hear the *but*…which was not going to be ego enhancing. Hers had taken quite a battering, and if it hadn't been for last night and Raoul making her feel… She pushed away the thought. She was not going to turn into the sort of woman who needed a man to tell her she was beautiful in order to be comfortable in her own skin… *Skin!* A tingle slid through her body.

Images began to tumble through her head, relentless details, vignettes that had been indelibly imprinted. She could hear the soft rasp of her quickened breathing as she relived strong hands against her skin, gliding, and lips warm and moist.

It required every last ounce of self-control she had to banish them, to resist the compulsion to live it over and over. It left her feeling drained and strangely disconnected from reality, which might, she admitted, looking at Mark, not be such a bad thing.

His lips were tight—Lara recognised his fall-back expression when Mark encountered any opposition.

'And anyway my CV could do with some polishing.'

Her comment succeeded in making Mark look uncomfortable; his eyes darted everywhere in the room except towards her face.

'I'll get the first flight home,' she informed him, and worry about how she was going to pay for it afterwards.

'You won't get a refund on your ticket.'

He was right, of course, she didn't, but the flight had not been as expensive as she had feared, even counting for the bus journey to the airport, which was miles out of the city.

Lara sat amidst frayed tempers and crying babies, sipping something that might have been coffee, when her flight was flashed up as delayed.

Just what she needed!

'Miss Gray?'

A tall man stood there, brown hair with some premature grey showing at the temples. He carried himself with an air of natural authority—of course, the captain's uniform helped.

She nodded, immediately wary; airports were not her favourite places.

'Is there a problem?' Her imagination went into overdrive, producing any number of disaster scenarios that would bring about this man knowing her name, seeking her out.

Did they send someone in a captain's uniform to inform you when your family home had burnt down or your mum was lying in hospital after a head-on collision with a bus?

He shook his head and flashed her a reassuring smile. 'Not at all. No problem, just a message.'

She touched a hand to her chest. 'For me?'

Her worried frown vanished as logic kicked in. There could be no message for her because nobody knew she was here. She hadn't explained her travel arrangements to Mark and nobody back home knew she was catching an early flight.

It was obviously a case of mistaken identity.

'I think you've got the wrong person.' And since when did men in pilots' uniforms act as messengers?

'No,' he said, looking at her hair. 'If you'd like to follow me...?'

When she thought about it later, Lara put her uncharacteristic docility down to a combination of the uniforms and airports, which were not the sort of places where anyone these days wanted to make a scene.

Airports! How she hated them! Though up to this point the worst thing that had happened to her was lost luggage.

'I hope this won't take long, my flight—'

'Thanks, Justin, I owe you. Give my best to AJ.'

Raoul placed a hand on Lara's arm before leaning forward, hand extended to the other man. Lara stood there, too stunned to protest the possessive gesture as she watched the two men shake hands like old friends.

'Any time, Raoul.' *Justin* flashed a sheepish apologetic look towards Lara before setting his cap on his head and walking away.

It was a set-up.

As she turned her head to look at the man who remained the life returned to her stiff limbs. Snatching her arm free, she took an angry step away from him.

'Is he even a pilot?' she asked bitterly.

'Yes, he's a pilot. I called him when I got snarled in the traffic.' When Raoul had dropped her off and driven back to his place it hadn't been too bad, but by the time he'd reversed back out it had been straight into rush-hour traffic.

In the interim he'd not actually got out of the car.

The automatic gates closing behind him had seemed to act like a trigger. Without warning the dark thoughts that he had escaped for a few hours last night had come rushing into his head, carrying with them a sense of searing desolation and loss. Unable to fight the downward spiral, he'd sunk deeper and deeper, struggling like a drowning man. Just as his lungs had felt as though they would burst, he had caught a whiff of the perfume that lingered in the confined space, and he had focused on that elusive fragrance, letting it carry him clear.

Over in seconds, minutes or an hour, he had no idea as he sat there feeling as though he'd just run a hard set of sprints, sweat trickling down his back. He leaned back in the seat, pushing his head into the leather rest. The face that belonged to the scent materialised, and he let it form and solidify, allowing the image to push away the feelings of moments before. Sex had always been that for him, an escape, and now the echo of it was doing the same thing.

It was just a shame he hadn't realised sex had nothing to do with emotions before Lucy. Now he enjoyed it for what it was, which was a better stress-releaser than track work and as good as—though a lot more fun than—solo climbing.

Last night—even for someone who enjoyed sex as much as he did—had been...*incredible*. He focused on the lips of the face in his head and released a sigh of regret. If what she did for him came in legal prescription form, the next few months would be a hell of a lot easier to get through!

And then it hit him. Like a jigsaw the pieces suddenly slotted together, and he ignored the fact that some of the pieces needed forcing, and thought... *Why not?*

And then the rest just became clear. He would make the gloriously sexy Lara Gray realise that this was a business arrangement she could not turn down.

Even when she'd been sparking up at him with antagonism he could see that she had been as aware of the crackle of tension between them as he was, just less experienced at hiding the fact. She would come to see that *not* sleeping with her boss this weekend had been a great career move.

It was also his winning card.

The information he'd requested had come during the airport traffic jam. Owning a law firm with access to first-class investigators could be useful, and these days—as in post-Lucy—he backed up his hunches and gut instincts with hard, researched fact.

The file he'd scrolled through had been thin. It turned out that she didn't have a criminal record or any skeletons in her closet. She did have a driving licence and a couple of parking tickets, but no fall-back position if she lost her job, and pretty much no qualifications. Lara Gray needed a pay cheque, and her boss was the CEO's nephew.

Raoul was brought back to the present. 'Luckily your flight was delayed.' Raoul had had his jet put on standby to cover that eventuality.

He'd had no trouble rationalising what might on the surface *appear* an extreme course of action. He never committed to any course of action unless he was willing to follow it through; half-hearted measures were not his style.

Not that his *heart* had been involved, in this or any other decision he made. It was impossible to remove the risk factor completely, but it could always be minimised.

'Lucky!' Lara echoed bitterly as she continued to rub her arm where his hand had lain.

She couldn't brush away the invisible mark of contact any more than she could brush away the memory of the previous night. It seemed laughable now that she'd spent the bus journey to the airport convincing herself that in time the face that was etched so clearly in her mind would fade, the details would blur. There would come a time when she wouldn't remember his voice.

She had found the thought soothing because, though she wanted to remember her *first*, she also wanted to move past it and him. She knew how special last night had been and recognised the danger of souring future relationships by subjecting them to death by comparison. The idea of becoming the dating equivalent of a soccer-team star, who got to be thirty and still considered the winning goal he scored in high school the pinnacle of his life, filled her with horror.

And now he was standing there and the lie was cruelly exposed. Her protection was stripped away and the truth was looking at her through his eyes, his beautiful eyes.

Time was not a factor. His simply wasn't a face you forgot. Each angle and plane of his face, the subtle shading of his deep voice, the scent of his skin…it was imprinted, indelibly imprinted.

'Very few people can carry off the open-mouthed look.'

Lara closed her mouth with an audible snap.

'I didn't say you were not one of them.' To his mind Lara Gray could not look anything less than luscious if she spent a day trying.

'I don't understand what this little stunt is meant to achieve. Actually,' she said, lifting a hand to ward off any potential glib or even outrageous explanation, 'don't bother. I don't want to know. Maybe you've got nothing better to do with your time, but I have.'

'You're not even *slightly* curious to find out why I tracked you down?'

'No,' she lied.

His sardonic disbelieving smile made her grind her teeth.

'I don't want to talk to you.'

He shook his head in sympathy. 'I'd prefer to take you to bed too but—' He stopped, a rumble of laughter vibrating in his chest as he registered the blush on her face that continued to deepen. 'Let's go somewhere you can cool down.'

She ignored his hand and tucked her own firmly behind her back. 'I am not going anywhere with you. I have no idea what this is about, but my flight could be recalled at any moment and I need to be there.' She didn't have the money for another ticket.

'Relax, you'll hear from the bar when it's called.'

'But—'

'If you miss it I'll provide alternative transport.'

'Oh, really? I suppose you have your own private jet?'

'Yes.'

Her jeering mockery faded. 'I've no idea why you're acting like some weirdo stalker, but if you have actually got something to say to me you can say it here.'

'And have you pass out on me? You're pale as a ghost. Did you have lunch?'

'I don't pass out.'

'Or breakfast?'

Her stomach gave a loud rumble and, ignoring his grin, she muttered, 'All right, a coffee.'

Raoul led her to a table in a corner of the crowded bar-lounge, looking out of place among the groups of cheerful tourists. Without waiting for him to pull out her chair, she sat down.

Raoul shrugged, walked around to his side of the table, and before he had taken his seat a waitress was there, eager to please.

'Coffee. *Grazie...* Lara?'

'Just a coffee for me.'

He responded in Italian this time and the girl bustled away after delivering a melting smile. 'I ordered you sandwiches.'

'Why did you ask if you were going to ignore me?'

A moment later, the waitress returned with their drinks and a plate of sandwiches, which she put in front of Lara, who picked one up. It would be churlish to waste good food just to prove a point.

She took a couple of bites; the slices of smoked salmon were interlaced with cucumber. 'So what is this about?'

'I have a proposition to put to you.' He saw her face and sketched a smile. 'Not *that* sort of proposition.'

Knowing her face was burning, she stirred her coffee and slung him a look of lofty disdain. 'I can't imagine I'd be interested in any sort of proposition you made.'

Unless it involved taking me to bed. She guiltily pushed the thought away and dug her even white teeth into the softness of her full upper lip, focusing on the pain, not on the ache low inside her.

'My grandfather is dying.'

Lara's eyes flew to his face. Her wary antagonism was crushed under a wave of inconvenient empathy. He looked as composed as he sounded, but she could intuitively sense the writhing emotions behind his mask.

She didn't know what she'd expected to hear but it hadn't been this. 'I'm sorry.'

His glance stilled on her face and she looked back at him through green eyes soft with sympathy. She hid behind a tough-cookie attitude and he could see why; it was inevitable that individuals who emoted that much frequently got taken advantage of.

Wasn't that what he was doing?

He shook off the moment of uncharacteristic doubt. He was not using emotional manipulation. This was a business deal, not a conventional one, admittedly, but he wasn't appealing to her soft heart, just her pragmatism.

'So am I.' He leaned back in his seat, his chest lifting as he exhaled and admitted, 'I've not really got used to the idea yet.'

'Has he been ill long?' she asked quietly. She'd been

a child when she'd lost her father but that had been sudden. Was it worse, she wondered, to know it was coming?

At least then you got the chance to say goodbye—something she'd always wished she'd been able to do.

'He's never been ill—at least, if he was I don't remember it.' His voice drifted away as he sat there seemingly lost in his own thoughts.

'Are you very close?'

He seemed to consider the question. 'He was more of a father to us than our father ever was.'

'So you have brothers and sisters...?' Maybe it was the lone-wolf thing he had going on that had made her assume he was an only child or even that he had emerged fully grown with designer stubble and a macho ego!

'I had a brother, Jamie.'

'Sorry,' she said again. His body language made it obvious that he wasn't comfortable with discussing personal matters, which begged the question, why was he? Raoul did not strike her as the sort of person who did anything without a reason.

'I'm not telling you this because I'm canvassing the sympathy vote. The fact that I'm the last Di Vittorio standing is relevant.' Perhaps he ought to tell her that people around him had a tendency to drop like flies, but on balance he decided this might not be a vote winner.

He paused and appeared lost in thought again as Lara, curious despite her determination not to be, sat there willing him to continue.

'Family matters to my grandfather. He feels strongly about continuity, about living on in his children, passing on his genetic blueprint through the generations, a form of immortality, I suppose. When I was married he assumed that I would provide the next generation.'

'You're divorced?'

'My wife died. There were no children.'

His voice was a little dead as he gave her the information, just the bald facts that probably hid a world of pain.

'What is this about?'

'My grandfather's dying wish.'

'Which is…?' she prompted.

'To have his name live on in my child.'

It took her a few moments to digest his words. He couldn't be…no…she couldn't even think it, surely he couldn't, wouldn't? Outrage mingled with disbelief as she shook her head. Her chair scraped the floor noisily as she made an attempt to rise but her knees would not support her.

'Which is where you come in.'

A gurgling sound left her throat. He could not be suggesting… *'Me!'* She started to shake her head and, hands on the table edge, she pushed her chair back farther as if to physically distance herself from this insanity. 'You are insane,' she told him with utter conviction. 'And this conversation is over. I'm not going to be a baby incubator for you!'

'I wouldn't bring a child into the world just to please my grandfather.' When he had been considering his options that had never even figured.

She remained wary as she subsided in her seat. 'What was I meant to think? You said—'

'I want you to marry me, Lara, not have my children.'

'Oh, well, that's all right, then.' She lost the mocking smile, unable to decide if he was serious or this was some sick joke as she directed a searching look of pained incredulity at his face… Hell, he made it sound as though he'd just requested nothing more outrageous than directions! 'When my flight leaves I'll be on it. This conversation really is over now.' She jerked her hands to underline the finality of her statement.

His broad shoulders lifted, the shrug negligent, but the dark gaze that held hers was intense. 'Hear me out.'

She shook her head slowly from side to side. 'Nothing you can say will change my mind.'

'Then you have nothing to lose from listening to what I have to say. Give me the consideration you'd give any other job offer.'

She lifted threads of hair from her eyes, tucking them neatly behind her ears. Were you meant to humour insane people? 'Do you drink in the daytime too?'

He leaned in, the unexpected action bringing his face within an inch of hers. 'Smell?' he invited, parting his firm, sensual lips.

As his mint-scented, warm breath brushed her cheek, Lara jolted back in her seat so fast she almost fell off her chair. 'I'll pass, and, in case you forgot, I have a job.'

'*Not* sleeping with the boss is generally a good thing but in this instance…?' He shook his head and studied her face, letting the blush of discomfort develop before adding, 'I see you have worked that one out yourself. Did it not occur to you to ask yourself if a weekend in Rome might have consequences beyond losing your virginity?' Recognising it was irrational didn't stop him feeling furious every time he thought of her throwing herself away on some loser—any man who let this woman walk away deserved the definition. 'Do you *ever* think ahead? At what point did it seem like a good idea?'

'How is your offer better?' she choked back, eyeing him with dislike. Where did he get off lecturing her?

His lips flattened into a hard line. 'Were you hoping to hook him?' he speculated.

'Hook?' she echoed. *Does he think I need reminding of what an idiot I was?*

'Was marriage what you were after?' he cut back, coldness seeping into his voice as other features superimposed themselves over her vivid face.

Lucy, his cold, calculating wife, had not done anything as extreme as save herself for him. She hadn't needed to... He felt a stab of familiar contemptuous self-disgust aimed more at his romantic, easily manipulated younger self than Lucy and her mind games.

'If I was out to catch a rich husband—which, by the way, went out with pearls and twinsets—I'd have chosen someone significantly richer than Mark.'

The furious flash of eyes like emeralds burnt away that other face and as she lifted her rounded, determined chin Raoul knew he had earned the dislike blazing in them.

Lara Gray was easy enough for a child to read! Not only could she not hide her feelings, she broadcast every emotion she felt on her beautiful face.

'It wasn't a judgement,' he said quietly.

She gave a snort. 'Not much!'

'If it's any comfort I think you got off pretty lightly. It can take some people a lot longer to realise the person they fell for doesn't really exist outside their own imagination.'

'Speaking from experience, are you?' she mocked, finding it totally impossible to imagine that situation.

He pushed his empty cup away from him, the action allowing him the time to smooth out his expression. 'Well, it wasn't all bad. Look, last night we had a good time.'

Lara struggled to fight her way out of the images that flickered relentlessly through her head.

He said, 'I made you forget.'

Where she began and he ended.

'And you returned the favour.' The dark glitter in his eyes was mesmerising.

The butterfly kicks had been a struggle to handle but now her stomach dissolved.

'So what do you think?'

She blinked like someone waking up and choked out,

'It was sex and it was one night.' She shook her head and loosed a shocked, incredulous laugh. 'What you're suggesting...beyond being certifiably insane—'

'Could work. I'm not asking for you to sign over your life.'

'Isn't that what marriage usually entails?'

'Have you read the divorce statistics? The contract I am suggesting would only last for...' he paused, the muscles around his jawline quivering before he voiced the grim reality '...my grandfather's lifetime, which according to the doctors is around six months, that or...' He stopped, cancelling the unnecessary codicil in his head: *until we want it to.*

He didn't like the vagueness of it, the sense that it was not within his control. No, there had to be a definite cut-off point.

His problem was thinking past the hunger she had shaken loose in him, a hunger he'd not felt, well, *ever.* Right now he felt as if he'd never be able to get enough of her. But inevitably he would; six weeks, six days...even this consuming passion had a sell-by date. It would not last as long as his grandfather, but, while it did, finding the sort of escape he had last night held a lot of appeal.

'He doesn't expect to see his grandchild, but being able to think there will be one will make his last days... It will give his life a purpose. Do you understand?'

Lara tried a change of tack, knowing that she was doomed to lose any argument that hinged on him *not* being the perfect lover and her *not* wanting more of what he'd shown her last night.

'I understand you're going to lie to your grandfather and you want me to help you.'

'You've never lied?'

She flung him a resentful glare. 'You know what I mean.'

'This is business. I'm not expecting six months of your life for free. You admit that you are going to be out of work…?'

She chewed on her lower lip. 'Probably,' she admitted reluctantly. 'But that doesn't change anything.' *Except my bank balance*, she thought gloomily.

'You're right, there are always jobs for people with the right skill sets and qualifications,' he agreed blandly.

'I look on this as an opportunity to go back to school.'

'I like your glass-half-full attitude, but of course university fees are not cheap and you have to live, pay the bills…or you could give me the next six months and walk away with enough money to put yourself through college without going into debt.'

He mentioned a sum that would do a lot more than that.

'It would be wrong.' But it would really be a solution to the situation she found herself in…

'Why? Who would be harmed?'

'You're paying me for sex. That makes me feel like—'

'The sex is optional,' he said, hoping he would not live to regret the gesture, but as risks went it was barely registered.

Raoul knew about sexual chemistry but just breathing in the fragrance of her skin ignited a hunger in him that broke new ground. And he knew it was mutual. Lara Gray didn't have the ability to hide her own responses. And, yes, it *was* a massive turn-on to know that he could make her quiver without even touching her.

The idea that they could live as man and wife and keep sex out of the equation was the equivalent to throwing a lit match into a pile of dry leaves and expecting nothing to happen.

'If you chose to sleep in another bedroom, so be it.'

'And you'd be all right with that?'

His grin flashed at the note of pique in her voice. 'No, I wouldn't, but it wouldn't be a deal breaker.'

'I couldn't do it. I'd have to pretend that I'm…I'm… I'm—'

'Madly in love with me,' he inserted helpfully. 'That's precisely why it *will* work. You can't hide your feelings.'

'If you think that one night in your bed makes me in love with you you're seriously deluded!'

Her vehemence drew a dry smile from him. 'If I thought you were in love with me that *would* be a deal breaker. I have no need of love.' The contemptuous curl of distaste on his expressive lips backed up the claim. 'But love and lust can look very much the same to an observer. The sensual side of your nature has just woken up. I woke it up… you look at me and you want me—it shows.'

An embarrassed choking sound left her throat; he hadn't even attempted to lower his voice. 'You have a very high opinion of yourself,' she retorted, failing to come even halfway to delivering the haughtily contemptuous tone she was aiming for.

'So none of what I have just said is true?'

Lara shook her head. 'Look, I understand why you came up with this idea,' she babbled. 'I'm sympathetic, but if you just stop and think about it you'll realise it would never work. Your grandfather sounds like an intelligent man…?'

A smile quivered across his expressive lips. 'His brain makes razor blades seem blunt.'

She threw up her hands in an 'argument won' gesture.

He looked at her; the gleam in his heavily lidded eyes was sensual and teasing. 'He'll like you.'

'For my good child-bearing hips?'

Her stomach lurched as she watched the smile fade from his eyes, leaving something much harder and more predatory.

She knew that he was thinking of her naked…and she was thinking of him the same way.

'Will you stop doing that?' she pleaded. 'People might—'

Her agonised whisper made him grin, dissipating a little of the tension. 'People might, what, know your knees are shaking under the table and your throat is dry; they might notice that your pupils are so dilated there is only a thin ring of green left?'

The finger he placed to her lips silenced a fresh rush of denial, but not the voice in Raoul's own head that without warning acknowledged the fact he had so far successfully dodged: he *liked* Lara Gray.

CHAPTER SIX

LIKE. IT SOUNDED BLAND, not a dangerous emotion, but even so the discovery threw Raoul. He had female friends—he had never bought into the popular belief that men and women could not be friends. There were women he admired, women whose opinion he valued in and out of the workplace, but none of those women were the ones in his bed, because *liking* was not a prerequisite for good sex. Was it something he subconsciously avoided in sexual partners…?

With a slight shake of his head he dismissed the possibility and the significance of his discovery as he allowed his hand to fall away. She closed her eyes as his fingers trailed down her cheek.

It had been the lightest of touches, but the chain reaction it set up was not! By the time he took his hand away she was shaking and struggling to catch her breath.

She forced her eyelids apart and folded her fingers around her coffee cup to stop herself touching the side of her face where the skin still tingled.

'That is what I mean—you can't hide the way you feel, the way *I* make you feel. You've only just begun to discover your sensuality—'

Mortified beyond belief by his comments, she had really thought that she was being discreet. She said the first thing that came into her head just to shut him up. Just to stop him saying those things, which she could have dealt with if they hadn't been true.

It was just sex, you couldn't fall for someone you barely

knew…just sex…just sex, she repeated in her head until the words became a meaningless hum.

'And I'm looking forward to continuing that process when I get back home with someone other than you.'

The words struck Raoul harder than a slap across the face. Without warning, images flashed across his retina, a stream of faceless lovers. Blood pounded in his ears as he fought to contain the outrage that threatened to spill out.

A couple of feet away Lara remained totally unaware of the effect her taunt had had on the recipient. It was the effect it had had on her that she was dealing with! The moment the words left her lips, the truth came crashing in—the thought of another man touching her as Raoul had made her feel… A shudder of revulsion rippled through her body.

'I don't want to have sex with anyone!' she cried out suddenly.

Her voice floated to him through a haze of anger. He shook his head to clear the low hum.

'Fine. As I've said that works too—you call the shots. I know marriage may seem extreme…hell, do you think I like the idea of going through with a farce? It feels like—'

'You're cheating on your wife?'

He gave an odd laugh. 'I certainly swore after Lucy died that I would never marry again.' His jaw clenched as he continued in a voice carefully devoid of emotion. 'But my grandfather means a great deal to me and if I can make him happy by disrupting my life for a few months it does not seem unreasonable.'

'He's not *my* grandfather.' It was ridiculous but she felt mean for pointing it out.

'Which is why I am offering an incentive.'

'You're trying to buy me.'

'Think of this as headhunting… You have a unique skill set that I want.' *I want you.*

'With sex as an optional extra?' she threw back bitterly.

'It would be a lie to say I am not eagerly anticipating sharing your bed,' he admitted, with a gleam in his eyes that sent a rush of receptive heat through her body. 'However, should the need arise the *palazzo* is a big place and you don't need to *see* me if you don't wish to.'

'*Palazzo?* I assumed we'd be living in your apartment... not that I'm going to be...living with... I'm not agreeing...'

He let her stumble on for a moment before permitting himself a smugly triumphant smile. 'See, a terrible liar.'

'For heaven's sake, being honest is not a defect, and I *can* lie.'

'I've never met anyone who wore her emotions so close to the surface.'

She lifted a hand to her temple, massaging the area to relieve a tension headache. 'No wonder I have a headache. You make me want to scream.'

'Now *that's* the truth, just as when you saw me you wanted to rip off my clothes...'

Before she could react to this casually voiced and deadly accurate observation he cast a look of critical distaste around the crowded room. 'I think we should go somewhere less crowded...'

'I'm not going anywhere with you. I'm catching my flight,' Lara said, unable to shake the feeling she was fighting the inevitable.

'That might be hard—your flight was called some time ago,' he said gently.

'You heard and you didn't say anything.'

Raoul rose to his feet. 'We both know you're not going to fly out of here—you're coming home with me.'

The denial on her tongue died as he caught her eye.

Unable to maintain contact, she looked away, shaking her head. 'It wouldn't just be your grandfather we have to convince. What about my family? They'll think I've gone mad.'

'You can't tell them the truth, Lara. You can't tell anyone the truth.'

'Then what do you suggest I tell them?'

'That I am your soulmate.'

CHAPTER SEVEN

'OH, MY G—!'

Lara took her eyes off the tree-lined, private road they were driving along—it wasn't as if they were going to meet any oncoming traffic—to look at her twin sister's face. She imagined that she had worn a similar look a week earlier when Raoul had brought her for the first time to the family estate—her new home.

It was all deeply surreal.

'Yeah, it is a bit, isn't it?' It wasn't just the size and sense of history of the golden-stoned palatial house, but the magnificent setting. Cradled by a backdrop of mountains, olive groves covered the gently sloping hills to the west and a river wound its way like a silver ribbon to the north with the *palazzo* like a jewel in the centre.

'It looks like an illustration in a fairy tale, you know, not quite real, a bit like you getting married to someone you've only just met…?'

Lara focused on the road ahead, not reacting to the unspoken question. 'Oh, there's Mum.' She nodded towards a plume of dust. 'We've almost caught them up.'

'It is incredibly beautiful, but don't *you* feel isolated here?'

The emphasis was not lost on Lara. She supposed it was her own fault. She had kind of played up how great the social side was when she had moved to the city for her job, but it was better than admitting that for the first six months she'd been terribly homesick.

'Without a night club within stumbling distance, you mean. I guess I'll just have to make my own entertainment, like in the olden days,' she mocked. 'I grew up in the country too, remember, only here there isn't a bus at the end of the lane, there's a helicopter.'

'And you have this.' Lily patted the deep leather upholstery of her seat.

Lara thought of all the cars in the garage that Raoul had given her the key code to on the first day, telling her she had her pick but warning her that the roads took some getting used to.

Up until now she had driven a 4x4 but this morning she had picked out the sleek sports car to pick up her mum and sister from the helicopter strip. Now she was regretting the impulse that might appear like showing off to Lily. In the end, when she'd arrived, Raoul's grandfather Sergio was already there with the limo.

'It is only good manners to meet your family,' he had reproached when Lara, already concerned that the hastily arranged marriage was going to exhaust him, had said he shouldn't have gone to so much trouble.

Her mother had been delighted to be driven to the house in the style to which she laughingly said she could easily become accustomed, but Lily had opted to go back with Lara.

Lara was glad it was a short drive. Lily had started in with the questions straight off, and Lara had avoided giving direct answers, then launched into a running commentary of the history of the house and estate. What she couldn't remember she made up, which, keeping in mind it was her inability to lie convincingly that had got her this gig, she felt she was doing rather well at.

If only Raoul were here to see her, she mused grimly, but he had flown off to Paris early that morning and wasn't expected back until tomorrow morning, barely an hour before the wedding.

He'd laughed when she'd accused him of avoiding her family but he hadn't denied it.

Wrapping a sheet around her, she had followed him out onto the balcony of their bedroom where he was taking his coffee. 'Even if Mum swallows this, Lily will know I'm lying. She'll definitely smell a rat. She knows even I wouldn't be insane enough to marry someone I've only just met.'

'*Even I?*'

'Lily is the sensible twin.'

He'd stood there with a look on his face that she had struggled to interpret. 'Sensible?'

'She wouldn't have agreed to this...and, no, you wouldn't have asked her.'

The odd look had come back, along with a smile. 'Then it is lucky for me I met the non-sensible twin. Relax, you do not have to prove anything to anyone, but if in trouble adopt the fall-back position.'

'What's the fall-back position?'

'Love is crazy, and we are deeply in love, *cara*.'

She'd tried to laugh but suddenly all she had wanted to do was cry.

She'd felt his eyes on her face as the silence had stretched. 'Try and relax. No one is going to question our motivation for getting married. Why would they? I suppose a few might wonder if the haste means that you are already pregnant.'

The possibility had not occurred to Lara, who had reacted with a moan. 'Oh, no!'

He'd seemed bemused by her reaction. 'What's the problem?'

'You don't have a problem with people thinking I'm pregnant?'

'Fictional pregnancies I can deal with. Now, a real one...'

His expression had left no doubt as to what his reaction to *that* circumstance would be. Not that it was going to happen—he was meticulously careful in that way.

'I really don't think I can pull it off, Raoul.' She hadn't been able to keep the panic from her voice.

'Of course you can.'

The irritation in his voice had been reflected in his face as he'd lifted his eyes from the tablet his glance had drifted to.

'I wasn't expecting anything like this place.' She'd waved a hand to encompass the view, the room, and everything that went with it. 'I won't be able to keep up the act.'

'Nobody expects you to. It's not as if you're going to be on show twenty-four-seven. You'll be living here. There are no cameras.'

'Oh, and there's nothing whatever daunting about that, and actually there are cameras.'

'Security cameras are there to protect you, not intrude.'

'Easy for you to say—you were brought up in a goldfish bowl.' She'd pressed a hand to her head and groaned out. 'This was a crazy idea.'

'Anyway, I doubt I'll be here more than one or two days a week.'

Her hand had fallen away.

'Did you think we were going to spend the next months joined at the hip?'

'Of course not!' she'd lied, trying hard not to examine the ambivalence of her reaction. 'Won't people think it odd…?' she had countered, keeping her voice light. 'Married couples usually—'

'Have a honeymoon, make babies…?' The mockery in his voice had morphed into a steely hardness as he'd spelt it out. 'This is not meant to be a real marriage.'

'How sweet of you to explain that to me.' Her glance had touched significantly on the sealed envelope that contained her copy of the prenup agreement that had been signed and witnessed the previous night.

He'd followed the direction of her gaze. 'You really should get a lawyer to look through those, you know.'

'I thought you were a lawyer.' Yet something else she hadn't known at the outset.

'I think they call it a conflict of interest.'

She'd shrugged. 'Why? Are you trying to cheat me?'

He hadn't smiled.

'Talking of cheating…if you want this to work it might be an idea if you're discreet…things like that might get back to your grandfather.'

'You are giving me permission to be unfaithful.'

Lara had felt her blush deepen under his sardonic stare. 'Oh, I know you don't need my permission.'

'You think after last night…' his dark glance had swivelled to the rumpled bed '…that I'd have the energy for other women? I will be *working* a twenty-hour day… jealousy is not part of your duties.'

Playing it again now, she could see how he had misinterpreted her comments, but at the time she had been utterly taken by surprise.

'Jealous…! I am not jealous!' Then, in response to the voice in her head saying she was protesting too much, she had managed a less emotional, 'It's just the responsibility of your grandfather when you're not here falls on me.'

She had been massively relieved to see some of the suspicion clear from his eyes.

'You will always be able to contact me; if he needs me I will be here, and later, when his condition worsens, obviously I will travel less.' He had paused and delivered a hard, level look at her lightly flushed face that Lara knew she would never forget. 'Don't fall in love with me, *cara*.'

Even thinking about the warning made her skin burn

with remembered embarrassment. Fall in love with him! She didn't even *like* him!

Lara shoved aside the memory of her response to Raoul, as beside her Lily continued to ask questions.

'So what sort of man is he?'

'He's the sort of man who would drag a woman off a flight to propose.' It was an inspired lie and, like all the best, had a basis in truth.

Lily's eyes widened. 'Seriously? He did that?'

Lara nodded.

'Wow, that is romantic.'

'Raoul is extremely romantic,' Lara lied cheerfully, before going on to invent several incredibly romantic gestures he had made. 'Here we are.' She released a sigh of relief as they drove through the last set of massive wrought-iron gates that closed silently behind them and pulled her car up beside the shiny limo that had preceded them. The massive main entrance door of the *palazzo* stood wide open, and presumably her mother and Sergio were already inside.

Lara got out of the car and waited for her twin, who came to stand beside her. The half an inch or so height advantage she had over her sister was cancelled out by the heels that Lily was wearing this morning.

Their tastes in fashion had always been different and today that difference was particularly apparent. Lily's floaty, flowered skirt fluttered around her calves, the top button of her simple sleeveless shirt was unfastened and her hair hung down her back in a shiny fat braid.

Lara wore a new acquisition, part of the wardrobe that Raoul had insisted she needed: a miniskirt in bold stripes of purple and lime green. Her silk top was sleeveless too but was cut low enough to show the upper slopes of her breasts and glimpses of her lacy bra. Her flatties were soft turquoise leather ballet pumps and on the way out she'd slid a haphazard selection of bangles on her arm, which jingled as she pushed her loose hair from her face.

She watched her twin as Lily tilted her head back to take in the full impact of the building. 'I suppose anyone would want to live here.'

Lara's expression froze over. 'I hadn't seen the place when I agreed to marry Raoul and once you've met him you'll realise that his bank balance isn't the attraction.'

'I didn't mean…'

Lara ignored the horrified stuttered denial. 'There would be a queue around the corner for him if he only had the clothes he stands up in!'

Her sister touched her arm and handed her a tissue—Lara hadn't even known her eyes were leaking moisture… *What was that about?*

'I wasn't suggesting that you're a—'

'Gold-digger? No, really? Well, call me sensitive but…?' She had gone several steps before she took a deep breath and calmed down. Sensitive, yes. She recognised her reaction had been irrational but when hurt, her natural response was to hit out and she had. She wasn't even sure why the suggestion had hurt her so much.

'You love him very much, don't you?'

The soft suggestion made Lara spin around. 'I—' She stopped herself just in time from informing her twin that Raoul was exactly the sort of man she *never* wanted to fall in love with, and somehow managed a smile she hoped was sincere and maybe a little soppy.

'Yes, totally,' she lied, pitying the woman who fell for a man who seemed to be in love with a ghost.

One of her first conversations with Sergio had confirmed her earlier suspicions.

'I am so glad he has someone. After Lucy died he became…a shadow. Not all of him was here, the spark had gone, but you have brought it back for him.'

'I've never seen any photos of…her?'

With the aid of the cane he had taken to using he had got up, walked over to a bureau and opened a drawer. He had pulled out a gilt-framed photo and with a sigh of regret handed it to Lara.

'Raoul took all the photos down after she died, couldn't bear to see her face, I imagine. I don't know what he did with them but I kept this one. He doesn't know I have it.'

Lara had looked at the woman smiling out from the frame. The photo had been taken in the *palazzo*—she'd recognised the fresco from one of the first-floor salons. The way the light fell made it seem as though she were part of the Renaissance scene behind her, and there was a something of the angel about her, the silky golden blonde bob, the cupid's bow mouth painted red and her smooth, pink-tinged cheeks.

'She was beautiful.'

Evicting the angelic image from her head, she swallowed a slug of guilt when her twin hugged her.

'Then that's all that matters, isn't it? I just hope this guy is good enough for you, Lara.'

Her twin had made up her mind on that score before she even met Raoul.

'What,' Lily demanded as she paced the room, clutching her bouquet of wilting flowers in a white-knuckle death grip, 'could be more important than being on time for his own wedding?'

'He'll be here.'

It was weird, but the more tense and angry her twin got, the calmer Lara became. Another time she might have appreciated the humour in the reversal of roles but not today. She was sure the stage nerves would kick in at some point, but not yet.

Maybe she wasn't nervous yet because it simply didn't

seem real. The entire event had taken on the quality of a lavish film production. From the setting in the *palazzo*, a backdrop more glamorous and lavish than any film set, to the sharp-intake-of-breath guest list. It was an understatement to say that the Di Vittorios were well connected!

'Lily, dear, will you sit down?' Elizabeth Gray, looking too young to be anyone's mother, caught her daughter's arm just as the door opened to reveal the head of Security.

'Buongiorno.'

'He's arrived?'

'Signor Di Vittorio landed five minutes ago. He sends his apologies for any delay—apparently there was a bomb threat at the airport. Don't worry, it was just a hoax. He says the ceremony can begin when you are ready.'

'Grazie, Marco.'

'Signorina.'

'Is that man carrying a gun?' Lily asked when the door closed.

'Probably.' It wasn't until she saw her sister's expression that she realised how quickly the abnormal had become normal for her. What would normal life feel like when she returned to it? She closed off the thought, determined not to think that far ahead. She was committed now and there was no turning back. 'The security staff are not normally armed while Sergio is on the estate but with the guests here today...'

'Sergio apologised for it being a modest affair,' Elizabeth confided.

The twins both looked first at their mother and then each other before they all simultaneously burst into laughter.

The very *modest* affair was to begin with a service in the fifteenth-century chapel, while the wedding breakfast that followed was in the grand salon with priceless frescoes on the walls and views of the Tuscan hills. The doors had been flung open to allow the guests to mingle outside in the knot garden, where an orchestra entertained the guests.

'So that's it, then…' She gave her mum a tremulous smile and felt guilty when her mum's eyes filled with tears. Lara knew there would be another sort of tears six months down the line when the fairy tale ended.

'You look absolutely incredible, darling.'

Lara smiled and glanced down at the dress she wore, smoothing the ivory silk with her hand. 'It is beautiful.'

It was possibly the simplest of the creations that had been brought for her to choose between. Lara had expected there to be a few, but when she had walked into the room she had found racks and racks of amazing gowns, none bearing anything as tasteless as a price tag.

'No, my darling, *you're* beautiful.' Elizabeth pressed a hand to her trembling lips.

Lara smiled and thought of the face of an angel…an angel with blonde hair and red lips. Whose face would Raoul see when she walked towards him down the aisle: hers or his dead wife's? Did he close his eyes and think of Lucy when they made love?

The image in her own head leeched the colour from her cheeks until she stood there several shades paler than her dress.

She started as Lily leaned in and said softly, 'You can walk away now if you want to. It's not too late.'

Lara squeezed her hand, wishing she could tell her twin the truth. Would Lily understand? 'I'm fine, Lil.' Then turning to her mum, she held out her hand. 'Ready to give your daughter away? And with these around my neck…' she touched the string of matching antique emeralds that Sergio had presented her with '…nobody is going to be looking at me.'

And after the ceremony the emeralds would be safely

back in the family vault along with the other Di Vittorio heirlooms.

It made her nervous to be walking around with the national budget of a small country around her neck, even for a short time. But there had been no question of throwing Sergio's gesture back in his face.

Infected by his mood, she had responded by asking him if he'd walk her up the aisle along with her mother. It wasn't until after he'd accepted with obvious delight that it had occurred to her it might not be the wisest idea. After a week here she knew that Sergio had good days when it was difficult to believe how ill he was, but he had bad days too.

The chapel was the opposite side of the *palazzo* from the suite of rooms where they had changed, separated by miles of marble-floored corridors, which today were lined with flowers and row after row of crystal vases, so many that the scent of orange blossom filled the air. She was aware of the occasional grim-looking suited figure as she walked along, smiling when she caught sight of one of the staff peering out from behind a door or around a corner to catch a glimpse of her.

Nothing about this could be less like the quiet wedding in a register office somewhere that she had imagined when she'd agreed to the plan. Not that it mattered really, the setting didn't alter the thing, and no amount of pragmatism could alter the fact that she was making sacred vows and she didn't mean a word.

Sergio stood waiting outside and smiled when he saw her.

'My grandson is a lucky man.'

Just when she thought she couldn't feel any *more* guilty.

'Thank you.' Lara laid her hand on the arm he held out just as the massive metal-banded doors swung open and a sea of faces appeared. Beside her she heard her twin gasp.

'It's Hollywood meets the United Nations! Oh, my God, is that…? Lara, there's *royalty* here…!'

'I know,' Lara gritted through a clenched smile.

Ironically it wasn't royalty that was bothering her—it was the less tangible presence of Raoul's first wife. How many of the people here today had watched when Raoul had exchanged vows with Lucy?

She gave herself a mental shake. It really didn't matter if there were people here comparing her unfavourably with the blonde angel—for some weird reason she couldn't see the woman's face without seeing a halo—what mattered was getting through this without being outed as a total fake.

The trick was just taking one step at a time.

As she began to move down the aisle, outwardly serene, inwardly she was panicking because two steps in it had become clear that this was *not* one of Sergio's good days. She could feel the tremors that moved through his body and the fingers that gripped her arm dug deep enough to make her bite her lip.

Now she wasn't worried about getting to the altar without falling flat on her face, she was worried Sergio wouldn't make the short distance without collapsing. She continued to smile, determined that the people watching would see her leaning on him and not the reverse.

Lara knew that for this proud old aristocrat to appear weak in front of these people would be devastating for him, and Raoul would blame her, and he'd be right to. She should never have made the offer.

Raoul stood there knowing before the organ burst into life that the reverent hush was for his bride.

It was a moment he had sworn would never happen again. The last time was enough for ten lifetimes and the poison it had left behind had burnt into his soul.

He took comfort in the fact that he would not fall in love this time—that this time his emotions were not involved. He'd fully expected to feel trapped at this juncture, he'd been *prepared* to feel it, but the emotion that separated itself out from the others was…actually, he couldn't name the feeling that tightened in his chest.

The circumstances ruled out pride, not that it was an unpleasant feeling to know you were the envy of every man in the room. She was beautiful. She was about to become his wife.

For six months anyway. The thought was chased up by a vague sense of dissatisfaction, but before he could analyse it he realised that, though she was acting her head off, looking at him as though he were the man she wanted to spend the rest of her life with, all was not well with Lara.

For a split second he thought she was on the brink of doing a runner, then he realised what message her eyes were flashing as she turned her head slightly towards his grandfather.

Raoul stood ready to step in should he need to, right up to the point that Lara helped Sergio into his seat.

Lara felt as if she'd been holding her breath the entire length of the aisle. It wasn't until Sergio and her mother safely took their places in the front pew and she handed her bouquet to Lily that she could actually breathe properly.

She allowed herself a small congratulatory smile before she turned to face Raoul.

Their eyes connected and the lie hit her hard. The look in his eyes, the promises they were about to make. She felt the tears swim into her eyes and wished she'd opted for a veil.

The ceremony itself went by in a blur of emotion. She could remember Raoul's responses, his deep, clear voice, but not her own. Presumably she had made her vows because Raoul was bending his head for the first kiss, brushing his lips across hers and not acting surprised when she whispered the unromantic message against his mouth.

'It's your grandfather—I don't think he's well.'

His eyes held understanding but he just nodded as, hand in hand, they moved on to the legal part of signatures and witnesses.

At some point she saw Sergio leaving through a side door, his shrunken frame looking frail between two bodyguards.

She could feel Raoul's impatience as they stood welcoming their glittering guests, and by the time they reached the end of the line her hand was aching and she was way beyond awed and star-struck.

Once they were seated, Raoul got to his feet and the place fell silent, all eyes on the tall, commanding figure.

'I wish to thank all my friends and family for being here today, and most of all, naturally, my beautiful bride...' He paused for the ripple of applause. 'However, as you have probably already noticed, one person is not with us. Our host today, my grandfather, is feeling unwell, so I will leave you for a moment in Lara's capable hands. Please enjoy yourselves.'

Lara watched him leave, noticing him pause to say something in the ear of a striking-looking brunette on the way out.

The woman nodded, then approached Lara with a friendly smile.

'Tell me, Lara, do you ride?'

She took a deep breath and thought, *And now I start earning my severance cheque.* 'I love horses, it's just heights I have a problem with. My sister and I did used to help out at stables near where we were brought up—the place is run by a charity that helps children with disabilities get an opportunity to ride.'

* * *

'I'm sorry.' It was close on nine when Raoul came to sit on the bed where Lara was wearing a pair of silky pale green shortie pyjamas.

She looked up when he spoke and shook her head. 'What for?'

'For walking out on the wedding reception...'

'How is he?'

She had got the message that Sergio's doctor had insisted that he go to the hospital to get checked over.

'They're keeping him overnight. They seem to think that there hasn't been any deterioration. It's his drug regime that's the problem.' He rotated his neck to ease the tension that had climbed into his shoulders.

Lara pulled herself up onto her knees and shuffled across the bed until she was in a position to slide her hands under the neck of his shirt. His muscles were like iron. 'Wow, you really have some knots there.'

Raoul grunted as her fingers dug into muscles. 'So how was it after I left?' He had felt guilty as hell leaving her to cope alone. Talk about throwing her in at the deep end!

'Oh, people were happy and there was plenty of booze. Actually, I left early myself.' Lily, who was at drama college, had a screen test for a TV show the next day, so she and her mum hadn't stayed late. Once they'd gone, Lara hadn't known a soul and Naomi, the woman Raoul had spoken to, who had introduced herself as a family friend, had assured her that she wouldn't be missed.

'Don't worry, I'll deputise,' she had promised as Lara had slipped away.

Raoul's silence made her wonder whether leaving early wasn't a bigger thing than the other woman had suggested.

'Did I do wrong? Naomi said she'd—'

'Oh, I'm sure it was fine.'

'Her husband is in a wheelchair?'

'She was one of Lucy's friends.' Actually the only one he still had any contact with. 'And Leo has MS. She's devoted and he's not an easy man. Ouch!'

She dug her teeth into her bottom lip. 'Sorry, got carried away,' she admitted guiltily.

He reached out and pushed his fingers into her hair. 'You make it sound as though that is a bad thing?'

His tone was light but the glow in his dark eyes was anything but. 'You looked beautiful today.' It was rare for his accent to surface; it only happened in moments of passion. 'I'm sorry the day was ruined.'

'There's nothing to ruin. After all, it's all make-believe, smoke and mirrors.'

'Well, you played your part well.'

'Did I? I don't really remember. I was just scared that Sergio was going to collapse, and this is all about Sergio.'

Recognising this didn't mean that she hadn't wondered a little about how it might feel if this were happening for real…oh, not with Raoul, obviously. When and if she ever married again she knew it would not be a man like Raoul.

Even *without* the perfect-dead-wife thing there was the fact that he was the sort of man who could have any woman he wanted. She pushed away the thought—trusting him to say no was not her problem.

'Yes…but here, now, it is all about us…' His voice was a throaty caress as he leaned in until their lips were almost touching, then with slow deliberation skimmed his tongue across her mouth, tracing the full outline.

Lara was breathless, capable of nothing but gazing at him, the longing that infiltrated every cell of her body shining in her eyes.

'I'm going to be gone most of the week.'

She ignored the sinking feeling in the pit of her stomach. 'What will your grandfather think?' No honeymoon was one thing, but the groom leaving his bride alone the day after the wedding...?

'No problem, he understands.' He had understood better than Raoul the massive task it was going to be to bring his knowledge up to a level where he could take the helm of the family businesses.

That makes one of us, Lara thought, stifling a stab of irrational resentment.

'Oh, that's all right, then.'

Hard not to contrast her calm acceptance with the reaction of a *real* wife. Right now he'd be being made to feel as guilty as hell—a marriage based on sex and a contract definitely had its plus points.

'Feel like being carried away?'

Lara curled her hand around his neck immediately, totally caught up again in the burning need of the moment. 'Oh, yes, please.'

The next morning she woke at around six feeling groggy on the couple of hours' sleep she'd snatched between lovemaking. The space beside her in the bed was empty, but on the bedside table stood a note, her name on it in bold, slanting lettering.

Unfolding it, she read it.

Meeting in Geneva at noon. Calling in on the old man on the way. Any problems arise let me know. If not should be back Fri p.m.

It was signed with a flourish—but no *love*.

CHAPTER EIGHT

Three months later

LARA GAVE HERSELF over completely to the explosion of
sensation as it hit, savouring the sweet release from devouring hunger.

Still breathing hard, she forced her lids apart as Raoul
rolled off her and lay next to her.

'Oh, wow, that was—'

'Just sex.'

The words had pretty much the same effect as a bucket
of cold water; they usually did.

She hid her hurt in sarcasm. 'And there was me thinking it was the start of something special, but I'm terribly
grateful that you keep reminding me, because you're so
irresistible I might not be able to stop myself falling in
love with you.'

Raoul didn't react. He just levered himself out of bed in
one fluid motion and began to collect the clothes he had
dropped on the floor when he had not quite made it out
of the door earlier.

'As you're a god among men...a—'

'Cut it out, Lara.'

She smiled and added sourly, 'Unfortunately no sense of
humour, so that's it, I'm afraid. I'd never fall in love with a
man who can't laugh at my jokes.' Or for that matter a man
she knew every woman he encountered imagined naked.
To marry that sort of man you'd need either impregnable
self-confidence or a lack of imagination.

'I could never love a woman who—' He looked into

the clear green eyes laughing up at him and his half-smile vanished.

There was nothing else to add. He *could* never love a woman. Love had almost destroyed him once; love was never going to enter into this or any other relationship he had.

He had been uneasy about the sense of connection he sometimes felt until he realised this was down to the fact that, since Lucy, his time with women had been counted in nights whereas he had been sharing a bed and his body with Lara for three months. Another three and she would vanish from his life.

Lara sensed his withdrawal. He did that so often—the sudden mood change, the broody silences—she'd stopped reacting to it.

'You've lost a button,' she said, watching him fasten his shirt and thinking he'd need a sense of humour or a stiff drink when she finally told him her news.

He dragged back his dark hair with an impatient hand. 'It doesn't matter. I'm late.'

She smiled. Late was good; late was a legitimate excuse for not telling him.

'So, Friday…?' She managed to say it as if not seeing him for four days were no big deal, but the truth was she missed him—or, as Raoul would have no doubt explained, she missed the sex.

The first twenty-four hours of their married life had pretty much set the pattern of the days and nights to come: he would leave on Sunday evening or Monday morning and come back Thursday or Friday.

Lara recognised she was pretty much the classic mistress, just with a ring and the social recognition that went with that. Social recognition meant she got treated with respect, which in turn meant she could have lunched out every day, had she chosen to, and was regularly asked to lend her name to any number of charities and good causes.

At first she had refused, until she'd realised she was in danger of becoming the woman who only came to life when the man in her life deigned to share her bed. He shared nothing else though, which, as she frequently told herself when bitterness crept in, was a good thing.

She *couldn't* let herself develop any feelings for him beyond lust; she could not allow herself to feel things that would make her hurt when the arrangement reached its inevitable and sad conclusion.

She'd grown fond of Sergio, which was fine because she was *allowed* to be fond of him.

'No.'

Her eyes lifted to discover he was standing by the door. Lara shook her head. 'No?'

'I'm not going away this week.'

'Why not?'

His eyes slid from hers. 'I have a meeting with grandfather's oncologist later in the week.'

'Oh, right.'

'I should be h—back early.'

Now she was familiar with Raoul's work ethic and his relentless stamina, Lara was able to translate 'early' as somewhere between twelve and one a.m.

Too late to hit him with her bombshell.

Oh, she was delaying the inevitable, but why not? What was the hurry? Considering his attitude it was small wonder that she was dreading delivering the speech. She had tried a dozen versions, but nothing worked.

Maybe she should settle for a simple, 'I'm sorry,' because now it couldn't be just sex.

There was a baby.

After he left, she went back to the bathroom and pulled

out the pregnancy-testing kit she'd hidden under some toiletries. She'd bought six and this was the last one left.

Her last hope.

Only there was no hope—she knew that even before she saw the line appear on the strip.

She spent the morning with Sergio. Roberto joined them mid-morning and they spent time going through albums, looking at snapshots of Raoul and Jamie when they were boys. In all the photos she had seen, Raoul's elder brother looked like a softer, fairer version of him—Raoul without the hard edges or dark outlook.

Though in the one that had got to her Raoul had had no edges. Nothing much more than a toddler, he had stood beside Jamie, staring not into the camera but up at his brother with an expression of childish adoration on his face.

The poignancy of it had filled her throat with tears that she couldn't hold back. It was her hormones, she knew that, but the two men with her had tactfully pretended not to notice her emotional reaction as she'd excused herself and left the room, leaning against a wall in the hallway before she gave in to the gulping sobs that shook her body.

By lunchtime she felt so tired she couldn't keep her eyes open so, after playing with the food laid out for her, she went to lie down.

She only intended to close her eyes but when she woke the clock told her she had slept for three hours. She'd missed her riding lesson.

She splashed some water on her face in the bathroom and, brushing back her hair, rubbed her pale cheeks to put some colour back into them before she went through to the bedroom.

Her heart stopped when she saw Raoul, who was hanging his jacket around the back of a chair. He looked up as she entered, his eyes darkening when he saw her.

'You're here...now... I thought...'

'I thought you'd be out...you look...' Raoul reached out, clamped an arm around her ribs, and pulled her into his arms. His kiss was bruising and hungry, driving the breath from her lungs. 'Sorry about that, it's just I've been thinking about it all day.' He smoothed a copper strand from her cheek and kissed her again, more softly this time, his skilled lips gently moving across hers.

With a groan of reluctance he pushed her away from him and, heading towards the bathroom, growled, 'Hold that thought,' over his shoulder. 'I've been shut in an office with broken air conditioning trying to soothe senior management fears that I'm about to sack everyone just for the hell of it.'

Lara sat on the bed listening to the shower, wondering how he was going to react to the news. Not well was a given. Feeling dizzy with anxiety, she walked across to the chair and picked up his jacket, intending to hang it up properly. Raoul's phone slid onto the carpet and as she bent to pick it up she asked herself what she was scared of the most—becoming a mother or his reaction to the news he was to be a father.

For goodness' sake, Lara, just deal with it, because it really isn't going to go away.

A hint of defiance crept into her face as she looked at the phone, remembering all the times the shrill, teeth-clenching ringtone had proved there was always something more important than her in his life. With a determined little grimace she switched it off and guiltily slid it back into his pocket.

A moment later Raoul walked in, his dark hair slicked with water and his golden-toned skin gleaming like polished bronze against the dark towel he had looped low on his narrow hips.

Lara lurched from panic mode into weak-with-lust mode

even before he reached her. The towel vanished as he laid her on the bed and slid a hand under her shirt over the warm skin of her narrow ribcage.

'I want to talk, Raoul.'

He stopped nuzzling her neck long enough to smile his brilliant head-spinning smile and ran his tongue across her lips. 'We can talk later.'

She had tried, she really had.

It was an hour later when she sat up in bed, pulling the sheet up to her chin.

'We really need to talk, Raoul.'

'I do not need to talk.'

She responded with a hissing sound of exasperation. 'Now?'

She closed her eyes so she could ignore the invitation in his eyes.

'Yes, now.'

'Fine. I'm listening.'

'Put on some clothes first.'

He looked bemused by the request and then smirked when she growled gruffly, 'I can't concentrate.'

'Right, will this do?'

She nodded. She had used the time while he dragged on a pair of jeans and a sweater to retrieve her skirt and shirt from the crumpled heap.

When the silence stretched he arched an interrogative brow.

Lara nodded and began to clear her throat but before she could launch into speech there was an imperative hammering at the door.

Frowning, Raoul opened it, barking out a question in Italian to the member of his grandfather's security team standing there.

The other man replied in the same language.

'My grandfather collapsed and was taken to hospital

two hours ago! Why,' he responded in icily articulated English, 'am I only hearing this now?'

'It's my fault.'

He swirled back to a miserable-looking Lara. 'What?'

'I turned off your phone,' she admitted.

'Why the hell did you do that?'

Lara shot a glance towards the staff member, who looked as uncomfortable as she felt. Raoul ignored the hint and raised a brow, intoning heavily, 'I'm waiting.'

Resenting the fact that he was treating her like a naughty schoolgirl, she couldn't deny how guilty she would feel if he didn't get to say goodbye to his grandfather.

'You looked so tired.' This was one of those times when even part of the truth sounded lame.

'I looked—!' He bit off his incredulous rejoinder and grabbed his key. He spoke to the solemn-faced messenger in Italian too rapid for Lara to even begin to follow and waited until the man had gone before he turned back to her. 'You're in danger of taking your wifely duties a little too seriously. You're here to look the part, not actually be it.'

She felt the heat of humiliation sting her cheeks. She'd crossed lines she hadn't known were there before, and made inevitable social faux pas, but previously he'd never lashed out at her for it. 'Fine. I'll move into the guest room, shall I?'

'That question might be academic.' He gave her one last furious look before leaving.

It was past nine when the phone finally rang. Lara picked it up, a feeling of sick dread in her stomach.

'He wants to see you.'

'How is he? Has he...? What's happened—?' She was talking to herself. Raoul had hung up.

Five minutes later she got into her car—well, the documents said it was hers, but, like her life at the moment, she knew she had it on loan.

Babies were not for three months or even six. Babies were for ever!

She pushed the thought away. She could barely deal with the present, let alone the unknown and scary future!

When she parked her car in the clinic car park, almost immediately one of Sergio's security detail appeared to escort her inside, and the man's normally impassive face showed signs of emotion as he told her that Sergio had been watching his favourite horse be put through his paces when he collapsed.

'Do you know how...?'

The man shook his head and stood to one side as she walked through the glass doors ahead of him. Raoul was waiting on the other side; the sight of his grey-tinged, exhausted face made her heart squeeze in her chest.

She was anticipating his anger; the relief that spread across his face felt like a kiss.

She caught his hand between both of hers. 'I'm sorry I turned your phone off. It was not my call to make. If I'd any idea...' she said earnestly. 'But I was with him this morning and he seemed to be having a good day.'

He shook his head, seemingly unable to take his eyes off his hand sandwiched between hers. 'I overreacted,' he admitted. 'He collapsed at the stables, and they airlifted him here. It's this way.'

Realising she was still holding his hand, she dropped it, muttering an awkward sorry before falling in step beside him.

At the door of the hospital room Raoul stopped and drew her to one side, aware as he did so of the scent of her hair. 'Just to warn you,' he began abruptly.

Her eyes lifted and his hands fell from her shoulders. He dug his hands into the pockets of his tailored trousers. 'He looks...'

With a soft curse he pulled his mobile from his pocket and turned away, but not before Lara had seen the blank screen or the expression on his face.

Overwhelmed by a rush of compassion that threatened to crush her chest, she could see the muscles along his strong jaw clenching as he outlined the situation. 'He's had a stroke, a complication of the drug regime. He looks…'

When his harsh voice broke, Lara's heart ached with sympathy. She touched his hand and he looked at her fingers on his wrist. For a moment she thought he'd shake her off but instead he turned his wrist and threaded his long fingers in hers, oblivious to the crushing pressure he was exerting. He took a deep breath and finished huskily, 'Broken, he looks broken.'

'I understand.'

Raoul doubted it. The doctor's warning had not prepared him for the reality of his grandfather's condition. 'Just don't let him—' He directed a warning look at her.

What did he think she was going to do, Lara wondered, look horrified or run from the room? *Is that the person he thinks I am?*

The answer was depressing. That was *exactly* the person he thought she was—a selfish, shallow thrill-seeker, an individual incapable of considering another person's feelings, let alone possessing any herself that might get bruised.

The knowledge hurt more than she was prepared to admit, even to herself.

'He's a proud man and for him this…' Bad enough that the cancer was eating him alive, fate had not even allowed him a dignified, clean exit.

Lara's anger subsided as quickly as it had emerged, replaced by guilt and a painful throb of empathy as she watched Raoul close his eyes, the muscles in his brown throat working as he fought to contain his own emotions.

'Of course,' she said quietly as she withdrew her hand from his.

Raoul preceded her into the room, his body initially blocking her view of the figure in the bed.

'Lara's here, late as usual.'

Despite Raoul's warning, Lara was shocked by the appearance of Sergio. Since she had known him, she had been conscious of the slow physical decline that even the best tailoring could not conceal, but the man in the bed attached to tubes and monitors, one side of his face twisted and frozen, was a grotesque caricature of the man who had once walked into a room and caused heads to turn.

Then she saw the eyes in the wrecked face. They were alert, so, squaring her shoulders, she donned a smile.

Raoul watched as Lara went forward, bending close to kiss the stiff cheek, something he had been unable to make himself do, before taking a chair and pulling it up beside the bed.

His grandfather spoke. The words perhaps had meaning in his head but they emerged slurred and garbled. Lara responded as though she understood what he was saying.

Raoul had no control over the emotion that broke free in his chest, and no cheque in the world, he decided, was big enough to repay the debt he owed her.

Half an hour later they walked side by side, not touching, to the car park.

'Are you all right to drive home alone?'

She turned her head but the glistening sheen of tears in her eyes made his face a blur. 'I could stay if you'd like?'

He stifled his instinctive response but the impulse disturbed him. There were times when he was aware that she gave more than he should expect and got very little in return. She played her part so well that often the 'supportive wife' act seemed real, not that he knew a lot about supportive wives, but he did know a lot about women who could act a part.

And that, after all, was what he had wanted. He had to remind himself that this was a job for Lara, not a life choice. And anyway, who in their right mind would choose to share their life with him?

Suddenly disgusted with his inability to face the truth and too tired to maintain the illusion, he accepted it. No relief came as he acknowledged that life with Lucy had broken him, he couldn't give or receive love, and that was a disability as much as a lost limb.

The knowledge lay like a stone where his heart once was as he shook his head.

'That isn't necessary. What did you say that made him look so happy?'

She lifted her eyes to his face, took a deep breath, and admitted with a rush, 'I told him I was pregnant.'

She watched as Raoul's dark winged brows lifted and a shocked grunt vibrated in his chest. A series of emotions flickered across his normally guarded features, finally settling into an expression of warm approval that lit a responsive glow inside her.

Lara had never needed anyone's approval in her life; even now with the glow inside her it was frightening to realise, to admit, how much she craved Raoul's good opinion.

'That was kind.'

She paused. This was the moment, but was it the *right* moment? Did the right moment even exist…? Then right or wrong it was gone, and the correction stayed in her head.

'Are you *sure* you're all right to drive back alone?' he asked again, noticing for the first time the pallor of her creamy skin and the faint shadows beneath her emerald eyes.

Had she lost weight recently? he wondered, his suspicions aroused as he took in the prominence of her delicate collarbones.

'You're not on some stupid diet, are you?'

Lara responded to his glowering disapproval with an odd little laugh and moved her head in a negative motion.

'I'm fine.' Pregnancy was not a disease, though she suspected the person who had said that had never suffered from morning sickness.

He made no comment but didn't look entirely convinced as he pulled his eyes from the visible blue-veined pulse that beat at the base of her throat and directed a hard look at her face.

'I thought I'd stay a while, sit with him.' His dark eyes shifted to the low sprawling terracotta-tiled building behind them that looked more like a hotel resort than a private hospital. The one thing his grandfather had not wanted was to spend his last days in a hospital bed. But life was filled with things that a man wanted but could not have, he thought bleakly.

'Let me stay, Raoul…?'

He shrugged. 'What would be the point?'

She hid her hurt at the rejection under a smile and withdrew the hand she had extended towards him. 'No point at all.'

The phone call she had been half expecting came just after midnight. Lara was sitting on the balcony of their bedroom breathing in the fragrance of the pines on the warm night breeze. It was the call she had been expecting, but not the caller.

'Hello, Lara, I hope I didn't disturb you.'

An image of the elegant, petite Italian brunette flashed into her head.

'Not at all, Naomi,' she said, wincing at the stiff formality of her response and wondering why she could never relax around the Italian woman.

'Raoul asked me to ring you and let you know that Sergio passed away about an hour ago.'

Lara's sadness was alleviated by the knowledge that the proud old man would not have to suffer any longer. 'Thank you for letting me know. Raoul, is he at the hospital still? I'll come—'

'That's fine, Lara, he asked me to tell you not to come. Don't worry, I'll look after him.'

It was around three in the morning when Raoul arrived back at the *palazzo*. Lara heard him and called out from the library where she'd been awaiting his return.

'I thought you might come.' He struggled to keep the note of irrational accusation out of his voice. Naomi had relayed Lara's message that she wouldn't be coming.

'I don't blame Lara one bit. Who wouldn't want to stay in their warm bed? The last section of that road would be any tourist's nightmare, Raoul.'

He felt a stab of guilt. Naomi had been really supportive and his response to her comment had been a lot sharper than he'd intended.

'Lara isn't a tourist, she's my wife.'

But for how much longer?

Finally acknowledged, the question refused to go back to the dark corner he had consigned it to. Such avoidance was not like him. Raoul could only suppose that his behaviour had been influenced by his grandfather's determination not to live his last days in fear of the future but instead extracting every last ounce of pleasure from the time he had left.

Not that the future involved any fear for Raoul, not even any major inconvenience. He had left nothing to chance;

the arrangements were in place to painlessly dissolve this marriage when it had served its purpose.

Admittedly, knowing that *the moment* was passing made him realise just how much pleasure it had held. And though he had refused to acknowledge how risky this strategy was, he admitted now that this could have turned out very badly indeed. Marrying Lara to make his grandfather's last days happy could have been a major crash and burn.

But though living with a woman who threw herself at everything, be it a pasta dish, a walk on a beach or sex with uninhibited enthusiasm, might be at times exasperating, it was also exciting. She perfectly encapsulated living in the moment.

Thinking about a future minus that excitement deepened the furrow between his strongly delineated brows but a woman like Lara demanded more time than a man like him could offer.

Couldn't, wouldn't, won't...?

His comment and his accusing attitude bewildered Lara. 'Naomi said you didn't want me to.'

The furrow between his dark brows deepened even more; she had obviously misunderstood. 'I took her home.'

Of course you did, she thought, standing motionless as the sick, angry jealousy grabbed her in a chokehold. 'How come she was at the clinic?'

'Her husband is there having some treatment.'

The explanation immediately made Lara feel ashamed of her gut response; the woman had never been anything but kind to her and if Raoul had friendships with other women it was not her business. If it was more than friendship? It still wasn't really her business.

'You look tired.'

He shrugged and walked across to the bureau. She

watched as he poured brandy into the bottom of a heavy tumbler and raised it to his lips. 'To you, you old bastard.'

Her nostrils twitched as the aroma produced a wave of acid nausea in her stomach. 'It might help to talk.'

Catching her worried gaze, he emptied the glass in one swallow. 'I don't want to talk.' He dragged a hand through his dark hair. 'I don't want to think... I just want—' He reached out towards her, his eyes burning with unvarnished need.

Then before she could react his hand fell. A spasm of self-loathing contorted his dark features as he slammed the glass down. He was using her and acting as if it were all right.

'I'll sleep in the study tonight.'

Lara was utterly confused by his mixed signals but also by the morass of conflicting emotions. She put it down to crazy hormonal changes and cried herself to sleep in the bedroom alone.

CHAPTER NINE

How was Raoul?

'I don't know,' Lara admitted. 'It wasn't really unexpected, but no one expected it to happen so soon. Raoul has been busy with arrangements…with the funeral.' The event, which was being attended by more than one state leader, required a lot of planning, yet another excuse for her to delay telling him about the pregnancy. And anyway it seemed to Lara that he was avoiding her.

Maybe as far as he was concerned the contract between them was already over?

'Ring me tomorrow when it's over…?'

It's already over! 'Sure,' she managed dully, suddenly feeling more alone than ever before.

'Look, you know I'd really like to come, to support you if I could, and so would Mum…'

Lara closed her eyes and fought back tears. 'It's fine.'

'It's not. It's just that I have a hospital appointment tomorrow and Mum is coming with me.'

Lara's stomach muscles tightened. 'You're ill?'

'No, the thing is, I'm pregnant.'

'Pregnant!'

'Yep, and at the moment I'm as sick as hell.'

Tell me about it!

Lara just stopped herself, biting her tongue hard enough to make her wince. It was so tempting to offload, to share something she had in common with her twin, but she couldn't tell Lily before she told Raoul. She would tell him…when the right time came.

'I thought it was supposed to end after three months.'

The implication of the comment hit Lara. 'Three months…so how far along are you?'

'Twenty weeks…it's not just you I haven't told, Lara. I've not told anyone. I think I was pretty much in denial, but now I've kind of exploded overnight.'

Lara barely registered the forced humour in her sister's voice. 'You're *five* months pregnant.' She pressed a hand over her own still-flat stomach. 'You were pregnant at the wedding?' There had never been any psychic connection but shouldn't she have sensed it? How could she have, when she'd been too busy keeping her own secrets to guess her twin might also have something to hide?

'It was *your* day, Lara.'

My day… She stared at her hands, feeling the tears that flowed too easily well hotly beneath her eyelids. She blinked them back and focused on the gold band that encircled her finger, suddenly aware her sister had been talking and she didn't have a clue what she'd said.

She lifted the gold band to her lips, remembering him sliding it on and how *right* it had felt. Without warning, the protective shield she had been hiding behind slid away, revealing a truth she could no longer run away from. She was staring at the truth…the glaringly obvious truth.

She'd told herself she was acting, that it wasn't real, but it *was* real. She was in love with Raoul—he had warned her not to but she had anyway.

He was *everything* she'd been determined to avoid in a man and yet he was everything she needed, she craved… She closed her eyes, wishing herself back to a time when she had imagined you could control who you fell in love with, that you could choose *safe* love, when in reality you had no more control over love than the colour of your eyes.

The level of her blind stupidity seemed incredible. Love had nothing to do with self-control or common sense; she had no choice whether to love Raoul and it didn't matter if he wanted that love, if he rejected it *and* her.

She loved him with a soul-deep passion and would carry on loving him even after he broke her heart.

The rest of the phone conversation was stilted and awkward but Lara barely noticed. It wasn't until she put the phone down with a shaking hand that Lara realised she hadn't even asked her twin who the father of her baby was!

The day of the funeral was warm, thunder rumbled in the distance but the rain waited until after Sergio had been laid to rest in the family vault.

The afternoon sun hit the study at the *palazzo*, and it was still uncomfortably warm as Raoul entered, putting his glass on the desk littered untidily with papers. He pulled open the French doors and stood there, eyes closed, breathing in the cool evening air before taking a seat in the padded leather chair beside the desk.

The mourners who had come back to the house after the service were gone...and so was his grandfather. His eyes went to the open door. Even now, he half expected to see the old man framed in the doorway.

But he wasn't.

Raoul had stood up and told the mourners that for Sergio Di Vittorio family came first.

He could with equal honesty have added that the old fox had also been a master manipulator who could be utterly ruthless when it came to getting his own way.

He had died thinking he had got his way one final time, Raoul thought as he lifted his glass in a silent salute.

The twisted smile on his face vanished as he put down the glass, his thoughts sliding back to earlier when she had told him that they needed to talk. It was obvious what that would be about.

Her future, the one she would have without him. It

would be a good one. She had talent, though he doubted she recognised yet how much. She deserved good things, he told himself, ignoring the sinking feeling inside. If he analysed it he'd have to admit that he wanted her to stay—not for ever, obviously, because there was no for ever, but just for a while, just so that he could carry on enjoying her.

When he'd met Lara his life had been disintegrating around him. He had lost or been losing everyone he'd ever cared for, but she had kept him afloat. Of course, having her around was going to make the next few weeks easier, but after that what…?

After that, nothing, because Raoul knew he had nothing to give. He was disgusted with himself for it, but he knew that what he was good at was taking. He knew it would be easy to persuade Lara to stay longer; he knew he was good at manipulating her feelings. But for once he was not going to put his own selfish needs first.

And then he could get back to life as usual.

I thought you'd fallen off the planet, darling!

At first he hadn't even recognised the woman who had virtually collided with him in the street. Her name had continued to elude him as she'd pressed a kiss to his mouth. Just in time to save embarrassment it had come to him, along with the location of their fling a year or so ago.

She'd looked at his wedding ring and aimed a speculative look at his face. 'Married, but how married?'

He'd made an excuse and left without responding to the question or the unspoken invitation in her carefully made-up eyes.

That was *his* life, the one he had chosen, the one he would go back to, just as soon as he was done with Lara.

Refusing to acknowledge the feeling that gathered strength inside him until it came perilously close to icy panic, he clenched his jaw and slowly rebuilt the barriers he had put up in order to survive his first marriage.

He was better off alone.

Not yet though; for the moment Lara was still here.

Was she still asleep? It had been three when she had finally confessed to not feeling well and then only after a lot of prompting.

Naomi had offered to help her to her bedroom and Raoul had looked in on her later, after the last of the mourners was gone. She had been fast asleep.

A sound made him turn his head. Framed in the doorway where he had just imagined his grandfather was Lara, her hair long and loose, glowing against the black fabric of the simple shift dress she still wore. She didn't move as their eyes connected.

'Are you feeling better?' he asked, refusing to acknowledge the tightening in his chest as anything other than a natural protectiveness. She nodded and walked into the study, her bare feet silent on the wood. Her eyes looked enormous in her pale face and the milky pallor of her smooth skin emphasised the delicate purity of her cleanly drawn features.

'I'm fine,' she lied, struggling to throw off the lethargy that seemed to weigh down her limbs. 'I slept.'

She had fallen into a deep sleep only to wake and find Naomi standing beside her bed, causing her to let out a startled squeal of alarm.

'Sorry, I didn't mean to wake you, but Raoul was worried and he asked me to look in.'

If Raoul was so worried why couldn't he look in himself? Even acknowledging the thought made her feel guilty; Raoul had buried his grandfather today and she was acting like an attention-seeking brat.

'Thank you, I'm fine.'

To her dismay the other woman sat down. 'I hope you don't mind,' she began hesitantly, 'but I've noticed… Well,

I've got the impression,' she corrected, 'that you feel you're living in Lucy's shadow.'

Lara was simply too astonished to respond.

'You have nothing to live up to. Lucy was a bitch,' she said simply.

Lara thought she had misheard. 'Pardon? I thought—'

'She was a bitch.'

'I thought she was your friend?'

'She didn't have friends, just people she used. She made Raoul's life a misery, and she knew all along that he loved someone else, but they cannot be together. I am so happy to see that Raoul has someone to make him happy now. I'll let you rest.'

Lara watched her go, not knowing what to make of the one-sided conversation. It wasn't just *what* she had said, it was the way she had said it…the secret little smile… She shivered, very much unsettled by the woman's manner.

Naomi hadn't actually meant that *she* was the person Raoul couldn't be with…*had she*? Lara thought about all the occasions she had seen them together or at least in the same room. There would have been signs, she'd have picked up the signals, wouldn't she…?

On the other hand, she had managed not to know she was in love with him for months. Maybe signals weren't her thing. Did any of this even matter? She'd be out of his life soon…except that there would always be the baby… Would he even want to be part of the baby's life?

Just what she needed—another unanswered question to add to all the others!

With a deep sigh she sat up and propped a pillow behind her head, running over Naomi's words in her head again and again. The more she thought about it, the more it felt *off* somehow. As was the idea that Raoul's marriage had not been happy, that his perfect wife had not been quite so, well, perfect.

It seemed much more likely that Naomi had a thing for Raoul and was making up stories about a poor woman who couldn't defend herself. The only way she'd know for sure was to ask him.

'Now there's a revolutionary thought, Lara,' she whispered mockingly to herself, and made her way downstairs to find Raoul.

'Sorry I skipped out like that.'

He shrugged, dismissing her apology as he dragged a hand across the dark stubble that already dusted his jaw and lean cheeks. He closed the laptop that had been sitting open on the desk. It was all for show—he hadn't been able to focus on work or even read his emails or any of the messages of condolence.

'I coped.'

'It's been a hard day for you.' Her heart ached for him; he looked so tired, so sad.

After a pause he acknowledged this with a tiny tip of his dark head, while privately acknowledging the fact that she had made it easier. Her quiet presence beside him, support expressed with a touch and a look.

'I should have been there.'

'Naomi was only too happy to stand in.'

He felt ungrateful but he'd found it impossible not to compare Naomi's practised social skills with Lara's more instinctive ones… Oh, there was no doubt that the woman could work a room and she never said the wrong thing, but then her smile was never genuine either and her laugh never uninhibited or too loud.

Not that there had been much to laugh about today, he thought sombrely, but Lara had not just *given* the impression of listening to the long-winded reminiscences of the elderly friends of his grandfather's, she *had* listened. It didn't matter who had been talking; he was pretty sure that mostly she didn't have a clue who they were—or how important. At one point he had seen her spontaneously grab his godfather and hug the man!

Just after Lara had slipped away the elderly but still-influential Greek shipping magnate had taken Raoul to one side and shaken his hand, telling him that he was lucky indeed in his wife: *'A keeper, my boy, but if I was thirty years younger you'd need to watch your back!'* he'd chortled.

For a man who would have preferred to walk in front of a bus than get married again, this arrangement with Lara was actually suiting him. Plus, the sex was incredible.

He wished they could extend the arrangement, but he had come to see the real Lara, to know her, and she deserved more...

Lara deserved better than him.

Closing the open French doors on a breeze that had sprung up, he missed Lara's flinch at the mention of the other woman's name.

'Has she gone?'

'Who?'

'Naomi.'

He nodded, making a mental note to have a tactful word—she had been dropping around a little too much lately.

'You should have stayed in bed.'

'Were you happy?'

There was a hushed, husky vehemence in the abrupt question that made him look at her sharply, sensing suppressed emotions that showed their physical presence in the restless twisting of her long fingers. Something was going on in that beautiful head and he didn't have a clue what it was. He allowed frustration to mask the protectiveness that made him want to take her in his arms.

'Was I happy when?'

'People say that you had a perfect marriage.'

'Do they?'

'Did you love her…your wife? Were you happy?'

In a voice edged with steel he cut across her. 'You're my wife.' The word had always carried with it negative connotations…yet there had been times when he had said it recently when he had felt…*proud*…?

The interruption didn't stop her; she'd gone too far and she *had* to know. 'You know what I mean.'

He turned his head and directed a flat stare at her face. 'No.'

'I was asking—'

'I know what you were asking.' He gave a twisted smile. 'I was answering. No, I was not happy, well, for about five minutes, but once I woke up, or grew up, or both, I was not.'

'If you were unhappy why didn't you just get a divorce?' *And marry the woman you apparently love so much but can't have?*

His mouth twisted into a parody of a smile as he turned to face her, dragging off the tie that was still looped around his neck as he did so. 'In a perfect world I would have, but the world…' he let the tie slip through his fingers and fall to the floor '…and life,' he continued harshly, 'are not.'

'I don't understand.'

'Of course you don't.'

How could she? There were no dark depths to Lara—she was the diametric opposite to Lucy, who on the surface had seemed so wholesome and sweet but the moment she was crossed revealed herself to be spiteful and vindictive, a person who thought the world revolved around her.

'Then explain.'

Well, he certainly hadn't learnt from his mistakes with Lucy—he had taken Lara at face value, and ignored the sweet, vulnerable angel beneath the beautiful but hard shell.

He'd clung stubbornly to the image, but each day together had eaten away at it until he couldn't pretend any more.

Understand... How could she? Lara had a conscience and empathy; she had no desire to see those who thwarted her suffer; she didn't need a constant, exhausting supply of attention and admiration or react with vicious spite when she didn't receive the praise she felt she was entitled to.

'Please, Raoul, I want to understand.'

The court-enforced appointments with the therapist following the hushed-up 'incident' that had left Lucy's hairdresser with a black eye had been illuminating but not in themselves helpful.

At the end he'd known all about borderline personality disorders and malignant narcissists, but as Lucy had refused to accept she had a problem it had meant little in reality.

'When I was married Jamie was never officially out. When he was still a student Jamie fell for a man who was...in a position of power, a married man, and they had a long-term affair. If the truth had emerged this man's career, his marriage, his life would have been over. One night Jamie started to talk. We'd been to dinner, had a few drinks... Lucy was very sympathetic.

'So when I told her that it was over she told me that if I filed for divorce she would out Jamie and his lover, that she would give interviews to every scandal sheet and tabloid she could find.'

Lara was appalled. She simply couldn't get her head around anyone who wanted to hurt other people. 'Your brother...'

'Didn't know.' He rubbed a hand across his forehead. 'The irony was, a month after she was killed in the crash he and his lover broke up; the next month he met Roberto.

'Lucy was the heroine in her own life story. Every story heroine needs a villain and for her that was me. To understand Lucy you have to realise that she did not just need to win, she needed to take everything away from everyone else, turn their friends against them, strip them of pride; her lust for revenge was utterly insatiable.'

Lara shook her head, finding it impossible to reconcile the angelic image in her head with the...*evil* he spoke of.

'The deal,' he explained in the same flat voice, 'was that we stay together...the public act was part of her punishment; she liked to see me helpless. She enjoyed flaunting her affairs, telling me she had aborted my child... laughing...'

Lara had sat dry-eyed and composed through the remembrance service; even when Raoul had paid his moving tribute to his grandfather she had kept the tears at bay. But now they flowed. 'Oh, God!' she sobbed. 'How could she, how could anyone...be so...? A baby...'

'She sent me a scan photo for my birthday, inside a daddy card.'

Lara pressed a hand to her mouth to hold the cry of horror inside. Like everyone else, she had looked at Raoul and seen the aura of power that he wore like a second skin, the cynicism, the edge of ruthless determination.

Now she saw the idealistic young man he had been before his first wife, the man he had been before he had been subjected to emotional torture by the person he had thought he loved. Her heart ached for him, the man he was and the man he could have been, had the evil woman not torn away his belief in goodness and love.

Would he ever heal?

Raoul felt an unfamiliar helplessness as he watched the silent tears fall down her face.

'It is in the past and gone,' he said abruptly. 'I am the man I am now, and it's better that I stay alone. I know not every woman is like Lucy, but I can't trust anyone, and even if I could I have nothing to give that sort of woman, not the things she needs.' His dark eyes held hers for a long moment. 'Do you understand what I'm saying, Lara?'

'You want to be alone. Doesn't that mean she has won?' He said nothing and she gave an angry sniff, choking out another gruff, 'I'm sorry,' while wiping away the moisture from her face with the back of both hands. 'I would like to tear her hair out... She's dead, that probably sounds terrible, but I don't care!' she cried.

'I know terrible, and, trust me, that is not.' He studied her pale face. 'You look like you could do with a drink,' he said, losing the battle to hide his concern.

'You should have told me.'

'Why? You think I want to advertise the fact I was a fool? I've never told anyone before—the whole world but you swallows the party line.'

The contempt in his voice made her wince. It was clearly aimed at himself. She didn't say anything because there was nothing she could say. Instead, she watched him pour brandy, wondering how she could refuse without it seeming odd.

'No, thanks, I won't. Actually I think Naomi knows.'

'*Naomi?*' He thought about it and nodded. 'I suppose she might know some—she and Lucy were close at one time, though I think she dropped her before the end,' he recalled with an uninterested shrug. 'And Lucy liked to boast about her triumphs.'

'I know now is not the right time, but I really don't think there's ever going to be a good time.'

'You want to make arrangements to leave.' Eyes dark and bleak turned her way but his shrug was casual. 'There's no hurry.'

'Good, no, I mean...' She took a deep breath and thought, *It's now or never.* 'That is not what I wanted to say. I've been trying to speak to you for a while... You see... Actually there's a...complication.' She swallowed. 'Oh, Raoul,' she husked out. 'I'm so sorry.'

His jaw clenched. 'Will you stop saying sorry?'

'Sorry.' She bit her lip to stop another sorry falling out. At least *sorry* was better than *I've fallen in love with you*. The words were so clear that for a moment she thought she'd spoken them out loud.

He arched a brow.

'I didn't lie to your grandfather.'

Comprehension spread across his face—how like the Lara he had come to know to get hung up over a lie. 'You lied for the right reasons.' He reached for her hand but she didn't take it; instead she brushed a few fiery, silken strands of hair from her brow.

'Our marriage was a lie.' On more levels than he knew.

Her use of the past tense deepened the frowning line between his dark brows.

'At times a lie is the kindest thing.'

'Not a kindness. You see, I *am* pregnant—not pretend, for real.'

The delivery was everything she had intended, measured, calm, but then she spoilt it all by bursting without warning into tears, loud sobs that seemed to be dragged from somewhere inside her. 'I'm s-sorry!' she managed between choking gasps.

Raoul didn't move; he just stood there with the look of a man who could see a ten-ton truck approaching and couldn't get out of the way.

Lara's knees folded and she sank down into the nearest chair. 'A shock, I know, and I'm sorry, but when you've had time to take it on you'll realise as I have that it doesn't have to change anything.' *He still didn't love her.*

Raoul, who had been standing silent, surged into motion, dropping down on his knees beside her chair.

'It changes *everything*.' He knew this, though the details of these changes remained beyond him at that moment. His brain just kept coming up against *baby* and stalling. 'And will you stop saying sorry?'

The absent afterthought made Lara lift her head. 'I can't stand women who cry all the time,' she sniffed, wiping the moisture off her face with the backs of her hands and missing the tender expression that momentarily broke through the shock on Raoul's lean face.

'Here.'

She took the laundered man-sized handkerchief and with a prosaic sniff she straightened her spine and looked into the face that was level with hers. She forgot what she had been about to say as a wave of love washed like a soul-deep sigh over her.

'I know this is the last thing you need right now—I—'

'*We!* It's not as if you didn't have a bit of help.' *When...?* Raoul pushed away the thought. It didn't really matter when it had happened; the way forward was to deal with this reality. He pushed against a crushing tide of guilt— *he* had done this to her.

'It's not really so terrible. I quite like the idea of being a young mother. If you like, I can keep you in touch with what is happening, milestones, you know, the birthdays and—'

'Keep me in touch...?'

'If you want?' Was she assuming too much?

'Where do you think I'm going to be?'

She made herself look at him, while struggling for a modicum of composure—better late than never!—and shook her head, not wanting to think about where he might be or, more specifically, with whom.

He dragged her to her feet then slowly but inexorably pulled her towards him until they stood thigh to thigh. 'Has it not occurred to you that I might want this child too?'

'To replace the one she took away?'

He didn't say anything but the words hung between them.

It was Lara who broke the silence. 'No, it hadn't occurred to me,' she admitted honestly. 'How could it? You've just finished telling me that you want to live your life alone.'

'This is about responsibility.'

'Is that all it is to you?' she flung back, wishing as much for him and their unborn child as for herself that it could be more.

'I'm not going to lie to you, Lara, pretend things I do not feel, but I had a no-hope father who always put his own needs ahead of his children's. I will not do that to any child of mine.'

'And if that's not enough…?'

'For who…you?'

'Yes,' she admitted in a quiet voice.

'It might turn out that way,' he admitted. 'But don't you think we should try…for the baby?'

'What do you mean by try? Do you mean that we should stay married? Because that was not part of the plan.'

'Having a baby wasn't part of the plan either,' he retorted.

'I thought you'd be angry.' Weirdly it seemed to her he was recovering from the shock quicker than she had.

'People *get* married because of babies, they don't get *unmarried*.'

'You wouldn't be suggesting this if there wasn't a baby, would you?'

'No.' She deserved a truthful answer, but she also deserved a man capable of love.

'No.'

Lara tried to tell herself that if he'd lied she would have

refused his offer, but she knew she wouldn't. She simply didn't have the strength.

'I've actually come to appreciate what Grandfather meant when he spoke of continuity, of wanting to pass on the name, the genes...'

'Oh, how convenient, now you suddenly *want* a baby? When did this happen? In the last five seconds?'

'I would never have made the conscious choice to have a child.' He would never have brought a child into the world merely to give his life meaning; the selfishness of the idea repelled him. 'But now that I am going to be a father I will be the best one that I can.' It would never be good enough, but luckily for their child he or she would have Lara for a mother to make up for it.

She gasped when, without warning, he placed a hand over her flat stomach.

Lara caught his wrist, felt a rush of emotion and hope. 'You think this could work.'

'We will *make* it work, *cara.*'

CHAPTER TEN

'A WEEKEND?' Raoul's ebony brows almost hit his hair-line as he watched Lara close the lid on another suitcase.

Lara turned, her heart skipping a beat as she met his smiling eyes. 'I'm nearly ready. It's not all mine—I have presents for everyone.'

Raoul crossed the room and sat on the bed, causing a pile of neatly folded silky underwear in rainbow colours to slide to the floor. He hooked a provocative thong and swung it on his finger.

'Do you mind? I spent…ooh!'

She landed with a throaty giggle on his lap. Framing her face, he kissed her deeply. When he finally drew back she laid her face on his shoulder, inhaling the warm scent of his skin as she looped her arms around his neck.

She focused on the moment and felt happy, though not totally relaxed. If she did that she might fall off the emotional tightrope that she'd been walking for the last few months. It was simply a matter of focusing on what she had, not on what she longed for. So long as she didn't expect too much, this could work.

And she had a lot to be thankful for: the baby growing inside her, the anticipation of motherhood, which she had never expected to feel so right.

'I need to finish packing.'

Raoul let her disentangle herself and lay back, hands behind his head, watching her finish her packing.

'Won't your mother and sister be hurt you haven't told them until now?' He had fallen in with Lara's decision to keep her pregnancy a secret from everyone including her family, actually *especially* her family, despite the fact it had always made him uneasy.

He still didn't understand it.

He felt the bed give slightly and heard her troubled little hitch of breath as she climbed onto it beside him. She tucked her feet under her as she adopted a kneeling position, looking down on him with her hair falling in a glorious fiery cloud around her face.

'I told you, I'm not ashamed.' She brushed her lips over his then, anchoring her hair with her forearm, and added, 'But I'm not the only one having a baby. Lily is pregnant.' Her sister's due date was approaching fast.

'Then surely that gives you something else in common.' Beyond the fact they were virtually identical to look at. It still bewildered him how his reaction to two women with the same face and body could be so totally different. One made him yawn…no, that wasn't fair, or even strictly true.

Lara's twin sister was not boring, she simply wasn't Lara, who ignited an insatiable desire in him that seemed to bypass every logic circuit.

His feelings for her might go deeper than desire? He pushed away the question, knowing that there was a limit to how many times it would go away unanswered.

How long could he keep dodging the issue?

Was he going to allow Lucy's poison to reach out from the grave and infect his future?

He closed down the internal dialogue—things were all right, better than all right, as they were. Why meddle with something that was working?

'Lily is facing being a single parent. Her situation couldn't be more different than mine and I don't want to make her feel—'

Raoul looped a hand casually around the back of her head, rubbing a caressing thumb across the angle of her jaw. He drew her down, pressing a hard, hungry kiss to her lips.

'You're a good sister.' He landed a kiss on the tip of her nose as she pulled away. Shaking her hair back, she laughed, a hard little sound that drew a frown from Raoul.

'Care to share the joke?'

'I'm not the good twin, that's Lily.'

She turned her head sharply, causing her hair to fall in a concealing curtain across her face. That she didn't want to make Lily feel bad *had* been true and it still was, but the real reason Lara was delaying the moment was not to spare her twin's feeling but her own.

They definitely weren't the type of twins that had some kind of psychic bond, it was just that her sister had the ability to instinctively ask the right questions—all the questions Lara was avoiding. She knew the conversation was inevitable but it was one she wasn't ready to have, or she hadn't been until now.

At the wedding she had kept Lily at arm's length for that very reason. She had known that Lily had been hurt but she also knew that her sister would never understand what she was doing... Who would?

She'd gone away to lose her virginity with one man and ended up falling in love and marrying another, and in the end neither man had loved her even the slightest bit.

Her hungry emerald stare shielded by a heavy fringe of lashes moved over her husband. There was bewilderment mingled in with the need and love that swept over her in a tidal wave of emotion.

The truth, or rather the public lie their relationship was based on, never went away, but there were some days when it remained a whisper in the back of her mind.

Admitting to her twin that their marriage had been a lie from the beginning and the only reason they were together was the baby would turn that whisper into a shout.

And she couldn't bear the thought of Lily looking at her with pity.

Her words were more revealing than she knew. Raoul felt a slug of anger and an image flashed into his head of a younger, more vulnerable Lara being asked why she wasn't more like her sister.

'Just because you've been assigned a role,' he roughed out softly, 'doesn't mean you have to live up to it.'

Her startled eyes flew to his face. 'Nobody ever did that.' There was defensiveness in the tilt of her chin as she tucked her hair behind her ears.

He angled a sceptical brow. 'I'm not saying it was deliberate.' He tried a different tack. 'Has it occurred to you that you're not so wild and she's not so sensible? Just that you're very different people?' He didn't want to encourage his Lara to compare herself to her twin all the time.

His...?

The possessive trend of his thoughts made him tense. *A figure of speech*, soothed the voice in his head. And what man with an honest breath in his body wouldn't like the idea of Lara being exclusively his?

'You think I'm not so wild?'

Her teasing was rewarded with a lustful growl. He curved a possessive hand across the back of her head and she went with it, allowing her body to fall across him as his mouth moved across hers in a slow, seductive kiss.

Several minutes later she sat back, pink-cheeked and dishevelled. 'I have to finish my packing.'

'What's stopping you?' he asked innocently.

Ten minutes later she clicked closed the lock on her overnight bag and gave a last glance around the room.

'I'll go tell Vincenzo we're ready—*finally*.' He huffed an irritated curse, fished out his phone and, glancing at the caller ID, signalled to Lara to go ahead.

By the time he had joined her she was already ensconced in the back seat of the limo. Raoul slung the case in the open boot and nodded to the driver before he slid in beside her.

He could sense her excitement.

'You miss your family?'

She nodded. 'Yes, I do.' She pressed a hand to her stomach. 'Especially now.'

'Are you all right?'

'Fine.' Lara stretched forward to relive the nagging ache in her back. She had read all the books and she knew this was normal. But she also knew the warmth, the spreading stain were not...

'Raoul...!'

He turned his head in alarm, then slowly followed the direction of her fixed stare.

For a few heart-thudding moments he was paralysed as he stared down at the crimson stain on her skirt and the seat, dripping onto the floor.

Lara whimpered. 'Something's wrong.' It provided the impetus for him to react.

Curling his hand over hers, he turned his head to yell at the driver, who threw the car into a screeching one-eighty-degree turn and set off at speed, ignoring the numerous horn blasts of complaint that followed him.

'Don't worry. Vincenzo drove tanks in the military. We'll have you there in five minutes.' Would five minutes be quick enough? There was so much blood. He looked away from it, focusing on her face, her white, tragic, pain-filled face, while he tried to channel calm.

Inside, Raoul didn't feel calm. He felt an icy fist clawing in his belly, tightening, spreading cold and fear... Could anyone lose that much blood and survive? Of course she could; this wasn't the Dark Ages—women didn't die this way any more. They could transplant hearts and rebuild shattered limbs...but there was so, so much blood!

'Faster!' he flung over his shoulder to Vincenzo, who was already breaking speed limits in a major way.

'Is the baby all right, Raoul…?'

Wishing he could take away the fear in her shadowed eyes, he took her hands between his; they seemed so small and white, and they were cold, so very cold.

He had never felt so helpless in his entire life.

He shook his head. 'Don't talk now, *cara*, save your— No, don't close your eyes, Lara, Lara, stay with me, *cara*.' His voice cracked as he pleaded, 'Stay with me!'

The lashes that lay against her waxen cheeks lifted and Raoul exhaled a gasp of relief. 'I've made such a mess of your lovely car.'

He swore with soft, savage fluency and lifted her hands to his lips, kissing her individual fingertips. 'I'll send you the bill.' He lifted his head in response to the driver's voice. 'We're here!' he said to Lara, whose eyes had begun to flutter closed once more. 'Everything will be all right, just hold on.'

'Who do you think you are? You can't park here! This space is reserved for ambulance emergencies.'

Raoul responded to the officious instructions in the same language, slicing out in a steel monotone, 'Can't you see it *is* an emergency? Get me a doctor! Now!'

Any inclination to argue the point faded as Raoul emerged and his interrogator saw Lara, who was drifting in and out of consciousness. He turned and shouted; in response two figures and a trolley appeared. They had transferred Lara to it when a doctor arrived and began to take charge.

The questions he shot at Raoul were reassuringly concise and to the point. In comparison, his own response seemed painfully slow as his tongue struggled to keep pace with his brain.

'I'm afraid you can't go beyond this point. Please take a seat.'

At the prospect of Lara being wheeled through those big double doors, away from him, something close to panic slid though Raoul. Then, as if she sensed what he was feeling, the little hand in his tightened and Raoul shook his head, barely recognising his own voice as he responded, 'No, I will not.'

The comment didn't throw the nurse, who made the request more firmly but still politely. She gave an understanding smile that made him want to yell at her—he didn't want smiles, he wanted someone to do something.

'I'm afraid, sir, that you—'

Raoul was afraid too, very afraid as the fingers in his suddenly went limp.

'Lara!' His yell of anguish diverted attention from him to Lara. It seemed to him that she was barely breathing. 'Do something!'

They *were* doing things, pushing him out of the way to get to the unconscious figure. When the doors swung shut moments later, leaving him standing the wrong side, he didn't move. He just stood there, hands clenched and white at his sides, feeling the weight of paralysing helplessness bearing down on him.

Raoul had lost count of the number of people who had walked through the door but on each successive occasion he braced himself only to experience a massive anticlimax as they walked on by. He was pretty much resigned for more of the same when a tall, grey-haired figure still wearing scrubs pushed the door open.

The man walked straight up to him and held out his hand. The grasp was reassuringly strong. 'I'm your wife's surgeon. She came through the operation well.'

It wasn't until the older man released his hand that Raoul realised his own was shaking. The screaming tension that held his body rigid released itself in a slow sibilant sigh.

The man looked at him with sympathy. 'You must have questions.'

'It happened so quickly.'

The doctor inclined his head. 'If you'd like to come through to my office...?'

Lara was dimly aware of being moved from the car to the trolley, but it all had a nightmarish quality. But the nightmare was not real, not while she had hold of Raoul's hand. So she held on tight as she was whisked along corridors, aware of the blur of faces, the glare of lights overhead hurting her eyes, hearing snatches of the buzz of conversation going on around her.

Then there was just black.

'No, leave it, Lara.' Fingers cool and firm stopped her pulling at the thing taped to her hand.

She knew the voice, the touch; she opened her eyes and Raoul was still holding her hand.

She was grateful he didn't wait for her to ask.

'They couldn't save the baby.'

She had known already, but hearing it made it real. 'What did I do wrong?'

It was not the response that he had anticipated but before Raoul could react to it a figure strolled into the room. The scrubs were gone and he was dressed in an open-necked shirt; it was only the badge he wore and the stethoscope protruding from his pocket that pronounced his medical status.

'You did nothing, Mrs Di Vittorio,' the doctor said firmly in his perfect English. 'Many mothers experience irrational guilt after a miscarriage.' He addressed his remark to Raoul and, after glancing at the chart at the foot of Lara's bed, walked around to stand closer to her head.

'And there was nothing you could have done to prevent it.'

'But I was nearly twenty weeks. I thought after the first twelve—'

'Miscarriages in the second trimester are not as common as those in the early weeks,' he agreed gently. 'But they do happen.'

'Why?' Lara forced the question past the aching occlusion in her throat.

'Many reasons. In your case, I'm afraid that the baby actually died a little time ago...'

'No!' Adrenaline of denial giving her a surge of strength, Lara struggled into a sitting position, wincing as the needle in her arm caught in her hair as she pushed it out of her face.

'It's not possible, I'd have known!'

The doctor placed a compassionate hand on her arm and, watching him, Raoul thought, *He knows what to do, so why don't I?*

She wouldn't be here now if he hadn't dragged her into his life. It had all been about him and his needs; his motivations had all been selfish and this was the result. Self-loathing tightened in his gut. She was better off without him.

'Did you have a bleed...something slight perhaps?'

Lara looked at him blankly for a moment and then blinked. 'No...yes...' She nodded, remembering the morning... If she had told someone, sought medical advice and not just put her symptoms into a search engine, maybe her baby would be alive.

The combined weight of *what if*s and guilt felt as if it were crushing her.

'As I have explained to your husband, you had what is termed a failed miscarriage. The complication came when an infection took hold, which caused the haemorrhage. Luckily we caught you before sepsis set in—that could have been very serious indeed. Look, I'll leave you two to talk, but not for long. You need to rest and, as I told your husband, all being well you can go home in the morning.'

Lara watched the door close; the gentle click echoed in her brain, over and over.

'I don't feel anything,' she said, dropping her head back on the pillow.

'They gave you pain relief, I think.'

'No, not that sort of feeling.' She pressed a hand to her chest. 'I don't feel anything.' She emphasised, 'I'm empty, it's like a vacuum.'

His eyes met hers, and the expression in them was guarded. Without warning, anger rushed into the vacuum she had spoken of, bubbling up.

'Say what you're thinking. You might as well, because it's obvious. The only reason we're together was the baby and now there is no baby, so there's no reason for us to be together any more. Don't worry, I'm not going to make a scene!' she shrilled, to the private room, empty but for the two of them, before her eyes filled with tears.

The sight made Raoul surge forward but Lara held up her hands as if to ward him off as she hissed, 'Don't you dare feel sorry for me!'

Raoul subsided back into the chair pulled up beside the bed and dragged a hand through his dark hair. 'I feel sorry...no, sad for *us*.' And it was true—alongside the guilt that he carried like a second skin there was a sense of profound loss.

His response threw her, but only for a moment before she shook her head and choked out bitterly, 'There *is* no us. You're probably glad this happened!'

'Don't be ridiculous! I appreciate that I wasn't the one who...the one who...' *Came close to losing my life.* He couldn't say the words but the acknowledgement of it added another layer to his guilt. 'The one who went through the physical trauma, but the baby was mine too. We will both grieve, so doesn't it make sense to you that we go through it together?' It was a logical response, he told himself. 'Who is better placed than me to know what you're feeling?'

Her lips quivered. 'I never thought I'd feel this way, but I wanted this baby... I *really* wanted this baby and it's fine, I don't expect you to understand.'

'I wanted this baby too.'

'Because you feel responsible, that's all.'

'I don't want to be the last Di Vittorio. I have been surrounded by so much death and misery. A baby... I have been able to look into the future for the first time in years.'

'I didn't know you felt that way...'

He gave an odd laugh. 'Neither did I. Look, life has kicked you, Lara, but you are strong, you will recover. I really don't think you should make any decisions until then. Let me take care of you.' *It's the least you can do*, mocked the voice in his head, *considering it's your fault she's lying there.*

'And when will that be?'

'I wish I could tell you.'

'And what then?' she asked dully, thinking that if they were going to split up anyway, if he was just waiting until she was stronger, what was the point? She'd never be *that* strong. It was always going to hurt, so why not get the hurting over in one go?

'That depends on what you want. The doctor says there is no reason we can't try again.'

'You're suggesting...'

'I'm suggesting we wait and see. Or would you rather go home to your family?'

Lara thought about seeing her sister with a healthy baby growing inside and shook her head.

'And if it makes you feel better to yell at me, blame me, that's fine. We will move on, and next time things—'

'Next time if we…things could go wrong again.'

The fear in her voice felt like a hand tearing at his chest.

'It's too soon, just focus on getting better.'

She didn't hear him. Lara was sound asleep.

The next morning, packed and waiting when he arrived, she was speaking on the phone. Conscious he was listening, she wound the conversation up as quickly as possible. 'Bye, Mum, and sorry, speak soon, give my love to Lily.'

'So when is she coming?'

Lara didn't meet his eyes. 'She isn't,' she said brightly.

He tensed. 'So you are going there?' He was afraid that if she went, she might not come back.

Raoul's philosophy in life had always been simple: predict possible outcomes before they happen and plan accordingly. It had helped him survive his marriage from hell and now, for the first time, he could think of no plans, not one. Denial was the only option.

'No.' This response was even less distinct.

What the hell was going on? 'Lara, will you look at me?'

With a heavy sigh Lara lifted her head, shaking back the curtain of burnished hair. 'Don't look at me like that. If you must know, I haven't told her.'

Raoul, who had been reaching into his pocket to switch off his own vibrating phone, let his hand fall away and just stared at her.

'You haven't told her?' She couldn't possibly mean what it sounded like.

'Well, I hadn't told her I was pregnant, so I could hardly tell her I'd lost a baby she didn't know existed.'

She screwed up her mouth, digging her teeth into her full lower lip as she pushed her hair behind her ears. The motion drew attention to the plaster on the back of her hand; the sight of it was an unwelcome reminder of the events of yesterday.

The flash of exasperation that tautened his sculpted features gave way to something between panic and tenderness as he watched a tear trace its way down her pale, smooth cheek.

Lara brushed the moisture away angrily and yelled, 'Don't look at me like that. It's my decision and if you go behind my back and tell them I'll never ever forgive you!' Her chest heaving with the strength of the emotions that were tearing her apart, she poked a finger at him and added a quivering postscript, 'I mean it, Raoul!'

'So I see.'

Anger she could have dealt with, but the half-quizzical smile that suggested he was pleased she was yelling at him drove a stake through her carefully crafted façade, cracking it wide open.

'Lily won't tell me who the father is, so she's keeping secrets too.' The hurt she hadn't even admitted to herself quivered in Lara's voice and she rubbed her hands up and down her upper arms.

Raoul pulled off the jacket he was wearing and laid it across her shoulders, not fighting the impulse that made him kiss the top of her glossy, burnished head.

Lara lifted her head and sniffed. Her beautiful eyes were red-rimmed and swimming, her full lips quivering. 'I w-want to be happy for her.' She swallowed hard and bit her lip. 'But I'm not a nice person. I just keep thinking, why should she get a baby and not me…why my baby…?' She bent her head again and covered her face with her hands, mumbling through her fingers, 'I must be a bad person.'

Her muffled words threatened to break through his control. Holding her would make him feel one hell of a lot better, but was it what she needed at the moment?

'Self-pity,' he drawled, 'doesn't suit you, *cara*. That's

better,' he approved warmly when her hands fell away and she shot him a teary but angry glare. 'I'm sorry that things are not good between you and your sister,' he added softly.

She sniffed and explained with husky, hard-won composure, 'I miss… I mean, I don't know what she's thinking or anything but we never used to hide things from one another, we shared.' She gave a loud sniff and made a pathetic attempt to smile that just about broke his heart. 'You don't want to hear this.'

It was true, he didn't, because he didn't enjoy feeling guilty. A major contributing factor in the situation that had led to the deterioration in the relationship between Lara and her twin must have been his insistence she not divulge the true circumstances behind their marriage. Hell, who was he kidding? This was his doing!

Since he'd walked into Lara's life he'd done nothing but cause her heartbreak and pain.

'If you like I could speak to her?'

'You!' Her incredulity at the casual offer was almost as great as Raoul's own. 'What would you say?'

He stayed silent because quite frankly he didn't have a clue and he had no idea what had driven him to make such a pointless gesture.

How about guilt?

'There's been no falling out as such…it'll be fine,' she insisted dully. 'I'm just feeling a bit fragile.'

'You're allowed.' His jaw clenched.

The trouble with Lara was she didn't cut herself any slack. Plus, she never asked for help, which, combined with her bloody-minded attitude, meant that if you did make a suggestion she was pretty much guaranteed to do the opposite. A 'no comment' policy was the safest bet—though not always the most fun.

A quiet life was overrated.

His half-smile faded as he realised what he was doing—

remembering make-up sex when she was some place close to hell. *You're a shallow bastard*, he thought.

Yes, she could be a total pain, outspoken, bolshie, opinionated…but he would have welcomed being on the receiving end of any or all of these undesirable qualities if it meant banishing the haunted look from her eyes.

Lara shook her head. 'Look, I know it's fashionable but I really don't need talking therapy.'

She had already rejected the clinic's offer to put her in contact with a grief counsellor. She really couldn't see how talking about something so personal, exposing her innermost feelings to a total stranger, would make anything better. No, Lara thought, she would do what she always had done with painful emotions and memories—she was going to build a great wall, shut them behind it and get on with her life.

'I just want to go home.'

CHAPTER ELEVEN

LARA REMEMBERED THE first time she had walked into the entrance hall of the *palazzo* and got her first impression of the grandeur and history of the ancient building. Her voice had echoed around the vaulted ceiling while Raoul's ancestors had looked down at her from the stone walls with varying degrees of disapproval.

She'd bumped into a suit of armour and tried to pretend she wasn't daunted, but she had been, even though she had grown up in the shadow of a very different but equally impressive historic house where her parents had worked, and where her mum was still housekeeper.

Today as she walked in, the smell of the hospital still lingering on her clothes, the stone walls lined with priceless tapestries felt like a haven. They felt like home.

When had that happened?

'What are these?'

'I have no idea,' Raoul admitted, walking across the room ahead of her to the items arranged on the heavily carved and inlaid table that took centre stage.

He turned and waved her to the table. 'For you.'

'Me?'

He watched the emotions on her face as she moved along the line, looking at one gift and then the next. She turned back to him holding the bouquet of prize roses grown by the *palazzo*'s head gardener, a surly, monosyllabic individual who grew them for the horticultural event he won every year—the blooms were normally off-limits to everyone.

She closed her eyes and inhaled the heady fragrance.

'Marguerite has cooked me my favourite biscuits, those lovely little almond ones.' Her throat closed over with emotion as she picked up an offering she had missed, a glossy magazine tied with a fluorescent bow.

'Rosa,' she said with a smile even before she glanced at the attached card.

'Who is Rosa?'

'One day she'll be famous, but right now she helps in the kitchen. She's halfway through a fine arts degree. I pass on my magazines to her.'

Small wonder she was so popular with the staff. In the comparatively short time she had been here Lara had come to know more about the people who lived and worked on the estate than he did.

'Everyone is so kind.'

'It would seem you have won their hearts.'

Lara looked away, burying her face in the roses before he could see the truth she knew was written on her face— there was only one heart she was interested in winning and that belonged to someone else.

If she couldn't have his heart, she could have his baby; she could give the man she loved that at least.

'Were you serious?' She fixed him with a grave questioning stare. 'Do you want to try again?'

'I do.'

The admission had been a long time coming.

Since Lucy he had not allowed himself to think about a family, not even when his grandfather had brought up the subject. A family came with love; you couldn't have one without the other. The logic was inescapable.

Almost having a child by accident had exposed the lie: he wanted an heir, a child…and he wanted it with Lara, who did not ask him for things he could not give.

'But maybe now is not the time to think about it.'

'I have thought.' She tipped her head up. 'I think I'd like that.'

'That is not a decision to make now. We will discuss this later.'

'When later?'

'You're asking me to give you a date?'

She pressed her lips together.

'Even if you do know your own mind, your body needs time to recover. If you still feel the same way in a year...'

'A year!' she yelped.

'All right, nine months.'

'I won't change my mind,' she said, thinking, *but you might*.

Raoul stood a little apart from the family group as Lara embraced her mother and then her twin, bending a head to brush her lips across the forehead of the baby. For someone who was looking for it, all the sadness and pain she had been struggling to hide all day under a bright, bubbly exterior was there glistening in her eyes.

Watching, helpless to do a damned thing, he felt as if a blunt knife were twisting in his stomach... Surely they *must* see...? But no, her twin and her mother were both focused on the baby.

He didn't know whether to applaud or weep when, a moment later, Lara was smiling, back in control and giving an Oscar-worthy performance of the self-absorbed, wild-child sister, and all the time crying inside.

'Well, rather you than me, Lily.' She laughed, patting her flat stomach with a complacent smile that made it seem as if she had nothing more to worry about in the world than her waistline. 'I don't fancy having to change my wardrobe.'

How often had she hidden her feelings this way in the past? he wondered? Maybe she wasn't so easy to read after all? He had debated whether to invent an urgent appointment and bring this visit to a premature end, but he was glad now that they had stayed longer. Not that Lara would have broken down, she was too determined to appear thrilled for her sister, but if he had to watch her being bright and smiley while her heart was breaking for another second…he doubted he would be able to fulfil his promise of silence on the subject of her miscarriage.

'I can't get over how much she's grown,' Lara said, retrieving a toy that had been tossed on the floor.

'They usually do in a year,' her twin responded quietly.

The stricken look that slid across Lara's face could have been caused by the undertone in her twin's voice, or the reminder of the previous visit, right after the birth, when Lara had insisted on flying over to see her sister.

Only a couple of weeks after her own miscarriage. Raoul had tried his best to dissuade her, but in the end she'd threatened to catch a flight on her own, so he'd taken her.

It had been a nightmare. Oh, Lara had managed to say all the right things at the hospital, had held the baby and told her sister how clever she was, but outside she had virtually collapsed in a heap.

She had sobbed uncontrollably on the flight back and pretty much for the next two days. Since then she had made excuses whenever a visit home was suggested, until today.

'Goodbye, Emily Rose, be good for Mummy.'

The baby, who was dressed in a cute pink outfit that she was almost too big for at eleven months, grabbed for Lara's hair.

'No, Emmy.' Lily clicked her tongue and detached the chubby fingers.

From where he was standing Raoul could see the muscles in Lara's pale throat working as she straightened up. Even someone with an armour-plated heart could not have failed to be moved by her struggle for control. He might not agree with her decision to keep the miscarriage a secret, but it was *her* decision, and he had to respect that. However wrong, misguided and pig-headed he thought she was being.

He cleared his throat and glanced pointedly at the time that blinked on the screen of his phone. 'I'm sorry to break up the party and drag you away, but we're on the clock here.'

It worked. Lara's twin and mother looked at her with sympathy and him with a lack of it—which was fine by Raoul. He was not seeking either their sympathy or approval.

He placed a hand on Lara's elbow and, projecting a level of callous impatience that he hoped was consistent with someone heartless and controlling—after all, was it a million miles from his actual character?—he raised his voice once more to be heard above the whirr of the blades of the waiting helicopter.

'Ladies.' He tipped his head curtly and pulled Lara, skipping along on her spiky heels to keep up with him, towards the door. She still retained her grip on his arm, though she no longer needed his support.

Behind them the two women exchanged worried glances.

Once they took off and the figures below vanished from view, Lara released a long shuddering sigh and leaned back, her eyes closed.

Sitting opposite her, Raoul sat waiting.

'There is no urgent appointment, is there?'

'No.'

She opened her eyes, which were luminescent with tears. 'I could have coped.'

'I'm sure you could,' he returned smoothly. 'But I probably wouldn't have if we'd stayed any longer.'

She shook her head as if the idea the day had been any-thing other than a breeze for him had not occurred to her. 'It was lovely to see everyone.'

People she missed…a life she regretted leaving behind? He pushed the thought away. 'Everyone said how lovely the baby was.'

He arched a brow at her quick defence. 'And nobody, not a soul, mentioned the father.'

Eyes wide with horror, she leaned forward in her seat. 'You didn't…?'

'What, after you told me the subject was off-limits? I wouldn't dare.'

She gave a disbelieving grunt and settled back in her seat.

'But the strain of not mentioning the elephant in the room was beginning to tell.'

'Lily hasn't told anyone.' *Not even me.* 'Raoul…? It's been nearly a year now, and I haven't changed my mind.'

Though she had been angry at the time, she was grate-ful now that he had insisted on the wait. For the last few months her emotions had been all over the place.

She knew she hadn't been easy to live with but Raoul had been incredibly patient, when she got angry with him, herself or life in general. And then there had been the sad times when all she could do was cry.

'Today—'

'Today was hard,' she admitted. 'Inside,' she said, press-ing a hand to her chest, 'I feel like a mother but no one can see that. One day I hurt, the next I feel as if it had hap-pened to someone else. I know I've been hell to live with and that was never part of the contract.'

'I broke the contract when I got you pregnant.'

'So your guilt is keeping us together.' She turned to stare at the clouds.

He wished he could have said yes, that would have made

things simpler to sort in his own mind, but though guilt played a part there was a lot more keeping him with Lara, more than he wanted to think about.

'A little while back I thought you'd changed your mind... Was I wrong?'

She turned her head and looked at him in astonishment. 'For a while,' she admitted, 'I did feel as though having another baby would be betraying the one I lost... I suppose that sounds mad to you.'

'No, it doesn't.'

Her eyes slid from his and she looked out of the window. 'It might never happen for us.'

He responded with an emotion-dampening positivity. 'Of course it will, and if it doesn't it won't be for lack of trying.'

'So you haven't changed your mind?'

His libido gave a lazy kick as she relaxed and laughed again; the sound made him realise how rare these moments were now.

'I want...' He wanted to see her happy, he wanted to repair the damage he had wrought after watching what she had been through during the last year. He would have done anything to make her laugh like that again. 'No,' he said softly.

'How about it, then...?' Holding his interested gaze, she slipped off her spiky heels and, tongue caught between her teeth in sexy concentration, her green eyes wide and mockingly innocent, she stretched out her bare foot and moved it slowly up his leg.

'You think...?'

He felt the heat rising up his neck, then the heat coalesced a little lower as her foot came to rest between his thighs. 'In a helicopter, *really...*?'

Eyes dancing, she gave a wicked chuckle and withdrew her foot. 'Well, maybe it can wait until the plane...

I mean, what's the use of having a private jet if you can't make use of the privacy?'

'I like the way your mind works,' he said, thinking now this was the way babies should be made!

CHAPTER TWELVE

Eight months later

IT HAD BEEN Lara's idea to revive the masked ball that had last been held at the *palazzo* twenty years before. If anyone had asked him his opinion, and they hadn't, Raoul would have pointed to the high wall that surrounded the property and said it had been built for a reason—to keep people out.

But she was so fired up about it that he hadn't been able to bring himself to throw a damper on her enthusiasm. His agreement to the scheme had been taken as read, though there had been several times since when he'd wished he had objected, not least when an army of caterers, musicians and assorted staff who were required for the smooth running of such a social event invaded his home.

Still, it looked as if the hard work had paid off. The night seemed to be a roaring success.

Raoul could hear his wife's throaty laugh from across the room. Her head was thrown back to reveal the lovely line of her swan-like throat, and the emeralds that had been dug out of the vault for the occasion lay glinting against the pearlescent skin of her breasts. That had been their first row tonight—the dress too revealing, too everything.

His thoughts slid back to when she had walked through from her dressing room carrying his mask in one hand, hers in the other.

The cut of the black dress had drawn a spontaneous low, feral groan from his throat; once he had started breathing again all he could think about was peeling it off.

'You can't wear that!'

In retrospect Raoul could see that he could have dealt with the situation better, but then hindsight was a marvellous thing.

The smile left her lovely face and her chin went up as she tossed his mask across. He lifted a hand automatically to catch it.

'You want to dictate what I wear?'

Hell, there was the *quiet voice*, the one that generally preceded a redheaded meltdown. He felt an answering flare of temper aggravated by extreme sexual frustration.

'Do you always have to get your own way?' he countered, thinking of all the times he had let her have it. *You're in danger of turning into a lapdog, Raoul.*

'Have you ever heard of compromise? Or patience?'

'I *beg* your pardon! And if I am a male, controlling jerk for wanting my wife not to wear something that could get her arrested—'

Her magnificent eyes flashed green fire up at him and her even more magnificent bosom swelled with wrath. 'You think I look like a hooker?'

'Do not put words in my mouth.'

'It's not my fault if some men have one-track minds!'

Raoul hooked a hand around her back and felt a deep responsive quiver run through her body as she dropped the hand-painted antique mask. 'I'm not *some* men, I am your husband.' The argument, the real cause, the hundreds of guests about to arrive burned away in seconds as the heat of primitive need consumed him.

'Shall I help you out of it…?'

He took her throaty little whimper as a yes and started to slide the zipper of the scandalous dress down. The image in his head of it falling in a silken puddle at her feet vanished as she suddenly stiffened and pulled away and, with hands raised above her head, began to struggle frantically to pull the zipper back up.

'You think all you have to do is get me in bed and I'll agree to anything!' she charged furiously.

Nerve-shredding frustration gnawed at him as he walked towards her. His control was perilously close to snapping. It must have been reflected on his face because Lara, matching his steps, backed away until her back was pressed into the canopy of their four-poster bed.

'It's getting you there, *cara*, that can be problematic.'

'You arrogant—' she gasped, her voice vanishing as they faced one another, panting, their mingled breaths crystallising into an electrical charge that vibrated in the air around them.

'Lara, I'm—'

She was leaning into him, her luscious lips a breath away from his, when a loud tap on the door made her blink like someone waking.

'Come in!' she yelled, before adding a warning, 'Hush!' as Raoul swore.

'Sorry to disturb you, but the caterers have a problem with the ice sculptures. They say they can't work with—'

Raoul's groan drowned out the rest of the woman's words. He didn't have a clue who she was but he'd seen her about the place the past week.

Lara shot him a cold glance. 'Don't worry, Sara, I'll come and have a word, just give me a moment, would you?' She waited until the door shut before she rounded on Raoul. 'Do you have to be so rude?'

'Me!'

'Yes, you! Would it kill you to smile? You make her nervous.'

'I don't seem to make you nervous.'

'You make me—!' She gave a little gasp that drowned out whatever it was she was going to say.

He found his anger shifting, giving way to reluctant concern as he realised how fragile she was looking. Her make-up might hide the shadows underneath her incredible eyes but it didn't disguise the sharpness of her delicately carved collarbones.

'Have you ever heard of delegation?'

Her determination to be involved in every aspect of this charity ball meant that there had been times when he had made time to be with her, and, rather than appreciate the effort he was making, she'd stood him up, for a florist! Oh, and, how could he have forgotten? A bottled-water supplier!

He liked to think his ego was fairly resistant but rain check…?

It wasn't that he felt neglected, it was not as though he expected her to be at his beck and call—the idea was laughable—but the dark shadows under her eyes were not. But as much as Raoul found the entire thing a pain, he couldn't help but admire the way she'd thrown herself into it.

But then, that was Lara. She never did anything at less than full throttle, he brooded, floating a glance over her sleek, sexy outfit. His opinion that the outfit was not fit for public consumption did not stop his blood heating and his body hardening. He frowned, imagining that he wouldn't be the only man she had this effect on tonight.

'What are you going to do, serve the soup and conduct the orchestra?'

His disdain brought an angry flush to Lara's cheeks. Not breaking eye contact, she lifted her chin to a determined angle. 'I want everything to be perfect. Would it have been too much to expect a little support?'

She had no intention of admitting that there had been many times when she'd wished she'd never started it.

Even if the person she was doing it for wasn't impressed… She blinked away the thought. This wasn't about impressing anyone, this was about charity.

'Why? What does it matter? People will get drunk and say things they regret the next morning. You're not being judged. It's all in your mind,' he said, tapping his own head.

'You just criticised the way I look.' She took a step towards him and lifted her chin. 'I'd call that judging, *caro*.'

She curled her fingers around the ornate handle of her mask and held it up. It covered the upper half of her face, leaving her lush, crimson-painted lips and rounded chin visible while through the slits her eyes sparkled like the green gems around her neck.

'I may not be able to make a baby but I can damned well organise a party!' Her defiance melted away as her words hung there in the air between them.

She was acting as though she'd just made some great reveal. But Lara was not telling Raoul anything he didn't already know. The timing had said it all. She had picked up the masked-ball baton and hit the ground running a day after their last big fight about IVF.

With a sigh, Lara dropped her hand. What good was there in hiding behind a mask when she'd just volunteered all her insecurities? Thanks to her big mouth. It would take more than some papier mâché to hide them now.

The siren had vanished, her face stripped bare of provocation; it was impossible not to feel her pain.

'Nobody has said you…we…can't have a baby.' He had humoured her with the tests but he might as well not have bothered. They had been given the all-clear, but every month her wild optimism gave way to dark depression. The cycle was relentless.

'Then why hasn't it happened?'

He closed his eyes at the constant cry. 'Maybe,' he ground out, 'because you are constantly so uptight! Relax and forget about it for a minute, stop taking your temperature every five minutes. Stop obsessing about getting pregnant and it might happen.'

Lara compressed her lips. Easy for him to say. He wasn't the one waiting for someone to call time on the marriage if she failed. It would be easy for him, he had no emotional investment in it, he could just shrug and walk away, find someone else to continue the genetic line. It was *his* line, not hers, that was important here.

She was not denying that he had put time and effort into their marriage, more than she had expected if she was honest, but he hadn't put his heart into it.

But she couldn't cry foul. She'd known what she was getting into, had agreed to it all with her eyes open, and he had never pretended he wanted anything other than a baby. The voice of reason in her head made her fling out bitterly, 'I'm not even sure you have a heart!'

This seemingly disconnected and unreasonable accusation made his sympathy shrivel and his paper-thin patience come closer to vanishing totally as he drawled, 'I didn't think it was my heart you were interested in.'

The irony of complaining about being treated like a sex object by a gorgeous and desirable woman was not wasted on him. He was sure that most men would envy his position and while there were many plus points—he had no problem with the fact that she couldn't seem to get enough of him, that she melted at his touch—he couldn't quite rid himself of the suspicion that was nagging at the back of his mind: was her desire real, or was it just the right time of her cycle?

You're just never satisfied, are you, Di Vittorio? What the hell do you want—love...? On that grounding mental observation he took a deep breath and decided to be reasonable. He might even wear the damned mask!

'Anyone would think you'd like for me to fail!'

Reason forgotten, he'd chucked his mask out of the window and hadn't responded to the accusation. To do so would have been to throw himself into an emotional minefield.

Instead, he had let her leave, her sweeping exit only spoiled by the fact that she'd had to come back for her shoes, which rather ruined the dramatic effect.

As he thought back on it now the memory twitched his lips into a half-smile that flattened out as the internationally renowned singer came to the end of the number she had been belting out, and above the applause that followed another peal of husky laughter reached him.

He swore, causing several of the nearest masked faces to turn.

Great, now he was the one raising brows while his wife flirted with just about every man in the room. Well, enough was enough!

On the specially constructed stage, the singer took another bow and in turn applauded the musicians. Raoul tuned out her voice as she bent to the microphone and explained why one of the charities this event was raising money for was so close to her heart.

That had been the response to his every negative comment about this event—*but it's for charity*.

On stage, the singer went on to speak of a change in mood that brought a spatter of anticipatory applause. He craned his neck to catch sight of his Lara. Ice slid into his eyes as he stared over the heads of people at his wife just as the guy she was with leaned in to say something in her ear. Raoul recognised him as the son of a media tycoon whose idea of a day's work was giving an interview to a magazine about the stress involved in being him.

Raoul could recall being seated next to him at a dinner once and having been narcoleptic with boredom before the main course was served.

Not that Lara seemed bored. Her eyes sparkled, the emeralds sparkled, the guy touched her arm…and he heard a snapping noise in his head. Blood pounding in his ears, he crossed the room, his progress impeded by the fact that manners meant he couldn't just push his guests out of the way.

He responded with a grunt to a couple of greetings and then the effort became too much and he adopted a selective deafness policy.

Lara laughed, even though she hadn't actually heard the punchline of the joke. She was really working hard at this hostess thing but, heaven help her, there were limits. This man was monumentally boring.

'Sorry, duty calls.' Lies were a lot easier when you had a mask to hide behind.

It was odd, but the more miserable she felt, the easier it became to laugh and act as if she were having a great time. And she *would* have a great time, she told herself, even if it killed her, which it just might. Or perhaps Raoul might—In the periphery of her vision she could see his dark head as he made his way towards her.

Across the sea of faces their eyes met. He was the only person in the room *not* wearing a mask, and as their glances connected she was very glad of her own to hide behind. Something close to panic broke free as he continued to weave his way through their guests. He not only moved with the elegance of a jungle cat, but he projected the same lethal grace you associated with that animal. It was all she could do not to run.

Lara took a deep breath, told herself she was being ridiculous, and turned back to the boring man who still hadn't got to the punchline of his next story. She struggled to pick up the thread of his conversation while wondering how this young man managed to say so much without actually saying anything at all.

Raoul reached her side just as the band struck up the opening bars of the famous hit. An expectant hush descended on the room as all eyes turned to the stage. Though not quite all eyes.

Raoul's were on her.

Raoul extended an arm towards Lara. 'My dance, I think.' He slid a look towards the other man who had faded away in Lara's mind the moment Raoul appeared, and in fact was already backing away looking distinctly uneasy.

Lara didn't blame him. If a wolf could smile it would have copied Raoul's.

'I don't want to dance.'

The singer's husky, mellow tones filled the room as couples around them began to gyrate and twirl.

'And I don't care what you want. This is about what I want.'

She pulled in a tense breath as he tugged her into his arms. He was an excellent dancer and she was swept along by the slow, sexy beat of the music and the thrill of being in his arms—that part never lessened. Lara wasn't aware of his intention until he danced her straight out of one of the big double doors that had been thrown open earlier.

The ribbons attached to her mask fluttered in the breeze as they stepped outside.

She spun around to face him, still clutching the exotic mask to her face. 'Will you take that damned thing off?' He took hold of her wrist and pulled the mask down, anchoring her arm to her side and jerking her towards him.

Without her shield Lara felt exposed under the ravaging intensity of his glittering stare.

'*Dio*, but you're so beautiful.'

She felt him shudder, a deep ripple of movement that exploded through his body.

His mouth, not hard but sensuous, his firm lips warm and seductive, moved over hers, his tongue sliding between her parted lips. When his dark head lifted his intense stare made her dizzy. 'Raoul, you can't, people are staring.'

'Can't a man kiss his wife?'

There was kissing and there was *kissing*, and that had definitely been the latter!

'I'm jealous.'

The abrupt declaration made her stare. He had never said anything like that to her before.

'Wasn't I meant to be?'

The question made her eyes wide. She opened her mouth to hotly deny the question and closed it again. Wasn't there an element of truth in what he said?

'You don't make me sound like a very nice person,' she returned, hurt quivering in her voice.

'I don't want nice! I want not to be pushed away, treated like the enemy. We do not seem to be making each other happy, Lara.'

Lara felt the tears press at the back of her throat.

'The only place we don't fight is in bed.'

She took a deep breath, her hostility falling away as she felt a sob rise in her throat. She had always known this would happen, she just hadn't expected it to be here, now.

'So you are saying you want a divorce? I think you might have chosen a less public place.'

'This is not a public place, it is my home.'

'You didn't want any of this, did you? I knew it and I still went ahead and—I'm sorry.' *Just like the baby.* 'I just wanted to do something that *I* could control...and if I don't fill the time I think about—' She lifted her hand to her head. 'It just doesn't stop.'

'I understand,' he said gently. 'I really do, but, Lara, we have to get on the same page with this thing. After all we both want the same thing, don't we? I don't want a divorce.'

Thinking of the way she'd been behaving, Lara wondered why not.

Raoul stood there wondering the same thing himself. What had happened to his safe compartmentalised life?

'Couldn't we take a day off from the baby thing? Does it have to dominate *everything*?'

Of course it had to dominate everything—it was the only reason they were together. Lara bit her tongue to stop herself blurting it out.

'I suppose so, but this is—'

'I know, for charity.'

'I'm sorry, I really am, I just got carried away, the dress...' The truth was she had not felt comfortable with so much flesh exposed all night.

'Are your hostess duties over for the evening?'

'Pretty much.'

'Then how about we slip away and have our own little party?'

'I'd like that.'

CHAPTER THIRTEEN

'CHARLES THINKS IT will be a good year, a vintage year. He also said he doesn't need a new assistant because you do more than the one he had. Should I put you on the payroll?'

'It's interesting,' she admitted.

Hot after the walk to the vineyard manager's office, Lara turned her face into the light breeze, though with Raoul standing there with his shirt open to the waist, a section of brown skin on show and the silver buckle of his jeans shining against the hair-roughened skin of his taut, flat belly, there was not much chance of her cooling down.

'The clearing-up operation should be done by now. We made a lot of money if that's any—'

'Forget about last night.'

There were parts Lara didn't want to forget. She pulled at the neck of her shirt as he tipped the remnants of the water bottle he'd been drinking from over his head.

Oh, my! She closed her eyes, willed her galloping hormones to get back in their box.

The sound of him crushing the empty water bottle between his fingers brought her eyes open. There were strands of glossy, wet hair plastered across his forehead and his shirt was splodged with moisture.

He raised a hand and pushed the wet hair off his face and, hooking one thumb into the belt of his jeans, nodded. 'That tree over there—I was six and Jamie was eight when we carved our names into the trunk.'

Her throat filled as she watched him stare into the distance as though he was seeing the day from his past.

'He cut his hand when he cut his name because I was pushing, trying to see.' Then, still staring at the tree, he seamlessly changed the subject. 'I will need to be in New York quite a lot over the next few months.'

'New York?'

'Yes, I had thought I could keep up the law side of things but it's not going to work. I'm selling up. I can delegate the satellite offices but I need to see through the New York handover myself as there are still outstanding commitments that need to be honoured.'

'I suppose that will mean a lot of travelling?' And a lot of nights alone.

'It could,' he agreed. 'But there are alternatives.'

She shook her head, suddenly sure what was coming next. He had decided to cut his losses.

'We could move there. I have a place.'

She opened her eyes. 'You want me to come with you?'

'I think a break would do you…us…good right now maybe? Look, I know it's easy for me to talk about changing the cycle, but maybe a physical move would help? And while we're there, the best IVF specialist in the world is based there…'

'What are you saying, Raoul?' Her heart lurched with wild hope.

'I'm saying that I'd be willing to hear what he has to say… I'll go in there with an open mind. I'm not making any promises, but I'm prepared to discuss it. I still think it's way too soon to go down that road.'

Her throat closed over with emotion. 'You'd do that for me?'

'It's only an appointment, Lara. Don't get excited…' he warned.

Eyes shining, she shook her head and flew at him, releasing a whoop as he whirled her around. 'When do we go?'

* * *

Their appointment with the specialist was arranged for the second month after they arrived in New York. Raoul arrived back early as arranged, only to find Lara sitting in exactly the same place she had been that morning when he'd left. She was still wearing her nightdress.

'What's happened?'

He dropped down on his knees beside the chair and took hold of her icy hands.

'I had a phone call from Lily.' She took a gulping swallow. 'It's Emmy—she's ill, in hospital.'

'Is it serious?'

She nodded. 'Very serious.' Her face crumpled. 'She might die...she's been ill awhile and Lily didn't even tell me.' It had brought home to her just how much her relationship with her twin had disintegrated.

'Oh, *cara*.' He pulled her into his arms. Lara pressed her face into his shoulder and sobbed. 'We'll fly out tomorrow. What about medical help? Tell her we will pay any—'

Lara lifted her tear-stained face and shook her head. 'I don't think she wants me there. If I were her I wouldn't want me there. And anyway, she doesn't need our help. Ben is loaded.'

'Who is Ben?'

'Ben Warrender. Emily Rose's father. I still can't believe it. We've known him for ever—his family own the estate...she didn't tell me. She sounded so...she must be going through hell!'

So, it seemed to him, was Lara.

'Have you cancelled the appointment?'

Lara looked at him blankly.

'The appointment with Dr Carlyle?'

'I forgot...will you ring them?'

'Of course I will,' he said, sliding his phone out and

moving away to stand before the big glass window with its stunning view of Manhattan and the Hudson.

Lara sat there trying to pull herself together.

'Sorted, we can reschedule.'

'Thanks.' She dragged her hands through her hair before pressing them to her face. 'My brain isn't working. I just feel so helpless! I can't imagine how she is feeling and if she loses Emmy…'

'You *can* imagine,' he said softly. 'You lost a baby, Lara.'

Her fluttering glance flew to his face. 'It's not the same.'

Raoul, who did not think this the moment to discuss semantics, shrugged. 'You look terrible.' His compassionate gaze moved over her face. He held out his hand. 'Come on, you need some sleep. You're exhausted.'

After a moment she took his hand and allowed him to lead her to the bedroom, but each step felt like an effort.

She looked at the bed but didn't move. 'Will you make love to me, Raoul?' She asked it without looking at him. 'God knows, I could do with a bit of sympathy sex.' And she wasn't too proud to beg, but then she never was with Raoul.

Her love for him suddenly welled up inside her like a solid wall of emotion, and the intensity of it brought tears to her eyes. He didn't want her love, the only thing he wanted from her was a child and she couldn't even give him that.

She heard the sound of his rasped exclamation and turned her head. As she did so his mouth found hers; the kiss was deep, filled with passion and yet incredibly tender.

He laid her on the bed and without a word peeled away her nightclothes before taking off his own clothes and joining her in the bed.

She felt his whisper-light kiss on her face, against her

closed eyelids. She kept her eyes closed as he pulled her to him, giving herself over completely to the pleasure of having his hands on her, his mouth on her. Raoul always knew where to touch her, how to touch her.

And when her body was ready, when the heat inside her built until only one thing could cool it, he slid into her, moving with deep strokes, letting them both enjoy being one. The combination of tenderness and passion brought tears of joy to her eyes as they shared the moment of ultimate bliss, their fevered cries blending into one.

As she felt him curl up against her back she reached behind her and caught his hand, curling it around her breast. She fell asleep with his hand on her heart and felt safe and loved, even though deep down she knew it was an illusion.

Finally, Lara got a tearful call from her sister. But the tears were good ones—Emmy was going to be all right. She rang Raoul immediately, wanting to share the good news, so it was frustrating when he didn't pick up.

She decided on impulse to cook him a special meal to celebrate. She had started to get to know some of the local stores and the novelty value of shopping in a new city had not worn off.

She got a bit carried away and bought way too much food. The bags tucked under her arms were bulging and heavy and there were still another few blocks to go before she reached the apartment building. About to admit defeat and hail a cab, she realised she was standing outside a coffee shop and realised why the name looked so familiar. A guide book she had bought had said that a coffee and Danish there while watching the world go by were an essential New York experience.

Seated at a table in the window, Lara savoured her Danish and her coffee. She wasn't convinced by it—the coffee tasted a bit funny—but she was definitely enjoying watching the world go by.

She was taking another bite of her Danish when she saw them. The pastry fell from her fingers.

Across the road on the steps of a hotel, her husband was kissing a dark-haired woman.

Lara felt as if someone had just thrust an icy hand into her chest. The merciless fingers were squeezing her heart until it felt as though it would burst.

Was this how her mum had felt?

But I'm not my mum!

I won't *be her, I'm* not *going to run away and pretend I didn't see.* Shoulders squared, she got to her feet, the smooth lines of her face set with resolve. She'd had enough pretending.

'You forgot your groceries! Your bill!'

'Keep the groceries…' She pulled a bundle of notes from her purse and pushed them at the waiter. 'Keep the change!'

The lights changed and she ran; she was panting by the time she reached the other side of the street. Then, weaving her way through the scrum of people, she almost collided with the woman who was no longer in Raoul's arms but only a couple of feet away.

Lara registered several facts. The woman was Naomi and Raoul looked furious.

'Lara!'

She held up her hand. 'Later.' Turning her back on him, she faced the other woman. 'Look, I have no idea what your problem is, and frankly I don't want to. Just get the hell out of my life and leave my husband alone!'

A strangled squeaking noise left the woman's throat.

'Never make a redhead mad.'

Swallowing, Lara turned slowly back to Raoul. 'Never kiss women who are not your wife in public.'

His smile died. 'I was not doing the kissing, *cara*, she's deranged...' Eyes hard, he turned to Naomi. 'I am sorry your husband is divorcing you, but *we* do not have a relationship, *we* have never had a relationship, and I am not in love with you.'

'Believe him, Naomi, I do.' Whatever came between them, it would not be Naomi!

She barely registered the other woman's leaving as she took a step towards Raoul. 'And I *was* angry and hurt and...pretty much the way any woman who saw the man she loved kissing another woman would feel.'

She saw him stiffen.

'Lara—'

She ignored the warning in his voice. 'You don't want to hear this, I know, but, you see, I have to say it anyway. I'm sick of pretending, Raoul. I love you, and I can't help it, and if you can't love me...' She bit her lips and shook her head. 'Well, I'd prefer to know—'

Looking at the appeal in the luminous eyes lifted to his, Raoul *wanted* to say he loved her, but the years of hardening his heart from the emotion, the knowledge of how it could destroy a man when it went wrong, stopped the words coming.

The seconds ticked by, and the fast thud of her heart slowed as her hope died, as Raoul stood there, silent, the muscles in his jaw flexing. A light drizzle had started, which was plastering his dark hair to his head.

She could wait for ever and he still wasn't going to say what she wanted to hear. Well, at least now she knew.

'It's fine,' she said, dying a little inside.

He squeezed his eyes closed to shut out the sight of her slender back as she walked away, fighting the irrational urge to follow her. It couldn't work, he reminded himself. He was the man he was, and incapable of returning what she had offered him.

And unworthy!
Why…*why* did she have to say it…?

Lara unlocked the door of the apartment and ran straight into the bathroom where she threw up violently.

After rinsing her mouth, she walked into the bedroom and, with a heart as empty as her stomach, she packed her belongings.

The note was short and to the point.

I'm going home. Please don't try and contact me. A baby deserves two parents who love one another.

There were no airport delays or incidents and her London-bound flight took off on time.

The hotel she booked into in the city was nondescript but it had everything she needed. Lara likened the instinct to a wounded dog crawling into a corner to lick its wounds—the trouble was a dog had better sense than to open and reopen the wound.

The concept of healing seemed a long way off. The numbness came and went in waves, and the rest of the time she was either murderously furious or depressingly self-pitying.

It wasn't until the third day that she realised that nausea and vomiting were not just the symptoms of misery and heartache.

She couldn't be! Life could not be that cruel. She spent the rest of the day in the small box-like room telling herself it couldn't possibly be true.

She finally fell asleep around three a.m., wearing the red dress she'd had on when they first met—despair had made her masochistic, like an addiction that slowly killed you from the inside.

She had no idea what had made her pack it, or why she had even brought it to New York in the first place. Probably the same stupid, sentimental reason that had made her try it on the previous night.

She woke late feeling utterly wretched and no longer able to bury her head in the sand. She had to know.

The only thing she paused for on her way to the door was a painkiller, and then realised as she swallowed it that she'd accidentally taken one of the antihistamines that she used for hay fever.

Ah, well, the chemist would have something for her headache—as well as for the *other thing.*

She was halfway down the high street when she realised she was still wearing the dress she had slept in. Such was the sense of urgency that gripped her she didn't even consider going back to change.

The chemist had a ladies' room, and, rather than suffer another moment of the agony of not knowing, she used it. Then she went out, bought another testing kit, and went back in.

The result was the same.

She began to walk back to the hotel in a daze, experiencing a bitter sense of déjà vu when she missed her turning and found herself lost.

Pull yourself together, Lara! She rubbed a hand over her face, and realised the extra antihistamine was kicking in. Then, as if that weren't enough, her path was blocked by a loud and boisterous wedding party emerging from a register office.

There was the sound of popping corks as the happy couple emerged. At least her dress blended in with the other guests. Head down, she was trying to ease her way through the group when a guest carrying an open bottle of champagne in one hand and two glasses in the other backed into her.

Lara cried out as he trod down on her foot.

He swung around, accidentally depositing half the bottle of fizz down her dress. He stood there, an appalled look on his face. 'So sorry, I'm so sorry. Here.' He poured some of the remaining fizz into one of the glasses he held and pushed it at her.

'Have some, please, no hard feelings.'

It was easier and quicker to take a couple of small sips and 'accidentally' spill the rest rather than reject the misplaced token of generosity and apology. Lara had taken a few steps before she realised her mistake. She had barely swallowed a mouthful but with the antihistamines already in her system…she *had* to get back and sleep this off.

During the next five minutes the sense of urgency lessened. She was actually feeling quite mellow and then she saw—it seemed like fate—the man who had fathered her twin's child.

He was standing at a hotel entrance but he wasn't kissing anyone.

He'd been there for Lily, and for Emmy, and she had to thank him.

She had a memory of the look of horror on his face as she staggered over to him, but after that it was pretty much a blank. As Lily said when she sat with her before she cried herself to sleep, it was probably better that way.

CHAPTER FOURTEEN

THE SIGHT OF her sister the next morning made Lara feel even more of a disaster. Lily looked like the poster child for health and contentment. She was actually singing to herself; she was glowing.

'You never could hold a tune.'

Lily put down the apple she was peeling and came across to her sister. She put her hands on Lara's shoulders and looked into her face.

'There's flour on your nose. Have you gone all domestic?'

'Not really, I just had an urge to bake. It's very fashionable—hadn't you heard?'

'I'm sorry.' Lara looked around the room. 'Is he…?'

Lily shook her head. 'Ben thought he'd give us some time to catch up. He's taken Emmy to the park.'

Lara arched a satiric brow. 'You mean he's running scared of his lush of a sister-in-law. I only had a sip, you know…really. It just reacted with my hay-fever meds.'

'I explained that to him. He'll fetch your things over from the hotel. I can't believe that you've been here for two days and you didn't—'

'I needed time to think. And I was too ashamed,' Lara admitted. 'I wasn't even sure you'd want to see me. I was jealous.'

Lily nodded. 'I kind of worked that bit out… If I'd known about the baby…you are an idiot, you know that, don't you? I binned the dress. I hope that's all right…?'

Her life was binned, so why not?

'Half a bottle went down the front. I only had a sip. I promise, it was the allergy meds.'

'I know.'

'I don't know why I kept the dress,' Lara lied, then immediately confided, 'It was what I was wearing the first time I saw Raoul. I was feeling very sorry for myself and kind of masochistic.' She gave a gulping sob. 'I told him I loved him.'

'Some might say that it was about time.'

'I just couldn't keep it in any longer. I couldn't pretend... he never pretended to love me but deep down I thought... hoped that he'd follow me. But he didn't.'

'Does he know?'

Lara lifted her head from her twin's shoulder. 'Know?'

'That you're pregnant.' She saw her sister's expression and shook her head, smiling. 'No, I'm not psychic and you're not showing. You told me last night. You told me a lot of things.'

Lara's eyes fell. 'No, he doesn't,' she murmured.

'From what you've said I'm guessing he'd come running if he knew.'

Lara nodded. 'Yes, he would. That's what makes it so hard... I... I... Thanks.' She gave a watery smile, accepting the wad of tissues Lily pressed into her hand, and she pulled out a stool at the breakfast bar. 'I was tempted. I thought I could settle but I want more, Lily.'

'You deserve more. Are you really so sure that he doesn't love you? I mean, whenever I've seen him he can't take his eyes off you.'

'It's a part he's playing, a part we both were, but for me it became real.' She stopped and gave a wild little laugh. 'No, I'm still lying. That's not true—it was love at first sight for me... I know, how crazy is that?'

Her twin didn't join in her laughter. 'I don't think it's crazy at all.'

'But then you always were the romantic…not me.' She ran her tongue across her dry lips and shook her head, her voice dropping to a grief-laden whisper as she admitted, 'If I hadn't been pregnant when his grandfather died the marriage would have ended then—that was the plan.'

'Well, if a baby was never part of the plan you both seem to have gone to a lot of trouble to make it happen,' Lily observed.

'I was devastated. I hadn't known how much I wanted it.' She swallowed down hard. 'He just felt sorry for me and there was the heir thing, carrying on his name.'

'I wish you'd told me.'

Lara gave a watery smile. 'How could I? You were pregnant and—I wanted to be happy for you, I *was* happy for you, but I was also jealous,' she admitted with a shamed sniff.

'If you don't mind me saying, Lara, your husband has never struck me as the sort of man who makes life-changing decisions because of pity.'

Lara blinked. 'No,' she conceded. 'But…he has a strong sense of duty, family. He can be very protective. You know, I used to believe that whoever I fell in love with would naturally love me back, because…because that's just the way it's supposed to be. But perhaps this is some of sort of punishment for being so conceited, because I've tried and I've tried and—' She squeezed her eyes closed as the anguished words emerged from her aching throat. 'But I can't make him love me.' Head bent, she closed her eyes. 'And I can't live without being loved.'

'Neither can I, Lara.'

She hugged her twin and added huskily, 'I'm glad that you have Ben, you sneaky old thing. If anyone deserves to be happy after all you've been through it's you.' She gave a sudden choking sob and wailed, 'Raoul deserves to be happy too.'

'You know you have to tell him about the baby.'

'Do you think I don't know that?'

He had let her walk away. As he turned and walked in the opposite direction he could still hear her saying it: *I love you*.

People took one look at his stony face and took hasty detours around the tall man as Raoul strode out blindly, feeding his anger as the emotions inside him built. She knew the rules, she was the one who had broken them, this *could* have worked…it *was* working.

Then his anger vanished and he clenched his jaw against the hit of guilt as he remembered the hope shining in her eyes, and how it had died and vanished as she'd waited for him to respond.

It had been a brave thing to do, a *Lara* thing. She'd had hope and he'd crushed it. Angry with her for saying it, but tortured by the thought of her hurting, he walked on, his black thoughts a swirl of self-loathing, anger and resentment.

He'd let her walk away.

Why?

He waited for the accusatory stream of responses to come—*she* wasn't being fair, *she* was asking for something he couldn't give, he was doing her a favour because *she* deserved—but they didn't come.

He stopped dead.

They were lies.

The truth flayed him and he didn't avoid the pain, he deserved it!

Lara was brave, and he was a coward, a gutless wonder who'd been too scared to admit his own feelings even to himself. And why? Because he'd stopped trusting his own feelings, and his solution was to pretend he didn't have any.

And it hadn't been that hard until Lara had appeared. She had challenged his accepted way of thinking from day one; she'd awoken dormant emotions inside him and made them blaze up like an out-of-control fire.

Once love had almost destroyed him, it had simply never even entered his consciousness that love, *real* love, could also be a salvation.

Lara was his salvation and he'd let her walk away.

He felt power surge through him as he embraced the truth: Lara was the love of his life. He was going to fix things, he was going to lay his heart at her feet and beg her to take him back.

It had been a massive anticlimax when he'd got back to the apartment and she wasn't there…just that heart-breaking note.

Raoul hadn't slept since. He'd traced her to London and then Lara seemed to have vanished. He felt as though he'd aged ten years in the last three days. He was crazy with worry; he'd tried everything…everyone.

If she wasn't here, he thought as the taxi driver pulled up outside a house in a leafy road, he didn't know what he'd do.

'Is this it?'

'I hope so,' Raoul breathed, paying off the driver. 'I really hope so.' He'd finally tracked down her sister, who was at a new address, and if she didn't know where Lara was then he wasn't sure what his next move would be.

He rang the bell and the door opened immediately. Seeing another woman with his wife's face, after so many days without her, was a jolt.

'Is she here?'

She looked him up and down, her eyes narrowed and assessing before responding. 'She is—she's through that way. No!' She laid a hand flat on his chest to stop his impulsive progress. 'Listen, Lara is…she's kind of fragile right now and if you hurt her, so help me, Mr Di Vittorio, you'll be singing soprano. Message received?'

'Received, and, for the record, though I am very attached to my singing voice I would sooner lose it than hurt Lara.'

Lily smiled and stepped back to let him pass, yelling after him, 'Don't mess it up!'

'I have been looking for you.'

With a gasp Lara turned, jumping up off the stool she sat on. She pressed her hands against her chest, fighting down the urge to reach out and touch him.

Instead in a flat little voice she said, 'It's over.'

'Let me finish! I have been looking for you *all my life*, though I didn't realise it. I would not let myself believe it. Lucy…she left me feeling toxic, like I had nothing left to give another woman, and then when I found you I was too stupid and cowardly…yes!' he said, reacting to her little whimper of protest with a shake of his head. 'Too cowardly to face the truth. I loved you, Lara Gray, from the moment I saw you. You are my life and I am nothing without you. I am here to beg you to have me. We will live where you like—move here to England if that is what you want— have IVF, adopt, do whatever you want. It is true, I am a bastard…a stupid, selfish bastard…' he said in a voice that throbbed with the depth of his conviction.

Raoul had been taking slow deliberate steps towards her as he spoke, but he stopped now that his dark eyes fastened on her face.

Could it be true?

Unable any longer to hold it in, she said the words he had ached to hear again. 'I love you, Raoul. I love you so much, I couldn't keep it in any longer. I thought all you wanted from me was an heir, and I wanted so…so much to give you one because I thought you didn't want me—'

The rest of her confession was lost in his mouth. Raoul crushed her to him, drinking in the taste of her, his hands moulding her body to his.

He framed her face with his hands and looked down into her eyes. 'I can't believe I just stood there. I can't believe I thought it would be easier to be alone and lonely than risk my heart. When I think what I could have lost... When I came back and found you gone I— Never, *ever* do that to me again. If you knew the things I have been imagining...'

'It was awful,' she admitted. 'It tore me apart...' She took a deep breath. 'I've decided against the IVF.'

A shade of caution flickered into his dark eyes.

'I found out yesterday that I'm pregnant.'

Joy filled his face. 'Perfect!' He kissed her and added throatily, 'You are perfect, and you must not worry this time—'

She pressed a finger to his lips. 'I am not worried, not while I have you,' she said simply. Whatever life threw at her, with Raoul at her side they would come through, together.

Neither heard the noise as the front door swung open.

Lily stood there pulling on her coat, blocking the way of Ben, who wielded a pushchair containing a sleeping child.

'We have to go back out!' she whispered.

'Why?'

'Lara is in there—'

'Oh, God, is she drunk again?'

'No, you idiot, she's not drunk. She's in love!'

* * * * *

LET'S TALK
Romance

For exclusive extracts, competitions
and special offers, find us online:

 facebook.com/millsandboon

@MillsandBoon

@MillsandBoonUK

Get in touch on 01413 063232

For all the latest titles coming soon, visit
millsandboon.co.uk/nextmonth

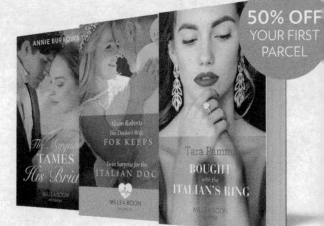

MILLS & BOON

THE HEART OF ROMANCE

A ROMANCE FOR EVERY READER

ODERN

Prepare to be swept off your feet by sophisticated, sexy and seductive heroes, in some of the world's most glamourous and romantic locations, where power and passion collide.

STORICAL

Escape with historical heroes from time gone by. Whether your passion is for wicked Regency Rakes, muscled Vikings or rugged Highlanders, awaken the romance of the past.

EDICAL

Set your pulse racing with dedicated, delectable doctors in the high-pressure world of medicine, where emotions run high and passion, comfort and love are the best medicine.

rue Love

Celebrate true love with tender stories of heartfelt romance, from the rush of falling in love to the joy a new baby can bring, and a focus on the emotional heart of a relationship.

Desire

Indulge in secrets and scandal, intense drama and plenty of sizzling hot action with powerful and passionate heroes who have it all: wealth, status, good looks…everything but the right woman.

EROES

Experience all the excitement of a gripping thriller, with an intense romance at its heart. Resourceful, true-to-life women and strong, fearless men face danger and desire - a killer combination!

To see which titles are coming soon, please visit

millsandboon.co.uk/nextmonth

JOIN US ON SOCIAL MEDIA!

Stay up to date with our latest releases, author news and gossip, special offers and discounts, and all the behind-the-scenes action from Mills & Boon...

 @millsandboon

 @millsandboonuk

 facebook.com/millsandboon

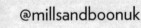 @millsandboonuk

It might just be true love...

GET YOUR ROMANCE FIX!

Get the latest romance news,
exclusive author interviews, story
extracts and much more!

MILLS & BOON
True Love
Romance from the Heart

Celebrate true love with tender stories of heartfelt romance, from the rush of falling in love to the joy a new baby can bring, and a focus on the emotional heart of a relationship.

MILLS & BOON
MEDICAL
Pulse-Racing Passion

Set your pulse racing with dedicated, delectable doctors in the high-pressure world of medicine, where emotions run high and passion, comfort and love are the best medicine.